Lara's
Journal

A. GAVAZZONI

Dedication

Again, I have so much to be thankful, I believe in order to thank everyone I'm grateful for, I will have to write a hundred books.

To my editor, Jill N. Noble-Shearer, you are the best editor ever! You are also a great and kind friend. Love you. Thanks for everything you are doing for me. To Kelly A. Martin, for the best covers and lots of patience. To my husband Mauricio—out of all the crazy men in the world, I chose you because your craziness is just like mine. Love you. To my parents, Olmar and Nilse—Happy 50th year of marriage! I just wish you two live forever, and I love you more than words can say. To my grandma Ida Gavazzoni, a teacher for forty years. I miss your hugs, your avocado ice cream, and your lovely letters. To Pedro F. Bretas, a great friend. Thanks for asking me, "When are you going to publish?" Hope you accept my invitation for a book written by both of us. To David A. Gurwin, wonderful musician and brilliant lawyer, thank you for fighting for my rights and becoming a good friend! To Edgar Amarilla, the true Doctor Edgar, thanks for all your support, my friend. To the author Catherine-Townsend Lyon, an example of a warrior and a lovely person others want to be near. Thanks for all the support. To Ual Bradley, former FBI agent, for your kind patience in helping me with all my questions and legal information, even though you didn't even know me. You have a kind heart and a great knowledge. To author Maxwell Ivey, Jr., for your help, support, and kind heart. Thanks to Marileusa dos Santos—your words are able to calm my heart. Thanks to Marcio Marcelino, for your patience and friendship.

PROLOGUE

The nightclub was dark, a few red lights barely illuminating the smoky, crowded dance floor. Music blared from the sound system, loud and shrill. People bounced wildly, unconcerned with keeping rhythm to the frenzied beat, only there to have fun.

At 3:00 a.m., there were very few sober people. She should be one of them, but not today; today she was enjoying life.

Life was unpredictable, she thought. Why not live intensely?

She was not really drunk. She'd had a few drinks— maybe five or six glasses of white wine. Or more...? In any event, she'd drunk enough to relax and loosen up a little but not so much that she slurred her speech or saw doubles.

A very interesting-looking man sat at a corner table, and he'd been staring at her for at least the last five minutes. Although she couldn't see his features well in the dimly lit club, she knew he definitely had dark-brown hair. He seemed young—much younger than she was—but so what? She wondered what color eyes he had, and decided, if given the opportunity, she'd find out.

He raised his glass in a silent toast, and she smiled back. Deciding to accept his obvious invitation, she nodded, and he was by her side in an instant, bringing two wineglasses with him.

"Hello," he said. "Would you like to dance?"

"*Hello,*" she answered, accepting the glass he offered her.

They didn't talk; the music was too loud for conversation. Instead, she stepped close to him and wrapped her arms around his neck, still holding her glass. They started to move slowly, following the music, trying to balance their drinks. He put his free hand on her waist, moving sensuously, then slid his hand up to caress her back.

She smiled as one phrase echoed in her mind. *Life is short, too short.*

He took her glass from her hand, put his and hers on a nearby table, took her to a corner, supported her against the wall, and lifted her arms. Holding them high, he leaned into her, effectively imprisoning her. Oh, she could easily break free if she wanted to, but at the moment, she wouldn't want to be anywhere else.

He lowered his head and captured her lips with his. His kiss was hot, hard, and aggressive and demanded an equal response. His tongue dipped inside her mouth, and he kissed her as if he wanted to dredge her soul. His mouth tasted of wine. Too much time had passed since she'd last received such passionate kisses.

He ran his hands over her body, trying to feel her through her dress. For a moment, she thought to stop him—someone might see them—but then she figured, *what the hell?* Who cared what people thought? No one there knew her, and there were several other couples doing the same thing in other shadowy areas of the club.

She kissed him back, her arms still draped around his neck, her body burning at his touch, her blood warming as her heart beat fast. He put his hand inside her dress and touched her breast, and a shiver traveled through her.

He might be younger than she was, but he certainly was not inexperienced. While kissing and nibbling his way down her neck, he pulled down one of her dress straps to expose a breast. Maybe in another time or place, she would have been ashamed, but not now. She felt only pleasure at being touched, at being alive.

He started to suckle her nipples, and she grew immediately wet. She closed her eyes to focus on his touch, a spinning sensation in her head brought on by her lust and the alcohol. She was moaning, but nobody could hear, the music drowning out the sound.

"Come with me," he said.

At least that's what she thought he said because he took her hand and led her to the men's bathroom.

There were a few guys hanging around the entrance and just inside, but nobody seemed to mind her presence. Her new friend took her into the largest of the five stalls—the one equipped for handicapped entrance—and closed the door. A sink and a toilet were lined up against one wall.

He lifted her dress, set her on the marble sink, and started to caress her again, sliding his hands up her legs. She whimpered and clutched at his shoulders.

Desperate to get her hands on his body, she opened the first few buttons of his shirt. She ran her palms over his smooth, warm chest then scraped his pecs with her nails. Her new lover moaned approvingly. She wiggled her ass on the countertop, signaling her desire for him to touch her, to take her.

He grinned before dipping his head to bite at her neck. He rained small kisses all the way down to her shoulder as he pulled aside her panties and put a finger inside her. Excited, wet, and ready for him, she moaned. He worked her for a while, moving his finger in and out, then he gathered the moisture from her pussy and rhythmically swirled it around her clit.

Breathing hard, she opened his zipper, took out his cock, and caressed its length, first with her nails and then with her fingertips.

"*Loca*," he said, his dick hard, moisture leaking from the tip.

"Fuck me," she commanded.

He reached into his pocket and withdrew a condom. After ripping open the little packet, he tossed aside the wrapper and sheathed his hard dick.

She spread her legs wide, and he stepped between them. He entered her in one long, smooth glide, and she gasped, digging her nails into his shoulders as her orgasm shattered through her.

Holy shit, holy shit, holy shit. She'd never come so easily or so quickly.

She wrapped her legs around his waist to allow him to go deeper inside her, and they started to move. He thrust into her brutally, his face a mask of desperate concentration as he sought his own release.

His charcoal-black eyes were wide open, and he held her gaze, one hand between them, massaging her clit, the other hand clamped on her waist in a bruising grip.

"Yes!" he whispered harshly, slamming into her.

They came together, him releasing a strangled cry and her biting her bottom lip to keep from shouting. Afterward, they stood there in silence, breathing heavily, the smell of sex permeating the air.

She glanced away. A moment ago, they'd been as close as two people could get, but now she felt uncomfortable...exposed. She uncrossed her legs, releasing him, and fixed her clothes while he got rid of the condom. He helped her to stand up.

She wanted to disappear as quickly as possible.

He asked her something, but thanks to the noise, she only understood the last word. Something about a "telephone"—had he asked for her number?

She refused him with a quick shake of her head, opened the door, and beat a hasty retreat. Without looking back, she lost herself on the dance floor.

CHAPTER ONE

Simone – Present Day

Simone sped down the dark hall. Behind her, the masked man drew closer.

Any minute now he'd reach her; she could practically feel his heavy breath on her nape. A staircase appeared before her, and she raced down, jumping the steps two at a time. At the bottom, she came to a closed red iron door. She grabbed the handle, turned, and yanked, but the damn thing was locked.

Simone spun around, leaning back against the door, breathing heavily and straining to listen for the man's footsteps in the darkness.

Heart racing, she searched her mind for a way out but came up blank. Above her, heavy footfalls sounded at the top of the steps. She opened her mouth to scream but found she had no voice.

Simone flew to a sitting position, eyes wide open, a sweat-soaked sheet wrapped around her waist.

"For chrissake," she said, pressing a shaking hand to her chest. "That damn nightmare is going to give me a damn heart attack."

A month had passed since Peter Hay had kidnapped and tortured her, and she'd dreamed of the insane serial killer nearly every night since.

"How much longer will he haunt my dreams?" she said. Although her partner—a psychiatrist who used to assist the police by putting together criminal profiles—had rescued her, and her physical injuries had long since healed, her emotional wounds still remained. The nightmares had started just before she'd left the hospital.

She looked around. What had she heard that had caused her to wake up? On the bedside table, her cellphone vibrated, signaling a call. Simone sighed and leaned over, reaching for the phone. The backlit display showed Edward's name and number.

Why would her partner be calling her this early? She would need to call him back later. Right now, she had to go to the bathroom.

She went into the white marble and glass bathroom, took care of business, then got her Pill case from her cosmetic purse. She removed one of the little yellow tablets, popped it into her mouth, and swallowed it down with a glass of water from the sink.

After grabbing a towel from the shelf, she opened the shower door, regulated the water temperature, and climbed in beneath the spray to take a good, long, warm shower and allow the water to erase all memory of the nightmare.

By the time she stepped out of the shower, she was feeling much better. However, a quick glance in the mirror revealed dark circles under her eyes, proof her nightmares were taking a toll on her physically.

She applied some light makeup then returned to her bedroom, where she dug out a pair of shorts and a t-shirt from her suitcase and got dressed. Only then did she feel well enough and awake enough to return Edward's call.

"Hello, Ed," she greeted him when he answered. "I'm sorry I missed your call. I was in the shower. How are you?"

"Well...to be honest, I'm worried about you. Your daughter told me you left Paris and were headed back to the US, but that was a week ago, and I hadn't heard from you, so..."

"Don't worry, my friend, I'm okay... I'm in Miami Beach. How could I be better?" Simone laughed.

"Miami? How come?"

"Do you remember that friend of ours from college— Arami?"

"Sure, I do. She was a Brazilian nut if I recall correctly..."

"She's still nuts, but she's from Paraguay, not Brazil. We ran into each other in France, and she invited me to come with her to Miami, and I couldn't say no."

Simone was at a point in her life where she didn't want to deny herself a little bit of adventure, and she'd accepted an invitation from Arami to come stay for a while. Simone was suffering from post-traumatic stress syndrome, but as a psychiatrist, she thought she could work her way through it...could at least handle her emotions.

"Just like that? You go from Paris to Miami...? That's so not you! Where are you staying? Just in case... The police are still investigating your case, and they may need to talk to you again."

"You're upset, Ed. Just give me a chance to get my head together a little bit. I'll be back soon; I promise."

"Okay, but I want you to be honest with me. How do

you really feel...?"

"From a layman's point of view, I'd say I'm getting better, but I'm still a little bit messed up. I can't sleep well if I don't take the pills. I have nightmares, but I feel safe here. From a medical doctor's point of view, I need to stop the pills..."

"Treat yourself like a human being, not as a doctor. You need the drugs right now. Take them until you feel ready to stop...and, Simmie...I miss you."

"Miss you, too."

She did miss Edward, her dear friend, her best friend and partner, but his declaration of love—delivered just before she'd been kidnapped—had changed things between them. She didn't know what to do or how to deal with his feelings for her. She couldn't imagine her life without Edward, but she couldn't imagine a life with him as her lover...at least, not now.

Simone had never been the emotional kind of woman; she always had a hard time dealing with feelings such as love and passion, but she really understood friendship, and Edward's friendship was very important to her. She couldn't loose that, but at the same time, she couldn't even consider anything like a love affair at the moment. She needed to focus on getting well.

They finished the call, and Simone realized her head was killing her—too much alcohol last night—and then she remembered where'd she'd gone and what she'd done. She and Arami had visited a Latin nightclub, and Simone had drunk a lot...and yes...for the first time in her life, she had sex with a stranger. She preferred to forget that part but knew she couldn't. Still, she didn't feel guilty...

Arami was one of those girls from high-class South American society. She belonged to a rich family. Before her father had been murdered, he'd been a general for the dictatorship. Arami had gone to the U.S. to study and had decided to stay. She was a plastic surgeon, a really good one, and she could speak English with almost no accent. Although her voice had an underlying, unique quality, she didn't sound like a foreigner.

Simone and Arami had run in to each other by chance in a café in Paris. Simone had taken her daughter Tamara to finish an exchange program, and Arami was participating in a Plastic Surgery Congress. They had started chatting over their coffee, and the friendship they'd formed in college came back as if they had only just seen each other the day before. Crazy, considering they hadn't talked since graduation. They had exchanged cards every Christmas and on each other's birthdays, but only that. Some friendships were like that, thought Simone; they would last forever even if you didn't see each other or talk all the time.

When Simone told Arami all about the serial killer, she'd invited Simone to stay in Arami's Miami apartment for a while, and Simone had decided to accept. Although spontaneity typically wasn't part of Simone's psyche, things were so confusing, she had decided to live life without analyzing every move and every act, and she was having a nice time with her old friend; Arami was an easy-going person, and she always seemed to be happy.

Arami's apartment was on Collins Avenue in Miami Beach. The oceanfront property was an example of what good money could buy. Big, luxurious, well decorated, and modern, the suite of rooms had glass walls everywhere that allowed one to see the ocean in all its splendor.

Arami refused to allow Simone to go to a hotel, explaining that Latin American hospitality would never allow a friend to stay in a cold hotel. "You can stay as long as you like," Arami had added. "Forever, if it suits you."

Of course, Simone wouldn't impose for much longer. She was actually thinking about leaving the following week. Not only did she not want to wear out her welcome, she also missed her house and her methodic life.

Someone knocked on her bedroom door, and when Simone opened it, Arami came in like a hurricane, crazy as ever, talking fast, and gesturing with her hands.

Arami was a short, pretty brunette, full-figured and

curvy, and she had beautiful, dark eyes that tilted up a bit at the corners, typical features of her countrymen. She really didn't fit the joke that used to go around college—the one about God saying a woman couldn't be a doctor and be pretty—because Arami had both brains and sex appeal.

"Let's go, let's go, girl." She moved her hands like a fan. "We have a lunch date today! Did you sleep well? What a party last night, huh?"

She kissed and hugged Simone enthusiastically.

Before Simone could answer either question, Arami went on.

"What a fantastic night we had! Never saw you drunk before, but I guess people change. That's nice!"

Did she see me with him? Simone wondered. While she'd been dancing alone, Arami had been in the corner, kissing some hot guy she'd picked up at the nightclub. Had she still been occupied when Simone had found her own Latin lover? She sure hoped so, and she wasn't about to say anything unless Arami indicated she'd noticed Simone disappear into the bathroom.

"Where are we going?" Simone asked. "My head is killing me..."

"To my uncle's house in Key Biscayne. They are vacationing here, but you can't go wearing those shorts—nice legs, by the way—but my auntie would kill you!"

"Who is this uncle of yours?"

"Cezar Benites. He is a retired general." She made a smart salute. "He is a dinosaur from the time of the Paraguayan dictatorship...old school...my father's youngest brother...you will see..."

"Really? Is he one of those tough, bossy men? I don't know if I can deal with someone like that right now. I've been feeling a little...fragile lately."

"Oh, he is bossy... But tough? With you? Are you kidding me? He'll act like a prince, and you'll have him drooling down your neck before you finish saying hello. Don't worry; he is very polite, but he is also a womanizer. Don't wear anything low cut, or he'll dive in...and then my auntie will poison your food." Arami's musical laughter filled the air.

* * * * *

An armored car sat waiting for them out front. Arami explained those were the general's security rules. He was always afraid of being murdered. The driver was also a private security guard.

"Is he really in danger?"

"I honestly don't know; I believe as a politician in Paraguay, he could be a target...as was my father...but in Paraguay, not here... I'm certain he is a little bit paranoid since my father was killed."

Arami's father had participated in the liberation of Paraguay. He had helped another general, Oviedo, to depose the dictator. Oviedo died in an accident, and her father had decided to run for the presidency after that, but before the elections he was killed in an ambush, and nobody had ever found out who had murdered him. Arami's uncle took his place, but he had lost the election.

They went to Key Biscayne, arriving at a property surrounded by high walls and a tall, iron gate. The sign on the gate read *Paraíso*—Paradise—and *No Trespassing. Private Property.*

The gate was opened for them, and Simone had the impression she was entering another country. They drove down a paved road lined with square, sculpted bushes. Beyond the bushes grew palm trees and a very lush green garden filled with colorful flowers—a real paradise. At the end of the drive, they came to a Spanish-style mansion. White with brown balconies, the home was huge and beautiful.

Two armed guards stood at the front door. As the car came to a stop, Simone and Arami climbed out. The front door to the house opened, and they entered into a gigantic foyer surrounded by arches. A natural garden stood in the middle of the room. They walked across the golden-brown ceramic tiles and through an archway, whereupon they exited into the pool area. Several women sat on deck chairs, drinks in hand, while two little girls played near another armed security guard. As Simone watched, he arranged his rifle on his shoulder and took one of the girls by her hands and spun her around. The children giggled, obviously having a blast.

I've fallen into a Gabriel Garcia Marque's novel. The Nobel Prize-winning novel, *One Hundred Years of Solitude*, was remarkably similar, she thought. *What kind of trauma will those young girls experience when they grow up, as a result of all this?* Simone's psychiatrist's brain asked. But then she pushed the thought aside. *Not my problem! I have my hands plenty full with my issues and those of my patients.*

The sound of dogs barking echoed in the distance, a parrot sat on top of a huge, iron cage, singing a Latin song, and the smell of a barbecue filled the air, but Simone didn't see a grill anywhere.

When she and Arami approached the women, all eyes turned toward them, especially toward Simone. She silently thanked Arami for advising her to choose a more conservative dress, because all the women seemed to be taking her measure, eyeing her from head to toe.

"Good morning, girls." Arami greeted everybody and

waved.

"*Buenos dias*, Arami," the women all said at the same time, speaking in singsong voices.

They all looked the same to Simone—dark hair, dark skin, all of them wearing similar, multicolored, expensive-looking dresses.

Where were the men? Simone wondered, feeling as if she'd stepped into a kind of girls' club.

"English, people, we have a guest here, and she doesn't speak Spanish." Arami pointed to Simone. "By the way, this is Dr. Simone Bennet."

A very classy, elegant lady, sporting a short, chic haircut, approached them. Her dress looked as if it was made of pure yellow silk, and she wore a beautiful pearl necklace. And she either had one of the best suntans Simone had ever seen, or she was naturally bronze, like Arami was. The woman kissed Arami and Simone on their cheeks.

"Nice to meet you, Dr. Bennet. I'm Magda, Arami's auntie. She told me she was bringing you for lunch. Welcome to our humble home."

She pointed to the house, no hint of sarcasm in her manner or tone, but Simone figured she had to be joking. Humble...? Hardly!

"Nice to meet you, madam. Please call me Simone."

"And you, young lady, call me auntie."

Impossible, Simone thought, but didn't say a word.

"Auntie." Magda took Simone by the arm and introduced her to everybody else, one by one. So many names and family positions…Simone would never remember them all. She compared them in her mind to the parade of names inside Gabriel Garcia Marques's novel. The more time Simone spent with these people, the more she felt she as if she'd stepped into the pages of the novel.

All the women spoke very good English, some with an accent, some without, but all of them perfectly understandable. After they'd spent some thirty minutes or so in pleasant conversation, a young boy came and said something in Spanish to Magda, and their hostess got to her feet.

"C'mon, ladies, the men wait for us with a nice *asado.*"

Simone looked to Arami, eyebrow raised.

"Barbecue," Arami translated in a whisper.

They followed a crushed-shell pathway around to the other side of another large building, which appeared to be some kind of gymnasium—where they found the men. Ten or more men stood or sat near an enormous brick barbecue grill that contained what seemed to be a ton of meat.

Arami kissed the oldest man there. He was very short, no more than five feet tall. She then introduced him to Simone.

"Uncle, this is Simone Bennet, the American doctor I told you about. Simone, meet my uncle, General Cesar Benitez."

"Doctor Simone." He grabbed Simone's hands and kissed them. "A pleasure to have an authority on the human mind in my home, especially when she is also a beautiful woman."

"A pleasure to meet you, General. You have a lovely house, and I would like to thank you for inviting me."

"No, on the contrary, the pleasure is all mine. Anything you need, you just ask."

He gave her a look that a wolf might give to a sheep...*a very hungry wolf,* Simone reflected.

"I would like to have a professional meeting with you next week, Doctor," the general said.

"Uncle, Simone is vacationing here..."

"It won't take long, Arami." He touched his niece's arm in a way that very clearly said "stay out of this" then turned back to Simone. "Once more, Doctor, welcome to my humble home."

Christ sake, what was this "humble home" shit? Simone

was intrigued.

"Arami, tell me, this house must be at least four thousand square feet. Why do your aunt and uncle refer to it as their 'humble home'?" she whispered.

"It's a Paraguayan saying, no matter the size of the house. There is no irony in their choice of words, I promise you; it's just a way to tell you that you are welcome."

"My darlings, our lunch is served. Let's go to the table, please," Magda called for them to join the others.

The "table" had at least thirty place settings. Everyone began loading up their plates with an abundance of food—all kinds of meats and side dishes, most of which Simone didn't recognize. She tried a little bit of almost everything, from the meats to *Chipa Guazú*—a wonderful pie made of corn and cheese—but she didn't have the courage to try a black sausage made of pig's blood called *morcilla*. She considered herself adventurous, but that would be pushing it.

"Not going to try our *morcilla*, Doctor?" the general asked, his eyes twinkling.

"No room, I'm afraid. I'm too full from all those other delicious dishes." She mentally patted herself on the back for coming up with a graceful way to refuse.

"You should try it; it's an aphrodisiac, you know." He

grinned.

Great! Simone thought. *Just what I need. I've already had sex with a stranger in the middle of a nightclub…a morsel of the morcilla and I'll go to work in a brothel.*

"Thanks, General, but we psychiatrists don't believe in aphrodisiac food…just aphrodisiac minds."

"So you are going to like men in Paraguay, Doctor. Latin lovers are the best."

Simone didn´t know how to answer to that remark.

Magda intervened and said something in Spanish to the general, speaking in a tone that sounded as if she was reprimanding him.

"She asked him if he's crazy or just senile, to say such things to a real doctor." Arami leaned close and whispered the translation into Simone's ear. "When they fight, they do so in Spanish, so they have more vocabulary to choose from…"

"I'm sorry, Doctor, my dear wife reminds me that it's not polite to brag about the prowess of our men in public."

"No offense taken, General. Don't worry, few thing are able to shock me."

Magda looked relieved, her shoulders relaxing.

But Simone could tell the general wasn't a bit embarrassed or regretful of his comments; rather, he was amused. *So,* Simone analyzed, *a man who likes to shock others...*

"And there he is! The latest man, ever," the general thundered from the head of the table as he pointed toward the door.

Everyone turned to look.

The newcomer wore blue jeans and a green shirt, and as he strode toward the table he took off his sunglasses and smiled. Simone gasped and grew lightheaded as she stared at the sun-tanned face of the stranger she'd had sex with the night before.

As the general, Magda, and the stranger began speaking to each other in Spanish, Arami translated everything for Simone.

"Father, I was taking care of business. Someone has to!"

"Today is Sunday. I've told you a thousand times...Sundays are holy days," Magda cut in.

The man approached Magda and kissed her loudly on the cheek.

"Sorry, Mamá! I promise it won't happen again."

"Sit and speak English, my son; we have a guest."

Magda pointed at Simone, who was praying—even though she was an agnostic—that the man either wouldn't recognize her or at least wouldn't reveal they already knew each other.

"Dr. Bennet," said the general, "this is my son Armando, also known as Always-late-for-lunch. Son, this is Dr. Simone Bennet; she is a friend of Arami and now a friend of ours. She is an authority on the human mind and also a published author."

My whole curriculum, thought Simone, hoping Armando wouldn't add something like, "And she's also a pervert who likes to bang strange guys in bars".

Armando looked at Simone. His eyes really were black, just as she'd thought last night, and shaped like Arami's were. He too had dark skin and black hair, but unlike his father, he was tall and very sensual looking. She remembered last night very well, and butterflies flittered in her stomach at just the sight of the guy, but what if he recognized her? She'd be totally mortified…

Tell me about bad luck and it being a small world, she thought. But maybe her luck wasn't so horrible. So far, Armando hadn't indicated he recognized her. Maybe he didn't. The club had been dark, and she'd been wearing a ton of makeup, and thanks to Arami's advice, Simone had also worn false eyelashes… A thousand thoughts flew through her mind.

"Nice to meet you, Doctor, welcome to our home! I

hope you are enjoying sampling our customary fare."

He took the empty chair near his mother—the one Simone had noticed and wondered about earlier—which had obviously been reserved for him.

Simone nodded. "Yes, thank you, everything is delicious. And you speak perfect English."

Simone had to say something, and a compliment seemed like a good way to start a conversation. She also hoped he wouldn't recognize her voice, but they hadn't exactly done a lot of talking last night, she reflected.

"He must speak your language well, Doctor; we invested a lot of money in his education, and he loves your country...he spends more time here than he should..."

The father and son rivalry sounded clear to Simone's trained ears.

"Yes, because we have businesses here, and I'm in charge of them. We have a cattle farm in Paraguay, but there's no point in farming cattle if you can't export the meat, and that's what I do in the U.S...."

Armando sounded at ease, not a bit worried or upset about his father's comments.

Ah, Simone thought, *nothing better than being raised by a dictator.* He seemed to be a man of strong opinions. A general would raise his children with rules and discipline, two factors that, in Simone's experience, produced strong people…the only chance he was a weak or spoiled man was if his mother had protected him from that discipline…but it didn't look as if that was the case here.

"Doctor, the life of a child who was raised by a general would make a nice subject for your couch. I could be your patient. Perhaps I could use a bit of therapy. You wouldn't happen to have an opening in your schedule, would you?"

"Cousin, Simone is here on vacation, not to work. What happened to this family? Suddenly, it seems as if everybody needs the services of a shrink!" Arami said.

Simone didn't disagree. She wasn't in the mood to deal with patients. Some of her more complicated cases she still handled through Skype. The others who weren't dependent upon prescription medication, she'd given some time off. For now, she needed to focus on and take care of herself. Just the thought of working on new cases increased her stress level. Memories of what had happened to her constantly filled her head.

"I really do need to relax while I'm here, but thanks for trusting me. I promise I will think about all your requests." *Maybe in my next life,* she added silently.

Magda seemed to realize the subject was making Simone a little uncomfortable and changed it.

"Where are you from, Doctor?" she asked.

"I was born in New Haven, Connecticut, where I still work, but now I live in Woodbridge."

"Have you ever been to Paraguay?" the general asked.

"No. I've never been to South America, unfortunately."

"You would love it there. My country and my people are very welcoming."

Simone noticed how often the general used the word "my". My son, my country, my people... The habit was typical of powerful men. On the way to lunch that afternoon, Arami had explained that the general used to command both his business and his family with an iron fist.

The conversation now took a more diplomatic rhythm, appropriate for a lunch. Afterward, Simone asked Arami for directions to the restroom.

"There's one right inside there," Arami said, nodding toward the big building they'd passed on their way to the table.

Simone excused herself, got up from the table, and walked back to the entrance of the building. To her surprise, she found she'd guessed correctly. The building contained a complete gym, and there were two restrooms and a sauna.

She finished up in the bathroom, washed her hands in the sink, and then opened the door. She jumped back in surprise. "Oh! It's you." Her face grew hot.

Before her stood Armando. She had the distinct and immediate impression he'd planned to meet her alone—he must have followed her. She hadn't fooled him a bit—apparently, he'd recognized her from the start.

"What game are you playing here, Doctor?" he asked.

"Game?"

"You do remember me, don't you?"

"Unfortunately, yes."

He grabbed her arm. "Unfortunately? Why do you say that?"

"Because..." She paused and sighed. "For the first time in my life, I decide to cut loose and do something crazy, and what happens? The very next day, I run into the man I did something crazy with! What are the chances? Next time, I'm going to try playing the lottery."

"I looked for you. Why did you leave in such a hurry? I would like to get to know you a little better. You seemed so...carefree and uninhibited. Today, you're completely different—straight-laced and formal. Who are you, really?"

"It's a long story. But I suppose the real me is closer to the person you're looking at right now. Last night...well,

I've been under a lot of stress, and I'm afraid I drank a great deal of alcohol..."

Her actions of the night before were so different from how she normally behaved; she found it difficult to explain.

He released her arm. "Can we talk again?"

"I don't know...your cousin is my friend; I'm a guest in her house. At this point in my life, I don't need any more drama." She felt tired and distressed, and she couldn't think about relationships right now.

"Are you married?"

"No...no it's not that."

"Then I would like to see you again."

He was definitely his father's son. Simone could hear the similarities in the commanding tone. Although phrased as a request, he was not asking her.

"Let's have dinner tomorrow," he said.

"Okay, call me at Arami's apartment. But I'm warning you; don't expect to meet the woman you were with last night. She doesn't exist!"

"Yes, she does...inside here somewhere..." He pointed at her chest.

The powerful sexual energy between them was

impossible to deny. Reminding herself she was there on vacation, Simone decided to abandon reason for a while.

"Okay, let's have dinner."

"I'll pick you up at eight o'clock. Be ready. Wear a dress." He used his father's commanding tone again.

Welcome to the world of macho men, she thought.

They spent the rest of that Sunday at the general's house and returned to Arami's apartment late that evening. Thankfully, the rest of Simone's visit with Arami's family had passed without incident.

* * * * *

The next day, Monday morning, Simone organized Arami's office, a very modern room in the apartment but a messy one. The décor was probably quite sober under all the disorder, guessed Simone. Grey shelves lined the walls. They were full of haphazardly stacked books, old magazines, picture frames, and all kinds of souvenirs Arami must have gotten while traveling.

There was a glass desk with a modern white computer sitting on it, sharing space with thousands of envelopes, pens, post-its, and a dry, half-eaten apple that looked as old as Simone was. A comfortable black office chair sat behind the desk, while two armchairs faced the front of it. Arami had told Simone she could use the space as long as she wanted to.

She spent more than an hour trying to arrange a space for herself on the table without disturbing Arami's order...or lack thereof. Simone loved organization—some might call it an obsession—and to work in an environment such as this one was a challenge to her nerves. And these days, it didn't take much to make her feel nervous.

Even while on vacation, she had reserved a portion of each day to listen to some of her patients over the internet. It was important to them to know she was available to them, but in a week she'd be back in her office in Connecticut.

Today, she had scheduled a meeting with Carl—the first time they would speak since she'd been attacked. Thanks to the work she'd done for him, her life had turned upside down. He had hired her to analyze a journal, to give him her expert opinion so he could defend a client—at least, that's what he'd told her at first—but the truth had been something altogether different, and in the end, his friend and ex-brother-in-law Peter Hay had kidnapped and tortured her.

Friday, he had contacted her, asking for an appointment. She'd felt apprehensive with his request, her heart racing at the idea of getting involved in his problems again, but she couldn't say no to him.

She consulted her clock. In addition to being organized, she was also a stickler for punctuality. Time to talk to

Carl... She opened Skype on her laptop, connected to the program, and waited for him to come online. To her delight, Carl was on time.

"Good morning, Simone." He greeted her in his normal, charming way. His chestnut hair looked shorter, which made him appear younger and very handsome in his blue suit, white shirt, and blue-and-yellow tie. Despite the fact his brown eyes had gained some small wrinkles at their corners since she'd met him, he was all charm and magnetism, as always.

"Hello, Carl, how've you been?"

"Fine, and you? I'm still feeling guilty about everything that happened to you..."

"You know it wasn't your fault. Relax."

"You almost died..."

"But I didn't."

She didn't want to continue talking about it, and she certainly didn't need his pity. She had a hard enough time keeping thoughts of the kidnapping out of her head; talking about the subject was too much for her.

"Tell me what's going on with you. You told me it was urgent that you talk to me."

"Yes, sorry, I know you're on vacation, but I really couldn't wait."

He began to talk, his words spilling out in a torrent that showed his anxiety. Normally, he was very discreet and restrained in his emotions.

"I´m not okay. I didn´t want to involve you again in the drama that has become my life, but you're the only one capable of really helping me. Selfish, I know, and I´m very sorry to do this to you."

"Don't worry about me, Carl; I'm a professional, and I'm used to dealing with other people's issues. Please, go on...tell me what´s disturbing you so much."

"Lara´s past is back to haunt me..."

Lara had been the love of Carl´s life until she had died during a sexual game they'd been playing one evening. Carl had never really fully recovered from her loss.

"What happened? Is it the usual...you missing her...or something new?"

"Sean, Lara´s brother, called me and told me he wanted to talk. During the trial, he had a few harsh words for me—called me a murderer, killer, vermin, and so on. He always blamed me, and we hadn't spoken since my acquittal. Needless to say, I was very apprehensive about any conversation we might have, but I couldn´t say no...he said it was important..."

"And how did it go?"

"Hard...first of all, he looks a lot like Lara. Same greenish eyes...it was as if she was looking at me through him, and I could barely stand to look at him. The pain was like broken glass piercing my heart... I'd never noticed the similarities between them before because he used to have a beard, but he'd shaved, and this time, it was as if someone had taken a magnifying glass and held it up in front of him. The likeness was uncanny. They even have the same long hands. If he was a girl, I would have fallen in love with him at first sight."

"You'll never forget Lara..." she told him, thinking what a pity it was that the woman would most likely haunt him forever, and a man such as him would never be available to love again. If she weren't the professional she was, she would have fallen for him, and she had to admit he disturbed her; she was not immune to him.

"You're right. How can I? She was the love of my life. I think I'm just like my father; I can love only once."

His words just confirmed her thoughts. Simone redirected the conversation.

"And after the initial shock of seeing him, were able to talk?"

"For at least two hours. It was bad, and it was good...he asked me to explain what happened. He told me he'd hated me for a long time because he was certain I had killed his sister, and not accidentally, but now he believes in my innocence."

"What made him change his mind, and what caused him to seek you out and tell you that?"

"He told me he'd always had a romantic image of his older sister as he was never informed of her situation with the senator's son and all she had been through up until only a few months before her death. He had no idea she'd led such a depraved life full of sexual encounters and other craziness. To see her lifestyle exposed in front of a jury right after losing her was too much for him. He couldn't believe what people were saying, and he thought my defense attorneys had embellished the truth to make me look better and get me off the murder charge.

"Sean and his sister Deborah decided to sell Lara's New York apartment, and they had to go through her things before they put it on the market. They found a locked box filled with diaries. Do you remember I told you I started to write because I was inspired by her habit of always keeping a journal at hand?"

"Yes...I remember."

"They decided they needed to read them. Sean told me he thought he might find some kind of proof of my guilt in one of them, but what he discovered was something altogether different. Apparently, what was revealed about her debauched lifestyle in court was just the tip of the iceberg. She'd written about her entire life...her childhood, her life in Paris, everything..."

"Those poor people! I truly pity them! But at the same time, I´m grateful they found a way to see the truth. It wasn't healthy for them to continue hating you. The truth can be liberating, even if it hurts. Hate is a horrible feeling, worse for the hater than the one who is hated most of the time. It can eat you up inside."

"He wanted to give me access to the whole story of her life...he gave me a copy of everything. That´s why I need your help."

"Have you read it?"

"I started to, but it was too much for me to stomach. When I came to the part about what that scumbag did to her...I was so angry, plagued by homicidal thoughts; I couldn´t sleep for two entire nights... I realized I need your help, or I was going to find him and kill the piece of shit. The idea of doing so rarely leaves my mind."

"Don't you even think about doing something like that, Carl; it won't bring Lara back, and you would end your life in prison."

"I know! But you have no idea how tempted I am. I would like to hire you to help me through this, Simone. I'll understand if you say no, but I really trust you, and I need your support."

Oh, god, she thought. Could she do this all over again? To read the journals, to analyze them was not the problem; her mixed feelings for Carl were what worried her. From the first moment she'd met him she'd been attracted to him, but they weren't on the same page. He was a lost cause—she'd bet he would never love again... At least, not the kind of passionate love he had felt for Lara—but how could she deny his cry for help? Before her kidnapping, she had promised to help him, to take him on as a patient, but she hadn't had the time to start the job.

"Okay, Carl, what do you suggest?"

"I would like for us to read it at the same time...kind of like a book club mixed with therapy sessions. We'll read a few chapters, and then we can discuss them. Of course, I will pay for your services as I did before, and I will respect your time. We'll work around your schedule, okay?"

"Yes, I´m going to help you. This story haunts my days, too. It will be good to know what happened to her in the beginning...why things turned out the way they did."

"When do you want to start?"

"Let´s do it this way; scan the file, if you can, and send it to me as an email attachment."

"Sure! No problem... Actually...I already did that. You can find the files in your e-mail... I don´t know how to thank you!"

So he'd counted on her help and didn't bother to deny it... *Too sure of himself*, she thought.

They talked for another half an hour, ironing out the details regarding her fee and other practical matters.

When they hung up, Simone sat back in her chair and sighed. She then opened her email box and located Carl's e-mail. Attached to it were scanned files of Lara's diaries. *Progress,* she thought. They hadn't signed a contract yet and hadn't even discussed a confidentiality clause this time. People change, she supposed. The last time Simone had worked for Carl, he'd had her sign a contract filled with confidentiality clauses.

Here I go again, she thought, *losing myself in the mysterious Lara's distorted life.* Simone felt a pang of apprehension, breathed deeply to take courage, and opened the first file.

Lara's Journal

They say everyone has a story to tell, and I suppose that's probably true, but some people's stories are more bizarre than others. I would like to tell you mine. If I had to choose a genre for my life story, I'd have to pick erotica...maybe a little romance...with a healthy dose of horror thrown in for good measure... It's definitely not a fairy tale, although I did have a fairy godmother, of sorts…but more on that later.

Part of the reason I'm writing this is to attempt to organize my mind and my feelings. Homework from my shrink, with love. He advised me that this might be a good way to come to terms with my past… I don't know if that's possible…but I hope so.

What I'm about to tell you is based, in part, on my diaries—I've been keeping a journal since I was a kid. But I'll also have to rely on my memory, as I apparently ripped out some of the pages in a few of my journals— no doubt while in a fit of rage…or out of shame—and some years' journals are missing.

And so, here we go…

About me… My name is Lara Parker… I'm blonde, my eyes are an indefinite color between blue and green, depending on my mood, and I'm very tall—five foot, nine inches. Yes, a gladiator. I'm an architect, and I'm also an interior designer. I love to build homes, and I'm quite good at my work.

I was born in Washington D.C. on June 6, 1978. We lived at 4709 Foxhall Crescent Northwest, in a beautiful, two-story brick house with a big, lovely yard. I don't know if the house is still there; once I left Washington, I never went back, not even for a vacation.

From my early childhood in D.C., I have some good memories. I'm the oldest of three siblings. My brother

Sean is five years younger than I am, and my sister Deborah is nine years younger.

My parents were working toward acquiring their piece of the American Dream. My father had a prosperous construction firm—he used to build for the government—and my mother was...well...a butterfly, forever trying to make it to the top of elite society through her social contacts. We were very well off, financially. Although we wouldn't be considered rich, we lived very comfortably, and every year, Father seemed to become a greater success in his industry.

For most of my early years, I was raised by a nanny, and as soon as I was old enough for pre-school, my mother made certain I was enrolled. I don't believe my mother wanted me around very much. I always seemed to be getting yelled at for being in her way. She was never a model of maternal devotion. Quite the contrary—and I don't remember getting along with her...ever. She thought I was a strange kid, and I thought she was a complicated person. We didn't find it easy to live together under the same roof.

My father, Laurence Parker, was a nice and very kind man, but he was also a hard worker, and I barely saw him around. He used to leave the house early, and sometimes he got back when I was already sleeping. He wanted to give us the best, and the best had a large price tag. But I always knew, deep in my heart, he loved us.

My mother, Sabine, did nothing but party and go shopping. Um, to be fair, she went to the hairdresser quite a bit, too.

By the way, I refer to my mother by her given name... A little later on, I'll explain why.

My parents didn't get along very well; they used to fight a lot, which, when I was a little kid, used to scare the shit out of me.

Thankfully, I had someone else in my life, someone who truly cared for me...someone who didn't believe children should be seen and not heard and who would take time to answer my dozens of curious question. Emma Parker, my father's mother and my paternal grandmother, was half French and half American. She was also the most fantastic person I've met in my whole life, the best influence a kid could have, and a really wonderful woman. She and Sabine didn't get along— probably because they were such complete opposites— and sometimes, Sabine would refuse to allow me to see my grandmother. But my grandmother was the only real mother I had. I didn't know anything about my grandfather—my father's father—until I was an adult.

Grandmother Emma preferred I called her Emms. She didn't want to be called Grandma, not because she thought it made her sound old—Emms was not like that—but because she wanted me to call her the same thing her friends called her. I guess she wanted our relationship to be based more on friendship than anything else.

Sabine's mother—my grandmother Shirley—was an alcoholic and didn't get along with her daughter or her grandchildren. The few times I saw her, she was weird, mean and bitter, and no one wanted to be near her…not even Sabine, who was a weirdo herself. My grandfather—Sabine's father—had abandoned her when she was a kid. To be honest, I can't say I blame him…

I received my very first diary as a birthday present from Emms one year. I remember thinking what a strange gift, especially compared to all the other fabulous presents she used to give me… She must have noticed my disappointed expression because she took me aside and explained. I remember the conversation as if it happened just yesterday.

"My darling girl, some of the best things we have in life are our memories. Everything else can disappear—people can steal from you, you can lose all, but what you have here"—Emms had pointed to her head—"you will never lose. I want you to take notes of the most important things that happen in your life, and when you grow older, you will read your journals, and you will understand how important it was to create a biography."

"What's a biography, Emms?" I had no clue what she

meant.

"It's the story of someone's life, the importance that person had in this world. But open your diary and see... I have another gift for you..." Emma told me.

Quickly, I had opened the diary with its red, faux-leather cover and tiny golden padlock, wondering what would be small enough to fit inside. I flipped through the pages until I reached the middle, and my eyes grew wide. Heart racing, I removed the airline tickets.

"Paris!" I shouted then looked at Emms. "Is this for real? Are you really taking me with you this time?"

Emms had been born in France, and she used to go back there every year. She'd told me dozens of stories about Paris and the Louvre and all the other sites. I'd pestered her for years to take me with her. France sounded like magic to my ears.

"Yes," Emms had said. "You and I are really, truly going to Paris this summer."

That birthday was one of those days a person never forgets. I wrapped my arms around my grandmother and hugged and kissed her.

"Emms, I love you more than anything!" I told her.

"I love you more, my little sunshine."

That's another one of my fonder memories. She used to

have all these beautiful nicknames for me—such as sunshine, my heart, and so on.

I really loved the diary because it had a real padlock and a key, and I could protect my ideas from Sabine, who always loved to snoop around in my things.

Even though Emms had explained the importance of me making certain I journaled on a regular schedule, I still had a rough time getting into the swing of things...until I gave my dairy a name. I had decided it wouldn't feel quite so much like talking to myself if I pretended each entry into my journal was another letter to my new friend Martin. Looking back on this now, I have to smile. Who names their diary Martin? But at that time, my favorite movie was *Back to the Future*, and Michael J. Fox played the lead character, Martin. I had so few friends at that time, and I was desperate to have one. Marty—my little red diary—became my best friend, and I used to write to him as if I were sending him letters.

I don't have many friends, Marty. Sometimes, I believe it's because I'm a little bit weird, different from other girls my age, and I spend a lot of time reading. I don't like to play very much, and I think kids are dumb. I also love to listen to music. I got a stereo on my birthday from Uncle Ruggiero and Auntie Valentine...now I need some CDs. I just have one—and here I'd drawn a little sad face. This birthday was super cool! There weren't many children, but a lot of nice people came—friends of my father, mostly—and the gifts were just great!

I used to hide my diary in a hole I'd found behind a drawer and had enlarged, by digging out the drywall with a knife because I was so afraid Sabine would find it and read it. I had explained this to the diary, apologizing as if it had feelings:

Sorry to hide you, Marty, but even if you do have a lock, my mom will find a way to open you... She's like that...nuts...but I believe most grownups are crazy, don't you think? All except Emms; she is the best grandma in the world, and sometimes, I don't believe she's a grownup, she's so cool. I can talk to her, and she treats me like a friend and not like a silly little kid the way other adults treat me. Most grownups think kids don't know nothing. I hate them. But I believe I hate children more because they do act so silly and stupid. I wish I could snap my fingers and become an adult. I want to have a car and go wherever I want.

Back then, to me, having a car represented independence. I thought adults went where they pleased, when they pleased because they could drive.

In the days leading up to the Paris trip, I barely got any sleep.

Martyyyyyyyyyyyyyyyyyyyyyyyyyyyyyyyyyyyyyyyyy, I wrote in my journal, *tomorrow I'm going to Paris! Just me and Emms. I'm so happy; I can't sleep. Today, Emms and I talked about the trip.*

"Ems," I said, "I'm so happy we are going to Paris. I'm

not going to bother you while we're there; I promise!"

"But who told you that you bother me, my sunshine?"

"Mother told me I'm a bother, and she thinks you are going to complain about me after the trip."

"She told you that?"

"Yes...but please don't tell her I've told you. She will ground me. She loves to do that."

"Don't worry, Lara," Emms said. "I will never tell anybody what you tell me; trust me."

She opened her arms and hugged me, and I was there, in her arms, listening to her heartbeat while we talked about Paris. To this day, I can still remember how she smelled, a perfume mix of flowers and vanilla, and how warm I felt in her embrace, and those memories bring tears to my eyes—me, a woman who rarely cries.

"Can we go to the Eiffel Tower and Triumph Arc?" I asked her.

"Of course. We can go anywhere you like. We are going to see many things in Paris—museums, statues, paintings. There is wonderful art over there. Art is an expression of love. The artist leaves a little bit of his heart in every canvas, every piece of marble, so we can have a little bit of his soul, of his feelings, and then when you have recorded that piece of art in your brain, a little bit of the artist's love will stay with you forever, too. Those memories will give you happiness because you'll know there are beautiful things in the world."

Emma always had a poetic way to explain things.

My First Trip to Paris...

Paris is a party! It's not just a phrase; it is a reality. I fell in love with the city from the moment I first stepped foot there. I adore everything about it—the smells, the food, the people, the crowds.

Visiting there with Emms was like opening a gigantic gift box. She took me every place a kid could go. Museums, galleries, parks, stores, libraries.

My first visit to *Champs Elysées* with its *caffés* made me think I would like to live there as an adult... I didn't know how right I was—or that it would happen long before I became an adult—at least, age-wise.

Emma took me to the Triumph Arc as she had promised. The elevator was broken—nothing unusual these days, I know.

"Madam," a policeman told Emma, "the elevator is broken. You have to use the stairs if you want to go to the top."

Of course, he spoke French, so Emms had to translate for me.

"Thanks," Emms told the officer, and then she turned back to me. "I believe we have to climb three hundred steps, young lady, what do you think?"

"I really would like to go to the top, Emms, can we?"

"Well then, what are we waiting for? Let's go."

Emms laughed and we started to climb. By the time we reached the top, we weren't laughing anymore, though...and we still had to go down...

But first I had to look at the view. I ran to the edge, which was surrounded by a fence to keep people from falling off, but I grabbed the bars and stuck my face in the middle to look down. It was beautiful! All those avenues that meet in the Arc and all so gorgeous. The day was clear, the sky a pale blue with a few clouds, and a gentle breeze caressed my face and lifted my hair, making it fly in the air. My heart was full of joy.

"How about it, Lara?" Emms asked me. "Worth the climb?"

"Oh, yes! I'm so happy I could shout with joy!"

"Well, go ahead. What's stopping you?"

I looked around us at the other people who'd braved the stairs to experience that amazing view.

"What about them?" I asked, turning back to Emms. "What are they going to think?"

"Do you know them? Are they very important to you?" She gave me a serious look.

"I don't know them at all." I shook my head.

"So shout. Go ahead and scream, kid! Never let other people prevent you from doing something that makes you happy. Their opinions don't matter."

I studied Emms's expression. Was she serious?

She grinned at me and nodded, so I took a huge breath.

"Ya-hoooooooooooooooo! I'm in Parissssssssssssssssssssssssssssssss!" I shouted at the top of my lungs.

People looked at me, some started to laugh, others turned their face, but Emms was laughing hard, and so I started to laugh, too. I was very happy. I didn't ever want to go home. I wanted to stay there forever with Emms.

Ah...life was so simple then...

In the evening, we went to a nice restaurant Emms knew. It was near the apartment she had there, Fontaine de Mars. Once we were seated at the table, Emms asked me what I was going to order.

"Steak!" I answered quickly. "My favorite!"

Emms frowned. "Don't you want to try something new? I think you're old enough to experience something a little different."

"Well, okay. But what if I order something I've never had, and I don't like it?"

I thought about a big, juicy steak, and my tummy rumbled. I was very hungry.

"Then you'll know you don't like it. But you'll never know until you try. And then you can order a steak and say, 'This is much better than anything else.'"

I nodded. I had never thought of it that way. "Okay...what we are going to try?"

"Hmm...let me choose? Trust me?"

Again, I nodded. I trusted Emms more than anyone else I knew.

Emms ordered, and a short while later, our waiter came over carrying a little round bowl covered in holes. Inside the holes was something brown and juicy looking. I watched Emms use a little fork to pick one up. It looked weird, like a little piece of brown rubber.

"Try this, Lara," she said.

"What is it?"

"Try it first, and then I'll tell you..." She held out the fork.

I leaned forward, closed my eyes, and sucked the little bit of food into my mouth. My eyes flew open at the delicious, buttery taste. It was a little soft but very salty. Some people have a sweet tooth, but I must have a salt tooth because I loved it!

"Well? Do you like it?" Emms asked.

"Oh, yes! Quite a lot. May I have more?"

"Sure. It's called escargot."

"Escargot is good, much better than steak," I told her around a mouth full of another one of the delicious morsels and some bread.

"It's a snail," she told me and waited for the information to sink in.

I stopped chewing. "A what?"

"A snail." Emms smiled.

"Like the ones in our garden? People really eat that?" I asked.

"Yes, you just finished yours and mine, so I'm guessing you really like it."

I glanced down at the empty plate, and my cheeks grew hot.

"I'm sorry," I said. "They were really good. But I can't believe I ate snails!"

"Don't think about what you are eating; just savor the flavor."

I thought about this for a moment and decided Emms was right. After all, I never thought about where steak came from, so why should I think about the snail?

That was how I fell in love with escargots, and to this day, whenever I can, I introduced that food to people I care about. And as usual, Emms had turned the whole experience into a lesson. One I still remember.

"Lara...over the course of your lifetime, you will face many new things. Just because you aren't familiar with something doesn't mean you won't like it. You cannot form an opinion unless you give it a try. Never judge before knowing—we can only make a judgment based on knowledge, okay?"

"Okay, Emms," I told her.

To this day, her words have had an impact on my entire life. I have never judged anything before first trying it, and thanks to Emms, I have always loved Paris and trying different things.

On Being "Normal"...

Early on, I discovered I couldn't concentrate very well in classes I didn't like. I was a genius when I enjoyed what we were learning and a total disaster when I didn't. One day, when I was on my way to biology—one of those classes I hated—I decided to skip school with a new friend. He was alone and sad, and I invited him to go fishing with me. We didn't go far; there was a little lake behind the school, and we went there.

Later that day, Sabine had a fit. The principal had found out I'd missed class and had called her, and she'd had to come to the school to get me. She told me I was stupid for cutting classes instead of studying. I had tried to tell her I had a hard time concentrating—that my mind refused to focus on my work. Instead, I'd find myself daydreaming...imagining I was an adult and lived in Paris, or I would think about the concerts I'd been to with Emms. I really had a hell of an imagination.

When we arrived home, my parents began shouting at each other. I'd been sent up to my room, but of course, I'd snuck back down and was behind the door, listening.

"Lara is totally irresponsible. I don't know what to do with her!" Sabine said to my father.

"C'mon, Sabine, she's just a kid. Kids do things like that. If you spent more time with her, you could talk to her about responsibility, but then again, responsibility isn't one of your strong suits, is it, so how can you teach her?"

I couldn't stifle my laughter at this, and they caught me eavesdropping. They both shouted at me, Sabine ending by yelling one of her most favorite sayings.

"You're grounded!"

Grounded. Again. Whenever that happened—and it happened a lot—I could read in peace, and I didn't mind being locked in my room.

CHAPTER TWO

Simone – Present Day

Simone had to close the file but not before she sent it to the printer. She really was one of those persons that preferred to read the paper. *Maybe I'm too old for technology,* she thought. She consulted her watch and opened her Skype again. She had another meeting in five minutes, this time with Phillip, her beloved, masochist patient. He was simply adorable, very gentle, very kind but completely disturbed regarding his private life.

His wife had abandoned him just before Simone´s kidnapping, and he was having a love affair with a dominatrix. He was an accountant, and he looked like one—serious and trustworthy—and nobody would guess that behind his professional façade existed a man full of kinky passion.

"Hello, Doctor, I've really missed our sessions. Thank you very much for allowing me to impose on your vacation."

"No problem, Philip. I've missed our sessions, too, but I'll be back soon. I also miss the goodies you always brought with you."

Philip loved to cook and always brought samples of his pastries for Simone, appearing at her office with a different recipe each week. As his sexual practices were weird, Simone never ate the things he cooked—one could never be too careful—but it was nice to receive such presents. She'd begun to miss those kinds of normal, day-to-day life events.

Maybe I really am ready to go back, she thought, *I'm getting soft, missing pastries I don't eat just because they remind me my old life.*

"I just learned a delicious new one called Paris-Brest. It's wonderful. When you come back, I will bake it especially for you."

"Thank you, Philip, that would be lovely. I believe I'll be back next week. But tell me about you. How is life? What's new?"

"I'm a new man! Having two women fight over me is crazy-good for my ego. Me...the epitome of a nerd. I'm delighted. I've never experienced anything like it, and I feel like Superman!"

On the monitor, he closed his fist and pumped it. Superman, indeed! Simone shook her head.

"What do you mean, you have two women fighting over you?" she asked.   Last time they'd talked, he'd been happy about his love affair with the dominatrix, but he suffered from a broken heart over his wife having left him. What had changed in a few weeks?

"My wife wants me back. She told me I'm the one, she loves me, and she wants to resume our life together. She even promised me to be more understanding about my fantasies...and Leonora is obsessed. She also said she loves me, and she is threatening to kill my wife, and so—"

"What? Oh, Philip. Sounds to me as if you have a real mess on your hands. Do you know what you're going to do?"

"I was hoping you'd help me figure that out. It's complicated... I like Leonora—we have fun together— but I don't feel the same way about her as I do about Jane..."

"And what do you feel for Jane?"

"Oh, my feelings for her run deep. She excites me—I'm always horny around her—she is the prettiest girl in the world to me, she is sexy...but at the same time, I've always felt as if I'm not good enough for her... Just the sound of her voice makes my heart melt... I'm always trying to make her appreciate me."

"And Leonora?"

"Ah, she makes me horny, too...but it's different. I feel safe when I'm with her."

How secure could he possibly feel, Simone wondered, with a woman who tied him up and beat him mercilessly?

"She acts as if she loves me. She wants to know if I'm okay, if I'm hungry, if I've had enough sleep... She worries over me. When we're at home and she's not working, she acts like a geisha..."

From a professional sadist to a geisha, thought Simone. Not so easy to believe...but if there was one thing she'd learned a long time ago, it was that different people could view the same situation completely differently.

"So we could say Leonora is the mother you would like to have, and Jane behaves like the mother you had?"

"Ouch, Doctor! You are so crude sometimes... I never thought about it like that. I certainly never compared either of them to my mother!"

"No, I'm sure you haven't...but that's basically what you just described. In one of our previous sessions, you told me your mother was never satisfied with you, and the more you did the more she wanted from you. You were always trying to make her notice you, but she always favored your big brother. Sounds to me as if you have a similar relationship with Jane. You are always trying to please her and always feel as if you fall short. Leonora, on the other hand—and this is only based on what you've just told me—attends to all your needs, just like a good mother should do... Now you're swinging back and forth."

"Swinging back and forth?"

"Yes...going from bad mom to ideal mom and then back again..."

"Should I get rid of them both?"

"Is that what you think you should do?"

Simone could tell by the anxious look on his face that he wanted her to make a decision for him, but she would never do that.

"No, I´m asking you what I should do."

"It´s not for me to decide your life for you, Philip. I´ve only analyzed what you said. If I were you, I would try to figure out what gives me more pleasure—to spend a lifetime living in fear of losing Jane or to live with someone who tended my every need as if I were a baby. And yes...sometimes, the answer is *neither one*. Relationships are better when they resemble a two-way street. But you have to evaluate the circumstances and come to a conclusion."

But can we ever find that perfect, balanced relationship? I haven't been able to do so... Simone added, but of course, she kept her thoughts to herself. After all, one of her roles was to give hope not only convey life's crude reality.

"As usual, you are correct. I suppose I have a lot of thinking to do! I believe I'd be better off with someone who loves me and who I love back without fears or dependence. Which would be the ideal relationship...but those are hard to find..."

* * * * *

After talking to Philip, Simone grabbed a pear from the kitchen, ate it, and then went to her room and changed into a bikini. She was going to the pool to lie in the sun for a while. She grabbed the print copy of the journal to take with her, intending to read a little bit more of Lara's story. Luckily, the pool was deserted, and she chose a reclining chair, spread sunscreen over her body, and lay down to feel the warm sensation of the sun on her skin. It gave her energy and yet relaxed her. With a contented sigh, she picked up the text and started to read.

Lara's Journal

All my life, people have said I am pretty. One day, a friend of Sabine's came to visit. Her name was Maggie, and I really liked her. She was short and chubby and had chestnut hair and a friendly, round face. She was always kind to me, and I liked being around her, but Sabine told me to disappear because she wanted to be alone with her friend. I hid to listen, making certain they didn't see me.

"Lara is getting prettier and prettier," Maggie said.

"Do you think so?"

My mother didn't think I was pretty; imagine that!

"Yes, she is already adorable, and she reminds me of a young Brooke Shields, straight out of *Blue Lagoon*, only Lara is much blonder than Brooke is."

I didn't stay around to hear more because I suddenly had to know—who was Brooke Shields, and what was blue lagoon?

That same day, after discovering from the maid that *Blue Lagoon* was a film and Brook Shields the main actress, I went in search of my father.

"Dad, can I watch *Blue Lagoon*?"

"Of course not, babe. You are too young for that."

Shit and double shit! Always too young.

I remember how badly I used to hate that phrase. I decided to call Emms, and she asked me why I wanted to watch it. When I told her what I had overheard, she promised to get the movie.

Some days later, Emms came to take me for a ride. It was a Saturday, and she took me to her place. I loved her apartment; it always smelled of cinnamon and was so pretty with its vases, flowers, and paintings.

Located on the fifteenth floor of a skyscraper, Emm's apartment was very bright and cheerful. She loved to decorate with a variety of colors. The living room had two cream-colored velvet couches and two beautiful chairs covered in gold-and-rose-colored upholstery. There was also a brown wood dinner table that seated six people. The cream-colored tablecloth was covered in small roses, golden flowers, and tiny green leaves. Many, many gold-gilt-framed paintings covered the walls. Almost all depicted images of women, some of whom looked exactly like Emm.

That day, we went directly to her room. She loved to watch movies while lying in her bed. Her room was so chic! She had an antique, brown wood bed, and the wallpaper was a light shade of rose, a color she told me was called *ceindres de roses*, which is French for "rose ashes". There were also many beautiful rugs on the floor and many paintings on the walls in there, too. When I drew in a breath, the scent of warm vanilla tickled my nose. I felt so comfortable there. How vivid that room is in my mind; I close my eyes, and I'm there.

As I went to lie down on Emma's bed, which was covered in throw pillows and cushions, she opened the door to her armoire, revealing the television she kept inside. She put the tape in the VCR and joined me to watch the movie.

Oh my gosh... Brooke Shields was gorgeous!

"Do you think I look like her, Emms?" I asked, full of expectations.

"Prettier, little one. But Brooke is ten years older now. This is not a new movie. I'm pretty sure it was released a decade ago, at least."

"So she's an old woman now?"

I was a little put off about that. I wanted that beautiful girl to be my age. Kids always tend to think grown-ups are old; I was no exception.

Emms laughed.

"We can say she is older..."

We continued watching the movie. During one scene, I pointed at the couple on the screen who were kissing and rubbing each other.

"What are they doing, Emms?" I asked.

Emms got the controller, paused the movie, and looked at me.

"They're having sex," she told me.

"Um...what's sex?"

"Nobody has talked to you about this yet?" Emms seemed surprised.

"No...I read something about it in a book but didn't understand very much."

"Well...let's talk. I'm going to explain this to you because I don't think anyone else will do this properly, and you are growing up fast." She took my hand and started to explain. "Have you seen you little brother naked?"

"Sure!" I laughed. "I've seen his little dick."

"Yes, he has a penis, but you can call it a dick if you want to, and you have a vagina but you can call it a pussy."

"Yes...vagina is too ugly...I'd rather say pussy."

"Me, too. So sex is like this...when a man likes a woman, they kiss, they caress, and the dick gets hard."

"I've seen Sean's dick hard when he is going pee!"

"Exactly! That's how it gets, and then the woman gets excited, too. So they join...the man puts his dick inside the woman's pussy, and they move together."

"But that's not what they're doing in the movie!" I was curious to see this thing she had described.

"No, Lara, of course not. People don't do that in public; they do it in closed places, like a bedroom."

"My mom and dad do that?" I couldn't imagine such a thing. Especially because most of the time I didn't think they liked each other.

"I believe they do."

"Ughhh, I don't want to think about it."

"About sex?"

"No, about my parents doing that; it's nasty!"

"But they had to do it for you to be born."

"How come?"

"Sex makes babies. The man leaves a seed inside the woman, and then she can have a baby."

"So...they did it three times?"

Emma laughed. "I believe much more than that because sex is a good thing, and a woman doesn't have a baby every time she has sex. People can have a certain control over it—there are means to prevent a pregnancy. Your mom never explained any of this to you?"

"No...I asked once...when she had Debbie in her belly, but Sabine told me I was too young to know and that I shouldn't ask those kinds of questions."

"And so you stopped asking?"

"I was ashamed. She told me it was shameful to ask people about things like that."

"Okay. Never, ever be ashamed of asking me anything, okay?"

"All right, Emms, love you more than pizza!"

"Pizza?"

"Yes! I love pizza! Emms, is it good?"

"Sex? Yes! Very much."

"Can I do it?"

"Not now. You are too young. But one day, yes, with the right guy, someone you love and care about and when you are grown up."

"Can I ask you another question, Emms?"

"Sure, my little sun, anything!"

"Can we have pizza for dinner?"

And then we went back to the movie.

* * * * *

Sabine used to throw fantastic parties for our birthdays. They were not kids' parties; they were adult parties with kids—just another excuse for her to throw a huge gala and gather high-society-type people around her.

During one of those birthday parties—I don't remember which one—I met Arthur. He was the son of Ruggiero and Valentine Eberle, two of my parents' best friends. Ruggiero was a banker and then a politician; Valentine was a socialite like Sabine...only they were filthy rich, and she really was part of the in-crowd, while Sabine merely struggled to attain that kind of status. Arthur was the Eberleses' only child, and he was twenty years older than I was.

He had been abroad to study and had come back to work in his family's bank.

He approached me during the party and started a conversation, to my surprise. I was not used to adults' attention. He was very clever and knew the right words.

"So you are the famous Lara..."

"Me? Famous?"

"Yes, my parents always talk about how beautiful and intelligent you are. I was anxious to meet you."

67

"Really?" I had a difficult time believing someone older would be interested in me.

"Yes. And I can see with my own eyes they were not exaggerating. Indeed, you are beautiful."

"And smart," I told him. For some reason, it was very important to me that he thought I was smart, too.

"Do you like ice cream?"

"Sure, who doesn't?" Strange question, I thought.

"One of these days, I'm going to take you to get the best Italian ice cream in town, and we can talk, and I'm going to discover if you are as smart as you are pretty, okay?"

"Done!"

I didn't think he would keep his promise, but some adults were like that; they promised things they never intended to fulfill. But I was happy with his attention. I felt as if I were finally growing up, and back then, that thought made me happy.

CHAPTER THREE

Simone – Present Day

Simone stopped reading to turn in the chair as she analyzed Lara's words. So far, Lara described a relatively normal childhood, a fantastic grandmother who—at least based on what Lara had written—seemed very experienced and wise, an absent father—considering she barely mentioned him—and a mother who couldn't deal very well with her. Nothing abnormal until now.

My mother didn't know how to deal with me, either, thought Simone, and thinking of her mother made her sad, as the older woman had died years earlier. They hadn't had an easy relationship... But I'm not going to review that story now, she told herself.

The thought made Simone restless. She got to her feet. She'd continue reading the journal later. She'd spent enough time lounging in the sun. Time to go back inside and check her business email, fill her head with work, and push her sad thoughts to the back of her mind, where they belonged...

As she walked in the front door of Arami's apartment, Simone heard the phone ringing.

"Hello?" she answered, a bit out of breath from having run to catch the call.

"Dr. Bennet, good afternoon." General Cezar Benitez was on the phone.

"Good afternoon, General."

"Doctor, I'm sorry to insist, but I really need to talk to you," he pleaded with her in a very gentle tone. "It's very important, and I won't bother you for long."

Simone couldn't think of a way to turn him down. The family had treated her too well...it would be rude to do so. And at the same time, she hated herself for allowing proper behavior and etiquette to dictate her reactions, rather than going with her feelings.

"Okay, General, can you come to Arami's place at 5:00 p.m.?"

"Sure, whatever time is good for you."

After hanging up with the general, Simone headed into the kitchen, a large and modern space with grey cupboards, a glass table with silver iron chairs, and modern stainless-steel appliances. Unlike the office areas, the kitchen was impeccably organized, probably because Arami couldn't fry an egg.

Simone dug around in the refrigerator, looking for something to have for lunch. Arami's maid, Eliza, had left Simone a plate filled with thin slices of perfectly grilled, pink roast beef and a mixed greens salad. Simone ate and then decided to rest a little while longer before checking her email. Her vacation would soon be over, and she would need all her strength to face real life.

The general arrived promptly on time. One of Arami's maids opened the door and led him back to the office, where Simone was waiting for him.

"Good afternoon, Doctor."

"Good afternoon, General. Please, take a seat."

He studied the two available chairs and chose the one nearest to Simone.

"Please, call me Cezar."

She would do that, but she would not tell him to call her by her first name. To do so would give an impression of intimacy she needed to avoid.

"Right...Cezar. Why don't we discuss why you're here? I'm listening; please, tell me how can I help you."

"You have developed a very good practice," he said. "I did a little research about you, and Arami told me how serious you are and that you're also a professor. I know you can help me."

Simone analyzed his wording—*I know you can help me*... Very positive... She heard the underlying *you* should *help me* behind the words...

"I have problems, serious problems. And I can't go to a regular shrink. I'm afraid I'd be betrayed. The last thing I need is someone selling my secrets. One can never be too careful..."

Add "paranoid" to your list, thought Simone.

"But, General, I'm going back to Connecticut next week. How could I treat you?"

"Well, I've been thinking about that... I'm seventy years old, but I'm not an idiot. I use the internet and computers regularly. If you agree to see me, we could talk online, if necessary, and you also could see me more frequently while you are still here..."

"Therapy is about reflecting, Cezar. Meeting every day is not necessarily a good thing because you need time to think about things between our sessions... Let's try this; I'll see you three times this week, and then we can discuss whether we need to continue. I still don't know your problem. Maybe it's easy to solve..."

"Should we start now?"

"Yes, you tell me your problem, and I will listen, take notes, only for my personal use."

"I'm impotent." He went directly to the point.

Well, she thought, impotence at his age was not an unusual thing, but the general seemed in good health.

"Have you ever been to a doctor for analysis?"

"Sure, I've gone to see my personal doctor. He is very trustworthy, but he told me there is nothing physically wrong with me. He even said that if he didn't know me and saw only my blood tests, he would think I was a seventeen-year-old boy. So he told me to see a shrink..."

"Okay. I would like to see your medical records. But tell me...when did you start to feel impotent?"

"I'm not sure. Some time ago. First, I was too tired, and I didn't want to be bothered. But then...when I was rested, I found I couldn't."

"You couldn't *what*?"

"Get a hard-on...an erection...a boner...not even to start a game...not even with girls in their twenties, thirties, or forties. Believe me, I tried everything, but it was no use!"

Talk about a guy who didn't worry about a girl's age...or his marriage.

"And I used to be a stallion," he went on, "I'd see a pretty lady and grow instantly hard, ready for combat. I could have sex three or four times with only a few minutes' break between sessions... And now this old friend of mine"—he pointed to his penis—"seems to be retired. I can't stand the idea! I never thought it would happen to me."

He punched the arm of the chair, a clear sign of his despair.

"Well, it's too soon to come to a conclusion, but if it's not physical, we need to understand what happened to change your life..."

"I believe I'm old. Now I have to just wait around to die!"

Oh, how dramatic! Simone fought not to roll her eyes.

"I would rather die than live as a useless, old man, good for nothing!"

Yes, thought Simone, if his life was directly connected to his dick, better to die...

"Why were you so tired?" she asked.

"Well, I ran for the presidency of my country in the last election. I lost, but it was close, and I believed I could win in the future. I decided to start campaigning again, starting earlier this time, and prepare for the elections in two years. So I was travelling, trying to gain sponsors, and I was not leading a healthy life. Not until I decided to stop...take a break...rest...come to Miami..."

"And your sexual appetite disappeared when you were campaigning?"

"Yes. But only gradually. There were too many trips, dinners, and lunches. I usually sleep eight hours a night, and I couldn't sleep more than four."

"So you decided to stop campaigning?"

"No. Not completely. I just cut back a little, following my doctor's orders. At first, he thought I couldn't perform due to my lack of sleep. But that wasn't it."

"Before you started this campaign, you were having sex normally?"

"Well...I was already tired from the elections, and I stopped having sex during the last month of the last campaign."

"When was this?"

"August, 2013. It's complicated because the press is always trying to dig up dirt on your life, so you have to be careful. I was being cautious."

"But how could they create a scandal over you having sex with your wife?"

"Well, Doctor, I'm a man... I have sex with my wife, but we've been together for many years. So you could say I fool around a little bit..."

"So you haven't had sex in three years—not with your wife, not with any other woman?"

"No! I had sex eventually in the past three years, but it was nothing like it used to be...and then in the last eight months, nothing."

"How do you feel about losing the elections?"

"I feel like a loser!"

He was very upset about her question; she could tell by his irritated tone and his red face.

"Can you explain to me how that happened? I heard you are a hero in your country."

"Yes, but I was just the pilot on the plane...the man who replaced his dead brother, who was also a replacement for the *true* hero, Oviedo. My name was not very recognizable."

"But don't you think you can win next time?"

"I'm not sure." He seemed sad and tired.

"Cezar, I believe we'll need to talk more about the

elections. I'm going to need more information in order to treat you. Can we meet in two days?"

"Sure. Whenever you want me to be here, I'll be here."

They talked about her fees, and the general explained he never touched money—he'd have his driver pay her—and although he didn't explain his reasons for this, right after he left, the driver appeared with an envelope filled with cash.

Carrying a handful of twenty-dollar bills, Simone went to her room, trying to remember when she'd last had a patient pay with anything other than a check or credit card. Looking for her cellphone, she found it on her night table. She checked the display to see if anyone had tried to reach her and found at least ten missed calls from Armando. *A very anxious and impatient person,* she thought. *Not a good sign.* She dialed his number right after listening to three messages—all from him—asking her to call him back.

"Hello, Armando, I saw you called me."

"Playing hard to get, Doctor?"

"I was talking to a patient, and I'm too old for games. I don't play, Armando," she said emphatically, letting him know in no uncertain terms how displeased she was by his statement.

"I'm sorry, Simone…I would like to confirm our dinner

tonight…" He quickly changed the subject.

"Yes, we're still having dinner. Is 8:00 p.m. okay with you?"

"Sure!"

"Do you like seafood?"

"I love it!"

"Great. I'll see you at eight. Good-bye, Armando." She knew she was being short with him, but she had a bad feeling about the way he'd obsessively tried to reach her.

They hung up, and Simone decided to go for a run. A bit of exercise always improved her mood. After she returned, she showered, washed her hair, and then blew it dry until it lay soft and shining around her shoulders. She would wait until a half-hour before they left to put on her makeup.

She sat in a confortable, soft leather reading chair near her bed, put her feet up on a matching stool, turned on the floor lamp, and resumed reading the journal. This particular project didn't really feel much like work, anyway. Lara's diaries read more like a novel—albeit a disturbing one, at times—and Simone couldn't help but be drawn into the dramatic events.

Lara's Journal

How to Lure a Girl...

A few weeks after the party and meeting Arthur, Sabine came to see me in my room—a rare thing, to be sure, and rarer still for her to be in such a good mood. I looked at her suspiciously.

"Hey, Lara, I think you have a new friend," she said in a singsong voice.

"Me? Who?"

I couldn't imagine what she was talking about because I hadn't met any previously unknown kids recently.

"Arthur just called to ask me if he can take you for a ride. He wants to take you to his golf club to have Italian ice cream or something like that. He said he promised you."

"Are you serious?"

"Do you know how exclusive that club is? I always wanted to be a member, and you get an invitation to go! Lucky girl."

Sabine was as excited as a kid waiting for Santa.

"It's weird...he is too old to be my friend." Why a man

that much older than I was would want to take me for a ride, I couldn't imagine.

"He's not that old! And he is adorable and so polite!"

"I don't think I want to go... I don't know him..."

"But you are going, and then you will get to know him. I'm going to tell you something, little miss, luck won't knock on your door twice."

I couldn't imagine why she thought I was lucky for being invited to go get ice cream, but before I could question her, Sabine slipped back into her true self, an annoying, bossy woman, and she threw open my closet door. She reached inside, grabbed a dress, and tossed it at me.

I stared in shocked surprise. Since when did she begin selecting my clothes?

"Wear that one; it's pretty!"

I picked up the dress—a pale-blue, sleeveless number with a waist-slimming, pleated skirt—and decided not to argue. After all, Sabine might have been a horrible mother, but she had excellent taste in clothing, and this happened to be one of my most favorite dresses.

When Arthur arrived, I was ready—polished, perfumed, and waiting, having followed Sabine's orders. I was not happy about that, but he arrived in the coolest red convertible car!

Back then I was crazy about convertibles and cars in general.

He opened the door for me, and when I climbed inside, I found a little gift box next to the seat.

Today, when I look back, I can separate my resentment, and I can give him credit for being intelligent. He knew exactly how to gain my sympathy.

"A gift for a beautiful girl."

I opened the yellow box quickly and discovered he bought me five CDs! All the most popular bands of the time. Of all the presents he could have bought me, he'd managed to hit on the thing I loved above almost anything else—music! I don't remember the names of all the bands, but I do recall he'd chosen two of my favorites—Roxette and New Kids on the Block were inside the little box. What a cool guy, I thought. Maybe Sabine was right for once, and he really was a great guy.

"Thank you, thank you, thank you, Arthur! I really love them!" I smiled at him.

"I'm glad. Now, let's go have that ice cream."

We went to his club, and he bought ice cream, and we chatted. He was nice and not boring at all. He was very interested in my life, my tastes, how things were at home.

From the rat's point of view, the cat was sniffing out the

rat's life in order to discover its weak points, its tastes, and its allies…hoping to use the information to the cat's advantage. He was preparing to have dinner…I would be dinner…but that thought never crossed my mind back then. At the time, I thought he was kind and considerate.

"Do you have many friends?" he asked me.

"Me? No…kids my age don't like me."

"Why not? You are pretty and smart!"

Flattering someone is the best way to his or her heart… It was to mine… Not nowadays, but when I was a girl, oh, how good it was to hear a compliment.

"I believe it's because I'm too tall and because I like to read more than play."

"You are not tall; you are perfect. And reading is a great way to pass the time. Do you want my opinion?"

I nodded.

"If that's why they don't like you, they are idiots."

"Yes, they are."

I thought a little bit about my friends and remembered Emms.

"I have my grandmother; she is my friend."

"No, kid, grandparents are not friends, they are just…grandparents. They will be by your side if they think you're doing the right thing, but a friend will always be there, even if it doesn't look good."

He'd changed the subject and told me about living abroad, about how he'd missed home and how he'd felt lonely after returning home. I'd felt sorry for him, knowing firsthand how it felt to be lonely. Looking back now, I realize what a great actor he was!

"So… You might be surprised to know I don't have many friends either…" He looked at me and made a sad face.

"I'm going to be your friend, and you can call me when you feel alone."

"Thank you, Lara!" Then he ran his fingers through my hair.

By the time he drove me home, I had decided he was nice, and I liked him… Boy, was that a mistake.

Many Rides, Ice cream, and Gifts

Two days after our first trip for ice cream, Arthur called me.

"Hey, beautiful, I'm here, sad and all alone, and I

remembered you told me I could call you."

"Sure. Are you feeling blue?" I had just discovered the meaning of the phrase, and I felt mature and grownup using it.

"A little bit. Do you feel blue sometimes?"

"Yes, I do."

"And what do you do when you are feeling blue?"

"I read. A good book can make me forget all my troubles. You should give it a try." I felt so great giving him advice.

"And can you recommend a good book for me to read?"

"I'm reading *Dealing with Dragons*; I can lend it to you when I'm finished."

"Sure. What's it about?"

"A bored girl who runs away to live with a dragon. It's really very cool."

"So you love fantasies, like dragons and fairies?"

"More dragons than fairies!"

I remember scoffing internally at the idea of a guy his age being interested in dragons, but he played his "nice guy" role so well; I had no possible way of knowing he was not being sincere.

We talked another half hour, and he thanked me, told me he wasn't upset anymore. Nice, I thought, thinking I had a friend.

Arthur started to send me tons of gifts! Nothing too expensive but all things dear to a girl's heart. From hairclips to books and CDs, day in day and out, I received something from him. Every day was like Christmas with him around. One specific day, he sent me a new book, exactly the kind I loved to read. It was called *Castle in the Air*, and it was about a princess named Flower-in-the-Night and a magic carpet. I called him to say thank you, as Sabine would insist I do every time he sent me a gift.

"Hey, Artie," I said, using the nickname he'd asked me to call him.

"Hey, beautiful, what's up?"

"Thanks for the book! How did you know I wanted to read this one?"

"A little bird told me you had finished *Howl's Moving Castle*..."

"Who told you?"

"A dragon..."

"Be serious."

"Well...a dragon...your mother told me..."

I laughed hard. He was funny, and I had started to bond with him. He seemed to understand me so well. He even knew Sabine was a dragon and how complicated my relationship with her was.

How to Catch a Bird

Arthur used to call me almost every night, and at least once a week we would go out for pizza or ice cream in his little convertible red car. I was happy because Emms was abroad, and I had someone to talk to who really seemed to understand me.

One day, he took me for a ride, and since it was a nice day and he knew how crazy I was about his convertible, he dropped the top. We ended up along a deserted road.

"What are we doing here?" I gazed around at the empty landscape.

"Beautiful, you are very tall for a girl your age, did you know that?"

"Yes, a giraffe, as the kids say." I frowned, thinking about how much I hated when kids called me that.

"Don't be sad about that. You are beautiful, and they are all envious little gnomes."

I giggled.

"And since you're so tall, I believe you could learn how to drive."

"What? Are you kidding me? But that's illegal. I'm too young."

"Well, yeah, it's illegal for kids your age to drive because if it wasn't, all those dwarf classmates of yours would want to learn, and they wouldn't be able to reach the pedals and still see over the dashboard! But I'm sure you're tall enough; now, come here. Switch with me."

He opened the door and came around to the passenger's seat, while I slid behind the wheel.

My hands were damp with excitement, but I felt so grown up, so powerful driving a car. It was one of the happiest sensations I ever had. To have full control of a beautiful machine, to be able to transport us. It was a feeling of freedom.

"Lara, you drove beautifully! But you have to promise not to tell anyone, okay? It's our secret! Grownups wouldn't understand, so we'll keep this between you and me."

"Sure, Artie. Can I do that again?"

"Next week. I have to take you back today, or the dragon is going to burn us."

I could imagine that. Sabine never learned how to drive. She said she simply couldn't do it. She had tried and failed several times, and once she'd driven the car into the trashcans. If she discovered I was driving, she would kill me. Arthur was right—I had to keep my mouth shut.

Indeed, I have to give him credit. Talk about Machiavellianism! He started by making me believe I could trust him, but I couldn't trust others, and he taught me that secrets were a good thing if you used them because you were having fun, and that others wouldn't understand. As my therapists used to say, Arthur had started to create bonds with me.

CHAPTER FOUR

Simone – Present Day

Yes, Arthur was definitely an intelligent predator, thought Simone. From Lara's report, Simone could bet he had lured other girls. He knew how to attract them, how to bond with them... Most likely, Lara wasn't his first victim.

He was slowly but poignantly creating a relationship with the girl, teaching her to lie, to hide things from her family—a perfectly sick pervert, in Simone's opinion.

Not to mention, back then—the things Lara described had taken place around 1990—people hadn't been so serious about pedophilia, or her parents would have stopped a grown man from taking a young girl out with such a frequency. But if the story went on in the direction reported by Mark, Lara's mother knew very well what she was doing. *Wait and see,* thought Simone. She set aside the journal to put on some makeup and get ready for her date.

She needed a break from the intensity of Lara's writings. This was not an easy read, and she felt as if she was always holding her breath every time she turned a page. Tonight, she would go out and have dinner with a handsome man, and that's what she would like to focus on now.

How long had it been since she'd gone on a date, Simone wondered. Too long, for certain, unless you counted professional get-togethers with clients and business associates. She didn't expect to form any kind of a relationship with Armando, but for once in her life, she planned to live in the moment, and she found the idea highly liberating—*especially for someone as uptight as I am,* she thought.

Simone chose a sleeveless, blue silk dress that had a deep V in the front and showed a great deal of cleavage without being vulgar. Envelope style, it fit her tightly, hugging her curves to perfection. A positive point from her life's dramas: she had lost at least ten pounds. A touch of makeup—she didn't like to wear heavy makeup, although last Saturday night she'd made an exception—diamond stud earrings, a nice ring, and a bracelet, her Coco Noir parfume, and she was ready to go.

Unfortunately, she discovered she had to wait, and she absolutely hated to wait. Unlike his punctual father—and to Simone's despair, considering she had a love affair with her watch—Armando apparently didn't pay much attention to the time. At twenty minutes after eight, he still hadn't arrived. Had he forgotten their dinner engagement, or did he simply have very poor manners?

She was pacing her room, fuming, her annoyance rising as the time passed, when she finally heard the front bell. Arami was not home, and the maids had all gone at five o'clock. Simone opened the door to a very charming man wearing a dark-grey blazer overtop a lighter-grey shirt. He looked really handsome, but she wasn't about to forgive him for not arriving on time.

"Good evening. You're late," she said, forgetting her manners and giving him an icy glare.

"Good evening," he said, and then quickly added, "you're pretty!"

He had no intention of making excuses; instead, he thought he could flatter her into a good mood. Even if she felt mistreated by his behavior, she sighed and decided to let it go. She wasn't going to make a scene; after all, theirs was not a serious relationship. She intended to just have fun for a change.

"Shall we go?" he asked and gave her his arm.

They went to a restaurant called La Cote, a nice, modern place on the oceanfront, surrounded by an abundance of green vegetation. They served Southern French-style seafood. Simone and Armando ordered oysters to start off, along with a bottle of Bourgogne white wine.

"Simone...just before leaving home, I received a call from my dear cousin. She told me that if I touch you or molest you, she will kill me. Do you believe that? What does she think I am? Some kind of maniac? She also told me all about what happened to you. Unreal! I heard about the serial killer on TV, of course, but I didn't link the story to you..."

And he continued making remarks about her kidnapping, another point against the man—he talked too much for Simone's taste.

"I'd rather not talk about that...if you don't mind." No way was she going to spoil a nice evening by discussing a topic that still had the power to make her hands shake. There was a light breeze, the weather was fine, the sky was showing its first stars—she would focus on the good in life, and forget about the bad.

"That's fine, but I wanted to tell you I now understand why you acted the way you did the other night..."

Shit and double shit! she thought. She'd been naïve to

think he wouldn't mention the nightclub.

"Gallons of white wine could explain that better and also because I realized life was too short to not try something new... Bad luck I decided to risk an adventure and stumbled on it the next day..."

"It was great, and I'm happy you considered me for your adventure!"

Subtle guy, she thought, her cheeks growing hot with embarrassment. They'd barely started their evening together, and already she felt a bit uncomfortable. But maybe she just lacked practice when it came to dating? "Armando...let me explain some things to you... I'm a forty-year-old woman. Most of my life, I've lived for my work and to study human brains...I'm not an adventurous woman. I don't do casual sex—or rather, I didn't, and I'm suffering from post-traumatic stress syndrome. None of that explains my behavior the other night, but I think it's only fair I let you know."

He laughed. "Calm down. I did my research...I know who you are, and I'm happy you decided to have that adventure with me. I understand you were inebriated— hell, I was too! So don't worry, okay? I don't expect to carry you like a caveman to the restrooms after dinner."

Simone had to laugh as she imagined him grabbing her hair and dragging her to the bathroom.

In the end, she was happy he had brought up what had

happened between them in the nightclub. Their conversation cleared the air between them, and after that, the dinner went really well. He had a great sense of humor and told her interesting, entertaining stories about his country and his family. He told her he had two kids and had gone through a very complicated divorce.

By the time they left the restaurant, they were chatting and laughing, her spirits made lighter by the alcohol she'd consumed. He had been the perfect companion for the night. He drove his black, X6 BMW directly to Arami's apartment without asking Simone if she'd prefer they went somewhere else. When they arrived, he turned off the engine and turned in his seat to look at her.

"You are a beautiful woman. I really appreciate you having dinner with me tonight. You were a wonderful companion."

"Thanks to you, Armando, I had a great evening, and I didn't think about my problems. You, too, were great company."

Armando leaned in and gave her a light kiss on the lips. He then climbed out of the car and came around to open her door for her. He gave her his hand and helped her out, and then, like a perfect gentleman, he escorted her to the front door, opened it for her, and waited for her to go inside. He didn't attempt to follow her.

"Thanks for dinner, Armando." Funny, considering how

the night had started, she was feeling a bit sad now to see their date coming to an end.

"Thanks for the company. I would like to see you again..."

"Absolutely! Call me. Good night!"

"Good night, my dear girl!"

He gave her a peck on her lips and left before she could react.

She didn't know if she was disappointed because he didn't try to sleep with her or if she felt great because he'd treated her like a lady. If she were honest with herself, she had to admit to feeling a little bit let down!

She closed the door and turned then jerked to a stop, her heart racing, until she realized it was just Arami sitting there in the living room. She wore a long gold nightdress; so obviously, she'd been waiting for Simone to get home from her date.

"God, you scared me sitting like that, Arami!" Simone's legs felt like jelly.

"Sorry, girl, come here," she said, waving Simone over to the sofa. "How did it go? You must tell me everything!"

Simone crossed the room, and Arami grabbed Simone's arm and dragged her down to sit on the couch.

"Well, we went to a restaurant called La Cote, and we had oysters…"

"*Dios mío!* I don't need to hear every boring detail. Just the hot parts," Arami said, shaking her hands in the air.

"No hot parts, Ara… We just had a nice chat, good wine, and great food."

"With my cousin? I don't believe it…he is the talk of Asuncion. In his younger days, he acted like a *Don Juan*, and then he married and settled down… But now that he is divorced, he is back to his old ways. I was positive you would have a very spicy night…"

"Well, I'm sorry to disappoint you," Simone told her with a laugh. "We had a nice evening…but not a pepper in sight…" *Unfortunately…*

"Are you sure you went out with my cousin?" Arami grinned.

"Yeah…pretty sure."

"Well," Arami huffed and sat back on the sofa. "If that's the case, then I can tell you, my friend, he must *really* like you. I know this, because when he likes someone, he waits…he is very good at the game of seduction."

"No." Simone shook her head. "No way. I'm leaving Sunday… I have to get on with my life, and I'm not going to start a long-distance relationship. I don't believe in them."

"I do… And besides, why are you leaving so soon?"

"Time to face reality. My patients really need me. I can't be on vacation forever… I feel much better now. You helped a lot, my friend."

"No, no, no, stay, Simone; you need a rest!"

"I've already had a rest. Now it's time for me to get back, to face real life, or I will never get rid of these feelings that are still haunting me."

"I understand, I suppose. Here is my advice: don't think about the future so much. Give my cousin a chance. In my country, we use to say that we don't know God's plans… Who knows what tomorrow will bring?"

"This is true…" For people who believed in destiny and chance…and Simone did not.

"I'm going to sleep now," Arami said. She patted Simone's knee. "I have an early surgery tomorrow."

She got to her feet, leaned back down to kiss Simone on the cheek, and left for her room.

God's plans… Simone sighed. She was agnostic—no plans from a superior being for her…just real life. She would like to be able to find solace in the idea of some all-knowing being that was sitting up there somewhere looking out for her, but she had a scientific mind. She counted on herself and her own judgment—and her instincts, which told her that Armando was trouble. Big trouble, and she didn't need any further disruptions in her life just then.

* * * * *

Simone slept until 9:00 a.m., and miraculously, she didn't have any nightmares. It had been a great night, indeed!

She took a bath, chose a pair of shorts and a t-shirt then went to the kitchen. She had a substantial breakfast of eggs, bacon, cereal, and a large cup of coffee, finding she was hungry enough to eat every bite—a novelty for her these days.

After breakfast, she went to her room, which she found already tidied up—the bed made and the pillows fluffed. She said a silent thank you to Arami's super-efficient and practically invisible maid Eliza. Simone scooped up Lara's journal from the nightstand, set the bottle of mineral water she'd brought with her from the kitchen nearby on a low table, and then got comfortable in the big leather chair.

She heaved a sigh. Back to the drama...

Lara's Journal

More Secrets...

I recall a day soon after I first learned to drive when I was sitting in biology class, daydreaming, as usual, and I sensed a presence over my shoulder. I glanced behind me and then quickly tried to cover the picture I'd been doodling on my homework sheet—an image of a bright-red convertible. But I was too late... The teacher had caught me, and since this wasn't the first time, she sent me to see the principal—who looked like an old frog with his thick glasses. After shouting at me for twenty minutes, he called Sabine, and I had to face another storm at home!

"Step outside your room, and you are going to be there for the whole week," Sabine told me.

Okay, I thought, *no problem.* I would read a book or write in my diary...but ten minutes later, Sabine appeared at my door again.

"Lara, Arthur is on the phone. Go say hi to him."

"I can't!"

"Why not?"

"Because I can't leave my room, remember?" I loved to annoy Sabine.

"Get out of that room, and pick up the phone right this instant!" She sometimes lost her classy veneer and shouted like a longshoreman.

"Hi, Artie," I said, twirling the long, curly cord on the

phone in the upstairs hallway.

"Hello, beautiful. What was all the discussion with your mom just now?"

"You heard? She locked me in my room, and then she told me to come out and answer the phone..."

"Grounded again, Lara? What did you do this time?"

"Zero, nothing! I was drawing during biology class, and that ugly teacher of mine caught me."

"Hey, now...you have to be more careful. Always remember what I told you about adults. They can't know what we do, or they'll spoil all our fun."

"But you're an adult, and you're cool."

"Naaaa, I'm going to tell you a secret. Only my body is full grown. Inside me there is a kid younger than you are, being held in captivity."

I started to laugh, imagining a boy locked inside Arthur's body.

"Don't tell adults," he repeated, "they don't understand!"

"No, they don't! Emms would, though. She's like you...nice and fun."

"When does she come back? Do you miss her?"

"I don't know. She's been in France now for a while. Sometimes, she goes there forever, and, yes, I miss her so much. She listens to me...she is my friend."

"Hey, I'm hurt. I'm your friend! I listen to you."

"Sure! And you're fun, too!"

"Okay, kid, behave, all right? I'm going to talk to your mom, so you won't have to go back to your room."

"I don't mind. I'm going to read in peace. She doesn't like to see me reading; she says it's not normal for a girl my age to read sooooo much. When she grounds me, I can read without having to listen to her whine about it."

"Smart cookie! You are my little intellectual thing. I'm proud of you."

Arthur had developed a habit of getting me out of trouble. He would talk to Sabine and resolve things. To this day, I still don't know for sure if he convinced her to allow me out of my room or if they were in cahoots, playing some kind of an obscene game of good cop-bad cop. Looking back now, and knowing them both as I do, the second option seems more reasonable.

A Person to Trust...

My brother is gay, and he started to show his inclinations very early in life. He loved to play with dolls, he was delicate, and he was not aggressive or messy like most boys are.

My parents forbade him to play with dolls, and I felt sorry for him. Why couldn't he play with them if he wanted to? I couldn't see what was wrong with it or why it should matter, so whenever I could—and when Sabine wasn't around—I allowed him to play with my dolls.

He was very smart and sweet, and I loved to play with him.

"You are cool, Lara. I love your doll. She is blonde and pretty like you."

"Hey, Sean, just don't let Dad and Mom know, okay? Or else we will both be grounded."

By then, I had learned from Arthur that secrets were very good, and good things should be kept from adults.

"What can't your parents know, and why would you both be grounded?"

I almost fainted, thinking it was Sabine behind us, but it was just Dorothy, the kids' nanny, and we could always count on her to help us.

"Hey, Doty, you almost gave me a heart attack! Thought you were Mom!"

"What are you two up to?"

"Just playing with my Barbie. Sean here is making her cool outfits."

"Christ sake, Lara! Your mother is going to kill me if she finds out about this!"

"If you don't tell, she won't find out."

I had learned very well from Arthur that a good secret was a great triumph, and you can convince people to lie for you. I just didn't know that yet, I was doing it unconsciously back then.

"I won't tell, of course, but take care, you two. And you, little man, time for a bath and a snack."

"I want chocolates!"

"No, not chocolates. But I'll fix you a nice peanut butter sandwich."

"With jelly?"

"Sure, kiddo. Hey, Lara, I almost forgot...there is another gift from that guy Arthur for you."

"Really?"

"Yep, it's in the kitchen, but, Lara...you need to be careful with that guy, okay? He's way too old to be messing around with a kid like you."

"No, Doty, he's great! So cool, like you and Emms. He's not a boring adult like the others..."

"Yes, but if he does anything weird, you tell me, okay? You know you can trust me!"

"Sure, Doty, he is not weird, and don't tell Mom about Sean playing with Barbie, okay? You know how adults are…"

"Yes, complicated people…don't worry…it's our secret." And she blinked at me.

As I recall this conversation now, I have to wonder why the nanny knew bad things could come from my "friendship" with Arthur, and my parents didn't?

But back then, I just figured Doty must be wrong. Still, she was also a great person, and I really liked her, so I filed her advice away in a corner of my mind…just in case.

CHAPTER FIVE

Simone – Present Day

Simone sipped some water, took off her reading glasses, and put the journal aside. She reflected that Lara was probably right—the volume of punishments she'd been receiving were connected to some sort of agreement between Arthur and Sabine...both sick people... Sabine's behavior was too icy to be normal; she really seemed to be a psycho, cold and determined to have what she wanted, no matter what, and Arthur...a pedophile, for sure.

The nanny saw what this was—or at least saw the possibility of trouble and had tried to warn Lara—but kids usually don't have the necessary judgment to mistrust people, and Lara liked Arthur, so no advice would make much of an impression on her.

The next day Simone would talk to Carl and give him her first impressions. She sent him a message to schedule a time, and he quickly answered her.

How anxious he is to solve the puzzle of Lara's past, Simone thought. *And why do I feel such envy over that?*

She decided to take in some sun and went to the beach, but as her skin was too fair, she couldn't stay out long, and after half an hour, she went back to the apartment, took a shower, put on a pretty red sundress, took a cab, and went to the mall. She was in need of some shopping therapy.

At 4:00 p.m. she called her daughter Tammy. It was night in France; Europe was at least five hours later than the U.S., and Simone caught her daughter at home.

"Hello, baby, I've been missing you." An understatement. The longing she felt to see her only child cut deep, but she did her best to hide her true emotions.

"Hi, Mommy, I miss you, too. How've you been? I'm so worried about you!"

"Don't be, Tammy. I'm all right, and to prove it to you, I'll let you in on a secret... Yesterday, I had dinner with a gorgeous man."

Tammy and Simone had a really close relationship. Now that her daughter was an adult, Simone treated her more like a friend, and they'd developed strong bonds of trust between them. Simone's mother had always been distant and cold, and even if Simone thought she had inherited her mother's aloof nature more than she liked, she tried to be as warm as she could be with her own child.

"That's cool! What's he like?"

Simone talked to Tammy for several more minutes, filling her in on the date with Armando. When they hung up, Simone checked the time. She had less than an hour before she had to be ready to go out for dinner with Arami, so she hurried to take a quick shower and freshen up. With only a few more days left to her vacation, Simone planned to make the most of every minute.

* * * * *

The next morning, the general returned for another appointment with Simone. He arrived exactly on time, unlike his son. Of course, Cezar was a military man, and they were known for being punctual. Simone really liked that aspect of the man's personality.

He showed up dressed impeccably, as always, wearing a summer-weight, cream-colored suit, his hair carefully combed and smoothed into place with some kind of gel. He looked extremely elegant, and as he stepped inside the apartment, she caught a whiff of his subtle cologne. Yum! He might be seventy, but he could pass for fifty. Even his skin was flawless. Simone guessed he might have had a Botox injection here and there, or even undergone plastic surgery.

Good morning, Cezar! How've you been? How did you feel after our first meeting?" she greeted him.

"Good morning, Doctor! I've been thinking a lot...remembering my political defeat. I must admit, it leaves a bitter taste in my mouth."

"Hmm," Simone said. "Well, let's go into the library and get comfortable so we can talk about things, shall we?"

He followed her down the hallway and into her makeshift office.

"Take a seat." She waved toward the chairs before the desk then went around to sit in the big chair behind it.

She waited until they were both seated, then asked, "Why would you want to be president? I understand the power, but I can see you are a successful man. Have you ever wondered why you want to subject yourself to all that additional stress?"

"I never wanted the power. Actually, I would like to help my people. We had so many big ideas. General Oviedo would be president, my brother would help him, and I would help my brother, but Oviedo died, so my brother would run for president, and I would be his right-hand man, but then he was killed. When that happened, I decided to go on with our plans. My homeland is beautiful, Doctor, but it's also very poor. Roughly a hundred and fifty years ago, we had an awful war that destroyed the country. Then came a dictatorship. I was in the military, and I was part of all that, and to this day, I regret being involved. So I wanted to correct my mistakes...to help my people get back on the right track."

"That's very noble of you. But haven't you already helped your country? I mean, you helped reverse the dictatorial system, didn't you?"

"Militaries follow orders, Doctor. We are very good at obeying, but General Oviedo, my brother, and I saw that the country was not progressing. The old dictator was going to die occupying his seat, and we started to think about a solution. In the end, we decided what we needed was a democracy, so we started to gather an army to take power."

"How did that go?" Simone had never met someone like him, and she was curious.

"To make a long story short, one day—and I remember this as if it was yesterday—General Oviedo, some colleagues of mine, along with my brother, entered the old general's room, weapons in hand. Oviedo had a grenade. They grabbed the general and put him on a plane. I was the pilot, and we took him outside the country for asilum...and that was the beginning of our democracy.

"Very risky."

"Yes, we could have been sent to prison for high treason, but the country was tired of tyranny, and God was by our side."

He pointed to the ceiling, showing he believed in a superior entity.

"And then you went into politics?"

"No. Not immediately. I was just like Armando—an executive in my family business—but with democracy came serious problems, such as corruption. Oh, it was always there but more controlled. There was a lack of security, a lack of direction...then my brother decided to run for president, replacing Oviedo after his death, and he wanted me by his side, so I entered into politics but still in my role as a businessman. I traveled abroad; I made alliances with businessmen and agriculturists. I was convincing foreign investors to invest in the country. I was the man backstage."

"You should try again, Cezar. That's your dream."

"That what I thought, too, and that's why I started campaigning again, immediately after the elections. But then...I got so tired, and I have to face reality, Doctor.

I'm old. The elections are this year. I don't know if I will find the energy to face all that again."

She shook her head. "Don't give up. Try again."

Clearly, the general had everything it took to win the elections if he wanted to do so. He was in excellent health and no doubt had great plans for his country. He would lead with an iron fist, but that was another matter, she thought.

"I'm old. People don't want an old man. The current president is young, around fifty, a good president, he knows how to make the country grow... I have to resign myself to the idea that I'm done...finished...washed up."

"Aging frightens you?"

"Aging terrifies me! There is nothing worse than sagging skin, wrinkles polluting your face...and every new day I see more evidence that I'm getting closer to death's doorstep. My face is cracking like earth under a white-hot sun. I look like a broken vase someone tried to fix." He gazed at Simone and frowned. "I feel like a rotten fruit that has lost its lushness and taste. I feel as if I'm withering away, a little bit more every day, but what makes me feel worse is to know I haven't achieved everything I wanted to do with my life."

Simone chose not to comment on the man's overly dramatic speech. Instead, she prodded him.

"So do it, Cezar."

"No." He shook his head. "I'm an old man, and nobody wants an old man. Just look at our society. People treat the elderly as if they've got the damn plague...as if it was our fault we grew older...as if we shouldn't be allowed to parade around with our ugly old faces. It hurts, Doctor; you can't imagine how bitter it is to be run over by the years."

The general put his hand over his heart, and his face was a mask of pain and suffering. To Simone's surprise, there were tears in his eyes. No doubt, his sexual issue was linked to his inability to accept the fact that he was growing older... That, and he was obviously dealing with depression. Some people had a hard time handling the aging process.

Simone had to deal with growing older—which was even more difficult for a woman in this day and age. There was a huge difference between how the world treated a woman of twenty and how they dealt with a woman of forty. Life could be harsh if you couldn't accept the fact that everyone gets old, sooner or later...whether they liked it or not.

Cezar, you are depressed; that much is obvious."

"You may be right. But sometimes, I feel as if this is karma...some kind of revenge for the way I treated older people... I had little respect for them when I was young... Of course, I never thought I would grow old.

When we are younger, youth seems eternal; we will never die... Old age is the debauchery of life."

"If it is of any consolation to you, many young people suffer from the same pathology...it wasn't just you."

"Thank you for that..."

"I'm going to prescribe some anti-depressants for you."

"Is that necessary?"

"I believe it is."

They discussed various medications and chose one for him to fill and begin taking, to combat his depression. They concluded their session, and Simone said goodbye, after agreeing to see the general again in a couple days. She had a feeling there was something beyond the elections disturbing the man, but only time would prove if she was correct or not.

After the general left—and his driver had come to the door to deliver her fee—Simone jotted down a few notes into the case file she'd created for Cezar. The rest of her day was open, so she decided to read a little bit more about Lara.

She'd just settled into the leather reading chair when her phone rang. She answered with a satisfied smile.

"Hello, Armando."

"Hello, Simone. How are you today?"

"Great! And you?"

"Very well, thank you. How about dinner?"

"Sure, let's enjoy the rest of my vacation."

"Okay, can I pick you up at eight?"

"My eight or yours?"

"Excuse me? I'm not sure what you mean."

"Eight o'clock for me means eight o'clock. For you, it means eight thirty...maybe eight forty-five."

He laughed. "I won't be late; I promise."

"Hmm. We'll see about that. I'll see you tonight." Simone suffered a pang of guilt for admonishing him about being on time, but then thought, so what? She was tired of being the good and polite girl and having to take other people's shit!

Simone disconnected the call and turned her attention to the stack of printed sheets on her lap, feeling very happy about the prospect of dinner that evening.

Lara's Journal

Every once in a while, Arthur took me to the movies. On one particular day, he took me to an adult movie. With my height, no one could tell I was underage. The name of the movie was *Ghost*, and there were some scenes that embarrassed me a little, but Arthur had the good sense not to say a word.

"Remember, Lara…"

"If anyone asks, we went to see Gremlins II," I finished his statement for him.

But I wasn't worried. When I went out with Arthur, Sabine never asked anything, and my father was always busy working and had no clue what I was doing. The way he looked at it, he did his job by working to pay the bills, and my mother did hers by taking care of their three children… But boy, was he wrong…

"Smart girl," Arthur told me.

When he dropped me at home, he leaned in close, kissed me on the cheek, caressed my hair, and smelled my neck. I felt a chill.

"Wonderful perfume," he said.

"It's called Beautiful."

"Like the woman wearing it."

I didn't think much about his behavior that night. To me, it was okay for a friend to appreciate my perfume. I couldn't have predicted this was the first step—the first glimpse of dark clouds on the horizon, if you will—in what would amount to a storm of torment.

I Don't Know what is Happening

After a while, I began to think of Arthur as my best friend. I could talk to him, I could laugh with him, and he was truly a nice person. I didn't see him as an adult but as an older friend.

One afternoon, he called and invited me to go for a ride. It was one of the last warm days of September, and I recall he had bought a new car—a black, convertible Mercedes this time—and he wanted me to drive it. I was so happy! I loved to drive, and I could do it so well after only a few practice sessions.

I asked my mother if I could go.

"Yes, of course, wear a nice dress," she said without even a glance in my direction.

I chose a nice, strapless dress—little red flowers on a field of white—applied some gloss to my lips, added a few spritzes of my perfume, and went out front to wait for him.

He arrived shortly thereafter, wearing shorts and a blue

polo shirt, and although he gave me his usual smile, he seemed very serious and looked older, as if something was wrong.

He let me drive for a few minutes, and then we went to Rock Creek Park. He parked the car, and we went out for a walk near the lake. The entire time, he was silent, and when we stopped on the lakeshore, he grab some little rocks and started to throw them into the water, making ripples of ever-widening circles.

"Are you sad?" I finally asked him.

"No, babe, just thinking."

We walked a little bit more, and he bought us some ice cream, and then we went back to the car. The park was empty, so we sat there listening to music and licking our ice cream cones.

The sun wasn't very bright, but he told me was going to close the top and turn on the air conditioning so our ice cream wouldn't melt. Once he'd done that, he turned and looked at me.

"You have ice cream on the corner of your mouth." He reached out and cleaned it with his finger, then he licked it off his fingertip.

For some reason, I thought it was funny, and I laughed.

"Ah, Lara, you are a beautiful woman. How can I resist you?"

I didn't understand what he meant, but before I could respond, he leaned in and kissed me on the lips. I didn't know what to do. I had never been kissed before! I didn't want Arthur to give me my first kiss—we were friends!

I tried to push him away, but he held my head and pulled my hair, and I couldn't move. My heart was beating fast, and my legs were like jelly.

"What are you doing, Arthur?"

"I'm done resisting you, you little sorceress."

Then he started to kiss me again, and he kept my head still, firmly holding my ponytail. He inclined my head back and kissed my neck and my bosom, and I was lost. I didn't know what to do, I was afraid, and he wouldn't let me go.

He was breathing hard, and he was kissing me everywhere, and I wanted to escape. I was getting really desperate.

My dress was strapless and had an elastic band holding it up to cover my chest. He pulled it down and grabbed one of my little breasts and then started to lick it. My teenager's brain couldn't comprehend why he was sucking my breasts like a baby.

I was dizzy, my breath short, butterflies were in my stomach, and I was shaking. He gently bit my nipples and then licked them, alternating back and forth from one to the other.

I tried to push him off, but he was too strong.

"Don't even think about it. Stay quiet."

Not knowing what else to do, and praying he'd hurry and finish whatever it was he was doing if I listened to him, I fell silent and still. He pulled up my dress and put his hand inside my panties and touched my pussy! He made circles with his fingertips, and I clenched my eyes, utterly embarrassed and astounded.

Then he put a finger inside me. It hurt me, and I moaned in fear and pain. Arthur must have decided he'd done enough, because he stopped and sat back, breathing hard. I was so ashamed I couldn't look at him.

"You are beautiful, Lara!"

He helped to arrange my dress, my hair, and still I couldn't speak. I was so ashamed.

He opened the glove compartment and gave me a little box wrapped in silver paper with a rose-colored bow. My hands were shaking so much I couldn't open it, so he opened it for me. It was a beautiful gold bracelet with a gold heart pendant.

"This is to celebrate our love, babe, so you will always know I'm crazy for you."

"What happened, Arthur?"

"Something beautiful between us. We are bonding, and we are going to bond even more. You are going to be mine, forever."

"But why?"

"Because we love each other."

Love? I didn't know what love meant...

To this day, I believe I still don't, but certainly I didn't love him; he was my friend. I couldn't understand why a friend would do the things he'd done to me. Emms had been clear—only adults did those things and only when they loved each other!

"You can't talk about this with anyone, honey. You know how grown-ups are; they would never understand. Well, they might, because they love to do this, but they will say they don't just to punish you. I love you!"

"I can't even talk to Emms?"

I couldn't face him. Instead, I was looking at my hands in my lap. I was wringing them.

"No, of course not. She doesn't see the woman I see in you. She will tell you you're too young. It's one of our secrets, right?"

I didn't say anything. I was afraid he would start touching me again, so I kept silent. He took me home, and I didn't say a word on the way back. Then I left the car quickly and said good-bye, but I didn't have the courage to look at him.

As soon as I got inside the house I ran into Dorothy.

"Are you okay, Lara? You look strange..."

"Just sleepy. I'm going to my room."

"Okay, girl."

I took a shower immediately. I wanted to get rid of the smell of Arthur's cologne, which seemed to be clinging to my body. The aroma was making me sick. I felt dirty and ashamed.

Writing about that day now makes all those sensations come back to me—the fear, the anger, the shame, and confusion. Even now, those memories make me feel violated, and whenever I think about that day, it hurts me.

CHAPTER SIX

Simone – Present Day

The image of a young and beautiful girl being abused haunted Simone's mind, and she wanted to throw up. Arthur was a real sick bastard, certainly a child molester. He was not in love with someone younger. He'd known very well what he was doing; Simone was sure about that.

She decided she couldn't handle spending anymore time with Lara that day and instead went to lie down for a while.

Two hours later, Simone awoke to get ready for her date with Armando. She decided on a simple pink dress, but she chose her lingerie with care, added a few drops of perfume, and she was done. She glanced at the clock. Almost eight.

To her surprise, Armando arrived exactly on time.

"Hello, gorgeous, you are stunning, as ever," he greeted her.

"Hello, sir, you don't look too bad yourself."

Armando was wearing a pale-yellow shirt and jeans, and a delightful citrusy perfume that pleased Simone's senses.

"How was your day?" he asked.

He took her arm as she exited the apartment, pulling the door closed behind her.

"I've been working a little bit but also resting, and you?"

"All about business and thinking about you..."

Simone bit back a grin. Although it would be so good to believe someone had spent his day thinking about her, she wasn't about to buy into his compliment. At her age, she was too smart for that. Still, she squeezed his arm in response to his effort to please her.

They went to Armando's building, which was only a few blocks from Arami's apartment, talking about inconsequential things. When they arrived on Ocean's

Drive Avenue, she and Armando crossed the wide lobby to the elevator. The doors swished open, and they stepped inside the car. Armando pushed the "P" button on the panel, and the elevator began its smooth journey to the top.

"It's a very nice building," she told him.

"Yes, it is, and best of all, it's new. I hate old buildings."

"Even if they are historical?"

"The only antique I can stand is my father."

He laughed at his own joke, but Simone didn't join in. As far as she was concerned, our elders deserved at least some respect, and she loved antiques.

The elevator came to a stop, and Simone followed Armando out into a large foyer area. He opened the massive, oak French doors for her, and they entered into a wide-open entry with grey marble on the floor covered almost entirely by white area rugs. So far, the suite reminded Simone of Arami's place, surrounded as it was by glass. Simone presumed Armando would have an amazing view of the beach during the day, and now, as it was night, she could see the dark sky above Miami, full of glittering stars.

The penthouse entry allowed access to three different levels. Two stairs down were four sofas—two deep blue and two beige—along with matching loveseats in dark blue with red and white flowers. There were two glass coffee tables, one holding an arrangement of white candles, and several pictures and books on the second one.

On the main floor—level with the entry—there was a square glass dining table and eight navy-blue chairs. A brilliant chandelier made of different sizes of hollow crystal balls hanging at various levels hung from the high ceiling above the center of the table.

Two steps up there was a kitchen with blue cabinets, a blue-and-grey tile backsplash, and stainless steel appliances. The countertops were made of silver granite and included a breakfast island surrounded by four tall barstools upholstered in blue.

The place was immense—the first floor alone had to be at least fifteen hundred square feet. The décor was very masculine but extremely tasteful, like something out of the pages of an interior design magazine.

"I like your home, it's very elegant."

"Thank you, but I have to give Arami credit for the decorating. She helped me find everything and decorate after my divorce. Do you want something to drink? I have wine, whisky, champagne, tequila, and vodka."

"A glass of wine would be fine."

"Come with me." He grabbed her hand and led her to

the kitchen. "Take a seat while I choose some wine for us."

He opened a two-door acclimatized wine cellar and brought out a bottle of white wine, opened it, and served her some in a goblet-shaped, crystal glass. She took a sip and smiled.

"Hmm, it's perfect!" Just the right temperature, and the taste was light and sweet.

"I love this cellar. It has three temperatures—one for red wines, one for white, and another for champagne. The bottles are always at the perfect temperature, ready to be consumed."

She could tell he was proud of his wine cellar. At that moment, a uniformed maid came in.

"Good evening, sir; Good evening, madam."

"Good evening, Amelia. This is Dr. Simone Bennet, a friend."

"Good evening, Amelia, nice to meet you."

"Nice to meet you, madam."

"Amelia is my precious helper here. She's an incredible cook, as you will soon find out." He turned to address the maid. "What are you preparing for us?"

"I'm going to cook filet mignon medallions with

Argentinian malbec wine reduction sauce and some potatoes."

"Sounds delicious," Simone said. Her mouth watered at the description.

"Yes, it is, and you are going to get a taste of the meat I produce in Paraguay!"

"That would be great."

"Come with me, and bring your glass. I'm going to show you the view," he said after refilling their glasses.

They left the kitchen to Amelia, and he guided her to a glass staircase, leading to the second floor. Upstairs was another spacious room with a well-equipped home theater. They crossed a floor made of the same grey marble, and he opened the glass doors. They stepped out onto an open, rectangular terrace with an infinity-edge swimming pool and several chaise lounges. Out here, the view was even more beautiful than it had looked through the glass walls.

"Come here, look how beautiful Miami's sky is."

"It's really wonderful!"

The weather was fine with a light, warm breeze. The perfectly chilled wine had begun to go to her head, because in this lighting, Armando looked remarkably like Antonio Banderas...from the time of Almodovar's movies. What more could a woman want out of life? A rich, handsome, divorced man. Her suspicious nature rose to the fore. He seemed almost too good to be true, and she knew better than to be fooled by outward appearances, but just for that evening she wanted to relax, stop being so suspicious and wary, and have a good time.

"What am I going to do with you, Doctor?"

"What do you want to do with me, Armando?" Wine talking, she thought.

They went to stand near the glass railing at the edge of the terrace. He took the glass from her hand and put it on a nearby table, took her by her shoulders, and caressed up and down her arms. He put one finger under her chin and lifted her head.

"I'm dying to kiss you, Simone."

She answered him by lifting her head a little more and pressing her lips against his. *Mmm...* He tasted like the wine.

He kissed her slowly, at first, as if he was savoring the taste of her, and then with a soft moan, he deepened the kiss, dipping his tongue inside her mouth. He caressed her tongue with his expertly and only stopped to lick her lips and distribute tiny, exciting bites.

They stood there kissing, hugging each other, occasionally pausing to sip their wine and look up at the stars. Perfectly relaxed, Simone enjoyed his company. His attention, while passionate, didn't make her feel pressured or as if he were rushing her into anything. She felt more like a teenager, enjoying her boyfriend's kisses, she thought.

The intercom on the wall by the French doors buzzed, interrupting them.

"Amelia," Armando explained. "That's her way of letting us know it's time to go downstairs and eat."

"Great, I'm really hungry." *And I still don't know what I'm going to do with you,* she thought.

The table had been set for two. The dinner was exquisite, the meat cooked to perfection—pink on the inside and charbroiled on the outside. The sauce was divine, and the rosemary-seasoned potatoes melted in Simone's mouth. For dessert, Amelia served small pears cooked in wine sauce with whipped cream on top.

"Thank you, Amelia, the dinner was perfect!"

Simone complimented the maid as the woman served their coffee.

"Let's sip some Armagnac on the terrace, shall we?" Armando suggested. "It's a wonderful sort of old brandy produced in France."

Let him be the man, and don't tell him you know what Armagnac is, thought Simone. She smiled. "Sounds great!"

Armando filled two goblets with Armagnac, and they went back to the terrace.

"What a marvelous dinner, Armando; I really enjoyed it. Thanks for bringing me here."

"I would have liked to have brought you here the other night, but I didn't want you to think I wanted to molest you."

"But now you think I've come to trust you enough to know you won't try to take me to bed?" she teased him.

"If you do, you're making a mistake. Today, I would definitely like to pick you up and carry you into my bed. There's something about you that drives me crazy...an understated sexiness I've never noticed in any other woman."

He gave her no time to analyze what he meant by "understated sexiness" before he took her in his arms and captured her lips in another passionate kiss. Without lifting his head, he scooped her into his arms. Still kissing her, he crossed the terrace and entered through another glass door on the opposite side of the pool. He carried her to an enormous, king-size bed situated in front of a wall of mirrors.

He gently set her on the bed and began to undress her, slowly. When she was completely naked, he took off his cloths, tossing everything onto the floor where he'd thrown her dress minutes before.

What a disorganized man, thought Simone and fought off the sudden desire to gather up their clothing and hang them neatly over the back of the nearby chair. Now was *not* the time to indulge her compulsion for orderliness.

"What do you like?"

"Why don't you caress me all over and try to discover all by yourself?"

C'mon! What kind of a question is that? The man was what...an inexperienced little boy? Simone groaned inwardly. Maybe she should write an instruction manual for him?

Armando joined her on the bed, leaning in to place small kisses down her neck, along her shoulder, and then farther down over her breasts. He slid his tongue around one taut nipple, flicked it, suckled it, and blew on it, and then he did the same to the other breast.

Simone moaned in approval. He was no boy at all; he knew what he was doing.

He took his time, seemingly in no rush to do more. Simone enjoyed his efforts, growing restless beneath his touch. She shifted, lifted her hips, silently encouraging him to continue his journey south, her pussy hot and wet from the delicious foreplay. *Definitively a man,* she reflected.

He finally seemed to get the hint and slid down to lie between her legs, kissing and licking her belly along the way. He went to work on her clit and pussy, setting the same leisurely pace, as if they had forever instead of only the night.

"Yes, you are on the right track," said Simone to encourage him. She felt like an airport employee—one of those people with the flashlight-type things who show the pilot of a plane where he should park...

Slowly, carefully, he stroked her with the tip of his tongue, stabbed the length of his tongue deep inside her pussy, lapped at her juices, and nibbled on her hardened clit. Simone writhed beneath him, grasped his hair, and lifted her hips. She started to feel the growing of pleasure sensations, the hot feeling through her veins, her clit throbbing as the orgasm approached, and suddenly, that wonderful sensation of a stellar explosion hit her, and she came in his mouth.

She rested a little bit, breathing hard, while he continued to cover her body with small kisses. She wanted to return the favor, and she told him.

"Let me taste you." Simone tried to reverse their positions.

"No, stay right there."

He positioned his cock in the middle of her breasts, pushed them together to embrace his shaft, and then started dry-humping her tits. Simone watched, astonished. She'd never done such a thing, and she had to bite her lip to hold back a giggle each time the head of his dick peeked out the top from between her smooshed-together breasts. So weird!

Thankfully, his interest in fucking her breasts didn't last long, because she was beginning to feel very uncomfortable with that.

A moment later, he jumped from the bed, opened a drawer, and took out a condom. He ripped open the packaging and slid the condom down over his cock, then came back to bed. With no further warning, he climbed between her legs, positioned his dick at her pussy, and drove inside. He fucked her furiously, the slow, gentle passion having been replaced by what seemed to be an urgent need to fuck her.

She liked his roughness and joined his movements, meeting each of his hard, downward strokes.

"*Cadela! Eres una puta, una rica puta*," he said in Spanish, his pace increasing.

She didn't know what that meant, but she knew the word "puta" from the movies. Why had he called her a prostitute?

She forced herself to disregard his words—she didn't

like those kinds of kinky words at all—and instead focused on how she felt. His rhythm increased, and she shook her head.

"Oh, no you don't," she told him and pushed him over until he lay on his back.

No way would she allow him to come before she had a chance to come again. She climbed on top of him, lifted to her knees, and guided him back inside.

"It's my turn now!"

She rode him hard, varying her rhythm and appreciating the view of his sun-kissed body. As her orgasm approached, she moved faster and faster. Chills covered her body, and her heart raced, blood pumping quickly to her extremities. A sense of buoyancy filled her, and she grew lightheaded until she came with a shout. Her toes tingled, either from the orgasm or from a lack of circulation caused by sitting on her knees. She was still immersed in her orgasm when he pushed her off him and onto her back. He got to his knees beside her, ripped off the condom, and finished masturbating over her breasts.

"*Soys esquisita!*"

Spanish again! Dammit, she thought...the guy was weird but being weird in a foreign language was even worse.

She remained silent and still, but some of his actions

disturbed her. He had some sexually deviant behaviors, apparently, but it was too soon to know how extreme they might be. Besides, this was nothing more than a vacation fling. She'd had two intense orgasms, and she refused to ruin the moment by overanalyzing.

"Damn, woman...you were perfect. I really enjoyed the ride."

Simone stared at him. How was she supposed to answer that?

A knock sounded on the glass door. "Sir, please answer your phone. Your cousin Arami is calling, and she says it's very important she speaks to your friend."

"*Hija de puta*, I'm going to kill Arami, what can be so important now?"

He snatched up the phone from the night table and dialed. He said something in Spanish and then gave the phone to Simone.

"Hi, Simone, sorry to disturb you, but you are not answering your phone, and Edward is calling. He sounded desperate and said something is wrong with one of your patients."

"Thanks, Arami. I'll call him right now."

Simone took the bathrobe Armando was holding for her and went downstairs for her purse. She pulled out her phone and looked at the display. Edward had called her ten times at least, and someone else had called once from an unknown number. She called Edward immediately.

"Hi, Ed, I was having dinner. Sorry I didn't hear the phone. What's going on?"

"Simmie, hello. I'm afraid we have a huge problem here! Your patient Philip Raymond destroyed a nightclub, hit his wife, and I'm afraid he's now in jail. His lawyer is trying to bail him out, but as he is in psychiatric care, the judge wants to talk to you first. He will need monitoring."

"Philip? Are you kidding me? That man is as passive as a lamb. What happened to set him off, do you know?"

"I really don't. I'm sorry. Can you come back?"

"Sure, I'm going to get the first possible flight. I'll let you know as soon as I make my reservation."

"I have a better idea. I'll buy a ticket for you. How long do you need to pack your suitcases?"

"I think I can be ready in two hours, and I'm a about half an hour from the Miami airport. If you can handle making my reservations and purchasing the ticket, that'll definitely save me some time. Thank you, Ed."

"You're welcome. I'll see you soon."

When Simone returned to the bedroom, she found

Armando lying on the bed caressing his cock. She explained the situation and told him she needed to shower and dress quickly and had to return to Arami's place.

"C'mon, come here, let's do that again! Your patient is already in jail; he is not going to escape…he is just spoiling our fun."

"That would be really irresponsible of me!" She couldn't believe someone could be so cold and self-centered.

She turned and headed for the bathroom, intent on ignoring Armando's childishness, but he followed her. She hated company while bathing!

Simone crossed the gray ceramic tile floor and opened the shower door. As she stepped inside, Armando moved in to stand behind her. Still ignoring him, she turned on the water and adjusted the temperature.

"Here… Let me help you."

He got the soap and started to wash her, running the bar up and down her arm. At this rate, it'd take her three hours to get clean and get out of there. Simone's irritation grew.

"I have this fantasy…" he said. "I would love you to pee on me while you stand under the spray. I will come quickly; I promise."

Simone balled her hand into a fist. She wanted to slap

him. What a bastard. What a selfish son of a bitch, and how deranged! But she didn't want to cause a scene, and she had no desire to fight with him. With effort, she recovered her temper.

"Armando, let me explain one thing to you," she told him, speaking to him as if he was one of her patients. "I'm not into kinky sex. I'm really a normal person, with normal habits. I like regular sex, and I don't like doing anything too...different. And if I were you, I would consider getting into therapy, because that 'fantasy' is a paraphilia called urophilia...you must resolve your mommy issues..." Her patience had neared its end.

"Hey, calm down," he said. "I was just trying to have a little fun, that's all..."

A little fun when she was so upset and worried? *How considerate,* she thought, and worse, she was pretty sure he hadn't been joking. She said a silent prayer of thanks that after today, she'd never have to see him again if she didn't want to, and she certainly never had to be alone with him. Okay, she thought, he was great in bed, despite of his kinky habits, but outside the bed... She had many doubts about him and a bad feeling he was not the type of guy she would like to have around for very long.

Simone finished bathing as quickly as she could, dressed with lightning speed, and was ready to leave the apartment as her phone rang again. It was Edward, calling to explain the flights to her.

"Hey, Simmie, I just got this crazy flight that departs at 1:30 a.m. It goes through La Guardia and arrives at 4:33. It's a direct flight. I'm just sending you your boarding pass because I already checked you in. I will be there waiting for you."

"Thanks, Ed. That's perfect for me... I... Thanks again." She'd started to say their usual, "I love you, my friend," goodbye but stopped herself just in time. After Ed had declared his feelings for her, she hadn't been able to tell him she felt the same way. To say "I love you" now might give him the wrong idea.

She looked to her watch. 11:20 p.m. She had enough time to pack and get to the airport.

* * * * *

When Simone and Armando arrived at Arami's apartment, she was waiting.

"Simmie, Ed explained everything to me. I took the liberty of packing your luggage, and I put aside some clothes for the flight—a pair of jeans, a shirt, and a sweater—so you can change from your dress."

"Arami, you are an angel, thank you very much." *What a friend,* thought Simone, and she made a mental note to send some flowers as soon as she arrived home.

"Hon, you would do the same for me! Hey, let's hurry

up; I'm going to take you to the airport. Your flight leaves in two and a half hours, and we don't have time to mess around, or you'll miss the plane." Arami said.

"No, Cousin, I will take Simone. Go to bed. You must have to cut open some old lady in the morning."

The last thing Simone needed was more time alone with Armando, but before she could say anything, Arami settled the question for them.

"Thank you, Armando, I actually do have an early surgery, but it's an old man..."

Simone didn't have the heart to drag Arami out so late when she had to be at the hospital early, so Simone bit her tongue. She could handle another thirty minutes or so of Armando's company...maybe.

"Arami, how can I thank you for everything? Your help and your invitation were all I needed to recover. You are a great friend, and I'm going to miss you." She spoke with absolute sincerity. Arami was funny and warm to be around, and this time spent with her was exactly what Simone needed now.

Arami pulled Simone in for a hug. At first, Simone stiffened, but then she forced herself to relax and return the embrace. Somehow, she would have to retrain herself to be warmer with those she cared about—to offer hugs and kisses instead of impersonal handshakes.

"No, on the contrary," Arami said, "it was such a huge pleasure to have you here. Promise we are not going to be apart for so long again!"

"I promise!"

They said goodbye, Simone thanked a tearful Arami for everything and then left.

On their way to the airport, Armando decided to chat, but in her head, Simone had other, more important things on her mind. She kept going over what Edward had told her about Philip. What could have happened to cause him to go off the deep end like that? Had he been drinking? The medications she'd prescribed him were strong, and alcohol tended to amplify their effects. But Philip should know better... She'd always been very clear about the side effects caused by mixing some medications with alcohol. She had no way of knowing what had caused him to behave so irrationally...to become violent. Frustrated, she wished she could wave a magic wand and be home already.

"When am I going to see you again, Simone?"

Armando's question drew Simone from her thoughts.

"I don't know...when our paths cross again, I suppose..." She continued staring out the window as he drove.

"I want to see you again... Can I come to your place next weekend?"

This caused her to give him her full attention.

"Listen to me, Armando, I don't want to be rude, but I'm not prepared to have a relationship. I'm still dealing with a lot of emotional issues. I'm in the process of healing, and having an affair is the last thing on my mind right now. I'm simply not interested."

"I don't want an affair; I want to date you...on a regular bases..."

"It's not you Armando, it's about me. I can't right now, sorry." She tried to keep her voice calm and professional and her face neutral to disguise the shock his words provoked in her. Date? On regular basis? They barely knew each other.

"Oh...but you could fuck me, right? Are you saying you just used me?"

She could tell by his angry tone of voice he didn't like her answer. This was an unstable man; he could go from sweetness to anger as fast as a racecar could go from zero to sixty.

Oh, God, thought Simone, *accused of using someone...there's a first.* Seemed as if life was full of them lately...

"No, it wasn't like that, and I'm being sincere here...and besides, I don't think we have much in common."

"That remains to be seen..." he said, speaking through

clenched teeth.

Simone didn't know how to respond. What could he possibly mean? She had no idea.

They arrived at the airport departure area, and Armando couldn't find a place to park—thanks to her silent prays for him to vanish, she thought.

"You can just drop me off at the curb out front," she told him.

She breathed a sigh of relief when he didn't refuse. As they pulled up in front of the airport terminal, she turned to him.

"Good-bye, Armando, it was nice meeting you."

He grabbed her by her neck and kissed her deeply.

"It was not nice meeting you, lady, it was a pleasure. I hope you have a safe flight. I will see you soon."

His "see you soon" would have disturbed her more if she didn't have to think about Philip.

They both exited the car, and Simone waited on the sidewalk while Armando lifted her luggage from the trunk and set it on a cart.

"Thanks again, Armando, and goodbye," Simone said.

Travel bag slung over her shoulder, she pushed the cart and entered the airport in a hurry. She didn't look back—not because she was late but because she wanted to leave Armando behind as quickly as possible. Since Edward had already checked her in, she headed to the security area, where she stood in line for what felt like forever. Finally cleared to enter the main airport area, she hurried to find her gate. They'd already begun the boarding process, and a few minutes later she took her seat on the plane. It was already one o'clock in the morning, but she was too restless to sleep. She decided she would read to calm her nerves, so she pulled out Lara's journal.

Lara's Journal

Secrets I Need to Tell...

After my shower, I ran a bath and started to think about everything that happened that day. Arthur's kiss and...the other things he'd done to me. I remembered when I was younger and Emms had explained sex to me, she'd told me I was too young to think about that. I'm still too young to think about it, I decided, and I'm definitely too young to do it.

I don't know why, but I knew in my heart that kind of secret couldn't be kept; what Arthur had done to me was wrong!

I tried to call Emms' house, but nobody answered, and I had no idea when she was coming back.

So I decided to talk to Sabine. She might be crazy, but she was my mother; she would know what to do.

I found her getting all dolled up for a dinner, but I told her it was urgent, and I had to speak with her. She gave me a dirty look but told me to wait in my room, and she would be right there.

"What is so urgent, Lara?" She was standing near the door.

"Mom, can you sit down, please; it's a little complicated to explain."

"I can't sit! I'll wrinkle my clothes, you silly child. What's the matter now? What have you done this time?"

"I haven't done anything, Mom... I don't know how to say this... I'm so ashamed..."

"If you don't know how to say it, then say it in the morning. I'm going to be late!"

"No, Mom, please!" I grabbed her by the arm.

"Then hurry up and tell me!"

She was totally impatient, tapping her foot, arms crossed, and when she got like that, it meant she was near to losing her temper, but I had to tell her.

"I bet you broke something, didn't you? Oh God, you are so stupid!"

"I didn't break anything, Mom! It's not that!" I used to be a little bit clumsy.

With my height, I was not the most coordinated person.

I looked down, unable to face her, and I almost lost my courage. Finally, I just spit it out.

"Arthur took me for a ride today. We went to a park and then he...he kissed me, he put his whole tongue into my mouth, and then he touched my pussy! I don't want to see him anymore!"

"What are you talking about, Lara?" She got up and closed the door then she approached me.

"Exactly what I just said! He kissed me, he licked me, and he put a finger inside me!" I shouted the last few words.

In the next moment, a resounding slapping sound filled my ears, and my cheek felt as if it had burst into flames. I blinked, unable to believe she had hit me. She was totally furious with me! As if it was my fault.

"You are never to say that again, you little liar! Where did you come up with such a horrible story? Imagine a weird thing like you getting the attention of a man like that! He was being kind to you, taking you for rides because he saw your inability to make friends. He is a good man, and here you are telling lies about him."

"I swear, Mother, that's the truth! He even gave me a bracelet."

I was pleading with her, begging her to believe me. I put my hands together as if I was praying, and in a way, I guess I was...praying for my mother to see the truth.

Instead, she pushed me, and I fell backward onto my bed.

"Stupid liar! Nasty little girl. I curse the day I made you. Damn! I won't listen to a single word about this, and if you repeat this story to anyone else, you are going to be in deep trouble. And you are grounded! Stay here until tomorrow, and no dinner for you!"

She left the room, slamming the door behind her and leaving me alone and feeling miserable with nobody to talk to about what had happened. My heart was broken. What did I do wrong? Why couldn't she believe me?

Half an hour later, Dorothy came to my room with a tray. "Eat this quickly, little girl, nobody can see me feeding you!"

"Thanks, Dottie, but I'm not hungry!"

"You've been crying? What happened?"

My eyes must have been swollen with all the tears I'd

cried that day. Dorothy always helped us when it came to Sabine. I knew I could trust her, and besides, she had warned me about Arthur, hadn't she? She'd told me if he did weird things, I should talk to her. Well, he'd definitely done something weird. I needed to talk to someone, and I decided to trust her.

"Dottie, do you remember the other day when you said if Arthur did something weird, I could talk to you?"

"Sure! What did he do to make you cry a river?"

"He kissed me! And then he licked my breasts and touched me...there..."

"On your pussy?"

"Yes."

"That man is a pervert! He's much older than you!"

"What he did is wrong, isn't it?"

"Yes. What he did is very wrong, honey. He can't touch you; you're just a kid! Only adults can touch each other, and you might be tall for your age, but you're still just a child. You have to tell your mom! She must forbid him to come anywhere near you!"

"I just did, and she slapped me and grounded me!"

"What? But why?"

"She didn't believe me! She thinks I'm lying. I'm not

lying, Dottie."

"I know, sweetheart! Come here, let me give you a hug."

I went into her arms, and I started to cry again, and she caressed my hair until I stopped.

"I'm going to talk to your mother, make her believe you're telling the truth!"

She hugged me again. Then she waited for me to eat and took the tray away. I felt better.

CHAPTER SEVEN

Simone – Present Day

Simone paused in her reading when the flight attendant asked if she wanted to have a drink. She'd been so deeply engrossed in the story she had tried to ignore the girl the first time she'd asked, hoping she'd think Simone hadn't heard. But the attendant had been insistent, and even though Simone hated to be interrupted when she was concentrating, she felt obligated to respond.

"A glass of water, no ice, please."

She thanked the attendant and went immediately back to reading the journal, more awake than ever by the impact of Lara's story.

Lara's Journal

The next day, the moment I arrived home from school, I went in search of Dorothy, anxious to find out if she had spoken to Sabine. I didn't find her, and the maid told me she didn't work there anymore. Something about a sick family member and having to return home. I felt so alone again! All my expectations of her convincing Sabine disappeared. Dorothy had been with us for years, and she hadn't even said goodbye!

Many years later, I discovered that Dorothy had spoken to Sabine, and my mother had fired the girl on the spot, sending her away with a thousand threats. Sabine wouldn't allow another person to know our "little secret".

During the following week, I tried to avoid talking to or seeing Arthur. He called me a few times, but I always found an excuse to not answer the phone. To my surprise, Sabine never forced me to speak to him, and I thought maybe she understood, after all.

On the first Sunday after the park episode, my parents had a barbecue to attend at Arthur's parents' house. I told them I didn't want to go, and nobody insisted. They left me home alone. It was the maid's day off, and

Sabine still hadn't found someone to replace Dorothy, so she had to take the kids with them. I could imagine how "happy" she was about that... I remember feeling safe and protected and thinking Sabine was not the kindest of the mothers, but at least she hadn't forced me to do things I didn't want to do.

I was sitting in our living room—my favorite spot in the house, with its large windows and beige silk curtains— watching TV on our big screen. We had an amazing surround-sound system, and I loved watching movies in there. I was reclining on the soft leather couch, legs on the seat, hugging a red cushion against my chest and staring at the television screen. I had the volume up high and didn't hear any noises, so when I saw Arthur standing beside me, all dressed in black like some kind of an outlaw, I nearly had a heart attack.

"Christ sake, Arthur, you scared the crap out of me!"

"Are you running away from me, little one?"

I just stared at him, wondering how he got inside the house. The door was locked, I was sure. I had locked it myself after my parents left the house.

"How did you get in?" I managed to say.

"Through the door...with the key..."

He showed me a key. How did he get it? At that time, I couldn't imagine, but later on, I figured out Sabine must have given it to him. No one else would have done so.

"What's going on, Lara? You avoided me all week, after everything we shared..." He made a studied sad face.

I didn't know how to explain...my feelings were confused. I had missed him, his friendship, his attention, but I was also afraid he would touch me again. I thought what he'd done was wrong, and besides, Dorothy had told me it was wrong. And I felt bad when he'd done what he'd done.

"No...I had to study today..."

"I can see..." He pointed to the TV.

"Ah...I already did my homework; now I'm free."

Arthur sat beside me on the couch. He took my hand and started to caress my forearm. My heart was beating fast, and I was afraid he would start kissing me again.

"Little girl, what am I going to do with you?"

"Why? You don't have to do anything with me; we're friends. I didn't like what you did the other day!" I spoke bravely, at first.

"Of course you liked it, and of course I would like to do a thousand things with you. And it's all your fault! You are haunting me. I can't get you out of my head. I can't forget our kiss...then I remember you are so young... I'm going crazy... Since we kissed, I can't sleep because I want you, I want to touch you, I can't fight myself anymore, and I'm obsessed with you!"

He seemed very nervous, wringing his hands, and his face was red.

"I want you! I want you in my bed, I want to know your taste, I want you in my life!"

"I don't understand half of what you are saying, Arthur; it doesn't make sense to me." I felt like a cornered animal, and I scanned the room, looking for a way to escape him. I braced my knees in a very defensive position.

"I know you understand. You are not a stupid little girl; you are clever and mature. You have ideas, and you know very well what I'm talking about...you know what happens between a man and a woman, don't you?"

I was positive he was talking about sex...

"I know, but Dottie said I'm not a woman yet, and what we did is wrong!"

"Who the hell is Dottie? Didn't I tell you this was our secret? Can't I trust you? What does this woman know about us, anyway? How could you? I never revealed our secrets to anyone!"

Suddenly, despite my fear, I felt bad. He was right; he had never betrayed our secrets. Ah, that hell's bond he had developed with me...all those little secrets we had shared...

"Dottie is...she was Debbie and Sean's nanny. I told her everything that happened at the park."

"Where is she?"

"I don't know. She doesn't work here anymore."

He looked relieved because he sighed, but then he grabbed by my wrists and shook me. "I told you, never tell anyone what we do!"

He shouted near my face, and he had foam in the corner of his mouth. I was afraid of him. He had never shouted at me before. He was acting strangely. I suddenly thought I had the answer—whenever my mother had too much to drink, she got crazier than she usually was.

"Are you drunk, Arthur?"

"Drunk? Only with your smell."

"Arthur, stop, please, you're scaring me."

"Sorry, babe, I don't want to scare you. Understand, I'm desperate, and it's your fault!"

"Why? Why is this my fault?"

What had I done to him? He was mad, and he blamed me.

"Because you are a sorceress, and you have bewitched me!"

"I'm not!"

I tried to get away from him, but he hugged me and started to kiss me. Like the last time, he put his tongue inside my mouth, and when I couldn't push him away, I bit his lip.

"Savage little thing!" He grabbed me by the shoulders.

"Stop, Arthur!"

He grabbed my hands and lifted them, locking my arms up and against the wall, and he kissed me again. I tried to push him with my bent knees, but he didn't move an inch.

"You are driving me insane, and I have to have you, or I'm going to be mad."

He was strong, and he held me tightly as he began kissing my neck. I didn't know what to do, and I thought he might stop if I stayed quiet, just as he had the first time. So I tried to calm down and stood there silently, not responding to him. My heart drummed against my ribcage.

"Kiss me, Lara."

I didn't react.

He bit my earlobe and put his tongue inside my ear, and I shivered in revulsion at the feel of his spit. He started to caress me. I felt like jelly inside. I couldn't think, and terror filled me. He seemed to have turned into an octopus because his hands seemed to be everywhere, all at once, up and down my whole body.

He moved away a little bit, and I jumped and started to run. I had no idea where to go, so I headed toward my room, thinking I could lock myself in there. Bad choice. He followed me, and before I could shut him out, he put his foot between the door and its frame, and he easily pushed his way inside the room. Then he locked the door behind him, both of us inside.

In that moment, I stopped thinking clearly. Panic took me.

He pulled me into his arms, and I started kicking and slapping him. Apparently, he didn't mind. He was too strong. Effortlessly, he lifted me and carried me to the bed, where he placed me in the center of the mattress. He took off his shirt, and I closed my eyes, not wanting to see. I knew where this was going, and the thought scared me to death.

"Stop fighting, Lara, I just want you."

He ripped my t-shirt, exposing my breasts, and I was so ashamed. I tried to cover myself with a pillow, but he took it away from me.

"Never hide from me, babe, never. You are mine."

He took off my shorts while I struggled to prevent him. I was wearing a pair of Mickey Mouse panties, and he laughed when he saw them. Realizing my efforts to fight him were futile, I started to cry. I was naked, ashamed, and frightened, and he wouldn't stop touching me. I didn't want to have sex with him! I was not an adult, and I didn't love him; those were my only clear thoughts.

"Shhhh, don't cry, you are going to like this."

He pressed me against the bed and began kissing me again. I couldn't move, and he started to caress my pussy... My fear went through the roof, and I began crying even harder. He opened my legs and positioned his dick near my pussy, and then he pushed it inside me with no warning, and I shouted in pain. He started to move inside me, and I felt as if he was tearing me apart.

"You little slut, you are so hot and tight."

He called me the strangest things, names I didn't know—slut, bitch, horny, dirty...finally releasing a huge groan and falling over me. I kept crying.

"Calm down, babe... Don't cry... It only hurts the first time. The next time will be good."

He cuddled me and let me cry. I couldn't understand the man—one moment he was a monster, and then the next he was acting like my friend again. My feelings were a mess. I liked the person who was soothing me; I hated the man who had molested me. I felt physically and emotionally torn to pieces.

When I'd grown calmer, he stood up, went to my bathroom, filled up the tub, took me in his arms, and put me in the bath. He began washing me with a little sponge he found.

Water had the effect of calming me a little more. I could think again.

"Why did you do that to me?" I finally asked.

"Because you bewitched me, and I needed you, and because I love you."

"But it's so wrong. I'm still a kid, Arthur."

"You are not a child anymore, my love. Now that I've made love to you, you are a woman. I know you felt pain, but next time, I'm going to control myself, and you are going to like it."

Like it? I thought. I hated it; how could I ever enjoy that? I felt dirty, so I took the sponge from his hand and started to rub my skin until it turned red. All I wanted was for him to get out of my room. I felt ashamed of my naked body, I felt ashamed over what had just happened, and I thought I'd never be able to face my friends and family again!

Arthur got a fluffy white towel from beneath the sink, took me from the water, wrapped me in the towel, and carried me back to bed in his arms. My bed was a mess; there was blood and ripped clothes, and it looked like a battlefield.

After he tossed the quilt to the floor, he went to the bathroom, and I heard sounds of water running. Apparently, he had decided to take a shower. Good. Maybe he would leave afterward. But when he exited the bathroom wrapped in a towel and sat down next to me, I turned my face. I didn't want to look at him. He had been my friend, and now I felt betrayed.

"Lara, look at me."

"No."

He made me turn my head toward him and started to kiss me again.

"Stop, I don't want you to touch me!"

But he ignored me, and over the course of the evening, he raped me again and again. I stopped responding and just closed my eyes, allowing my mind to drift and think about other things. I didn't want to see him; I didn't want to feel him.

Finally, he grew tired, or maybe he decided it was getting late. He grabbed all the clothes—his and mine— took the linens from my bed, and after asking where my mother kept the clean ones, he made up the bed. The room was in order again. As if nothing had happened.

I was sitting in a chair, not knowing what to do. I was in a state of shock.

"Lara, sit here."

He sat on the bed and tapped the mattress beside him. I got up and went to sit on the bed.

"Do you understand what we did today?"

I didn't answer. I didn't want to talk. The guilty sensations had returned with a vengeance. I felt dirty. I want him to leave, and I wanted to get rid of the goop between my legs, to wash away his smell.

"We didn't just have sex. You became my woman today. You are going to be mine forever. When you are older, we are going to marry. But now...people won't understand... You can't tell them... You know that... When you and I have fun, you know they won't understand...like when I taught you to drive. It's the same thing. If you tell, they are going to blame you. Did you understand?"

"I don't know...you hurt me, and I didn't want you to touch me."

"You wanted me, baby. Your body wanted me. Since the day we became friends, you went out of your way to seduce me with your perfume, your little dresses, your movements...you are a seductress, Lara. I have to go now. Here. Take these." He gave me two pills he took from his pocket. "You are going to feel better."

He filled a glass of water from my bathroom sink and gave it to me, then he waited patiently for me to take the pills.

Today, I know they were birth control pills, but back then, I thought he was being considerate and giving me some pills for pain.

"Now I have to go, but remember, it's our secret!"

He left, taking our clothes and the sheets with him. I went to the bathroom, filled up the tub, and spent a very long time bathing, not getting out until the water had grown cold. Not only did I still feel dirty, but I also felt different. And worst of all, he'd convinced me I was somehow responsible for everything he had done to me.

I knew my life would never be the same. I was an adult now. I started to cry again, full of regrets over becoming friends with Arthur, for liking his attentions and spending time with him.

When I look back on that day, I imagine I was like an innocent woman who'd just received a life sentence for something I hadn't done. Every word Arthur said to me was like a bomb exploding inside my head, sending my thoughts in all directions.

CHAPTER EIGHT

Simone – Present Day

Simone was so deeply immersed in Lara's horrors, she didn't feel the flight begin its approach, and she only came back to reality when the plane touched the ground. She was feeling very disturbed by what she'd just read.

Over the course of her career, Simone had studied many cases of child abuse, but no medical report approached the intensity of Lara's words. They were so vivid, Simone found herself suffering right along with the kid through her pain! Unfortunately, for now, she had to put away the journal and get ready to disembark.

She got her purse and left the plane, and walked to the baggage claim area in a state of stupor, where she had to wait almost fifteen minutes for her bag to arrive.

Simone met Edward after she got her luggage at baggage claim, and the moment she saw his face, she realized she'd missed him more than she had realized. He saw her, waived, and waited for her to reach him. The moment she did, she dropped her bag and drew him close for a hug.

She'd learned with Arami how good it could feel, being in the arms of someone you loved and who cared about you.

She breathed in deeply, a sense of calm washing over her. Being in Edward's arms felt like coming home, and the sensation surprised her. Maybe she had to seriously analyze her feelings for this man sometime soon.

She couldn't avoid comparing the good sensation he provoked within her to the bad, bitter taste her quickie affair with Armando had left in her mouth.

"Hey, girl, I missed you so much! And you are beautiful...look at that suntan! All you need is some pasta to put a little more meat on your bones..."

"I missed you, too, Ed." She released him and stepped back to look into his face. "It's so good to see you."

"My car is parked a little far from here. Wanna come

with me, or wait here and I can come back and get you?"

"Let's go together. I'm really anxious to get home."

They went out to his car and chatted about her time in Miami. She didn't mention Armando, she felt no need to bring that up, and to her, that was already in the past. They also talked about Philip and other things that had happened around their office as Edward drove them into the city of New Haven.

"I didn't get a chance to talk much with the police officer who arrested Philip, but it seems to me the guy was under the influence of some kind of drug."

"It's not possible Ed, he is not a junkie. To tell you the truth, he never mentioned drugs to me. I need to see him. Let's go directly to the police station."

"C'mon, Simmie, you look as if you need some rest."

"I can't sleep until I see Philip."

Simone wanted to go directly to the jail to talk to Philip, even though she was exhausted after going almost twenty-four hours without sleeping.

"Okay, you're the boss. Let me call one of my friends to see if you can get in to see him as soon as we get there."

Edward made arrangements with one of his police

associates for her to see Philip. They arrived at the New Haven Police Department and parked in the lot outside the brown brick building. Edward led the way inside and took her to one of the police officers on duty.

"Aaron, this is Dr. Simone Bennet, Philip's doctor. Simone, this is Officer Aaron Stewart."

"A pleasure, Dr. Bennet." Aaron gave her his hand.

"Nice to meet you, Officer. I'm really anxious to see my patient. How is he?"

"He's calm now. I'm going to take you to him, and we can talk later."

"That would be great." Simone tried to hide her impatience behind a polite smile.

"Edward, could you show Dr. Bennet to interrogation room four, while I go get the prisoner?"

Simone cringed inwardly at hearing Philip referred to in such a manner.

"Sure, Aaron," Ed said.

Edward used to help the police by creating criminal profiles, and he was familiar with the police department layout and the people there. He conducted Simone to a cold grey room with just a steel table and two aluminum chairs. A few moments later, Officer Stewart returned with Philip. His hands were cuffed behind his back, and when he saw her, he started to cry.

"Would you take off the cuffs, please?" Simone asked Officer Stewart. "I give you my word I can control him."

"If you're sure, Dr. Bennet."

He removed the cuffs from Philip's wrists but made no move to leave the room.

"Could you leave us alone, please?"

"I don't know..." Officer Stewart hesitated. "This guy made quite a mess last night..."

"It's okay, we can leave them alone," Edward said. "I don't think there will be any problem."

"Okay. I'll take your word for it."

After Edward and the officer left the room, Simone took a seat in one of the metal chairs. "Sit down." She waved a hand at the other chair on the opposite side of the table.

Philip took a seat, and after waiting a few moments for him to calm down, Simone reached across the table and took his hand.

"Hi, Philip, what's going on? What happened? Can you tell me?"

"Doctor, thank you very much for coming! I was desperate! I really don't know what happened.

Somehow, I went crazy and destroyed a nightclub."

"Did you mix alcohol with your medicine?"

"No way! You were very clear about not drinking, and I swear I haven't touched a drop! All I drank that night was iced tea. I didn't have anything else."

"Are you taking any other medications, other than the ones I prescribed?"

"No, Doctor, nothing!"

"Can you tell what you do remember?"

"I don't know... I was at Bali's—that's a nightclub where Leonora works sometimes—and I went there because I was going to break up with her. She was working when I arrived...tying up some girl...and I decided to wait for her. I was sitting in a corner, alone at a table, sipping my stupid iced tea. After that, all I remember was becoming a little bit dizzy, and then I saw something like a dragon."

"A dragon? Dragons do not exist, obviously. You were hallucinating. What happened next?"

"I really don't know. When next I came to my senses, I was here in the jail, and they told me I had destroyed the place. They said I was throwing chairs and glasses and that I'd hit my ex-wife!"

"Why was your ex-wife there?"

"That's the thing; I don't remember her being there...and I sure as hell don't remember hitting her!"

"How do you feel today?"

"Awful...like a rat! To think I hit the woman I love, that I wrecked a place. That's not me!"

He sounded desperate. Simone could easily read his anguished expression. His eyes were enormous, and he appeared panicked and aghast at having done something so against his beliefs.

"Did the police run a drug test on you?"

"I sincerely don't remember."

"I'll check with them." Simone made a mental note to ask Officer Stewart about this later.

"But I swear, Doctor, I didn't take anything!"

"I just need the tests to discount any physical reactions, Philip, and I'm going to keep an eye on you. Your lawyer is already on his way, and I'm going to take responsibility for you, but you have to promise to report anything unusual to me. You have my personal phone number."

"Thanks again, Doctor. I apologize for making you cut short your vacation."

"Don't worry about it, Philip. It was time for me to come

home anyway."

Simone said goodbye to Philip and left the room. She talked to Officer Stewart about drug tests.

"We already had him tested, Doctor. We used a Breathalyzer first, but those results were negative, so we ran blood and urine tests, but we don't have those results back yet. He looked completely intoxicated when he arrived, and he kept shouting, 'Kill the dragon, kill the dragon!'. But a few hours later, he was like he is now, totally normal."

"I really don't understand. I've known him for years, and he's a trustworthy, good person. Please let me know when you receive the results of those tests, okay?"

"Sure, I'll call Dr. Reynolds when we have them."

Edward had been talking to another officer, and as Simone headed toward the front desk, he hurried to catch up with her. Philip's lawyer arrived, and they did all the necessary paperwork to get the ball rolling to bail out Philip. Simone accompanied Philip in front of a magistrate and agreed to take personal and professional responsibility for Philip upon his release.

Once they finished up there, she and Edward left the police department, and Simone asked Edward to take her home. Ed headed toward her house house in Woodbridge, and within minutes she fell asleep in the car, more relaxed now she had talked to Philip.

"Simmie, wake up, you're home."

She opened her bleary eyes and saw they were parked in her driveway. She looked at Edward.

"I'll see you to the door, and then I'm going home to shower, rest a little bit, and then head back in to the office. You need to rest, please, okay? You look tired. This afternoon, I'm going to interview a new secretary—the last one was a disaster. If you're up to participating, that would be great."

"Sure, Ed. Thank you very much for everything. I'm always indebted to you."

"No, you're not. Just rest." He kissed her lightly on the cheek. "Come on; let's get you inside."

He walked her up the sidewalk, carrying her suitcase, and the waited while she found her keys inside her very organized purse, opened the front door to her house, and stepped inside.

"I'll see you later?" Ed set her suitcase on the floor just inside the foyer.

"Yes. Thanks again."

She hugged him goodbye, but he acted as if he hadn't been expecting her to touch him and disengaged himself from her embrace subtly yet quickly.

He turned without another word and hurried back to his car.

She watched him walk away, a bit curious about his reaction, and then she shut the door and went into the living room. The familiar, classic furniture gave her a sense of security. God, she was happy to be home, but she was too tired to do anything more than shower, grab something quick to eat, then crawl into bed, and that was exactly what she did.

Later that afternoon, having gotten some rest and feeling more refreshed, Simone went to her office in New Haven. As she pulled up in front of the Tudor house she and Edward had bought and restored, she couldn't help but admire its beauty. How good it was to be home, she thought again as she opened the front door and stepped into the empty waiting room. She crossed the Persian rug and paused in front of the secretary's desk.

Simone felt a pang in her heart at the sight of the empty desk. She missed Mona, her former secretary, one of the victims of the serial killer who had kidnapped and tortured Simone. She glanced at Edward's closed door. *He must be in with a patient.* She went down the short hallway to her office. Inspired by one of Empress Josephine's castles in France, which Simone had visited while studying in France, she had decorated her office in dark wood and a thick, Persian carpet in different shades of red. Paintings in wide wooden frames hung on cream-colored walls.

Simone sat on her leather armchair, caressing it and looking at her oak shelves full of books, so different—so classic and comfortable compared to the modern décor that had surrounded her in Miami.

Her heart was heavy; she was feeling a little odd but figured that had more to do with her having to get used to her old life again than anything else. She didn't know what to do without a schedule to fill every moment of her day, and Edward probably had to deal with his patient, so she was on her own.

She took her copy of Lara's journal from her purse, determined to make some headway in her reading. Better to be productive than to sit around here torturing herself with these unfamiliar feelings and thoughts.

Lara's Journal

When my parents arrived home that night, I was in my room, and my father came to say hi and ask how my day had gone. My eyes were swollen from crying, my face was all red; I looked a real mess and felt even worse. I didn't know what to do. I couldn't tell my father—I couldn't face him in my shame.

"Hey, baby, what's up? You look sad. Are you okay?" My father appeared sincerely worried, his forehead a mass of scrunched-up wrinkles. "Are you upset because you were alone at home?"

I could barely find my voice to say no, and I continued sobbing.

His kindness and concern made me feel even worse, but I still couldn't tell him. All I could do was cry and sob.

"Sabine, come here, please."

My father was a good man, but as with almost all men, he had a difficult time dealing with a woman's—or in this case, a girl's—tears.

"What now?" Sabine asked, obviously not in the mood to deal with me.

"There's something wrong with Lara," he told her.

"And what else is new?"

She strode into my room in a huff, but the moment I met her gaze, she hesitated and turned to my father.

"Leave us, Larry. I'll speak with Lara and make certain she's all right."

My father hesitated, putting a hand on my shoulder. "Lara—"

"I said I'll handle this, Larry," Sabine insisted, still

sounding impatient. "I'm certain I can help Lara with whatever is bothering her."

I was still sobbing, and tears were sliding down my face, and I believe she must have gotten worried I'd say something to my father. Something she might have a hard time explaining her way out of...

But my father still didn't move.

"Larry, please, I believe Lara and I need to have a bit of a girl talk. I'm going to take charge now," she said, changing tactics, her voice soft and kind.

My heart filled with hope. Might I be able to trust her now? Despite what had happened the last time I tried to speak with her, I dared to believe she'd take me seriously now. After all, what I had to tell her couldn't be refuted. She'd have to accept the truth.

But my father, bless his heart, still didn't get up and leave right away. "Lara? Is that okay?"

"Yes, Dad." I offered him a watery smile in an effort to assure him it was all right, and he could go.

Besides, I couldn't imagine my father hearing what I had to say. I'd be mortified, and if he were to blame me for some reason, I didn't know what I would do.

He finally got up and left the room, closing the door behind him. The moment he was gone, Sabine came and sat beside me on my bed. She took my hand in a gentle grip, and I couldn't remember a time when she had acted so kindly toward me. I was touched. She could be a pain in the ass, but I was sure she loved me. She was my mother, and I could trust her.

These days, I feel like a moron for being so naïve.

"What's going on, Lara?" she asked me.

Her tone was soft and low, and I really needed to be comforted, and so I decided I could tell her, that I *had* to tell her everything, and so I did. I told her about Arthur, the way he entered the house with a key, the way he assaulted me, everything he did to me, even the bad words he'd called me. She sat there in silence, listening as I sobbed and cried and spilled the whole, sordid tale. Although she didn't speak, she continued holding my hand, and I felt safe and secure.

When I finally finished, she released my hand and turned to face me, looking me in the eye.

"Is that all?" she asked.

"He told me it was my fault, Mom!"

She didn't hesitate. "That's because it is, Lara."

I was so shocked, she could have slapped me, and I wouldn't have been more surprised than I was by her words.

"It's entirely your fault. Always trying to get his

attention. From the first day you met him, you behaved like a little bitch in heat, always following after him. Men are like that, Lara; if you give him attention, he wants something more, and now that you've given him what he wanted he will only want more."

"It's not my fault. I thought he liked me. You have to stop him, Mom. I never intended for him to do that to me! Emms told me a woman only has sex with a man she loves, and I don't love him!"

"Oh, Emms told you that? That old bat and her crazy ideas. People have sex when they want to feel good; love doesn't have anything to do with it."

"But I don't want to do it with Arthur! And you have to stop him, please!" I begged her.

I reached out to touch her arm, hoping to reestablish the warm connection I had with her when she'd first come into my room. But she got up and stood there, arms crossed, looking at me coldly.

"No, I will not do that. You started this, and now you are going to do what he wants. I don't want to have problems with the members of that family. They are good to us. Your father has many government business contacts, thanks to them; we have this pretty life, thanks to Arthur's family. I've already told you that! If you were stupid to the point of seducing a man you didn't want, that's your problem now, but you are not going to reject him. No way, miss!"

"Yes, I'm going to reject him; I don't want him! I never did. I thought he was my friend."

"Friendship between a man and a woman? That doesn't exist, Lara; you are so naïve."

"If you don't stop him, I'm going to tell Emms, and she will do something about it!"

My shouted threat must have made her nervous because she grabbed me by the shoulders and shook me. Her behavior reminded me of the way Arthur had acted earlier.

"Don't you dare raise your voice to me, you little brat. And if I were you, I wouldn't talk to Emms."

I tried to calm down and not shout because I was sure she was going to slap me as she always did when she lost her temper. But my tears had subsided, and I'd regained my courage enough to fight with her.

"Yes, I'm going to talk to my grandma. She always listens to me, and I know she won't approve of an old man having sex with a child."

"Okay, Lara, let's calm down here. I'm nervous, you are upset, and we have to have a long talk about some facts of life. I'm your mother, and I have to tell you the truth about a few things."

She was suddenly as calm and composed as she always was when she played the good mother in front of other

178

people.

"Lara, you know I was pregnant with you when I married your father, don't you?"

"No, I didn't."

"Well, I was, and we married in a hurry. But the truth is, I was having an affair with my gynecologist and also seeing your father. The gynecologist got me pregnant, but he wouldn't marry me because he was married, so…I decided to marry Laurence. You are not Laurence's daughter, Lara." She paused and looked at me pointedly and then went on. "Which obviously means you are not Emma's granddaughter. I was waiting to tell you this when I thought you were old enough to understand. So if you tell Laurence anything about Arthur and what you led him to do today, I'm going to tell Laurence you are not his daughter."

I stared at her, speechless for a moment, before I finally found my voice. "You're lying!"

"No, I'm not! But you can try your luck. Go ahead…tell him…tell Laurence about Arthur, and five minutes later, I'm going to tell him all about you. What do you think will happen then? He will kick you out on the street."

"He would kick you out, too," I said defiantly.

"Yes, but you'd have to go with me. We would both lose, but you—you will lose so much more than I because I'm going to live my life. Laurence would keep Sean and Debbie since they are his legitimate offspring; I would send you to live with my mother. If you think your life is miserable now, you'd learn quickly how blessed you really are! Your dear 'Emms' will turn her back on you; you won't be her darling son's daughter anymore—you will be only the daughter of the hateful Sabine… You know very well how much she despises me…how do you think life will be?"

My head was a mess, my imagination always very fertile and vivid, and her questions caused me to picture myself living with my bitter, alcoholic grandmother Shirley, but worse, I could see me loosing Emms and Dad and my little brother and sister, too. I felt broken inside. I had nothing. My whole reality had disintegrated. All the people I loved were not mine to love! The only thing I really had was the loathsome person in front of me.

But apparently, she still wasn't happy…didn't feel she'd done enough damage, because she continued with her hateful diatribe.

"So now you understand… If you want to keep this life, you are going to do what I say and what Arthur wants you to do. If you do what I say, your life won't change; if you don't…if I hear any complaints from Arthur…your life will be miserable. I personally guarantee that."

"God," I whispered. "How can you be so cruel to your

own daughter?" Foolishly, I thought my words might reach her, cause her to change her mind.

"Yes, unfortunately, you are my daughter, and I will not allow you to get in my way more than you already do." She pointed a finger at me. "You've never been anything but a burden, a huge mistake, like a sharp stone inside my shoe... But you are not going to stand in my way of getting to the top. If I have to kill you, I will do so with pleasure! And if I have to allow Arthur, his father, and his grandfather to fuck you in order for me to achieve the social status I deserve, then I damn well will!"

She turned on her heels and strode from the room like a prima donna leaving the stage.

For a long time, I stared at the closed bedroom door, completely lost. I had just endured the worst day of my life. I felt empty. I had no more tears to cry. I was a miserable hostage, my mother's prisoner—Sabine's prisoner...never again would I consider her my mother. I no longer had a father. I was alone.

That conversation with Sabine defined the rest of my life. From that day, forward, I was like a robot. I tried hard not to feel, but I was always sad and depressed. I'd changed from a girl who loved to read to a girl who depended on books to escape reality. I stopped socializing with the few friends I had—after all, what would we talk about? Sex? Rape? Betrayal? They were still young and naïve; I felt as if I had aged a hundred years in less than a week...

To separate me from my grandmother, Sabine picked a huge fight with Emms when she returned from Europe. I don't know what they fought about—I never asked. But as a result, Sabine refused to allow Emms access to our house and to my siblings and me. My father and Sabine had another huge fight about her fight with Emms, but somehow, Sabine emerged the victor, and Emms stayed away.

I still managed to stay in touch with my grandmother, however. Clandestine meetings, secret phone calls... Just hearing her voice made me feel better, but I couldn't imagine telling her the truth. Arthur and Sabine had taught me to mistrust adults; I'd learned I couldn't predict their reactions. So I kept Emms in the dark... Not only did I fear her response, I was terrified she would discover I wasn't her granddaughter, and I would end up losing everything of importance to me.

I know Emms always suspected things were not okay with me, but I always tried hard not to let her know my true feelings. And when I was with her, I could pretend I was the same girl I used to be—I could forget my life and be happy for a little while—and then I'd return home...back to my dungeon...

As for Arthur...he kept molesting me. He bought an apartment and called it our "love nest". We met there at least once a week, sometimes more, depending on his mood.

Sabine would find excuses to give my father...and my God, she was good at inventing them.

For the first few years after that first day, Arthur never hurt me...we had sex, and he was always kind, and I even learned how to appreciate the act. Every time we were together, I would close my eyes because I didn't want to see his face... Instead, I would simply feel, and then one day, much to my surprise, I realized I was experiencing physical pleasure as I imagined a handsome, famous actor on top of me, rather than my abuser.

It was never Arthur with me...with my eyes closed I was always with somebody else, someone I'd chosen...an actor...a singer...never Arthur.

But emotionally? Emotionally, I was a wreck. I became paranoid and suspicious, unable to trust, always looking for other people's hidden motives. If a man gave me a compliment, I got chills...and not in a good way. And as for Arthur, I felt like his puppy, a trapped animal with no way to escape. He used me how and when he wanted. He treated me as if I was his personal doll, told me how to dress, how to behave, how to fuck. I was his; my mother had guaranteed it.

Our "arrangement" lasted for some years. Arthur ran for a political position, and when he lost, he decided he would leave the scene for a while. He would go to Paris. I was so happy when he told me because I thought I would be free, finally, but then he informed me he and Sabine had found a way for me to go with him.

Sabine had arranged a kind of exchange. It was important for a girl in my position to learn French and to experience life abroad for a little while before attending a university. My father asked me if it was okay with me, and of course I said yes...what could I say? "No, I don't want to go. Arthur is going with me, he raped me, he is my lover, Sabine approves, and by the way...I'm not your legitimate daughter?"

Days before my departure, Arthur gave me a huge ring and advised me that we were going to play the role of an engaged couple while we were in Paris. I couldn't have cared less; as far as I was concerned, it was just another lie to add to my phonebook-length list of lies.

CHAPTER NINE

Simone — Present Day

Forty-five minutes later, Edward knocked on the door, and Simone put the journal aside.

"Come in."

"Welcome home, Simmie."

"Funny you should say that—I've been thinking the exact same thing. I'm so happy to be home, and I'm ready to work."

"The new applicant arrived. Would you like to help me interview her?"

"Absolutely. Let's do it. In fact, you can bring her in here." Simone was excited about starting to work and participate in life around the office again.

Edward stuck his head out her office door. "Patricia, will you come back here, please?" he called out.

Patricia Bravesh appeared at the door. She was tall and slim, around thirty-five years old, had brown hair and green eyes, and she was dressed in a classic grey suit. Overall, she was very pretty and elegant.

"Good afternoon, Dr. Reynolds and Dr. Bennet."

Good start, thought Simone, *someone has been doing her homework; she already knows my name.*

"Good afternoon, Patricia." Simone got up and came around her desk, extending her hand in greeting. "Please, take a seat and tell us a bit about yourself."

"I've brought some references with me, Doctor." She handled Simone a curriculum vitae and then sat and waited, very still and composed.

Patricia had great references. According to her resume, she had worked for several well-known lawyers in town.

"And why did you decide to abandon the field of law?" asked Edward.

"My last boss retired, and I didn't want to go to a huge office. I would prefer something like this." She waved a hand, indicating her surroundings, and smiled. "Only two people to keep track of. I like to do a more personal job."

"Well, even a psychiatric office can get a little...excuse the pun...crazy. Are you sure you're prepared to deal with a little chaos now and then?" Edward no doubt had very fresh memories about patients acting crazy recently and knew they needed a firm hand to control them.

"What Edward means to say is that sometimes you are going to need to use a strong hand to bring our patients in line. Are you capable of that?" Simone asked.

"There were a lot of lunatic clients in some of the law offices, too." Patricia shook her head. "It takes quite a bit to scare me."

The woman was very firm in all her answers, and she seemed to be secure and controlled, two necessary qualities for the job. After a few more questions, Simone had heard enough.

"Can you give us a moment, Patricia?"

"Sure, Dr. Bennet." She left the room, closing the door behind her.

"What do you think, Simmie?"

"I haven't met any of the other candidates, but she looks perfect to me—almost too good to be true—but as you interviewed the other candidates, I don't have anything to compare her to."

"None of the others were as good as Patricia, and I had the same impression about her; she seems to be calm, controlled, and experienced."

"Let's hire her, Ed. We need help here. Things are going to be back on track in a few days, and we both know we can't do this by ourselves. If she isn't how she's portrayed herself, and if she doesn't work out, we can always just hire someone else."

"You're right. I was doing my best with no help at all, and it's hard."

They went out to the lobby to give Patricia the good news, and she agreed she could start the next day. When Simone and Ed had finished talking with their newly hired secretary, and Simone was heading to her office, Edward's cell phone rang. He pulled it from his suit jacket pocket and answered it. He lifted his hand, signaling for Simone to wait for him to finish. He ended the call a moment later.

"Philip's drug tests came back," he said. "I'm afraid the news isn't good. He tested clean for alcohol, but he had an enormous amount of Lysergic Acid Diethylamide present on his urine."

"What? LSD? Philip? No way!" She couldn't believe.

She knew Philip, and she knew him quite well. He would never take LSD! But the test results did explain the violent behavior and the hallucinations. LSD in high doses did sometimes cause some individuals to exhibit violent behavior. But Philip? She just couldn't believe he'd indulge in any street drugs.

"Are you sure, Simone? Those tests are usually very accurate."

"I have to talk to Philip, but that's so unlike him."

Edward excused himself and went to his office while Simone headed to hers to call Philip. She took a seat behind her desk, got her phone, and dialed Philip's number. He answered immediately.

"Doc, how are you?"

Having treated him for several years, she could recognize the sound of worry in his voice.

In her agitation, Simone tapped a pen rapidly on her desktop. "Philip, I have bad news... I've just gotten the results of your drug tests, and they found a substance called Lysergic Acid that happens to be the component of LSD... You can tell me the truth, Philip..."

"I've never taken LSD in my life, Doctor! I've never taken *any* illegal drugs! I'm afraid of them, and the only drugs I take are the ones you prescribe. This must be a mistake! I would never drug myself! Could I take another test? Maybe pay a different facility to do the testing or something like that?"

"I advise you to do that...but there's a good possibility they wouldn't find anything. LSD leaves the blood stream quickly...but it can't hurt to try."

"How could this have happened? It's impossible!"

"I really don't know, Philip, there is only one way drugs can get into a person's system; you have to take them, voluntarily or not. Do you have any enemies?"

"Me? N-no, n-nobody I can th-think of..." Clearly upset, Philip had begun to stutter.

"Do the test, and we'll try to figure out what happened," she told him. "And, Philip, I know you're having a difficult time right now, but please, try to stay calm, okay?"

"I will, Doctor. Thank you. I'll let you know when I've gotten the second set of test results back."

They said good-bye, and Simone set her phone on her desk. Poor Philip. She really believed him, but that could only mean someone had slipped him LSD when he wasn't looking. But what she couldn't understand was why...

To take her mind off her patient's problems, Simone decided to spend the rest of the afternoon reading Lara's journal. She still didn't have any appointments scheduled, and she didn't want to return home yet.

Lara's Journal

Paris...

Sabine escorted me to Paris. Her reasoning? Something bad might happen to me if she didn't come along. What a joke! To be her daughter was the worst thing that could have ever happened to me! I didn't exchange a word with her during the flight. In fact, over the previous few years, I had talked to her only when absolutely necessary, and I had discovered I didn't need her for much of anything.

We arrived in France on a grey afternoon. The Roissy Airport was crowded, tourists all over the place. I recalled how different things were the last time I had gone to Paris, when Emms had taken me with her. I had been full of hope and expectations; everything had been fun. Now I had no idea where my life was going...and I was entirely under Arthur's control.

As I walked through the airport, I felt as if my heart weighed a thousand pounds. I could barely breathe. Arthur was waiting for us with a driver.

"Good morning, Sabine."

He greeted her with a kiss on the cheek and then turned to me. He tried to kiss me on the mouth—his first public demonstration of affection—and I realized that far away from home, he apparently didn't feel the need to restrain himself. But I turned my face, and he kissed the air.

"I've missed you, babe; haven't you missed me?"

I really think Arthur was a pure masochist; he had to know I was going to be unpleasant. I may have been under his power, but I still had a rebellious vein inside me.

"Like I'd miss being bitten by a snake. You know why I'm here!" I chose that precise moment to make my first attempt at rebellion.

I used a low tone just for his ears. I knew if Sabine heard me, she would make some unpleasant remark or another. Arthur was perfectly aware of Sabine's blackmail. She'd made it clear to me she had told him, so he could use the same information if he needed to do so in order to make me comply with his wishes.

"I know...but you are going to be happy here; I promise."

Then he grabbed my hands, brought them to his lips, and kissed my knuckles. I thought it was so ridiculous and old-fashioned; I would have laughed if I'd had any humor left inside me.

On our way to Paris, I stayed quiet, staring out at the buildings and the grey sky, remembering how different it was when Emms had shown me every building and had explained what everything was as we'd driven past.

I could still remember her voice and my childlike giggles.

Traffic was slow, and it took us a while to reach Paris. We ended up on a tree-lined street. Platans, I remembered. How I loved those trees. In fact, I still have a dried platan leaf inside my first diary...my heart lifted a little at being back in the familiar city... I had good memories of Paris and couldn't blame the city for my current life.

I recalled one of the many wonderful things Emms had taught me:

"Lara, when all seems to be against you and you can do nothing...swim with the current for a while until you regain your strength and can find a way to swim against it again."

I would do that; I would try to be happy in Paris, despite Arthur. One way or another, I would enjoy the city until I could find a way out of this life.

We arrived in Ilê de Saint Louis, one of the more expensive places to live in Paris. Arthur's apartment was at number 12 of Quai d'Orléans. We entered through rue Budé, the building's garage entrance.

Built of beige stones and covered in black iron balconies, the old building was very charming and chic. A doorman dressed like a lawyer in his black suit and silk tie opened the huge black iron doors for us. The lobby was beautiful, brown marble floors and a wonderful crystal chandelier pending from the high ceiling, illuminating a round table with fresh flowers. The décor said, "Welcome to the high life!"

Inside the building, there was an elevator with gold doors. We packed inside, the fit a little bit tight, even for just the three of us, but that was Paris— preservation trumps technology every time.

The apartment was on the second floor. Later, I discovered it actually occupied two floors. A maid wearing a starched grey uniform waited for us with the door standing open.

"Bonjour, monsieur, bonjour, madam, mademoiselle."

"Bonjour, mademoiselle," I answered in French, using one of the few phrases I still remembered.

Arthur introduced us to his maid. "Claudette, this is my beautiful fiancée, Lara, and my future mother-in-law, Sabine."

Claudette's gaze searched my hand for a ring, and she gave a slight nod. No doubt, she'd spotted the huge diamond... Lies need to be based on some kind of truth...and the ring was very real. If she thought I was too young to be engaged, she kept those thoughts to herself.

Just inside the apartment, in the foyer, there was a huge, gold-gilt-framed mirror and two Louis XV chairs.

Well, I know that's what they were now, but I had no idea at the time.

The seat backs were framed in curved wood painted gold, with rounded medallion, cabriole legs. The upholstery was a deep green with gold embroidery. A round Persian rug in shades of green, blue, and *ceindre de roses*—rose ashes—was in the center, and on the left side there was a small mahogany table and on the right, a beautiful painting of Arthur's grandmother. I stared at the painting. *Are you proud of your grandson's actions?* I wondered.

Marble covered the entire apartment, and there were expensive rugs everywhere.

In the main visiting room, there were blue velvet sofas and gold-gilt wood armchairs. A chaise longue divided the room in two, and on the other side, there was a grand mahogany piano surrounded by more Louis XV chairs and small coffee tables.

The tall windows were dressed in cream silk sheers and gold velvet drapes, open to allow in the light. The room was very bright, even on that gray Parisian end of afternoon.

"Come here, Lara; I think you are going to like the view."

Arthur took my hand and guided me to a window. He moved the curtains away a little more and opened the window, which in reality was a door, and we stepped out onto one of the black iron balconies I had seen from outside. The view was splendid; it took my breath away. The Seine River was just in front of us; we had only to cross the avenue! There was a bridge nearby, too.

"Wonderful view!"

I could see Arthur was pleased by my reaction. He took me by the elbow and guided me on a tour of the apartment, Sabine on our heels.

The apartment had a beautiful dining room with a table big enough to hold twelve adults, and the walls were covered with many paintings and the same high windows. There was a library and to my delight, shelves full of books. I decided I would explore them all later.

Near the office there was a marble staircase with gold handrails, leading to the second floor.

When we reached the next level, another maid—Aline, an English girl with whom I could communicate—waited for us.

Arthur told Aline to show Sabine to the yellow guest room, and she followed the girl. I could see the light shining in her greedy eyes. She was acting so sweet and kind, pretending to be a lady, but I could see her calculating mind putting a price tag on every piece of furniture. And the price to have access to all that luxury? Her own daughter. I decided then and there I was going to finish her party quickly and send her back to the U.S.

Arthur's room, beautifully decorated in a blue that reminded me of lapis lazuli and gold, also had a view to the Seine.

"Lara, this is my room. It can be ours if you wish, or you can have your own."

He gave me those puppy-dog eyes, but no way would I share a room with him. And besides, I took great pleasure in saying no to him.

"Thanks, but I would like to have my own room. You snore!"

"I don't, but that's okay. If you want to have a place all for yourself, I would respect that."

"What a unique idea...respect me...would you send me back home? Would you vanish? Those would be great indications of your respect for me," I murmured.

He ignored my remarks and showed me to my room. I followed him, instantly falling in love with the place the moment I entered. The primary color was an antique rose color, the wallpaper had small flowers in a deeper shade of rose, and the décor reminded me of Emma's room back in the States. I felt at home immediately. The bed was huge, also mahogany, and the linens were a dusty-rose color. Pillows and cushions were arranged in a pile across the headboard.

The bathroom was perfect. Immense, all in rose marble, with a bathtub the size of a small swimming pool.

When I looked out the floor-to-ceiling windows, I discovered I had my own view to the Seine. Unfortunately, I also realized my room was next to Arthur's, and a door without locks linked the two.

I could tell he was waiting for me to express my gratitude.

"Your house is beautiful," I told him. "I really like my room, but I'm very tired. I would like to take a shower and sleep."

It was a huge lie; kids my age were never tired. I was full of exploratory energy, but I wanted to get rid of him.

"Sure…but wait for dinner, at least. It will be served soon."

"Thanks, but I'm not hungry. I'm just tired. And Arthur…"

"Yes, babe?"

"Send Sabine back; I don't want her around."

I was positive I could manage Arthur better without that woman around.

"Sure, she's going to spend a week, and then she'll go home. Don't worry, honey."

When he called me "honey", I cringed and thought, *okay...now we are officially an old couple.*

The following week flew by. I had to register for my French classes, and I really wanted to explore Paris. I quickly developed a habit of going out and walking around the city every day. First, because I didn't want to be near Sabine while she was there, and then because I fell in love with Paris again.

Friday of my first week there was a great day for me. I woke up, knowing Sabine was departing, and nothing could make me happier than I was, knowing that soon there would be an ocean between the two of us.

When the time came for her to leave, she tried to put on her Mommy act—probably afraid one of the maids was watching us—and reached to hug me. I pushed her away.

"Lara, how dare you disrespect me? I'm your mother! Come here, and give me a hug."

"Sabine...listen to me...and please listen carefully. You are not my mother; you are my pimp. Don't ever confuse your role."

"Don't say that. Look around you." She gestured around the room. "You would never have something like this without my intervention."

"That wouldn't bother me a bit... Material things are important to you... Do you know what would make me happy? To go back in time, years ago, and to be a normal kid. To grow up normally, to have a first boyfriend my same age, to have a first stolen kiss on prom night...to have a family... You took everything from me, stole every chance I had of being normal and happy, and you sold me for the best price you could get. Now that's the life I have in this golden cage... So never try to play Mommy Dear again, okay? You are not my mother, not in my heart, and you are not dear to me... If you were drowning, I would throw you a stone to help you sink faster!"

"You are going to regret your words, little lady."

"You are going to regret your life one day! It's a promise."

She left the apartment without looking back.

Great! I thought. I'd finally gotten rid of the first viper.

CHAPTER TEN

Simone – Present Day

Simone stopped reading and set aside the pages of the journal. *Some people,* she decided, *should be forbidden to have kids.* Unfortunately, anyone could become a parent—it was one of the easiest things to do and required no special abilities. And yet, the job one undertook after giving birth was one of the most important roles on the planet.

There should be a law that everyone has to pass a battery of psychological tests before they're allowed to reproduce! Lara was right; her mother was a true viper. Simone agreed wholeheartedly!

Simone left the couch and went to the window. The day was almost over. She felt strange, a little bit blue, maybe the result of Lara's story or maybe due to the return to real life... Simone had been so happy when she'd arrived, and now she was feeling weird. She wasn't hungry yet, and she wanted to read a little bit more and then talk to Carl as soon as possible. She and Lara had one thing in common, anyway—Simone, too, could escape real life by losing herself in a book. Maybe that was why she spent so much time reading—to avoid having to face the reality of a lonely life...

Someone knocked on her door, and she turned.

"Yes?"

"Hey, Simmie, are you staying late?" Edward asked from the doorway.

The sight of his familiar face gave her some comfort. Maybe he would invite her for dinner, since it was her first day back in town...

"I have to leave now," he said. "Will you be staying on a while?"

Trying not to let her disappointment show in her expression or in her voice, she nodded. "Yes, I am. I need to finish something here. Don't worry; I'll lock everything when I leave."

"Have a good evening."

"You, too, my friend." Their relationship had definitely changed. Used to be, she could predict Edward's actions, but now...? He was the same guy and yet a different person, and she didn't like that.

Edward left and closed the door behind him. Simone went back to her couch, took off her shoes, did a self-massage on her nape, and then put on her glasses and picked up the journal. She had to stop dwelling on all the negative feelings. Tomorrow, life would be better. She would be more rested, and things would seem different.

Lara's Journal

We'd been living in Paris for about a month, and the weather had grown very hot. The city was not very well equipped for hot weather. Back then and even now, the buildings are mostly too old for installing modern air-conditioning systems because to do so would ruin the architecture.

Our apartment had an old, useless cooling system, which seemed totally out of place in such an otherwise chic place. To make matters worse, Arthur had developed an allergy to it. One Saturday, we decided to open all the windows in order to try to catch a breeze, and I had dressed in shorts and a t-shirt to try to beat the heat.

It was a lazy day; nothing to do...that unbearable heat had been building up inside the apartment. Strange, some images never dissolves from our minds. I can remember that day so well, and I can even feel the unpleasant sensation of the heat on my skin. I had decided to take a stroll along the shore of the Seine, and then I would pick a book from one of the *bouquinestes* aligned there. The *bouquinistes* were small newsstands that sold old books and souvenirs, and I had developed a fondness for old books.

I wandered a while, but when the sun became unbearable, I went back home.

I found Arthur sitting on a couch, and he had a young man there with him. A very handsome young man. With his straight, shiny black hair that fell to his shoulders and black eyes, he looked like a gypsy. He gave me a beautiful smile when I walked in.

"So this is your beautiful fiancée, my friend?" He had a strong accent, but he spoke perfect English.

"Come here, Lara, meet my friend Adrien."

Arthur called for me, and I approached them, curious about the unknown—Arthur had never had a visitor before. Adrien stood up and kissed me on the cheek, as was the custom in France. And oh, my god, what delightful cologne!

"Nice to meet you, Lara."

"Plaisir de faire votre connaissance." Nice to meet you, I responded in French.

"And you also speak French... How nice!"

"I'm learning."

He looked at me closely, running his gaze from my head to my toes, and his expression took on the same famished look Arthur used to get when he looked at me.

"Sit with us, Lara."

Arthur patted the sofa beside him. I saw they were sipping whisky, and I decided to take advantage of the opportunity.

"I would like to have a whisky, Arthur."

He glanced at me with surprise in his eyes, but he couldn't say I was too young or anything...not without exposing at least a few of his lies. Particularly the ones he'd told everyone about my age.

Arthur didn't argue—obviously, he couldn't—so he went to the bar. I watched as he filled a glass with mostly soda and then added just a few drops of whisky. He handed me the glass. I took a sip and wrinkled my nose at the watered-down taste. It reminded me of when I was a little girl and my father had given me a taste from his glass, but only after the ice had melted and had diluted the whisky until I could barely taste it.

The memory made me miss my father, and since then, whisky always had that effect on me—comfort and the feeling of being near to my father.

The nostalgic moment didn´t last, and I flashed Arthur a smile, stood up, went to the bar, and added a generous amount of whisky under his attentive and reproachful gaze.

When I returned to the couch, I couldn't help but notice that Adrien was looking at me in a very appreciative way. I offered him a smile. God, he was a fox! Arthur looked at both Adrien and me, and I sensed he understood that we were checking each other out. I feared his reaction, but he didn't say a word. Maybe I had only imagined that he'd noticed Adrien and me looking at each other.

We exchanged a few pleasantries, and then the guy said he needed to leave.

As soon as he left the living room and crossed the exit, escorted by Claudette and leaving behind his intoxicating scent on the way, Arthur hugged and then kissed me violently. He ripped off his clothes in the blink of an eye, and in the middle of the living room, he started to run his hands over my body. I closed my eyes and began to imagine the handsome gypsy was touching me, not Arthur.

I could imagine Adrien's hands on me, and I got wet immediately. Arthur took off my clothes and bit one of my nipples—not a playful nibble but a real bite. It hurt, but it was also pleasurable. He was impatient and rude, not in the mood for sweet caresses. Instead, he bit me all over my body, scratched me, and wrenched my hair.

I don't know if I was turned on because he seemed so excited or because I was fantasizing about Adrien, but I wanted a dick inside me, quickly, and I told him so. A first for me, to beg to be fucked.

"Please take me…"

"Do you want me or Adrien to fuck you?"

I didn't answer, and Arthur entered me quickly and began to move.

"I want to see you with Adrien. I was so turned on when I realized he wanted you. I want to watch another man fucking you."

As he said this, and other less-coherent phrases—all of which added up to the fact that he wanted me to fuck someone else—he moved faster, and I could see his desire increase, as did mine. He went back to biting my nipples while fucking me. Despite the pain, I came hard, and yet I still wasn't satiated.

I pushed Arthur down on his back on the sofa and mounted him, riding his cock, faster and faster.

"I want you getting crazy on another man's dick. I want to see you use him to satisfy your lust."

I didn't trust Arthur enough to enter into his fantasy with him, so I remained silent, but his words had excited me and made my imagination run wild. I could picture Adrien, and I was almost coming when Arthur did something new... He reversed our positions and grabbed me by the neck and started to strangle me while still moving inside me.

I felt as if I was melting inside, a pleasurable sensation taking my whole body, my pussy throbbing, my heart racing, my blood rushing throughout my body, my eyes closed, my mind imagining the beautiful, dark-haired man. I could still smell his cologne. Then my lover came with a cry, and when I felt him shooting inside me, I came again.

When I opened my eyes, back from my fantasy, I was so disappointed to see Arthur and not Adrien over me that I pushed Arthur off, but he didn't seem to mind.

As he gathered up his clothes, he looked at me, still naked and spread on the couch.

"It's true...I really want to see you with another guy...you can choose whomever you want..."

"What?"

"I want to see you with Adrien...or someone else. I don't care. You pick. You can seduce him..."

I didn't understand. Sometimes, while we had sex,

Arthur would say things, and he told me he had fantasies, and they were normal between couples, but now he wanted his fantasies to become reality?

"Are you serious?"

"Completely. I was so horny when I realized he was sitting there lusting after you, I almost came in my pants... It's like having a Ferrari and everybody seeing you driving it...it's a shame to keep you to myself...you are too beautiful..."

"You would be jealous. You always say I belong to you! Don't you want me anymore?"

I felt so strange saying that. A part of me hated Arthur, and yet another part of me was connected to him. I felt mixed emotions...the fear of being rejected and despised. In some ways, he was the only person I had, and he was taking care of me.

Years later, one of my shrinks told me I suffered from a sort of Stockholm Syndrome—victims had feelings for their captors—and in that moment, when Arthur told me he wanted me to sleep with someone else, I was terrified at the thought of losing him and this hostile yet familiar arrangement we had.

"Silly!" He hugged me. "I love you! Sure, I'll be jealous. You are mine! But I want you to have fun; I want both of us to have fun. And one of the pleasures of having a Ferrari like you is to see the greed in other people's eyes."

Back then, his explanation hadn't satisfied me because I thought he was trying to trick me. But now...when I remember his words...he compared me to a car...he really thought he owned me like an object. At that age, I couldn't see that clearly. I knew so much about life I shouldn't have known...but how to analyze words wasn't one of them.

"But it's wrong..."

"Who told you it's wrong? The same people who told you not to have sex? And now don't you love having sex? We can just ask around...everybody does it...bringing in a third party can help keep a marriage fresh...but it'll be our secret."

I didn't believe him. I didn't think he would ever allow somebody else to have me.

CHAPTER ELEVEN

Simone – Present Day

Two days later, on Friday afternoon, Simone met with Philip at her office. He'd brought along his second set of test results—these ones from a private laboratory. Unfortunately, they only confirmed what the first tests had shown. Although the levels had decreased, as traces of LSD can only be detected for up to five days after consumption, Philip's blood work once again showed the presence of the drug. Simone was starting to have second thoughts about trusting Philip on this. She looked directly into his eyes.

"Philip, we're alone here. I need you to tell me the

truth."

"I am telling the truth, Doctor! I swear I didn't take any drugs." Sitting on the edge of his chair, Philip spoke quickly. "Hell, I've never even tried marijuana, let alone something as strong as LSD. Just the thought of losing control like that scares me half to death!"

Simone watched him closely, looking for signs of deception, but he appeared to be telling the truth. He wore the same worried expression he'd had months ago, when he'd become so upset over his sexual behavior. She couldn't be mistaken about him.

"Okay." She nodded. "I believe you, but we have to find an explanation..."

"Could someone have put that in my drink? I mean, I didn't notice any funny or different taste, but—"

"LSD is tasteless and odorless," she told him.

"But who would do such a thing? I have no enemies, Doctor."

"Maybe Leonora decided to hurt you after you told her you were going to break up with her?"

"I didn't have the time. I intended to tell her after she finished with her client, but I didn't. Then the next thing I knew, I woke up in a jail cell."

"Okay, then someone else must have given it to you

without you knowing. We have to find out who. When do you go before the judge?"

"In two weeks."

"That's great. You can take another drug test to show you're clean. By that time, the drug will be completely out of your system."

"I'll either be at my office or at home the next two weeks, and I promise you I will only drink water from sealed bottles."

"That would probably be wise."

"By the way, Doctor, I need a refill on my prescription. I'll be running out soon, and I'm happy to say I'm feeling very good on this last one. I'm less compulsive about sex, and I've been able to calmly analyze my romantic relationships in a more detached way."

They talked for another half hour, and she gave him his prescription. Then she talked to Patricia and asked her to call all Simone's patients, let them know she was back from vacation, and to try to book appointments with them for the following week. In less than an hour, she had a full schedule. She was happy to know all her patients had waited for her—that none had decided to move on to other therapists while she'd been away dealing with her personal issues.

She wasn't excited about the prospect of spending that

first Friday night alone, so she waited for Edward to finish up with his last patient and then caught him before he left for the day. Maybe he hadn't asked her to spend any time with him outside the office because he was embarrassed about telling her he loved her. If that were the case, she would take the necessary steps to put him at ease. Simone knocked on Edward's office door.

"Ed, do you have plans for dinner?" she asked him. Putting only her head inside the room, she saw he was already arranging things inside his briefcase, apparently getting ready to leave.

"Indeed, I do... I have a date." He raised his head to look at her.

For a moment, Simone was speechless. Right before she'd been kidnapped, he'd told her he was in love with her. Now he had a date? Just a month and a half later? She wouldn't stop to analyze the rush of disappointment brought on by the idea of Ed seeing another woman. At least, not just yet.

"Who's the lucky girl?" she asked with a forced smile.

"An FBI agent. Her name is Carla, she's investigating Peter Hay..."

"Oh...nice. Okay, well, maybe next time then." Simone didn't like the feeling of rejection she was experiencing in that moment. She wasn't used to it, especially not with Ed.

"Sure! Have a nice weekend, Simone."

She watched him hurry down the hall and out the front door. *Huh.* Not only did he have a date with another woman, he apparently had no interest in speaking to her again until they both came into work the following Monday. *Nice... And why the hell am I feeling so damn hurt?*

"Doctor? If there's nothing else, I'll be leaving now." Patricia peeked around the corner from the reception area.

"Oh, um, no. Nothing else. Thank you, Patricia. Have a great weekend," Simone told her. "Don't worry about locking up. I'll take care of it when I leave. I'm right behind you."

Simone stepped into her office to grab her purse and car keys off her desk, her thoughts still pre-occupied with what Edward had just said and feeling really hurt by his behavior. How dare he tell her he loved her and then avoid her now at every turn? He had spoiled their friendship, and she really needed her friend back! *Shit and double shit!*

She headed home, her heart heavy, even though she had no right to be upset. If she were honest with herself, she'd have to admit she missed the warm, close relationship she and Edward had developed. Although she hadn't been able to tell him she loved him, she liked knowing he cared about her.

He still cares about you, she told herself, trying to calm down. Just not as much as he did before she'd left town. But what did she expect? That he'd wait around for her forever? His seeing someone else was a good thing—a healthy thing.

So why was she feeling so depressed about his rejecting her invitation to dinner?

She stopped and grabbed take-out Chinese food. When she reached the house, she went directly to her room. She kicked off her shoes and then stripped off her work clothes and put them in the laundry basket in her bathroom. She took a quick shower, put on a silk robe, and went to put together a plate of food.

In the kitchen, she heated up the Chinese food and ate alone, sipping a glass of orange juice.

What a wonderful way to spend a Friday night, she thought, missing her vacation already, but she wouldn't lie to herself. What she really missed was Ed's company. He'd always been there for her.

I'm acting like a spoiled child who doesn't want to play with the toy but doesn't want another woman to have it, she reflected. But that knowledge did nothing to make her feel any better.

She took her plate and glass to the couch and turned on the TV. She surfed through at least a hundred channels before turning off the set, feeling restless, upset, and tired.

Nothing better than spending some time getting lost in another's person life to forget about my miserable existence, she thought. She took her empty plate and glass to the dishwasher and then went into her room, where she sat in her reading chair with the journal. She had scheduled a meeting with Carl the following week, and she decided to use her wasted Friday night to do something productive and advance a little further in her analysis of Lara's life. She adjusted the reading lamp and began to read.

Lara's Journal

During our stay in Paris, Arthur and I were invited to attend many parties and dinners. Arthur refused almost all of them. I don't think he wanted to have to explain about me.

However, we received one invitation for a particular ball, and suddenly, Arthur changed his attitude. I was lying on the couch reading when he arrived, obviously excited, waiving a golden envelop in his hand.

"Babe, we are going to a ball this weekend."

"A ball? Where?"

I put the book down, drawn in by his enthusiasm. Besides, I really liked parties.

"You don't know them; they are a middle-aged couple, friends of my parents."

I picked up the book and slumped back down to my reading position. "Nice," I said, unable to hide my sarcasm. "A ball in the asylum."

"Don't be like that, Lara, it's going to be fun... Adrien is going to be there..."

My heart accelerated at the mention of Adrien's name, but I knew Arthur. Better that I remain quiet. If Arthur had taught me one thing, it was to think through the consequences before speaking.

This is a lesson I've not forgotten to this day...

On Friday afternoon—the day of the ball—Arthur arrived, carrying a large white-and-black box.

"What's this?" I asked him.

"Your dress for tonight."

I opened the box and removed the tissue paper, revealing one of the most gorgeous dresses I've ever seen. A long, golden number with an open back that revealed my skin from my neck to the line of my hips.

"Try it on... I want to see how you look."

I took off my clothes in front of Arthur, right there in the middle of the living room, and slipped on the dress. By then, I no longer felt ashamed of my nakedness, and I was used to Arthur buying me clothes, asking me to dress then stripping me of them to have sex with me. I was anticipating the whole scene...only I was mistaken...

"Beautiful," he murmured. "Turn and let me see your back."

I turned for him, and he ran his hand along my spine.

"No panties, it's too low, and they would show. The hairdresser is going to arrive at seven. We leave at eight...and Lara, I hope you seduce Adrien tonight..." He stared at me, as if waiting for a reaction.

"Are you serious?"

"Yes, very serious."

I still couldn't understand his game, and until I solved it I wouldn't react.

"How do I seduce him?"

"You won't need to do much... Your body in this dress will play its part...but exchange glances with him, smile at him, touch him accidentally..."

"And what about you?"

"I'm going to watch, and you can be sure my dick is going to be as hard as marble"—he took my hand and put it over his erection—"see...it already is, and we are only talking about it."

"I don't think it's right..."

"Lara...it's perfectly fine when it concerns consenting adults. It's fun...you will enjoy yourself." He kissed my nude shoulder and left the room.

I am hardly consenting, I thought to myself, *and even less an adult...*

For the rest of the day, my stomach was in knots. Arthur was really serious about me seducing another man and determined that I comply with his wishes. I'd finally come to believe he wasn't just testing me. He honestly wanted to watch me fuck Adrien.

I could not eat, and I decided to go to Pont de La Tournelle, a beautiful old bridge close to our apartment. It has a kind of belvedere, and I used to love to sit there, gazing at the water, watching the boats passing whenever I needed to clear my mind.

And my mind definitely needed cleared that day. Was Arthur right? Was it really no big deal if I seduced another man? Was he telling the truth when he said lots of other people did it? Should I do what he wanted me to do? What were the potential consequences if I did? I didn't have anybody to ask. Sabine would tell me to do whatever Arthur asked me to do. I couldn't call Emms... I didn't have any friends. What could I do? Obey or jump off the bridge... No... one needed courage to kill themselves...

I wasn't brave back then, and I'm still not, although the thought crossed my mind many times when I was in despair, but I wouldn't be so selfish as to cause my family that kind of pain.

I went back to the apartment after almost an hour, my doubts still turning inside my mind. I took a shower, washed my hair, and waited for Louise, the hairdresser, who arrived exactly at 7:00 p.m. She was very nice, and I used her services whenever we had social functions. We often communicated in French—she allowed me to practice with her—and tonight, I was very clear about my hair...nothing complicated!

Louise brushed my long hair, leaving it loose and straight—I've always hated chignons and couldn't stand seeing beautiful women in those awful coiffures that made them unrecognizable when they went to parties.

After she finished my hair, Louise worked on my makeup. When she finished, I looked in the mirror. A beautiful, older girl looked back. Gold and black shadow made my indefinite eye color look sparkling green. My lips appeared fuller in red lipstick.

"Très belle, Lara," Louise said, telling me I looked very pretty.

"*Merci*, Louise. *Tu as fait un bon travail.*" I
complimented her on a job well done.

She said goodbye and told me she hoped I had a great
time at the party. I smiled and told her I would do that,
but I wasn't so sure...

Arthur decided to leave later than we should have if we
wanted to arrive on time. He wanted to make an
entrance with me on his arm.

He gave me a jewelry box containing a set of wonderful
diamond earrings set in yellow gold. They were long and
had a grey pearl dangling at the end. The box contained
a matching ring with two grey pearls, and a bracelet.
Very elegant. A display of his power to others...

I've always loved jewels, not for their value but because
they're beautiful.

We arrived at the party around 9:00 p.m. There were
other people arriving at the same time. The house was
beautiful; a wonderful marble staircase gave access to
the brightly illuminated entrance. The home was an
historical building—how I love historical architecture!
I'd learned to love all things antique during my stay in
France. This home was square and painted beige, and it
had square windows, reminding me of a small palace.
The host and hostess were waiting for their guests just
inside the carved oak door.

Arthur greeted their hostess. "Bernardette, this is my

fiancée, Lara. Lara, this is Bernardette, a great friend of my family."

The middle-aged woman took my hand. "A pleasure to meet such a beautiful woman!"

I smiled, liking the woman instantly. "Glad to meet you, Bernardette."

"But how could you get engaged and not tell anyone, Arthur?"

Great! I thought. *Let me see you get out of this one, Arthur.* I watched his face, waiting for his explanation. He didn't move a muscle, ever the good poker player.

"Bernie, dear, it's not official yet! We are going to make our announcement when we get back to the U.S., and you'll be invited to our engagement party, you can be sure of that. I just couldn't wait to put a ring on this little finger." He lifted my hand to show off the ridiculously enormous ring. "Or someone would steal her from me. But please don't say anything to my parents, or they will call Lara's parents, and I need to ask for her hand first—very traditional family, you know…"

"Of course, my dear! Count on me to keep your little secret, and congratulations to you both."

A line of guests formed behind us, and Arthur used this as an excuse for us to move on inside.

"Hmmm, you were almost caught there…" I said, amused by his flushed face.

Arthur didn't bother to reply, but I could sense his annoyance. No doubt he was already thinking on how to improve his lies…

The party was being held in a huge salon. Crystal chandeliers glittered from the ceiling, apricot-colored silk fabric covered the walls, and beautiful paintings hung everywhere. Dozens of waiters weaved through the crowd, carrying silver trays, offering champagne and other beverages, and colorful *hors d'oeuvres* that looked really tasty, but I was too tense to think about eating.

I accepted a glass of champagne from a passing waiter and sipped, trying to relax.

"Don't you think you're too young to drink? Whisky the other day…champagne now…" Arthur asked.

I stared at him, momentarily too stunned to speak. Finally, I shook my head. "No…I'm old enough to be engaged, have sex, live with a man twenty years older than I am… I think I'm quite capable of handling alcohol, thank you…" I gave him the most ridiculously cheesy smile.

Arthur didn't argue. Of course, he probably didn't want a scene right there at the party… I didn't, either, but there was no way I was going to give up my champagne.

About fifteen minutes later, I saw Adrien coming in our direction, a gorgeous brunette hanging on his arm. Disappointment rushed through me, but my heart accelerated at the same time.

"*Bonsoir, mes amis*! Good evening, my friends!" Adrien kissed my cheeks and said, *"Tu est ravissante, Lara*! You look gorgeous." He inclined his head toward the woman at his side. "This is my sister Annie."

I couldn't explain why I felt so relieved to learn she was his sister.

Arthur greeted both of them and started to talk with Annie. I had an opportunity then to speak freely with Adrien, but I was feeling shy. He must have realized my embarrassment because he smiled kindly and started to talk.

"Are you enjoying France, Lara?"

"I really love your country."

"Is this your first visit?"

"No, I was here once before...a long time ago...with my grandmother. It was love at first sight."

"So you will always come back. Love at first sight is a serious matter, and one that we never forget; it's forever."

He held my gaze with his very dark eyes, and I blushed.

"And what brings you back now?"

"I really wanted to learn French, and Arthur had to spend some time in France, so we agreed to travel here together." By that point, I'd said those words so many times I answered without thinking. Except for the part about my agreeing to accompany Arthur—as if I had a choice—the rest was true.

"And how about college?"

I hesitated, uncertain how to respond. My education wasn't something Arthur and I had ever discussed, so I had no prepared answer for Adrien's question. Apparently, Arthur and I needed to revise our lies, I thought. Twice in the same night...

At that precise moment, Arthur—having always been a much better liar than I was—came to my rescue.

"Lara had to delay furthering her education because her parents were frequently abroad, but she is going to start when we are back in September."

"And what are you going to study?" Adrien asked.

I had no idea until that moment, but I thought quickly and answered, "Architecture."

"Really? May I ask why?"

"I want to build beautiful things." And in that instant, with the all the passion in my young heart I decided on my future profession.

"A beautiful woman is going to build beautiful things of course."

I could see my body charmed him, as his gaze travelled my length from head to toe.

Adrien's sister excused herself to talk to a friend, and Arthur took the opportunity to speak with someone on the other side of the room, leaving Adrien and I alone.

"Have you been engaged for long?"

"No...just before the trip...and it's not official yet."

He looked from my ring to my face. "I understand...the perfect way to make it acceptable to drag a young lady out of the country..."

I glanced away, unable to meet his gaze. "We've been dating for almost three years..."

"Really? My friend is a cradle thief, and I didn't know... He is too old for you."

"Some people think so...but I'm not that young..."

"Sure..."

I could see in his eyes he didn't believe a word.

"And you?" I asked. "Aren't you too young to be friends with Arthur?"

"I'm twenty-five...and he is a friend of my parents...we have a business relationship, not a real friendship," he said. "So tell me...what do you do with your spare time besides study French?"

Relieved he'd changed the subject, I smiled. "I walk around, explore the city..."

"Alone?"

"Most of time, yes."

"Would you like to have some company? I could show you several beautiful places I'm positive you've never seen."

"Yes, I would like that," I said, telling myself I'd only accepted because Arthur had insisted I lead Adrien on and not because I had any real personal interest in the man.

"Arthur wouldn't mind?"

"No...why would he? You are a friend..."

"I am, indeed, but I'm also a man, and I wouldn't leave a girl like you alone to walk around with another man."

"Arthur isn't like that; he doesn't mind."

"I would..." Adrien shook his head. "But I suppose his foolishness is my good fortune. So may I call your house?"

"Sure. I have a private number…"

I had a phone line just for me. Arthur didn't want someone calling me and having an employee pick up the phone and give out unnecessary information… I even had an answering machine to collect messages, just in case I wasn't there. Emms called me at least once a week… Sabine never did, and every once in a while, my father would do his duty and check up on me. If only he knew…

"Can I take note of it, please?"

So I gave him my telephone number, and he got a pen from a waiter and wrote it on his arm. I laughed.

"Do you want to dance?" Adrien asked.

"I don't know how to dance very well." I shook my head.

I had never danced with a man. I had taken a few ballet classes, as all the young girls of my station used to do, but that was all. Arthur didn't like to dance; he used to say he didn't understand that "primitive habit" people had.

"That's okay," Adrien said. "I can lead you."

He didn't wait for an answer but grabbed my hand and tugged me along after him to the dance floor.

To my relief, there were already at least a couple dozen

people dancing alone, so I could lose myself in the crowd. I observed the moves made by a few of the women closest to me, and my confidence swelled. I could do that! I started to dance, imitating other people around us, and just when I had started to relax enough to enjoy myself, the music changed to a slow song. Adrien immediately put one hand on my shoulder and the other arm around my waist, pulling me to his chest and starting to guide me.

"That's right," Adrien said. "It's really very easy. You just hold me tight, and move your feet."

He spoke close to my ear, and I felt a chill all over my skin. He brought his face close to mine, and we were dancing cheek to cheek. I felt a wave of heat and realized I loved being in his arms.

"You lied to me, *ma belle.*"

I tensed. Which of my lies had he discovered?

"Me?" I asked. "How...? What do you think I lied to you about?"

"You are an excellent dancer."

I released a relieved sigh. "You are a good teacher."

We danced until they announced dinner. Despite being hungry—I had yet to eat that day—I felt disappointed as I followed Adrien and the other dancers off the floor. Not only had I enjoyed what Arthur referred to as a "primitive habit" much more than I thought I would, I had also loved being in Adrien's arms. In fact, if I spent the rest of my life snuggled up to the man's broad, muscular chest, I wouldn't mind one bit.

I met up with Arthur so we could find our assigned table, but I wasn't happy about leaving Adrien.

"Well done, Lara, very well played," Arthur said.

"Why? What do you mean?"

I had merely danced with the man, I told myself. Hardly what others would refer to as seductive.

I sat there daydreaming about the beautiful gypsy and how I'd felt when he'd wrapped me in his embrace. I had no desire to leave the paradise I'd created in my imagination...no inclination to return to reality.

"Adrien is fascinated with you...he is looking at you right now. Look to your left, three tables from ours."

I searched for Adrien, and he raised his glass in a silent toast and smiled at me.

"Lift your glass to him, Lara. When someone makes a toast like that, if you are open to advances, you answer by lifting yours..."

I obeyed, but I looked down. I was to new to that kind of game.

After dinner, I didn't see Adrien again, and we left early. As I stared out the window on the drive back to our apartment, I wondered if he would call...

CHAPTER TWELVE

Simone – Present Day

To avoid thinking and the inevitable self-pity, Simone kept busy the whole weekend. She organized her already super-organized house, went to the movies, to the mall, and to her manicurist. She relaxed and did some meditation. It was good to be back home doing trivial things, she thought.

She decided to take a break from reading the manuscript for the weekend. She needed to clear her head a little bit, and every time she opened Lara's story, she felt a mix of sadness and anger, and she didn't need to add that to her own dark mood for the next two days.

The weekend passed slowly, and Monday arrived to start a very busy week. On Monday morning, Simone woke up, took off her cream silk nightgown, went to her bathroom, and took a long shower to wash away the desire she had to go back to bed. She looked at herself in the mirror and decided she wouldn't start her week on a negative note. She was going to dive into her busy schedule, and let things take their own course. Stop pushing life and live at as it was, in the moment. She dressed quickly, ate a light breakfast, and then went to her office.

She arrived to find a very active Patricia giving orders to the gardener, and when Simone finally sat at her desk, she found all the files for the day piled on her desktop, categorized in order of appointment time. Simone smiled. *Efficient woman! Smart move to hire her.*

She was going to take on a new patient, Theodora Broombaker. Simone took the medical background she had on the woman and read it, making a special note of the patient's age—eighty years old. Doctor Shultz, a colleague, had referred Theodora to Simone, and the elderly woman's medical records showed she was in excellent health. Besides doing a lot of plastic surgery and having a C-section, she didn't have any other complaints of a physical nature. Amazing, thought Simone. What kind of sexual problems could a woman her age have? Lack of desire, probably…

Simone looked at the clock over the tea table near the couch. Time to meet her newest patient. She called Patricia on the intercom and asked her to bring Theodora in.

The elderly woman turned out not to be what Simone would have expected from a lady of such advanced age. In her black leather pants, red sweater, and high-heeled black boots, she looked thirty years younger. She wore her jet-black hair long and straight, and with her blue eyes sparkling with what could only be mischief, she returned Simone's stare.

What the hell? Simone thought. This woman certainly didn't look like anybody's grandmother! With great effort, Simone cleared her throat and pulled herself together.

Theodora marched into Simone's office.

"Good morning, Theodora, how are you?"

Simone offered her hand, and Theodora shook it vigorously.

She was definitely a strong woman. Simone could tell by her gestures and her decided way of moving.

"Hello, Doctor. But please...all my friends call me Thea."

Except, I'm not your friend, thought Simone. "Thanks, Theodora, would you have seat?"

Simone pointed to the couch in front of her armchair, but Theodora went directly to Simone's chair and sat. An oppositional person, analyzed Simone, but she allowed the woman to remain in the chair. After all, Simone was not going to play Sheldon Cooper from the TV show *The Big Bang Theory*, one of her favorites, even though she felt the same way he did about her armchair.

Theodora crossed her legs in a very elegant way. Her movements were precise and not a little bit restrained by age. She then looked directly into Simone's eyes.

"What brings you to my office, Theodora?" she asked, deciding it best to maintain a professional distance.

"I can't tell you my life story if you call me by my whole name... You sound like my mother, getting ready to reprimand me!"

"Okay, Thea. How can I help you?" Simone had to give in—this time, at least—in order to proceed. She hated that kind of intimacy, but if she had to call the woman by her given name in order to make the patient talk, Simone would do so.

"A man!" Theodora flashed a mischievous smile.

"Um...you have a problem with a man?"

"No, I'm the problem. I don't want to scare him, because I really like this one; I mean I *really* like him."

"Okay, but I'm not following you. What could you possibly do that is so bad?" She shook her head. "No...let's back up. First, why don't you tell me a little bit about your life, so I can try to understand what make you think you might scare him...?"

"Hell, is that necessary? To go back to the stone age?"

"You don't need to go quite that far, but a bit of background information would help."

"Well, Doctor, I'm not a girl anymore, and I've been married six times already...the last one twenty years ago...but the problem is that I don't like to be married. I enjoy the romance, the chase, winning a man's heart. I love weddings—especially wedding receptions—but after that...well, I'm afraid I begin to lose interest. The monotony of daily, married life drives me crazy. It's all too tedious."

"Do you have children?"

"Oh, God...yes...but not in the plural form, thanks to Zeus! I had one...we didn't plan on getting pregnant—my second husband and I—but you know how it is...passion gets in the way, and people forget to be careful. I learned very quickly that one child was enough for me. I'm not a very maternal person. Besides, I have a pact with happiness, Doctor, and being a mother doesn't bring me happiness."

If all mothers were that sincere about their feelings,

reflected Simone, kids would be spared years of therapy.

"A pact with happiness? Can you explain what you mean by that?"

"Sure... If something makes me sad, I walk away. I don't know how much time I have left to live, I don't know the future, but I don't have time to waste on being sad..."

"It's good you've made a decision to be happy, but sometimes, sadness is a part of life and makes us appreciate the good times even more."

"Yes...and sadness was part of my world—forty years ago. But the day I turned forty, I decided to live according to my desires, to stop explaining myself, and since then, I've been a whole lot happier. I get to be myself, regardless of what anyone else might think."

"And what does that mean—you get to be yourself?"

"I live according to my feelings, and my feelings tell me I looooove sex!"

Her blue eyes glittered even more than they had earlier when Simone had been appraising Thea's appearance.

"And you see, Doctor, I'm a sadist!"

Well, this is it. I'm done, thought Simone. *I can die right this moment because now I've seen everything!*

Struggling to keep a straight face, Simone pressed on.

"You are an active sadist?"

"Yes, I feel so much pleasure provoking pain; you can't imagine."

"What kind of pain?"

"Physical pain! I love to kick, to whip, to apply clamps."

"Men, women…children?"

"Oh, only men; I'm completely heterosexual. I gave it a try once—with a woman—but I didn't like it at all.

Thea made a face that clearly indicated her displeasure at the memory of her one lesbian encounter.

"How do you feel when you spank someone?"

"It's sexual, it turns me on, and I become really excited."

"And can you become excited with anybody, or do you need an emotional link?"

"Hmm. I never really thought about that. Let me see… I suppose I usually need some kind of emotional connection. After all, how could I explain my desires to a brand new lover or a casual acquaintance? But that's not entirely true, as I can beat the shit out of strangers, too, if I'm in the mood for that… She looked as if she was searching her memory and then said, "Okay…I don't think I need an emotional link, but I don't think I'd do anything to an innocent...like hit the maid or kick a cat or anything like that...it's purely for sexual purposes."

Simone was glad to hear the woman was not a psycho who went out looking for people to whip on the streets.

Theodora continued. "So now I have this new boyfriend, I believe I'm in love with him, after experiencing an emotional drought for so many years, and I don't know how to proceed, because I really like him, and I don't want him to go running if I show him a whip. However, for me, our relationship cannot be complete if I can't spank him a little bit..."

God, please, take me now. Simone sighed inwardly. She was having a hard time keeping a poker face lately— maybe because the deep emotions she'd been experiencing were rising toward the surface—but she should restrain herself, at least in front of her patients.

"How long have you two been together? Where did you meet him? How did you fall in love...? I'm sorry to ask a million questions, but I need more information to form a complete picture of what's going on."

"Of course. That's fine. Let me see... He is the son of a friend of mine."

"So we are talking about a younger man...?"

"Yes, thirty years younger. I never planned to fall in love

again—I never believed I *could*. I started advising him about some properties, as I'm a real estate agent, and we started spending a lot of time together—every day, really, because I was showing him properties, and suddenly, we were in love."

Theodora's eyes sparkled with the light only people in love had, and her face was flushed like that of a teenager talking to her BFF about her crush on some boy.

"He feels the same?"

"Yes, he does. He was married, but he's divorcing his wife, and he wants to have a serious relationship with me."

Simone had heard of and had treated middle-aged men who were suffering from mid-life crises, and all of them had been trading in their wives for twenty-year-old girls. The men saw this as an affirmation of their virility, and some were even having babies, but Simone had never heard of a fifty-year-old man divorcing his wife for an eighty-year-old woman...not even an eighty year old who looked as if she were fifty. *Maybe I haven't seen all there is to see...*

"So tell me...how is sex between the two of you now? Even though you can't indulge your sadistic side, is sex still enjoyable for you?"

"It's funny... He acts very uptight sometimes... I fell in

love with his personality; he's sensible, caring, and attentive, but sex is not his strong point. Not yet, anyway..."

And she turned her eyes toward the ceiling as if she was imagining how their future would be...

"Because you can't spank him, or because he is not able to perform? Why isn't it as good as you think it should be...or could be?"

"He's just...I don't know... Too serious. Too polite. I can imagine him writing a letter asking if he can please penetrate me!"

Simone bit her lip and swallowed back her laughter, fearing the elderly woman would take offense and walk out before they finished their session. After a moment, she managed to regain her composure.

"Despite his stilted approach, does he manage to satisfy you?" Simone asked.

"After we reach a certain point, he seems to let loose a little bit, and he's able to make me come... But if I could whip him just a little bit, my orgasms would be much more intense."

"Yes...but can you imagine a conservative man such as you've described being spanked?"

"No, I can't. And that brings us to my reason for being here; I don't want to lose him. For the first time in thirty years, I'm in love, and I don't want to chase him away. Let's be real, Doctor... I don't know how long I'll stay looking this way... Plastic surgery, cosmetics, working out every day...it's a constant fight. On the outside, I'm winning...but who knows what's going on inside this old bod? At my age, I'm like a time bomb, ready to explode at any moment. And I want to die happy, by his side, preferably immediately after I've had a huge orgasm..."

Poker face, poker face, poker face. Simone repeated the thought like a mantra.

"So you are here because you want help with your addiction to sadism?"

"Oh, no!" Thea shook her head. "I'm here because I want to find a way to convince him to go along with it—to allow me to spank him. I simply must find a way! Um, and also because my prescription for sleeping pills has run out, and I would like a refill. You have my medical records, so you should be able to prescribe them to me with no problem."

Great! A sadistic woman who wanted to die with her whip in her hand and who had only sought out a sex therapist to help her create a more convincing argument to support her plan... What other amazing things could Simone expect to encounter in this wonderful career? But despite the insanity she often ran into during the course of her job, Simone couldn't be happier to be back in her loony house! Being there gave her a sense of belonging—at least her patients really needed her.

"Okay, Thea, we are going to figure out something together, I'm positive. I believe the best way to start introducing the subject is by making some moves in that direction...and trying to figure out if your boyfriend has an inclination to participate in such activities."

Theodora grinned. "Should I beat him?"

"I believe you should try to be more subtle... Why don't you start small...a few slaps and scratches, just to see how he feels about mixing sex with pain...?"

They talked for another half hour, and Simone rechecked Thea's medical records. The old woman appeared to be as healthy as a twenty year old—maybe healthier. At this rate, she'd probably live forever. Simone wrote out a prescription for the sleeping pills.

When Theodora left, Simone thought about how she'd recommended the woman slowly introduce her lover to spanking. Simone had surprised herself. Had the drama she'd gone through changed her? Made her feel and react more practical and less theoretical? And if that was true, was it a good thing or a bad thing? Most importantly, would her patients benefit from this new and different Dr. Bennet?

Theodora, Simone thought, would probably never change. Not unless she wanted to do so. Simone was resigned to the fact that she wouldn't even try to resolve Theodora's spanking fetish. In fact, Simone thought, why not help the older woman be happy while she could.

* * * * *

After a very busy day, Simone was tired, but she was still happy to be back, to be taking care of her patients again. She couldn't lie to herself; she loved to listen to their stories, and she felt much better now that she was back to helping people. If she'd known that would make her feel better, she would have returned sooner. She was even a little less down in the dumps than she had been lately because being there made her feel useful and necessary.

The last patient had departed, and Simone decided to read. She had nothing to do at home at the moment, and she had no intention of feeling sad again, so she would go back to Lara's life before finishing the day.

She carried her copy of Lara's journal with her at all times, just in case she had a few extra minutes to read. She pulled the pages from her purse, took off her shoes, sat on her armchair, and sighed. *Time to climb back on the roller coaster,* she told to herself, and mentally fastened an imaginary seat belt.

Lara's Journal

I spent the next few days rarely leaving my room at the apartment for fear I'd miss Adrien's call. Monday, I was convinced I would hear from him, but he didn't call. I checked the answering machine at least a dozen times. By Wednesday, I had given up. Maybe he had washed his arm and lost my number. Thursday afternoon, he finally rang me up.

"Ma belle, how are you today?" His voice was strong and very masculine.

My legs turned to jelly just hearing him speak. "Fine, and you?"

"Okay, but missing you…how about going for a ride with me today?"

I hesitated to say yes. Arthur had said he'd be home around 7:30 p.m. I had to be back by then. "What time?"

"Let me see… It's one o'clock; how about in an hour?"

"Okay. Where would you like to meet?"

"At the front door of your apartment? Wear jeans and a pair of sneakers. I have a motorcycle."

"Can you meet me at the corner?"

"At the corner? But why? You told me Arthur wouldn't mind you hanging out with another man…"

"He doesn't…but I'm worried about the neighbors…"

Bad lie! We didn't have neighbors; we occupied the entire building…

"Which corner?"

"Rue budé and Rue Saint Louis en île…is that okay with you?"

"Sure. I'll be there."

I had never ridden a motorcycle, and I was excited about everything—going out with Adrien, riding a motorcycle…my head was spinning.

Adrien met me at the corner at exactly 2:00 p.m. He was riding a black motorcycle, and he looked so handsome in a pair of stonewashed jeans and a leather jacket. When I approached him, he took off the helmet and kissed me on the cheek. He smelled so good, like wood and some other indefinite substance.

"Put this on, ma belle," he said, handing me a helmet. He took my hand and helped me onto the bike. "Be careful. Don't touch anything with your legs, okay? Those pipes are very hot; they can burn you. And hold on tight to my waist."

I held on to him as we rode around Paris. The wonderful sensation of the wind, the beautiful weather, combined with Paris's landscape and Adrien's smell made me ecstatic.

We went to tour Eiffel, but instead of going to the tower, he took me to Champs de Mars, the landscaped area surrounding the tower. There were a lot of people...tourists and locals—some working on their tans, others reading, and some even sleeping. We chose an empty spot near the marionnettes du Champs de Mars—the Champs de Mars's puppet theatre—to sit on the grass, and Adrien bought us a couple of Cokes.

"Now that we have the perfect spot and something to drink, I want to know everything about you," Adrien said.

I stayed silent, not certain what to say or where to start. After all, my life was an entanglement of lies, and I feared I'd accidentally reveal something I shouldn't. The Lara he thought he knew didn't exist. I'd lied about my age, my relationship status... I'd lied about everything. Rather than answer his question, I flipped it around. After all, if there was one thing I'd learned it was that people loved to talk about themselves.

"You first. Tell me all about you... When you're done, I will tell you anything you want to know. How about that?"

He drew a deep breath and started to talk.

"I'm finishing up business school, but I still don't know what I'm going to do once I graduate..."

"Work with your father?" I suggested.

"I don't think so... I would like to do something on my own—be recognized for my own efforts—but I don't know where to start, and I don't have the capital. So...my future is sort of all up in the air right now..."

"Ask your father for some capital..."

"I'm afraid it's not that simple..."

"Why?"

He remained silent a moment, staring off into the distance. "I guess you could say I'm kind of the black sheep in my family..."

"The black sheep?"

"Yeah...my parents don't approve of my way of life and some of the choices I've made, and they think I take unnecessary risks..."

"And?"

"And I left home some years ago, and I don't intend to go back now..."

"But what would they like you to do?"

"Maybe marry, settle down, have a bunch of noisy kids...get a regular job with a regular company..."

"And how about you, what do you want?"

"Hmmm... To travel around the world with just a

backpack...to see all the beautiful sights there are to see...there are so many places to visit and so little time."

"Don't you want to marry?"

"Not now...one day, I suppose, if the right girl comes along..." He put his index finger on my ribcage and said, "But you...you are going to marry soon, I assume, judging by the size of that rock on your finger..."

"Just like you guessed the other day, it's a ruse. How else could I travel alone with Arthur? I will never marry him."

If there was one thing of which I was certain, it was that... I would never marry him, and I would not to be with him for the rest of my life.

"Never? Does he know that?"

"I don't know. We've been together for a while, but the subject of marriage never came up."

"Well, but the engagement ring tells the world a different story..."

"Yes...but it's just that—a story."

"Anyway, he is too old for you. How many years older?"

"Fifteen," I lied...again. Arthur was twenty years older.

"Too old! My god, he's from another generation. But

old or not, I don't believe he is going to give up on you."

"He will…eventually." I sounded more certain of this than I felt.

"Don't you love him?"

A good question. Did I love Arthur? No…certainly not. I cared for him, and sometimes, I worried about what I might do if I were to lose him. Other times, I couldn't stand the sound of his voice. I would never forgive him for all he had done to me. My feelings were confusing. I felt angry, despair, desire.

"I really don't know. I like him, I suppose."

"I like this Coke"—he pointed to the empty can—"Is that how you feel about Arthur?"

"I'm sorry…I don't know what love is."

"Well then, my darling girl, you've never been in love. If you had, you would know." He ran his fingers across my cheek and pushed back my hair that had fallen in my eyes. "Girl, you make me crazy. The only thing I would like right now is to kiss you."

"So…? Go ahead… Kiss me."

He pulled me close and captured my lips with his. He was only the second man to kiss me, but I could tell the difference. His mouth tasted sweet, like Coke. He kissed me softly, his lips touching mine slowly at first, then he intensified it, and I felt a wave of heat. I wanted him.

Adrien stopped kissing me and put some distance between us. I struggled to hide my disappointment.

"What am I doing? Kissing another man's fiancée. Encroaching on another's man property."

"I don't belong to him; I belong to myself."

I hoped to bring the magic moment back, but it was over.

"Yes, you are his property." He took my hand and lifted it, displaying the ring.

I thought about my life and realized he was right—I was Arthur's possession. He and my mother had guaranteed that, and until the day came when he no longer wanted me, I would be his. I had no rights, and I certainly couldn't choose to love another man...but I had a feeling it was too late... My heart was beating differently for Adrien.

I gathered my courage and said, "I want to see you again."

"Ah, little girl... I want...you."

And the magic was back. He kissed me, and we embraced and fell to the ground. We began to caress each other, our lips pressed together in the deepest of kisses. He put his hand under my t-shirt and touched my breasts with care. I touched him and could feel his erection beneath his jeans.

"Il faut aller à une chamber vous deux..." a man called out as he passed by.

His recommendation that we get a room destroyed the moment, and we quickly grabbed our helmets and left.

When I arrived home, to my relief, Arthur wasn't there, and when he finally did come home, he didn't bother asking about my day. Of course, I didn't offer any details. Just one more secret in my life...the souvenirs of that day and Adrien's kisses.

We began a routine, Adrien and I, of riding all over Paris on his motorcycle. We laughed and talked—Adrien made me speak French and corrected me patiently when I said something inaccurately, and thanks to him, my French was improving. I went to school every morning, and in the afternoon, after having lunch with Arthur, as soon as he left the apartment to tend to his business, I left home to meet Adrien.

On a Friday morning, I left home to go to my French classes as I did every day during the week, but that day, I decided to skip school in favor of spending more time with Adrien. He was waiting for me a few blocks away...without his motorcycle this time. Instead, we caught the subway and went to his studio on 28th, Rue du Faubourg-Saint-Honoré.

He lived on the fifth floor of a building near the American embassy. The building had one of those old-fashioned cage elevators that served only the first four floors. We got out on the fourth floor and from there we had to climb the stairs. We arrived laughing and out of breath.

"Welcome to my mansion," he said and opened the old oak door.

The room was small but nice. A big bed covered with a blue blanket, two pillows against the headboard, sat in one corner. Nightstands flanked the bed, one holding a lamp and at least five books. On the other side of the room—really only a few feet away from the foot of the bed—were two chairs and a small dining table. Several bottles sat on a tiny coffee table next to a fireplace.

He showed me the ridiculously small kitchen, which contained a two-door cupboard, a hotplate, a sink, and one of the littlest red refrigerators I'd ever seen. There was also a bathroom, which, compared to the rest of the place, looked huge.

Thinking back, I believe the architect definitely lacked a notion of space...but back then, I just thought the place looked a bit weird.

The décor was nice, bright and cheerful, the furniture modern, and there were a few lithographs on the walls. All in all, his place was nothing spectacular, but I immediately felt comfortable there.

"I like your apartment."

"It's not an apartment; it's a *studio,* Lara."

"What's the difference?"

"Size...lack of an elevator...one bedroom, top floor...colder in winter...hotter in summer...cheaper..."

"But the address is great."

Rue du Fabourg-Saint-Honoré was a very exclusive street. All the great *couturieres* had stores there. I'd been there with Arthur many times.

"Thanks to...my mom. She is the owner."

So he was not as independent as he'd made himself out to be the other day...a black sheep grazing in green fields...

"Well, I like the way you've decorated the place."

"Not my doing, either. I need to give all the credit to my mother. But the sink full of dishes is my own touch."

I laughed.

"Would you like something to drink?"

"No, thanks!" I was a little bit nervous. We'd spent a lot of time together in public, but this would be our first time alone in private. Still, I couldn't imagine drinking in the morning...even to calm my nerves.

He had taken a seat on his bed, and I went to his side. He immediately pulled me into his arms and started to kiss me. He hadn't touched me intimately since the day on Champs de Mars, and I had been dying to taste his lips. Just being near him turned me on.

His touch was so different from Arthur's. Adrien's hands were softer, his demeanor calmer. He ran his hands over my body and stripped me in a very natural way. I started to unbutton his white shirt, and he finished, moving back a bit to slip it off his broad shoulders. I began caressing his chest, marveling at how hot his skin felt and at the contrast between his dark tan and my pale-white complexion.

He eased me back onto the bed then kissed and licked my neck. He continued lower, running his tongue down my entire torso—while fondling my breasts—until he arrived at my panties. He took them off gently, as if he were undressing a baby. So sweet all the time, always searching my eyes for my approval.

This time, I wouldn't close my eyes. I wanted to see and feel everything, and I wanted to be with him and nobody else. No fantasies. Just Adrien and me together, touching and kissing.

He started to lick the outside of my pussy lips. I was crazy for him to tongue it, longed to be penetrated, but he was in no hurry and wanted to play. He blew hot air on my clit and nipped at the lips. He used his fingers to separate them while touching my clit with the tip of his tongue. I cried out, dying to be fucked, and then he started to suck it, caressing my entrance with one finger. My wet sex perfumed the air, ready to receive him, and I came in his mouth.

I changed positions, pushing him back to lie on the bed. I opened his zipper and took out his cock, stroking its silky-smooth but hard-as-marble length. I captured and held his gaze as I lowered my head and took his cock into my mouth. God, he tasted wonderful. I sucked him hard, bobbing my head. He moaned, and my heart soared at the sound. *I did that,* I thought. Reveling in my ability to bring him pleasure, I scraped my long nails over his chest as I continued to suck him.

"Stop, Lara, or I won't be able to hold back. I don't want to embarrass myself our first time together."

He pulled me up, reversed our positions, and I stretched out on the bed. He got a condom from the night table drawer, rolled it down over his dick, positioned himself between my legs, and slowly penetrated me. Before he was all the way in, I came hard.

My body synced with his, and I moved in time with him, searching for another orgasm. I quivered all over, my senses heightened, sensitive to his every touch. My nipples were hard as pebbles, my soaked pussy tight around his shaft. His musky scent increased my pleasure, driving me to the edge once again.

Never had I experienced such intense pleasure, my orgasm erupting like a volcano, molten heat dripping down my thighs. He joined me, his deep cry of release mingling with my whimpering sobs. We lay there on his bed, not moving, just holding each other, speechless, both of us drenched with sweat.

When we finally caught our breath, he lifted his head and smiled.

"That was amazing...the most intense sensation I've ever felt." He shifted a bit and then closed his eyes on a moan. "God...your pussy is so hot and so tight."

What should I say to that, I wondered. Thank you? I remained quiet but returned his smile and lifted my hand to cup his cheek.

After a moment, he kissed me on the nose then rolled off me to climb off the bed.

"Wait one moment," he said.

He went into his doll-sized kitchen, and I closed my eyes, listening to him rummaging around. A few minutes later, he came back and rejoined me on the bed.

I watched as he spread a blue-and-white checkered cloth and then began laying out a variety of food— cheese, ham, *confiture aux figues*...a fig jam...and pieces of crusty bread. We ate in silence, both of us needing to regain our energy. Appreciatively, I sipped the red wine he'd opened.

"I want to make love to you again," he said.

That expression—make love—sounded odd to me. I knew the term, of course, but I would never use it to describe what Arthur and I did. We had sex, we fucked, but we didn't make love. But with Adrien the term seemed appropriate.

We made love again and again until we noticed how late it had gotten, and I realized we'd spent the entire day together. We hurried, hoping I'd get home before Arthur did...but that didn't work out so well... When I arrived back at the apartment, Arthur was already there, sipping whisky and waiting for me.

He looked annoyed, his mouth turned down at the corners, and he was glaring at me the way he always did when he was pissed off.

"Hello, Lara, where were you?"

"Walking around..."

In my little universe of lies, I've learned that when you don't tell the truth, it's better to be economical with your words and stick as closely to the truth as possible. I really had been walking around...that much, at least, was true...

"A little bit late, no?" he growled.

"Is it? What time is it? I forgot my watch." I looked at him, keeping my expression as innocent as possible.

"Nice...take it with you next time...I bought it for you, so you could keep track of the time."

"I guide myself by the sun...problem is the sun sets too late here..."

"Sure you do... Okay. Take a bath, and let's have dinner."

"Yes, Dad!" I knew he hated when I did that—called him Dad, Uncle, or Grandpa—but I did it on purpose... That was another lesson I'd learned early on in life: disguise your fears behind a façade of confidence. This time, it worked like a charm.

After I'd showered and changed, we sat to have dinner, and I started to yawn. I wanted him to think I was sleepy because I had no intention to have sex with him that night—not after the day I'd spent with Adrien. We had dinner in silence, and when we finished, I told Arthur I was going to my room. Thankfully, he didn't protest or show any interest in following me. But I knew my good fortune wouldn't last. Tomorrow or the next day or the day after that, his interest would return, and I could barely stand the thought of touching him again—or having him touch me. I wanted Adrien only. I had to figure out what to do.

CHAPTER THIRTEEN

Simone – Present Day

Simone pitied Lara so much! Just a girl and she had to pretend, to put on an act to avoid a man's touch. She didn't have the right to fall in love like a normal young girl because she had an owner. The image of Simone's daughter...so different...crossed her mind. She'd always fought to give her daughter freedom, never forced the girl to do anything against her will—not even to kiss people when she didn't feel comfortable doing so... Hard to imagine a mother could put her own child in a situation like the one Lara had been thrown into. But Simone knew better than most people that not everyone was born with maternal love and instincts, and the relationship between mother and child was almost always a complicated one, full of contradictory feelings.

As she began to return her attention to the journal, someone knocked on Simone's door.

"Come in."

Patricia opened the door. "Dr. Bennet, it's almost eight o'clock; don't you need some dinner?"

Simone had lost track of time again—but why was her secretary still there? Office hours had ended long ago.

"Sorry, Patricia, I should have told you to go home already!"

"Oh, no, Doctor, I'm not going to leave you alone. If you have to work late, so do I."

I love this woman, thought Simone, but she shook her head. "No, Patricia, from now on, you can leave as soon as the last patient—mine or Dr. Reynolds's—leaves. I'm finishing up here, so you can go. I'll lock up the office, don't worry, and thank you very much."

"Have a nice evening, Doctor."

Patricia left, closing the door behind her, and Simone decided to go home.

* * * * *

Thursday flew by for Simone, her schedule so busy she barely had time to eat. At three o'clock, she was preparing to see one of her patients, Helen Northstrond. Simone had reread the woman's files, re-familiarizing herself with Helen's situation, as it'd been a while since she'd been to Simone's office. Even then, Helen had only attended sessions sporadically, but Simone was happy to see her again.

Helen was young, twenty-eight years old. She had short brown hair and blue eyes, she was not tall—only about five foot four—and she was very slim. Unfortunately, her tiny physique was due to her addiction to what she called "recreational drugs" and not healthy eating habits and exercise.

Helen entered Simone's office like a hurricane and threw herself onto the couch without saying hello. After tossing and turning to find the best position, she seemed to remember her manners and greeted Simone.

"Hello, Doc."

"Hello, Helen, it's nice to have you back. How is everything since the last time we talked? If I recall correctly, you were preparing to get pregnant..."

"Yes. It's good to be back. I'm actually doing really well, thank you. No babies..." She shook both hands to signal a categorical no. "I fell in love with my gorgeous neighbor, and I'm thinking about divorcing my husband."

"What a change...from starting a family to a divorce...in"—Simone did a quick calculation—"less than two months. And a new relationship? Who is this neighbor? How long have you known him?"

Helen contemplated her hands for a moment, picking at the skin near her thumbnail, and then she looked up at Simone.

"It's not a him; it's a her..." she said, speaking low, as if she feared someone might overhear. "And I've known her since I was a kid, but I've only recently really gotten to know her well, and we are deeply in love. I've decided to come out of the closet."

And all that in the blink of an eye—how mature, Simone thought.

"Well, that's a huge decision, Helen. Are you prepared to face the consequences? Can you imagine the reactions once you tell your family you're getting a divorce—and 'oh, by the way, I'm gay'?"

"I am. I'm truly in love, probably for the first time in my life, and I want the world to know!"

Okay then, Simone thought. Then why was she whispering...especially behind the closed door in her psychiatrist's office...? Something told Simone that Helen wasn't all that certain about her choices.

"What happened with the teacher?" Simone asked.

Helen had been in love with her teacher and had stalked the woman for a while even though the teacher claimed she was a hundred percent straight. Helen had pursued the woman for a long time, and Simone had spent many sessions trying to convince Helen that the woman felt maternal love for her, and she should leave the teacher alone.

"You were right..." Helen nodded. "She cares for me as a mother would...and she is part of my past."

"You stopped stalking her?"

"Well, I wouldn't use that term, but yes, I've ceased trying to seduce her and stopped all contact. I even blocked her on *What's App*!"

"Why did you block her? If it's over...you don't need—"

"Olivia told me I had to."

"I see. And was it your idea to tell the world about being gay?"

"Olivia is gay, and she said she doesn't want to be in a fake friendship relationship—she wants a real romance."

"How about you?"

"I want her, and I want her to be happy..."

"But that's not what I'm asking. I want to know how you

feel. Are you going to be happy with all the changes in your life? I thought you wanted to become a mother?"

"We are going to find a father for a baby if things go well."

"And the feelings you had for your husband? You told me you loved him, and you were preparing to have a child. Is that over?"

"No…in some ways, I still love him, but Olivia would never agree to share me forever…"

"Again, Helen, I'm not asking about Olivia. What does *Helen* want?" Simone pointed to Helen's chest. "What does your heart tell you?"

"I really don't know, Doctor. My emotions are in turmoil these days. I'm sure I don't want to lose Olivia. I love her… But I also have feelings for my husband. To be honest, one day I'm okay, and the next day I'm depressed and questioning all my decisions. But I can't say no to Olivia."

Simone already had a clear idea of how manipulative Olivia could be and was getting worried. Simone hated to be partial, but she was feeling angry with that girl, and she didn't even know her.

"Look, I think you're moving too quickly. Why don't you allow me to help you get your emotions under control— find a little balance, so you're not so up and down all the time. What happens if you walk away from your marriage and then find out this thing with Olivia was nothing more than a brief infatuation?" Simone held up a hand, preventing Helen from answering right away. "And don't tell me that's not possible; you've been there before…"

"Yes, but this time is different. It's strong, powerful…"

"If the teacher told you she was in love with you, would you stay with Olivia?"

"That's not going to happen…"

"Maybe not, but let's pretend… Use your imagination."

"Well, like I said, I don't know… I don't think it's possible…"

Helen's hesitation on the subject was as clear as day; she wasn't prepared to make such a big decision right now.

"Helen, you can't get a divorce right now. Let me help you get a handle on your emotions. You aren't thinking straight. Be patient, okay? Let your feelings for both your husband and your girlfriend foment for a little bit while you focus on what *you* want… In the end, you must be the one who's pleased with your life…"

"And if I lose Olivia?"

"If she loves you, she'll wait; she won't push you

beyond your limits."

"I *am* very confused... I wake up and look at my husband's face, and I tell myself I can't leave him, he is so good to me. But when I'm with Olivia, I tell myself I love her, and I should give our relationship a try."

The pain on the girl's face showed clearly. To be torn between emotions was one of the hardest situations in a person's life. It couldn't be faced lightly, and Helen needed help quickly.

"Okay, I'll make a deal with you here... You are going to live one day at a time, okay? And you are going to make a list of things you like in your husband and a list of things you dislike about him. Do the same for Olivia..."

"And meanwhile, if my husband discovers I'm having an affair?"

"Well, if you continue messing around with Olivia, that's your choice, and you'll have to face the consequences. But ten minutes ago, you told me you were going to get a divorce, so why worry?"

"I don't want to hurt him..."

"You're in a very tenuous position, I'm afraid. No matter how this turns out, someone is going to get hurt. It's not possible to make a choice like the one you're facing without expecting some collateral damage. You have to decide what you can live with and then choose...but

first, you have to discover what you, *Helen*,
wants...what makes *you* happy...*not* your husband, *not*
Olivia, just *you*. You are the main person in your world,
and you are the one who is going to suffer the most
with the consequences of your acts."

"In theory, I know that...but I'm so confused... Please,
Doctor, don't go away again. I really need you!" Helen
clasped her hands as if she were praying.

"My vacation is over, Helen, don't worry. I will be
here—and I'll see you at the same time next week.
What do you think about taking a mood stabilizer? It
usually helps to clarify the feelings."

"I was letting my body be free of any kind of drugs for
the baby."

"It won't damage your mind, and you've postponed
having a baby, or so you told me when you first came in.
Not only that, you need peace in order to resolve these
puzzles. You can't do that jumping from one emotion to
another like a grasshopper."

"Yes, you're right. Any unpleasant side effects?"

"Hard to tell, Helen; different people react differently to
each medication, but this one is pretty safe."

They agreed Helen would begin taking the medication,
and Helen left. Simone felt so sorry for the girl; she
seemed so lost all the time. But long ago, Simone had

learned not to suffer for her patients—if she did, she'd have to abandon her profession or go insane. But in truth, she still tended to think about them pretty much every day after office hours, always trying to figure out the best way to help them. Maybe she should take to her heart the advice she gave Helen—"You are the most important person in your world!" Easier to say than to put into practice. For better or for worse, Simone usually tended to put other people's needs before her own.

Simone had exactly an hour to rest between Helen and her next patient. Right after Helen's departure, Patricia entered Simone's office with a tray of tea and biscuits.

"Patricia, you are an angel."

"I'm glad you are pleased with my services, Doctor."

Despite the secretary's words, she didn't smile. In fact, Simone had never seen a smile on the woman's face. Patricia maintained a composed and serious demeanor, professional at all times. Simone didn't feel at ease with her...and it was impossible not to compare Patricia's rather dour behavior with the tenderness Mona used to display to everybody. Even though Simone had to recognize the qualities of her new secretary and remember all people were unique, she missed Mona, damn it. Still, Patricia did a more than adequate job.

"Very pleased," Simone said. "Please put the tray on the tea table for me."

Simone grabbed Lara's journal and went to the couch. She served herself a cup of tea and a biscuit. As the next client was an online session, she set the alarm on her phone to remind her ten minutes beforehand and then settled in to read.

Lara's Journal

Every time I saw Adrien, my heart grew light. He was handsome, smart, he always made me laugh, and one day—without warning—I realized I'd fallen in love. Crazy, I knew, considering we'd only known each other a short time, but there was no mistaking the feeling in my young heart. I couldn't stop thinking about him, and I wanted to be near him all the time.

Each time Adrien and I slept together, I'd avoid Arthur, refusing his demands for sex, and I could tell he was getting very annoyed with my excuses. I told him lies I didn't have any idea how to sustain.

"Not tonight, Arthur, I've got my period."

"Again? It's too soon!"

"Better soon than late, as you always say!"

"Come here. I don't mind."

"I do! I have cramps."

And so on... A bunch of lies...but so what? He had taught me how to lie...and I had always been a quick learner...

On a Friday afternoon, after being with Adrien the entire day in his tiny apartment making love and talking, we were sitting on the floor on an old rug, naked, wrapped in each other's arms.

"Lara, I would like to have you for myself... You are so pretty, so sweet, so hot... I want to be with you forever."

His words sounded like a declaration of love to me, and my heart soared. Lord, I was such a silly girl back then!

"I do, too. Tomorrow is Saturday, and we can't see each other, and that makes me crazy!"

"I will miss you, too, babe..."

"Let's run away together!" I twisted in his arms so I could see his face. "Let's go away some place. Let's travel the world. You want to travel, and so do I..."

Already, I could imagine our life together, somewhere far away from Arthur. I pictured what it would be like waking up in Adrien's embrace every day. The drudgery of everyday life—things like paying bills, washing clothes and dirty dishes—never even entered my mind back then.

"We can't. I don't have the money to do that, sweetie." He placed a kiss on my forehead.

"I don't mind! We can work."

"Doing what, exactly?"

"I don't know...but we would figure out something."

"I can't do that, babe."

"Why? You don't love me?"

He hesitated to answer, and he didn't meet my eyes. "If love was the only problem... But it's not that simple..."

Listening with my foolish heart, I interpreted his statement as a declaration of love! He may not have actually said the words, but he hadn't denied it. The world could have come to an end right then, and I would have died happy. I felt like singing and dancing, overflowing with joy.

"Come here, babe, let me hold you."

We went to bed and made love once more before I went home.

When I arrived at the apartment, I went directly to my room, and after half an hour the phone rang. It was Emms.

"Hi, Emms! So good to talk to you!"

And it was, because for the first time, I was happy, and I didn't have to pretend I was okay as I always did in order to not worry her.

"Hey, baby, you sound happy!"

"I am!"

"Tell your old grandma what makes you sound so joyful today."

"Emms...I think I'm in love!"

"Wow, Lara! Your first love! That's great. Tell me everything! I'm curious."

"He is adorable and handsome; he has a motorcycle, and we ride all over Paris on it. He is lovely."

"It sounds to me like you've found a nice man, but how old is he? Does he know how to drive a car, too?"

"He's only nineteen, Emms." I felt guilty lying to her, but what could I do? "And he is a great driver."

"You take care, kid. Wear a helmet, okay? Is he French?"

"Yes, Emms. And my French is getting so much better, thanks to him."

To prove my statement, I began speaking French to Emms, and she told me she was very proud of me.

"Baby, let me ask you a personal question."

"Yes, Emms."

"Are you having sex with this guy?"

She sounded worried, but I couldn't lie to her about that.

"Yes, and it's very good..."

"That's good. Sex is very good and healthy, but, honey, please take care... A pregnancy at your age would be a disaster."

"I know. I'm on The Pill... He took me to a doctor—" Another lie... God, I hated doing that with Emms, but it wasn't as if I could tell her that Arthur had gotten me on The Pill a long time ago...

"Okay, Lara, you are still so young, but if you are happy, what can I say? My baby is growing up. Take care and enjoy yourself. There's nothing better than a girl's first love. Even if it doesn't last forever, you'll never forget it."

"It's going to last forever, Emms; I love him."

We said our good-byes and hung up, and I was so happy I'd shared my good news with my grandmother.

CHAPTER FOURTEEN

Simone – Present Day

At least this last chapter was a better one, thought Simone. It was good to read about Lara being a girl again, experiencing her first love, her first real emotions in her life. Simone was sorry she had to set the journal aside.

She powered up her desktop computer. She'd scheduled an hour on Skype with the general—their very first online session—but he'd insisted he wanted to continue being her patient.

He was already logged in waiting for her when she

signed on.

"How are you today, Cezar?" she asked.

"To be honest, I miss your shining presence...you made me think about my life—and about running again—and I've decided I'm too old for that. Besides, it was not my dream; it was my colleague's and then my brother's dream. Those shoes are too big for my feet."

"But you know you can try again..."

"Yes, but I decided I don't want to. Doctor, let me ask you...why are we talking about my political life? I have an impotence problem, and I would really like to talk about that."

"Cezar, we've established that your impotence is not a physical problem. Therefore, we have to understand what provoked it. Often, when a man suffers some kind of defeat or a period of great stress, frustration, and rejection, he will become impotent. I need to know what really happened, and it seems to me you are hiding something..." She couldn't explain; it was just a feeling she had.

"Maybe frustration and rejections," he mumbled.

"What are you not telling me, Cezar?"

The general lowered his head as if he was considering how to answer.

"You are very clever. Tereza…"

"Tereza?"

A woman—bull's eye, thought Simone. She'd known there was another story behind all his sexual problems.

"Yes, Tereza, the most beautiful brunette on Earth."

"Okay. Tell me about her."

"She was my lover."

"But you told me you don't approve of a married man having lovers…"

"I don't. But I fell in love, just the same. She didn't want me, though—she thinks of me as an old man, and she is thirty years younger than I am."

"She told you that—that she doesn't want you because you're an old man?"

"Not in those words. She's too polite to say such a thing. She's a good girl, from a good family. She studied abroad, she is very cultured, and when her father passed away, she inherited a great deal of wealth. Her father was a friend of mine, and she came to me, asking for help with some business matters. I agreed to assist her, and things progressed from there. We spent a lot of time talking, and she made me laugh as no one else ever has. We began having lunch together, then dinner…she awoke a side of my personality I didn't know existed. She touched my heart—something I believed was no longer possible. She is sweet...she is intelligent...and her body was designed to take a man to paradise. I felt like a boy again...sex with her was complete."

"Complete? Explain that to me, please."

"I've always been very aggressive when it comes to sex. I never enjoyed making love... I'd rather fuck like a wild animal. With my wife, this was impossible. She would be terrorized if I asked to be spanked. And there was no way I could be with her like that—she's the mother of my children. But with Tereza... God... She is just like me. Sex with her was exactly what I love—she scratched me, beat me, dominated me."

Powerful men and their eternal desire to be dominated. Cezar wasn't the first of her powerful patients who professed they could only find pleasure when they were dominated, spanked, or humiliated by a partner...the general was not so exceptional... This type of behavior was a kind of compensation for dominating everything else in his life.

"And so?"

"And so, after some time, she started to avoid me...to give me excuses...and then she simply stopped taking my calls."

"That happened when?"

"Eight month ago."

Bingo, thought Simone, around the same time sex had become a problem for him. But the general continued.

"And I just can't forget her. I have no doubt she decided she didn't want to waste her life with an old man who could die in her bed!"

The general was far from dying; he was a strong man, but he was really a prima donna and tended to see everything in a tragic way. Perhaps this had more to do with his Latin heritage than anything—always so intense.

"Have you ever thought she didn't want to continue having a relationship with a married man?"

"No..."

"So go talk to her. From what you've told me, I believe the major part of your problem stems from the rejection... You were rejected by your people. You were rejected by the woman you love. Why did you fall in love with her? Can you tell me?"

"Before Tereza, I had lost my zest for living. Few things gave me pleasure those last years, fewer still made my heart race. I'd lived it all...seen it all... I didn't trust anybody, and suddenly, a young lady showed me my old heart was beating, that I could dream again...but then she cut me off cold."

"Did you tell her you were in love with her?"

"So she could mock me? So she could call me a ridiculous old man? No, of course not... All I have left is my pride..."

"Would you divorce your wife for Tereza?"

"For her, yes!"

"So...tell her that. She can't read your mind. You have a family, a long-term marriage... She probably thought you would never leave your wife, and she isn't the kind of woman—at least, based on how you described her—who needs to live from crumbs. You have homework here, Cezar, and I don't want to talk to you again until you handle this unfinished business."

"Say, Doctor, I'm going to take notes, so I won't forget your words!" He took a notebook and a pencil and was ready to take notes, like a good schoolboy.

"Talk to Tereza—that's the only note you need to take."

"I can't!"

"You can, or I can't proceed with you."

And now I'm blackmailing my patients... What is happening with me? Simone rarely lost control, especially in a professional setting.

"I will think about it."

"Think and then do...your pride is not going to improve your ability to perform sexually, and it's certainly not going to win back your lover..."

"I have to think...what do I have to offer this girl?

"How about yourself? How about your love? Think, and think well, Cezar...you don't have half your life to spend thinking what to do. Half of it is over...do now...or never..."

"I promise I will try."

"It will do you good. We are finished for today. Next week, same day, same time?"

"Yes, Doctor, thank you very much for today; it was very interesting."

"Therapy is much more interesting when all cards are on the table, Cezar. See you in a week."

They said good-bye, and Simone closed the live-chat software.

Cezar had been Simone's last patient for the day, so she decided to go back to her analysis of Lara's journal. Simone was curious to know how the teenager's romance had progressed. She picked up the stack of printed journal pages and went to her favorite armchair. She began reading, immediately becoming immersed in the story.

Lara's Journal

On a grey Saturday, I was feeling blue, knowing I'd have to wait until Monday to see Adrien again, and I was positive I would have to fuck Arthur. The thought made me sad. I decided to go for a walk and talk to my favorite *bouquinestes.* I was proud of myself; my French was much better, and I could carry on a normal conversation with anybody.

I didn't want to go back home, so I bought a tomato, buffalo cheese, and basil *baguette* sandwich for lunch and walked along the Seine eating it. But I had to go back at some point.

When I arrived, to my surprise, Arthur and Adrien where sitting on the couch sipping whisky. Arthur looked relaxed, reclined against the cushions, his legs crossed at the ankles. Adrien sat leaning toward Arthur, talking, and I immediately grew tense. But I was still glad to see Adrien.

"Hello, baby," Arthur greeted me. "I hope you don't mind... I invited Adrien to join us today."

"Hello, Lara, how've you been?"

"Great! How about you?"

I didn't know how to proceed, so I shook Adrien's

outstretched hand. My heart was beating fast, and I was afraid Arthur could see my discomfort.

"Do you want something to drink?" Arthur asked.

I stared at him, astonished by the question, thinking perhaps he was trying to prepare me for seducing Adrien. My hands started shaking. Although I'd used Arthur's fantasy when we had sex the other day, I couldn't imagine myself making love to Adrien in front of someone else in real life...

"Don't bother to stand up," I said. "I can fix my own drink."

I needed a whiskey. I'd discovered how well alcohol calmed my nerves. I took a crystal glass from a tray on the bar and poured myself a double with no ice. I took a long drink, and the booze burned its way down my throat. I started to cough, and tears came to my eyes.

"Slow down, Lara," Arthur admonished me.

"I'm okay!" I managed to say once I stopped coughing, my eyes full of tears from choking.

"Come here, sit beside me." He tapped the cushion on his side of the couch.

I thought about defying Arthur but changed my mind. I sat near him, and he put his hand on my knee. I immediately glanced toward Adrien to seek his reaction, but he wouldn't meet my gaze. Instead, he frowned and looked away.

"What were you talking about before I arrived?" I asked.

"About how beautiful you are, of course." Arthur sounded a bit strange.

"Yeah, right..." I scoffed.

"I swear it's true." Arthur put his arm around my shoulder and kissed me on the lips, a rare display of affection in front of other people.

"Adrien, this girl is my precious gem!"

I was totally embarrassed, but he didn't stop there. He pulled up my dress until my legs were almost complete exposed, and he started to caress my thighs.

"Not to mention, she is a delicious fuck!"

Before I could react to Arthur's statement, he went on.

"But you already know that, right, Adrien?" Arthur asked. "I mean, you two have been fucking behind my back the last...what? Two or three weeks?"

If I were a more fragile girl, I would have fainted. Unfortunately, I was strong, and I sensed I was about to face a huge humiliation. Arthur knew about Adrien and me! But how could that be?

"Have you been following me, Arthur?" That had to be it. I could think of no other reasonable explanation.

"Following you? Of course not, my darling."

He was no longer hugging or touching me, and he had turned so he sat facing me. I was terrified, and when I looked to Adrien, he had his head down.

"Then how did you know?" I was so nervous, it never occurred to me to deny his accusations. My stomach felt as if it was full of butterflies, and my legs were shaking uncontrollably.

"How did I know?" He turned to look to Adrien "Adrien? Should I tell her, or are you going to do the honors?"

"Please, Arthur...don't..." Adrien sounded as if he were begging. I'd never heard him use that tone before.

How would Adrien know how Arthur had found out about Adrien and me? I couldn't figure out the connection.

Arthur sighed. "I suppose it's up to me to speak the truth."

He paused for several long seconds while he looked from me to Adrien and back to me, an amused expression on his face, a small, satisfied smile lifting the corner of his mouth.

It felt like an eternity passed before he spoke again.

"How do I know? Well, you see, I paid this young man here to seduce you! I knew you wouldn't have the courage to seduce him. How was I to know you would lose your mind and start acting like a lovesick fool? I thought you were more intelligent than that." He tsked.

I stared at him, trying to wrap my mind around what he'd just said. He'd paid Adrien? To seduce me? No...that had to be another lie. Adrien and I were in love!

"You're a liar! That's not true!"

"No, baby, I'm afraid I'm telling you the truth. I paid Adrien to seduce you; I paid the rent on that little love nest, and let me tell you, he is an expensive gigolo! I fantasized about seeing you with another man, but you are so naïve, you fell in love with him! I can't believe how stupid you are! You fell in love with a man who sleeps with old women for money! A paid companion. You fell in love, and you were planning to run away with him? Then what would you have done, hmm? Embrace the same profession?" He shook his head. "You have nowhere near the necessary skills to survive in such a lifestyle."

He started to laugh. He laughed so hard, and all the while, I felt as if I was living inside a horror movie.

I turned to Adrien. "Please...tell me he's lying! Please tell me this isn't true!"

I was positive Adrien would say this all was a joke and that he loved me, and we would be happy together, away from this maniac, but he just looked at his shoes, his guilt written all over his face.

"No, this can't be true; it can't be!"

I felt a deep ache in my chest as if Arthur had ripped out my heart with his bare hands and smashed it to pieces. The pain was so intense I felt as if I might die. Betrayal, shame, rejection, humiliation—I couldn't be more hurt. I tasted my salty tears, only then realizing I was crying, but I couldn't stop.

"You are a monster!" I pointed at Arthur, and then I turned to Adrien and said, "And you? You are worse than he is; you are a worm, a scumbag. Do you know what you did to me? You used me, you crushed my feelings, you tore a hole in my chest, and nothing is left inside me, nothing."

By that point, I was sobbing hysterically. Arthur tried to approach me, a worried expression on his face.

"Babe...calm down; it will be all right! We'll get past this..."

"You call me 'babe' one more time, and I'm going to scratch out your eyes." My voice had changed, grown stronger, so much so that I barely recognized it, and in that moment, another person was born, a person with a big black hole where her heart used to be...

I went to my room. Nobody followed me—I imagine nobody had the courage to do so.

CHAPTER FIFTEEN

Simone – Present Day

Simone was astonished by what she'd just read. Just when she'd thought the poor girl would find a moment of happiness! *Christ, what a deranged world,* she thought. She'd had enough for one day. *I'm going home,* she decided.

Simone got her purse and car keys from her desk drawer and left her office to find Patricia still waiting. Didn´t the woman have a life? She seemed to be there more than Simone and Edward combined.

"Patricia, dear, please leave at six o'clock every day.

There's really no need to wait for me."

"No, Doctor... I know what you've been through, and I believe it's better for you to have some company. The police never caught the suspect, did they?"

"How do you know about that, Patricia?"

"Well, it was all over the news, of course..."

"And still you had the courage to come here and work for us...after what happened to our last secretary..."

"It won´t happen again, Doctor. You know what they say about lightning never striking twice in the same place..."

"Yes, but you were still very courageous to have applied for the position."

Patricia shrugged. "Don´t worry, Doctor, I will try to leave early from now on. I promise," she said, addressing Simone's original request.

Simone went to her car, and it was weird how every time she approached a closed vehicle, her subconscious expected her to find a dead body inside it. Apparently, she was still very traumatized by the events. She climbed in behind the wheel, drew a deep breath, started the engine, and headed to her house.

When Simone arrived home at around seven o'clock that evening, there was a black SUV parked in front of her house. She pulled into the attached garage, and from there, she entered the house. She was afraid of visitors these days. Ever since her kidnapping, she worried she might find herself facing an unpleasant surprise—like another serial killer! The house alarm was set, so she turned it off to go inside, but then she immediately turned it on again. She had barely set her bag on the kitchen island counter when the intercom sounded. She searched the monitor of her security cameras to see who was outside.

What in the world? She blinked hard. She had to be imagining things. Surely that wasn't Armando standing out there on her doorstep, a bouquet of flowers in his arms!

"What in the hell is he doing here?" she mumbled under her breath as she stalked to the front entry. She opened the door.

"For you, my lady," Armando said, charming as ever. He held out what had to be two-dozen roses.

"Armando. What a surprise. Um...thank you."

Although Simone had to admit he looked good in his faded blue jeans and a crisp white shirt that emphasized his tan, she couldn't keep her annoyance at his unexpected appearance on her doorstep from leaking into her voice.

"You knew I was not going to allow you to leave my

life!"

What the hell she should do now? She really didn't know and decided to be polite, at least.

"Would you like to come in?"

"Sure!"

She stepped back, allowing him to enter, and then she headed into the kitchen to find a vase for the flowers. She would hate to see them die.

Armando followed her, and when she set the vase of roses on the island, he wrapped his arms around her and hugged her close, dipping his head to capture her lips. He didn't give her time to think, kissing her senseless as he unbuttoned her blouse. She pushed against his chest and jerked back her head.

"Stop, Armando, we have to talk."

But he didn't listen and continued his exploration, running his hands over her body, touching her everywhere, teasing her, provoking a response, despite her anger.

He undressed them both before Simone could stop him, and to be honest, she didn't try too hard. His cock stood long and thick, ready to give her pleasure. Armando dug in his pocket and pulled out a condom, sheathed his cock, then took her back into his powerful arms. With no more foreplay, he supported her weight against the island and drove inside her. He fucked her, fast and furious, and they came quickly, like two teenagers.

And that was how it all began, Simone thought, thinking of that first night in the Miami bar.

When he recovered his breath, he hugged her. Holding her in his arms, he said, "Now we can talk."

She blinked up at him. What had she wanted to tell him? She had forgotten.

"I need a bath first, Armando. Let's go to my room. Please get your cloths." She was already grabbing hers from the floor and proceeding to her room, Armando on her heels.

"I'm going to shower," she told him.

"So am I."

To her displeasure, he followed her into her master bathroom.

This time, he didn't ask her to pee on him. Maybe he really was just a normal guy, and she was too sensitive after everything that had happened to her.

Again, he bathed her, taking the soap from her hand. After they finished, he got a towel and dried her body. She was not used to men doing that kind of thing... Maybe she was too independent to be taken care of, but she figured it wouldn't hurt to let him pamper her a little.

"Let's go to bed?" he asked after he'd finished.

He tossed the now-wet towel onto the floor, and Simone looked at it and frowned.

"Don't you want to eat something?" she asked.

"Yes. You…"

"Well… The come here, little boy!" She was going to have a good time, she decided. Once he left, she didn't know when she would find someone again. "Let's seize the moment."

They went to her king-size bed, and he dragged off her beige bedspread and tossed it onto the floor.

God, I'm going to kill him, she thought. Didn't he have a mother to teach him about cleanliness? Who comes into another person's house and starts throwing stuff all over the floor?

He began to kiss her, starting with her toes, licking them one by one. Rather than becoming turned on, Simone grew uncomfortable, but he proceeded to her ankles and then higher, until he had licked and kissed her whole body, from bottom to top and back again. As before, he seemed to be in no hurry. He climbed between her spread legs and pressed his mouth to her pussy, licking and sucking. Simone's breath hitched, and she grasped his broad shoulders. She closed her eyes, relaxing into his touch, but then suddenly he stopped. She looked to find him climbing to kneel astride her stomach, and as he'd done in Miami, he put his cock between her breasts and used them to massage the shaft. Simone groaned but not with excitement. Why couldn't he be normal? Why couldn't he just lick her pussy, fuck her, give her an amazing orgasm, and be satisfied with that? After several more agonizing moments, he finally climbed off, grabbed another condom from his pants on the floor beside the bed, and covered his cock. He moved between her legs and entered her, turning into the attentive lover he had been moments before. He moved with precision, not in a hurry at all. As she began to moan, he moved faster, driving her to her orgasm. But as she came, the freak inside him took charge, and he pulled out, removed the condom, and began fucking her breasts again. She watched in horror until he came all over her tits and chin! She was pissed off, but as she was going to get rid of him forever that night, she decided not to start an argument with him in bed.

"Now we need food," he told her and went to her bathroom to shower again, acting as if he owned the place.

She felt a little like a prisoner in her home, surrounded by the invading commander.

Rather than eat at her place, once they'd both gotten cleaned up and dressed, Simone invited Armando to go

to a restaurant. She needed to talk to him to put an end
to the situation, and she thought a public place would
be better for that particular conversation.

They went to a simple Thai restaurant called Thai
Stories. With its sparse décor, small, wooden tables,
and brick walls painted a greenish-grey, the place had a
homey ambiance Simone adored, and the food was
exquisite.

She chose a table far away from people, all the way in a
back corner.

"The place is not sophisticated, but the food is
amazing," she told him.

"I'm happy to hear that, but I'm not here for the food;
I'm here for you!"

She drew a deep breath to calm her nerves and began
to speak.

"Armando, we have to talk... I don't know what you're
thinking about all this, but I don't want a relationship
right now, and I told you that. I'm living through the
most complicated time of my life, and I can't cope with
having a boyfriend."

"Sure. And that's why you made love to me like you did
just half an hour ago..." He shook his head. "I don't
believe you. What's the matter? The distance? Until we
know each other better, I can come here every

weekend. If you want, you can come to Miami. And if we decide to stay together, I'll buy an office for you there, and you can move!"

"Um…you just decided my whole life?" She felt a wave of rage. God, how she hated macho men.

"No, it's not like that… I'm just simplifying things…there is no complication. If you don't have the money to travel, don't worry; I'll pay for everything!"

"I do have the money…but I don't want to travel all the time, and I don't want to move. I don't want a long-distance relationship because I don't believe in them…and most of all, I don't have those kinds of feelings for you!" There. She'd come right out and said everything she'd had on her mind. Obviously, subtlety was not going to work with him.

"Why not? What are you afraid of? Sex between us is amazing… I can make you come; I saw that."

"Sex is not enough. We don't have anything in common."

"You don't know that. You don't know me well enough to say that. I can be whatever you want me to be!"

"Understand me, Armando. You should be who you are and not try to change for somebody… To do so would be the same as basing a relationship on lies."

"For you, I would change. You must understand. I'm in

love with you!"

Oh, God, this is becoming more complicated by the second. "No, you are not...we've seen each other four or five times. You cannot be in love with me."

"I fell for you the first day we met! I want you, and I'm not going to give up on you."

"You are not going to make my life easy...I can see that. I don't want you, Armando."

He looked at her as if she had slapped him, shock and annoyance clear in his expression. His lips thinned, his nostrils dilated, and he appeared as if he was on the verge of losing his temper.

"Let's do this, Simone... I know you're going through a traumatic period right now. So we don't have to date. I can come here once a week. We can go out together—for dinner—we can have sex, chat, whatever you want to do. And then, after a few months, you can tell me if you still don't want me."

Yes, because you're such a hot commodity, there's no way I could refuse you. Simone's anger simmered. "Let's do this, Armando. You are not going to come here once a week. You can call me; we can try to get to know each other over the phone, but we are not going to have a relationship, understood?"

Simone was annoyed with herself for agreeing to talk to

him on the phone, but she had to try something to get rid of the guy.

"Okay, we'll do it your way since you are sick right now…"

I'm not sick, you bastard; I'm trying to find a way to get rid of you without creating a scene, and I'm trying to put you in your place.

They finished their dinner, and Simone told him he couldn't sleep at her house. He accepted her statement and left in his rented car. Finally, she could breathe, but she was worried. Christ, she didn't need another lunatic in her life right now. Maybe she'd be able to manage him from a distance. If she refused to answer his phone calls, surely he would give up.

Back home Simone knew she wouldn't fall asleep easily. She couldn't get Armando from her thoughts; she was positive he was going to be a pain in the ass. Why had she broken her rules and fucked a stranger? She knew nothing good could come from that. Her head was spinning, trying to figure out what to do. She paced from room to room while thinking. She tried to breath deeply, but she had no peace in her mind to even try to relax. Maybe some wine? But her ever-rational side reminded her that drinking never helped a person resolve their problems. Okay, then, how about a distraction?

She decided to read some of Lara's journal to calm her

nerves...or make them worse—*with Lara's story, one never knows,* Simone thought, but at least she wouldn't be stressing over Armando.

Lara's Journal

The weekend after the episode with Adrien, I couldn't leave my room. I cried so much I thought I might die of dehydration, but after a couple days, my tears dried up, leaving me in a state of emotional exhaustion. I felt nothing but hate. Nothing made much sense to me, but I could think, and I came to some nasty conclusions about my life.

First, I was Arthur's pet. He would do to me whatever he pleased.

Second, I was Sabine's ticket to high society. She would sell me out to the devil if he paid the right price, and it didn't necessarily have to be expensive—a good invitation to the "right place" would do.

Third, I had no one I could trust. Although I had Emms, I couldn't talk to her about all these things.

Fourth, I had to find a way out of the mess I was in.

Fifth, in order to get out, I needed money.

Having clarified all these issues in my mind, I decided to

formulate a plan to get my hands on some money. I wasn't sure how, but I had to find a way out.

I felt certain that once I got rid of Arthur, Sabine would tell my dad about my true father and Daddy wouldn't want me back living at home. I could try Emms, but she hated Sabine, and I thought Emms might hate me, too, when she discovered the truth...

Looking back, I realize how naïve and controlled by Sabine and Arthur I used to be. If only I had trusted Emms, my life would have been so different. But the fact was I didn't fully trust anyone, and I'd been lying to Emms for years because Sabine and Arthur had brainwashed me into believing the silly idea that only blood relations mattered. As an adult, I know better, and I would never doubt Emms's love.

I know now that it's too late to cry over spilled milk, as the saying goes, but sometimes, I'm so full of regrets. I have to forgive myself, I know, but it's so hard to do that, harder than forgiving others...or just as difficult... I believe I'll die still hating Sabine and Arthur.

Back then, for the first time in my life, I understood I needed to have money and things had a cost. I would need to find a place to live; I would need to buy food and be able to survive until I got a job. I had no idea how to go about doing those things.

Not to mention, it never crossed my mind I was a minor, and that would cause a whole other set of problems.

What could I do to survive? I had no skills, no college education yet. My head spun as I tried to find a solution. I could teach French, I thought. But to do that, I'd need to learn much more than I already had. That would be my first goal.

I could also sell the jewels Arthur had given me. I decided my second goal would be to get him to purchase more jewelry for me.

Arthur and my dear "mom" were going to pay!

* * * * *

I went to the school and talked to the principal, asking how I could learn more quickly. He suggested I take a six-hours class everyday instead of three—an intensive course. That night, I had to face Arthur for the first time since the confrontation with Adrien. I hated the idea of speaking to Arthur, but I had to if I wanted to move forward with my plan.

I found him in the living room, watching the news on TV. I planted myself in front of the television, and he looked at me. I could tell by his expression he was worried, no doubt anticipating another emotional storm after what he had done to me, but I kept my cool.

"I'm going to take six hours of French every day instead of the three."

I didn't tell him why. I had no intention of explaining, and I had a feeling he wouldn't dare say no.

"Sure. That's okay, what do you need from me?"

"Money."

"How much?"

I rattled off a number that was double the price, knowing he never checked those things. "And can you give it to me in cash? The principal told me they don't like checks."

"No problem."

I had the impression I could have asked for gold bars, and he would have agreed. The guilty little shit!

"And Arthur...?"

"Yes, my darling...?"

"I saw a beautiful pair of emerald earrings, and I would like to have them."

I suffered a pang of shame for making such a request, but I forced it away. My entire life was a shame...what was one more thing?

Arthur chuckled. "Yeah...you are really growing up...you already know how to punish a man through his pocket. But yes, of course, babe, tomorrow, we are going to get those emeralds for you. Anything more?"

"I will never forgive you...I want you to know that!"

"Aw, c'mon, babe…you are the one who needs to be forgiven. You betrayed me, right? I'm the injured party here… Or I would be if I was not smarter."

"The devil is the devil not because he is smart, Arthur, but because he is old… And you will not have my forgiveness for all you've done to me during my life…not just this little episode. Thanks to you, my life is shit. Don't you ever think, for a second, that I have any feelings for you!"

"Hate me, babe… That's fine. After all, hate and love are opposite sides of the same coin. If you were indifferent, I would be worried. So hate me as much as you want, but remember one thing." He stood up and put his finger under my chin and lifted my head to look into my eyes. "You are mine, and you always will be. So forget the insane idea of having a love affair and running away… I will get you back, I will find you…you are mine until the day I no longer want you to be."

Wait and see, I thought, but I didn't say anything.

"And, Lara… I really do want you to have sex in front of me. This will happen; you know that, don't you? I'm in the mood for that! Even more so now that you had your fling. You must pay me for that…"

He pushed me aside and turned back to the TV once more.

* * * * *

After that statement, Arthur didn't touch me or come near me for days. Then, on a Wednesday evening, I arrived home from school at around five o'clock to find Arthur there, waiting for me.

He was in the sitting room, and I had to pass by him to go to my room, but I would still try to keep my distance. He was sitting on the blue velvet couch, his usually whisky in hand, his feet propped on a low stool. I said hello to him from the room's doorway and turned to rush to my room, but he was quicker and left the sofa to intercept me. He tried to kiss me, but I turned my face away. No more kissing... I didn't want intimacy with Arthur kissing was too intimate for me. I had to fuck him; I didn't have to like him.

"I have a surprise for you." He seemed very excited.

"Yeah? My emerald earrings, at last? You promised me some days ago..."

"Those, yes...but something more..."

He picked up a green box from the coffee table and handed it to me. I removed the lid to reveal two beautiful emerald earrings lying on a bed of black satin. Nice. I admired them for the money they would bring me in the future.

"Thanks," I said without feeling. After all, the earrings were well earned.

"I have another surprise... Take a bath. I left some lingerie on your bed. Put it on. You'll find a new pair of shoes, too."

"And the rest? What should I wear? A dress?"

"Nothing."

"Hmmm..." Already, he was charging me for the earrings.

Arthur did that sometimes—asked me to dress in some outfit or another he had bought for me. Play out some fantasy he had...usually college uniforms... I wasn't going to deny him tonight. I needed to create a pattern—good behavior...great gifts... I hadn't known about Pavlov's dog back then, but that was kind of the same concept.

I went to my room and took a shower, put on some perfume, then dressed in the red lingerie he'd laid out on my bed. Minuscule lace panties, a lace bra, and silk stockings barely covered any skin. A new pair of super-high-heeled shoes—also red—sat on the floor, and I slipped those on, too. I decided to put my all into the role and put on some makeup like the lady had done when she'd helped me get ready for the party. I already had a considerable collection of makeup and brushes lying on my beautiful, antique dressing table.

I added some red lipstick to match my outfit. I looked at myself in the crystal mirror, and a much-older girl looked back at me. Maybe it was the makeup or maybe because I felt as if I had lived through and seen so much for my age...

Arthur came to me with a blindfold. "Let's put this on your eyes."

I shook my head and took a step back. "No. I don't want to! I want to see everything."

"You'll spoil the surprise." He wrapped the blindfold around my head, despite my resistance. "Hold still, and let me adjust this."

I started to get nervous. Why the blindfold? I was wearing lingerie, for goodness sake, what else did he have in mind? What was the game now?

He took my hand and led me to the living room and helped me to sit on the couch. He attached earrings to my lobes...probably my new ones—he loved to see what his money could buy, including me—then he pressed a glass into my hand, wrapping my fingers around the stem. I hesitated then took a sip. Champagne. What was this? Arthur was willingly giving me alcohol? Then I heard the bell.

"Wait here, Lara, your surprise has just arrived..."

Someone was at the door, and I suddenly felt vulnerable. I wanted to run to my room and wait for Arthur there, but he had specifically told me to stay there. I heard him speaking French to someone, and then a man replied, although I couldn't understand what was said as they were too far away.

Suddenly, I realized there was someone near me, and it wasn't Arthur. I tried to cover myself, putting my hands in front of me, to no avail. No way could I cover my entire body with only my hands.

"Lara, I want you to meet…" Arthur's voice trailed off.

"Claude," the man supplied. He had a nice, husky voice.

"Who the hell are you?" I was in no mood to exchange pleasantries with a stranger while I was sitting there half-naked. My stomach hurt, and my palms were wet. I felt as jumpy as a cat, ready to leap to my feet and run. Desperate to regain my composure and drown my fear, I drank down almost all of my champagne, and the heat of the alcohol warmed my body, but still I remained tense.

"Claude is a friend of mine. You are going to like him. I would like you two to touch each other a little bit. Enjoy each other…"

I took the blindfold from my eyes and jumped to my feet, pacing in the direction of the piano. A man stood in the center of the room. He was young and handsome—no more than twenty years old. He wore his chestnut-colored hair cut short in a military style, and he had blue eyes that matched his navy-blue polo shirt. He was wearing jeans, and his clothing hugged his muscular body. I noticed what appeared to be a tattoo of a scorpion on his upper arm. A lighter version of Adrien... I surmised Arthur had decided to hire another male prostitute.

"Allo, Claude, how much did he pay you?"

He didn't answer; he just smiled and then looked at Arthur, no doubt seeking his guidance.

"She is yours, Claude...take care of her... Lara, if you don't like something, just say no. I'll be watching you."

What to do? I would have liked to run, but then I decided why not? I needed to get rid of my memories of Adrien, and what better way than to have sex with another handsome man? Especially another man who was not Arthur.

Claude approached me and took up a position behind my back.

"*Allo, chérie*," he said. He then pulled up my hair and started to kiss and nibble on my nape.

I shivered, his hot touch giving me the chills, and my fears disappeared completely. Claude trailed kisses down my back.

"*Très jolie*," he murmured. Beautiful.

But I'd had enough of his compliments. "*Ne parles pas!*

Je ne ve veux pas écouter un seul mot," I said, telling him not to speak. I didn't want to hear a word from his mouth.

I wanted only to feel, and at that moment, I was feeling his hot lips on my back. Suddenly impatient, I turned to him, supporting my buttocks on the piano keyboard cover. I grabbed his hand and put it on my breast.

"Touch me here," I commanded him in French.

He put his hand gently on my breast.

"No, I want you to grab her breasts. Squeeze them. Pinch her nipples," Arthur said.

Claude did as he was told, and I moaned. He took my nipple into his mouth.

"Bite her! I want her to feel pain...she has not been a good girl lately..."

Apparently, Arthur had his own ideas about how we would proceed, and my earlier fears returned. I stiffened, preparing for the pain, but the guy lifted his head and brought his mouth close to my ear.

"Don't worry, I'm not going to hurt you," he whispered.

Then he took my nipple again and started to nip at my flesh, not too hard but in a way that made me grow wet. He eased my panties down my legs, and after I stepped out of them, he lifted me in his arms and sat me on top of the keyboard cover. He spread my legs and parted my folds then got to his knees. The first touch of his tongue on my pussy made me moan, and I leaned back to lie on top of the piano. Arthur joined us, leaning down to take my nipple into his mouth and bite me...hard. The pain was awful, but at the same time, Claude was tonguing my pussy and sucking on my clit, driving me mad with pleasure.

"I want you to fuck this little slut," Arthur said. "I want to see you banging her hard."

Claude's cock was rigid and he took me in his arms and put me on the couch.

He moved to lie between my legs, but Arthur stopped him and gave him a condom. Claude quickly slipped it on. He lined up his dick with my pussy and opened my swollen lips with his fingers. He slid one finger inside, his gaze locked on mine, and then he slowly entered me. I moaned. His dick was gorgeous, bigger than Arthur's and Adrien's, and it felt wonderful inside me. We started to move, slowly at first, then quickly until I came, moaning loudly.

Claude continued to fuck me, and when I looked up, I found Arthur standing there, just observing. I could tell he was excited, almost as if he was fucking me and not Claude. Arthur's pupils were enormous, his face red.

I looked away, refocusing my attention on Claude. I pushed him back, and his dick slid free of my pussy.

"Lie back," I told him.

He quickly complied, propping his head on a throw pillow against the arm of the couch. I straddled his waist, took his long, thick cock in my hand, and guided him inside again.

I closed my eyes and moaned, relishing the feel of his hard dick filling me. I started to move faster, leaning over his chest, my ass in the air.

Suddenly, I felt an acute pain on my buttocks and realized Arthur was hitting me. I glanced over my shoulder but couldn't see what he was using. My buttocks felt as if they were in flames, and my first reaction was to stop and tell him not to hit me again. I turned toward him.

"Don't you dare stop!" Arthur growled. "Fuck him, you nasty bitch. Fuck him hard!"

I obeyed his command and kept moving, and Arthur kept hitting me and to my amazement, a few minutes later, I came hard, all my body feeling as if it was coated in flames. My heart was racing like mad, my sopping-wet pussy clenching and unclenching around Claude's hard cock. I sagged, drained from such a huge orgasm.

Before I could dismount I felt something hot and wet on my buttocks. I looked back to see Arthur spreading his cum on my ass.

I dismounted slowly, my buttocks still burning. Thinking to make a quick getaway, I started toward my room, but Arthur grabbed my hand and stopped me. He slumped into a chair, dragging me with him. His cock was hard again, and he positioned me on his lap to take him inside.

I closed my eyes, as I always did when I was fucking Arthur. The sensation of having a different cock excited me again. My pussy was still quivering, my clit sensitive from Claude's condom-covered cock's brutal invasion, and now Arthur penetrated me with his naked dick. Just the thought of what I was doing with these two men heightened my excitement, and I knew I was going to come again.

My pussy burned from the condom, and the sensation of Arthur's dick sliding over the sensitive flesh was at the same time slightly painful and pleasurable. And as I continued to move, Arthur rubbing my clit while fucking me, pleasure won out, and I came hard, the orgasm a mix of sweet satisfaction, pain, heat, and relief.

Moments later, Arthur handed Claude a wad of cash, and I hurried to my room. I caught sight of my reflection in the mirror and wrinkled my nose. I was a complete mess. My hair was in knots, my skin all red and covered with bite marks. I twisted around and looked over my shoulder. My buttocks were covered in dark-red marks from the whip. Yes, Arthur had used a flat horsewhip on me; I had seen it lying beside the couch before I'd left the room. Worst of all? I'd liked it. I'd liked all of it...two men...the beating...this was the beginning of a new era for me, in terms of sex.

CHAPTER SIXTEEN

Simone — Present Day

Simone set aside the journal, went to her bathroom and prepared for bed. Dressed in a pair of silk pajamas, she climbed between the sheets and turned off the lights. Enough of Lara for tonight. If she kept reading, Simone feared she would have nightmares.

But despite her exhausting day, sleep didn´t come. She tossed and turned and finally got to her feet. It was late, and she had two choices— sleeping pills or a good, stiff drink... And since she was trying to get off the pills, she went to the kitchen and got a bottle of wine from the refrigerator and a glass from the cupboard. But as she pulled the previously loosened cork, she paused. Are you going to replace pills with alcohol? Really? She left the bottle sitting on the counter and returned to her room. She found a series she liked on Netflix, selected the first episode of the first season, and settled in to watch. At some point, she finally fell into an exhausted sleep.

* * * * *

The next day, a very tired Simone went to the office to find the always efficient Patricia already working, calling patients and apparently very busy at eight-thirty in the morning. Simone's surprise grew when she went into her office and found her tea and some toast on her table and all her files for the day stacked in order of patient's arrival on the corner of her desk. She said a silent prayer to all the gods on Olympus, thanking them for the secretary.

She had her tea while reading the files for the morning patients. She was going to see a new one this morning, and she wanted to at least have some idea about what was going on with him.

Alan was thirty-five years old, and he was a CEO for a French company headquartered in the U.S. He hadn't included the company name in his file. At nine o'clock, he entered her office, greeting her with a bright smile, and she thought she was receiving Nicholas Cage. Alan could be the man's stunt double. And he had a confident attitude that seemed to shout, "Women, God sent me to you."

"Hello, I'm Alan Zakiyev." He gave Simone his hand.

"Simone Bennet. Take a seat, Alan, and tell me how can I help you. Tell me a little bit about yourself, something that's not in your files."

He settled on the couch and immediately started to talk.

"Well, I'm thirty-five years old, I'm a CEO for a foreigner company in Unites States. I prefer not reveal the name..."

Sure, Simone thought with a smile, *because I might go there and tell them everything I know about you...*

"I'm divorced, I have an eight-year-old boy, which just so happens to be the exact number of years I've been divorced..."

"And what brings you to me?"

"I'm having problems in a relationship, and I don't know what to do."

"Which relationship...past or present, and what kind of problems?"

"I have a girlfriend—we've been together for four years, and we have a good relationship." He stopped and looked at Simone. "Can I tell you everything?"

No, thought Simone, *be quiet and pay me.* What a stupid question!

"Absolutely. In fact, I hope you will, because I won't be able to help you, otherwise."

"Well, our life together is great. She allows me a huge amount of freedom, and she has a unique outlook on our sex life..."

"Explain that to me, please..."

"Okay. Well. For example, the other day I arrived home to find her in sexy lingerie, and to my surprise, a girlfriend of hers—also wearing beautiful lingerie—was there, and my girlfriend allowed this friend of hers to suck my dick! Talk about amazing! So anyway, that's what I mean...that's how she is. And since I'm not into monogamy, I like that kind of relationship."

Oh...another Don Juan, thought Simone, already displeased with this patient.

"If you like it, and if she likes it, what's the problem?"

"The problem is that I met this other woman...a lawyer...a beautiful, smart, rich woman who doesn't need my money. She's very independent, but she wants exclusivity, and I don't know what to do!"

"Sounds to me as if you will have to choose, and all choices have consequences."

She should record that phrase; she had to repeat it some many times every day, she was tired of saying it.

"Yes, but I like my girlfriend...and the freedom she gives me. But I also like Izadora and the pleasure she gives me. She's crazy, and she has these delightful little feet that drive me mad. She allows me to worship them, lick them, and even cum on them."

"So, you have a foot fetish?"

"Yes, I do. As far as I'm concerned, it's the most erotic part of a female's body... Whenever I see her feet in high heels, my cock gets hard instantly, and Izadora wears the most delightful heels, super high, delicious, her nails always painted red. I can come just thinking about her feet."

"Okay, so you like the freedom the one woman gives you and the feet of the other..."

Well, who can have everything? Simone mocked mentally.

"Samara's feet are not pretty, and besides, she doesn't like me to cum on her. But Izadora's are delightful. The problem is that Izadora will suck my soul dry; I can see that... She's not the kind of woman you can deceive...not in bed, not outside bed..."

"And Samara?"

"Samara allows me to sleep with other women because

she's not so great in bed... She's easily satisfied, and she doesn't ask for much... On the other hand, Izadora wants to fuck all the time—once, twice every day, and I can't keep up with her!"

"Why can't you?"

"I have this blood pressure issue. For the last ten years, I've taken medication to keep it under control, which means my dick gets hard only with Viagra...and I can't tell her..."

"You are young to have that kind of issue."

"Yes, but I've had this condition, as I told you, for years."

"So how do you handle it?"

"Whenever I'm going to see Izadora, I take a blue pill, but my health conditions don't allow me to do that every single day, so I play this disappearing act..."

"Um...a disappearing act?"

"Yes, I act mysterious... I come and go...as if I'm not interested...but now, she told me to go to hell!"

"If you're not sincere, she's probably insecure. You have to tell her the truth."

"If I tell her the truth, that I really don't care all that much about sex, and that all I think about is her beautiful feet, she's going to think I'm a lunatic!"

Would she be wrong? She took a deep breath and blew it out.

"And what do you want to do? Exactly why did you come to me?"

"I need help deciding which girl I want to be with, because I would like to keep both."

"I'm afraid that is for you to decide, but in my opinion, you're asking the wrong question. What you need to do is face up to the facts regarding your sexuality, as it is now, or you can try to find a cure for your problem. The blood pressure issue can be controlled without damaging your sex life, if that's what you want, but it seems to me you're not worried about having intercourse all the time. Apparently, indulging your fetish is your primary concern."

"To be honest, Doctor, those are my thoughts, exactly. I couldn't care less about getting my dick wet. I don't need to fuck a woman; I just need to touch her feet. I would like to find a woman who was satisfied with just that—one who would let me worship her feet and we're done!"

"Women have their needs... Do you think you can keep a relationship with Izadora based on your needs? You told me she loves sex, she wants to have intercourse constantly, every day of the week... How long do you think you can disguise your lack of interest in the whole act?"

"I didn't think about that…"

"And besides…she must be letting you worship her feet just to please you… A foot fetish is generally a male thing."

"Really?"

"Yes…it's more common in men…"

"What's the cause?"

"There are many theories… Freud says it's all about the phallic form. There are other neuroscientists who say it's a physiological problem with the brain. No one is certain, but in your case, one theory fits better than the others. There are some doctors who believe men with foot fetishes also suffer from impotence. How long have you had this fetish?"

"Since I started to have problems achieving an erection. Holy shit! I think you may be right, Doctor!"

"So you may have replaced one thing with the other…but as I said, it's just a theory…"

"I've been very anxious about this, and I don't know what to do. I would like your opinion…"

"Okay, I can't tell you what to do, but if I were you, well, first, how about trying to solve your blood pressure issues? There are doctors who recommend exercises to control that, without any kind of medication. That would allow you to reestablish your sexual life after a while."

"Do you know someone?"

"Yes, I do, I can write a referral for you. Second, I think you should be clear with this woman, Izadora. Tell her why you disappear...tell her it's a temporary problem you are having. You don't need to tell her how long you've been dealing with this. But you need to be as truthful as possible, and then see how she reacts. Find out if she's willing to be patient and wait for you to resolve your problems.

"And third, even if you are not a monogamist—and I believe you feel as you do because you can't get any real satisfaction from just one relationship—you have to clarify your feelings for both women. You get one with all the freedom, or you get the other with all the restraints. Think...listen to your reason...what would make you happier?"

"Really, Doctor, you are the best. I came here all confused, and now I can see a light at the end of the tunnel!"

And I can see problems in my way if I continue impulsively telling patients what they should do, Simone thought.

They finished the session with a very happy Alan leaving her office, and Simone spent the rest of the day listening to the life stories of several more patients.

At the end of the day, as usual, Simone decided to take some time to read Lara's journal. As she started to sit in her armchair, it occurred to her to ask Patricia for some food. A short time later, the secretary delivered a tray laden with a variety of fresh fruits, a turkey and Swiss sandwich, and another pot of fresh tea.

Simone thanked her, then reminded her to leave by six o'clock. As Patricia left Simone alone again, she decided to move her armchair near the window. She loved the natural light that streamed in this time of the day. She tucked her legs beneath her and started to read.

Lara's Journal

Several days after our first "threesome"—although I didn't refer to it as that back then, since that was a term I'd never heard—I arrived at my French class early, so I decided to go wait in the cafeteria. There were two girls sitting and talking at the next table, their voices so loud I didn't have to strain to hear them.

"Hey, Louise, did you know Mary's boyfriend was arrested yesterday?"

"Which Mary?"

"The English girl from the advanced class."

This caught and held my attention; Mary was a girl from my class.

"Why? What did he do?"

"He had sex with her..."

"So?"

"So she's a minor! She is not fifteen yet, and he's eighteen!"

"But they've been together for months. I'm sure she probably agreed to sleep with him, don't you think?"

"She may have, yes, but that doesn't matter. According to the law, any adult who has sexual contact with a minor is committing a crime."

I was twelve the first time Arthur raped me. What he'd done was illegal. Of course it was. How could I have not known? Probably because my "mother" consented to it. And if it's wrong for an adult to have sex with a fifteen year old, I imagine it's much worse if the girl is only twelve. Dottie and Emms were right—only adults could consent to have sex. What Arthur did with me was wrong...so what had happened with Arthur and Claude was doubly wrong and most likely an even worse crime.

Beside me, the girls were still debating the moral and legal ramifications of Mary's boyfriend having slept with her, but I couldn't listen anymore. Their conversation had shaken me. With my limited knowledge, I'd had no idea how wrong my life was. Sure, Emma had told me that grown women can have sex with men they love...but apparently, it was not only a question of age—it was also a question of legalities... I felt guilty; I felt bad! I couldn't pay attention in class because my head was spinning.

How can I go on like this? I wondered. What kind of "surprises" would Arthur come up with next? First Adrien and then the guy the other night. Arthur had apparently discovered a new vein of perversion—one he very much enjoyed. Not that I hadn't liked the experience, too—I'm a lot of things, but a hypocrite isn't one of them. I loved sex. But Arthur had a sick mind, and I sensed he wouldn't stop with just bringing a third person into our sex life.

More than ever, I realized I had to end our screwed-up relationship. I'd been gathering money and jewels, but it was a slow process. Trying to figure out how much I needed to survive alone, I started to look at our bills, at the supermarket receipts, and so on. I had no idea how much it would cost to pay rent, so I needed as much money as I could get my hands on... I would also remember what I'd overheard about how having sex with a minor was illegal. When the time came, I suspected that information would be useful.

327

During the week following our threesome, Arthur bought me gifts but didn't say a word about what we had done. And then that Friday, he arrived home very excited about a party. I wondered why he seemed so happy—I mean, what was one more party invitation when we received so many?

"Here," he said, handing over a big, rectangular silver box. "Wear this."

I took the package but didn't bother opening the lid. No doubt it contained another new dress. Nor did I thank him. He never bought clothes for me because he wanted to please me; he bought them because he treated me like his personal, life-size Barbie doll, and when we went out, he dressed me as he pleased.

"What time are we leaving," I asked, wondering how long I'd have to get ready.

"Around eight."

I turned away without another word, heading into my room to call Louise, the girl I always used when I had to have my hair and makeup done for a special occasion. Hopefully, she didn't already have plans or another client booked for this evening.

My luck held, and by 6:30 p.m., I was dressed and ready to go. I stood before the full-length mirror in my room and stared. The heavily embroidered, beaded black dress with its deep cleavage was gorgeous. As with all the dresses Arthur picked, this one was tight and short but also, thankfully, tastefully chic.

I felt prettier than ever. Louise had done an exquisite job on my makeup. The kohl-black liner around my eyes gave me a mysterious air, and the curly hairstyle made me look fierce. The dress was the ultimate in elegance, and as we were getting ready to leave the apartment, Arthur handed me another box, this one much smaller. I lifted the lid to find a pair of earrings—tear-shaped black onyx center stones surrounded by smaller diamonds—a matching ring, and a diamond tennis bracelet.

I looked up to find Arthur standing there looking at me.

"Thank you," I murmured. Although I knew the jewelry was just another prop he had purchased to make me into the woman he wanted seen on his arm, I wanted him to think I truly appreciated his gifts, so he'd keep them coming. Who knew how many months worth of rent or utilities this set might cover once I left his sick ass?

I was wearing high, shiny-black heels, and Arthur had insisted I put on a beautiful pair of black lace string-bikini panties and thigh-high black stockings with black lace at the top. I began to wonder what kind of party he was planning. Why the need for sexy undergarments? Between the skimpy underwear and the way he kept looking at me, I began to suspect something sexual was involved. The thought made me grow tense.

My hands shook a little as I put on my new jewelry, using the mirror in the foyer to make certain the earrings were hanging straight and hadn't gotten tangled in my curls.

"Are you ready?" Arthur asked, moving close to stand behind me.

I glanced at the grandfather clock in the hallway. "It's still a little early. Is the driver here yet?"

"I'll drive."

I lifted a brow. What was he up to? Arthur hated driving in Paris traffic and almost always used a driver. He never allowed me to drive anymore, either... Apparently, that whole thing had just been a part of his plan to seduce me into bending to his will.

We left the apartment, and I stood on the curb while he went to get his car, a silver Jaguar. He pulled up in front of me, climbed out, and came around to open the door for me, and he was all smiles and pleasantries. My suspicions grew. When Arthur was overly kind, he usually wanted something... I climbed into the passenger seat and waited while he went around and got in behind the wheel.

"Where are we going?" I asked, as he maneuvered the car back onto the street.

"To Vaux Le Vicomte."

"Who is this Viscount?" I asked, referring to the name that ended with 'The Viscount'.

"Funny girl! It's a place near Paris; the party is at a chateau."

"Which one?" I grew excited about the idea of attending a party at one of France's historical chateaus and could already imagine the marvelous old architecture.

As an adult, I can see how the time I spent visiting all those old buildings while living in France with Arthur influenced my professional style. There is always a touch of French architecture in my architectural designs.

"No one you know. It's a private chateau called Chateau Garcin."

"There is a family living there like Chateau d'Ussé?"

I'd been to Chateau d'Ussé and had fallen in love with the whole "Sleeping Beauty" setup there. Apparently, my innocent romantic side wasn't dead after all...

"No, the family perished long ago. These days, they rent it out for parties."

He turned up the volume on the radio, which meant he didn't want to talk to me anymore about the party or the chateau or anything else. I gazed at his profile and shook my head. Yes...he was definitely up to something...

The chateau was located outside Paris, and it took us almost an hour to get there. The castle sat in the middle of a park, far from any other houses or buildings. Beautiful iron gates emblazoned with a gold coat of arms swung open at our approach, and one of two men dressed in burgundy, historical-looking livery stepped over to the driver's side of the car. Arthur showed him our invitation. The man nodded and resumed his post, allowing us to enter, and we drove up an unpaved road lined with torches until we reached a circular area with a fountain in the middle.

Several valets were waiting to park vehicles. Arthur turned and grabbed a small bag from the back seat. He reached inside the bag and pulled out two black masks—one lace and one satin—and gave me the lacy one. He adjusted the satin mask on his face.

"Put it on!" He nodded toward the bit of lace I still held in my hand. "It's a *bal masqué*"

Excitement momentarily overrode my fears. A masked ball! This was something I'd only read about. Of all the parties we'd attended since our arrival in France, none of them had required masks. Careful not to flatten my hair or get anything caught in my earrings, I slid my mask into place.

One of the valets opened my door for me, and I could see appreciation in his eyes. Yes, I was pretty, indeed!

I looked up at the outside of the enormous castle, and my heart raced. The architecture took my breath away. Made of *tuffeau*—the beige limestone used for the construction of castles in France—it had a long, central pavilion flanked by two round towers. The Immense *portes-fenêtres* were lacquered in white—a modern touch, of course. Lights illuminated every window, and somewhere inside, music played.

Two more valets were checking the invitation. Was the president of France inside? I'd never seen so much security!

We entered a vast ballroom, where some of the most well-dressed people I'd ever laid eyes on were dancing, sipping champagne, chatting, and gossiping. All were wearing masks, including the catering team and members of the orchestra. I just loved that!

The finely carved wood trim and heavy wooden doors, typical of what one might find in a castle, enchanted me. Gold-gilt-framed paintings lined the walls, and the high, dome-shaped ceiling was covered in colorful images of angels and flower garlands. The intricately painted scene was so beautiful; I couldn't help but gape as I imagined what it might have been like to live in this home all those years ago. How skilled the artist must have been to be able to paint something so amazing so high in the air!

"Welcome, my dear friend Arthur."

A man dressed in a black tuxedo similar to the one Arthur wore, approached us.

"Good evening, Fabian, thanks for the invitation. Meet my fiancée, Lara."

Arthur put his hand at the small of my back and gave me a little push forward.

Fabian took my hand and kissed it.

"A pleasure, Lara. Nicholas Fabian de Sevigné. My friends call me Fabian. Lara, you certainly are the beauty of the ball. Welcome to my masquerade. Enjoy. I hope we can find a few moments to get to know each other better a little later."

I took in our host's chestnut hair and blue eyes. Although he stood a bit taller than Arthur did, I judged them to be around the same age. I glanced around, looking to see if he had a wife or girlfriend lingering nearby and waiting her turn to greet us, but Fabian appeared to be alone.

He stared at me with unconcealed hunger, and rather than respond to his last statement, I looked away. I shivered slightly, bothered by the way he seemed to undress me with his gaze. Finally, he walked away to greet someone else, and I turned to Arthur.

"Your friend really liked me..." I stressed the last words, so Arthur would understand I was being sarcastic.

"He and all the men here if they have blood in their veins. You are really gorgeous tonight. I'm so proud of you."

As if to prove his point, Arthur took my hand and began to parade with me all over the room, showing me off as if I was a pureblooded mare!

Over the next several hours, he made certain my champagne glass never went empty. Odd, considering how he normally behaved when it came to me drinking alcohol. But tonight, he gave me no recriminations, no scowling looks. I began to grow lightheaded from too much booze and very little food. They hadn't served dinner, but caterers weaved in and out of the crowd, carrying trays of *hors d'oeuvres*.

A quick glance at a porcelain clock over the huge marble fireplace settled in a corner told me the hour had grown quite late, and I had noticed several couples departing over the last few minutes, but there were still at least thirty couples and maybe twenty more individuals left. I stood alone in a corner, sipping my champagne and looking around, when I noticed a commotion nearby and decided to go see what all the fuss was about.

Several people had formed a circle, and something was happening in the middle of that circle. I couldn't see anything, so I maneuvered my way in between a couple young men, my curiosity heightened. There, in the middle of the circle, stood a very pretty black girl I had noticed earlier. She was almost naked, her beautiful body bare except for her high black stockings and heels. Her two companions, both men wearing masks, were caressing her body. One had his mouth on her breast, and the other had his hand on her pussy. As I looked closer, I realized one of the men was our host, Fabian.

The people who had formed the circle stood staring, as if they'd fallen into some kind of trance. Some of the men reached out to touch the girl's body, while others simply watched, content to just appreciate the scene.

"My friends," Fabian began, "our party has now officially begun. Do as you please, but remember, it is forbidden that you take off your mask. No violence unless you have your partner's consent, and do not impose on anyone who indicates a lack of interest in whatever it is you propose. As for the rest...make yourselves comfortable."

What the hell was that! I turned my back to leave and nearly ran into Arthur, who stood just behind me.

He handed me yet another glass of champagne.

"Here," he said, pressing a pill into my free hand. "Take this. You haven't eat much, and I don't want you to be sick."

Without thinking, I took the pill and washed it down

with a swig of champagne.

Arthur leaned in close. "Did you like the scene we just witnessed?" He pointed toward the crowd and where I had just been standing.

"I…I don't know…" I looked away, unable to meet his gaze.

To be truthful, what I had seen had excited me. I had grown wet, and my legs felt like jelly. The whole scene—all those people watching that girl, the men touching her, all the masks, the champagne, and the surreal, medieval, luxurious environment were turning me on.

I glanced over my shoulder just in time to see Fabian make his way through the crowd and approach us. The way he looked at me, I had no doubt he wanted to touch me as he had touched the other girl. And I realized I was attracted to his dark-blue eyes.

"He is crazy about you. He's wanted you since the moment he laid eyes on you. So go…have fun," Arthur whispered in my ear while caressing my back.

"What do you mean?"

I wanted an explanation, but suddenly, I felt even more lightheaded and dizzy than I had previously, and I remembered the pill I'd just taken. As I look back on this night now, I have to wonder what Arthur had given me.

"Do as you please, Lara...touch people...be touched...that is the purpose of this party. All the guests have come here for the same thing—to meet different people, to interact without commitment. Nobody knows you...nobody cares what you do...and after we leave here, nobody will even talk about what went on here tonight..."

"I don't understand..." I murmured.   My brain was so foggy, I couldn't understand much at all.

"Fuck whomever you like, *capicci* now?" Arthur growled, having obviously become annoyed by my questions.

"Hey, Lara, I noticed you over there," Fabian said and pointed toward where the crowd still gathered around the girl. "Did you like the show?"

I didn't know what to say. Arthur then leaned in and kissed me on the lips. He touched my breast, but I was too dizzy to protest. Around us, many other couples were doing the same thing—touching each other, stripping.

"She tastes wonderful, Fabian, why don't you try?" Arthur said.

Had I heard correctly? Had Arthur just offered me to our host?

"I would like that very much. Would you mind?" He

looked to me for my consent.

At least he had the good sense to ask me. But I simply couldn't imagine putting on a show for everybody to see.

"No..." I told him. "Not...in front of everybody...no... I don't..."

"Come with me."

Arthur took me by my arm and led me to a mezzanine, Fabian following along behind us.

"Do as he commands you, or you are going to be in trouble with me, Lara, deep trouble," Arthur told me, speaking low so only I could hear him. He squeezed my arm as if to prove his point. He reminded me so much of Sabine years before. "I need that man's help, and if he wants you, lucky me..."

I couldn't think clearly, but the threat had the effect Arthur no doubt intended. I feared what he might do to me... And in my foggy-headed state, I didn't recall he had already done all the bad he could do...nothing could be worse. But back then...how could I know?

There were five or six people fucking in the mezzanine, and below them, the crowd reacted with frenzied excitement. Unbelievably, the orchestra played on as if it was a regular party.

We went to an empty corner, and Fabian leaned in

close, his face just inches from mine. I could sense Arthur behind us, watching, no doubt waiting to see what I might do.

"You are beautiful," Fabian said, and then he kissed me. Not a normal first kiss between a man and a woman who barely knew each other, but a kiss that was meant to ignite passion.

I closed my eyes and responded. His lips were firm, his mouth tasted of whisky and cigarettes—this was back when smoking didn't have such a stigma attached to it—and I found myself enjoying the very masculine way he kissed me. Between Fabian's sexy, somewhat aggressive approach and all the people around me—touching, fucking, kissing, moaning—there was no way I could resist becoming aroused.

Arthur moved in behind me, put his hand on my nape, and suddenly, I felt the front of my dress falling. By then, I was too high from the alcohol and whatever drug he'd given me to even think of protesting. Immediately, Fabian took one of my breasts in his hand.

"Small but perfect," he said. His hands were soft and slightly damp.

He caressed me, and so did Arthur, four hands roaming over my body. My head began to spin at the incredible sensations. Fabian posted himself behind my back, pulled up my hair, and started to lick my back from my shoulders to my waistline. Arthur fondled my breast.

Goose bumps covered my arms, and I shivered, my legs weak, my panties wet.

The next thing I knew, Arthur was helping me to step out of my dress. At first, I was ashamed, but then I saw almost everyone else around me was either half naked or totally nude. I stood there in my panties, stockings, and high heels, while two men caressed me. I closed my eyes to focus on all the crazy sensations, and a moment later, I felt one of them pulling my panties aside. A warm mouth covered my pussy, and I opened my eyes to discover we had an audience.

A fat man stood nearby, masturbating, and a couple— still fully dressed—watched us with interest. An unknown man was running his fingers over my body. I don't know how it was possible, but I felt no shame. In fact, seeing them there, watching me, touching me, added another erotic element to the situation and heightened my desire.

Fabian sucked my pussy without mercy. He licked and penetrated me with his tongue as deeply as he could. I could feel Arthur's cock rubbing between my legs from behind. Both men were obviously very excited.

Fabian stopped licking me, stood up, and put a finger inside me and turned it, imitating fucking me with his finger. After a moment, he removed it, brought it to his mouth, and licked it clean.

"You really taste wonderful!" he said and grabbed me

by the hand.

He led me over to a nearby chaise lounge and helped me to lie down. I stared up at him through half-closed eyes, and he slid a condom down over his rigid dick. Vaguely, I wondered when he had undressed and where he might have gotten the condom. Obviously, most people there had come prepared. He leaned over me, opening my pussy with his fingers, and I nearly came at just his touch. Then, without bothering to remove my panties, he positioned himself between my legs and penetrated me slowly. I came immediately, my deep moan of release rumbling in my ears.

He must have interpreted the sound as an invitation because he started to move, slowly, at first. Arthur found a way to position himself so he could lick my clit while Fabian was fucking me, and it was the most exquisite sensation, ever. I came and came. But Fabian didn't. He was an experienced lover, and he seemed to be taking great satisfaction in watching my pleasure.

"I want you from behind," he said suddenly.

Too excited and too drunk or drugged to think, I didn't understand what he wanted. I simply lay there, watching as he got up and grabbed something—a bottle of some kind—from a nearby end table. He returned to my side, slipped off the condom and replaced it with a fresh one, then upended the bottle over his still-hard cock. Thick, dark oil drizzled from the bottle, coating his dick, and he used his hand to spread it up and down the length of his shaft.

"Arthur, touch her for me…" Fabian told him as he pulled off my panties and flung them onto the floor.

Arthur reached between my legs and began to caress my pussy. My pleasure grew, and I shifted on the chair, wanting…needing to be filled. Arthur slid up to wrap his arms around me, turning me in his embrace, my back toward Fabian. Something warm and wet covered my ass—the oil, no doubt—and he started to spread it over my ass cheeks and down the length of my crack. His actions brought me back to my senses, and I immediately stiffened. What did he think he was doing?

"Calm down, babe," he told me. "I won't hurt you. You're going to like this…"

I was still tense, but Arthur got on his knees and began to lick my pussy, and I immediately forgot everything but the growing pleasure. Fabian slid his dick between my ass cheeks and slowly began to penetrate me. I gasped and tightened up immediately.

"No, babe, relax. The secret to enjoying this is to relax. I won't move until you are ready."

He did as he promised, slowly, patiently, pushing in a little at a time until he was all the way inside me. Then he started to move, again slowly, controlling his pace. Arthur was still working on my pussy, two fingers inside me, licking my clit. Fabian started to move quicker, and so did Arthur, fucking me with his fingers. My pussy and my ass felt as if they were in flames.

I sensed the approach of a huge orgasm, and I began to shudder. Arthur moved again, replacing his fingers with his cock, and both men set up a rhythm with me in between them. Moments later, I came like a cosmic explosion; I swear I left my body and entered another dimension. The pleasure spread from my brain, throughout my body and back again. I felt no shame, just a profound sense of completion with both of them buried deep inside me, their hands all over me, mouths kissing me, as I lost myself in the most amazing orgasm I had ever experienced.

I moaned and cried out loud, and then both men followed me over the precipice, coming simultaneously, and we had to clutch each other to keep from losing our balance and tumbling onto the floor.

When I opened my eyes, the old man who had been masturbating was cleaning himself with a napkin as he had cum over himself, the couple was kissing and touching, a man was fondling my breasts, and three other men I hadn't seen before stood across from us, masturbating, and as I watched, all three of them started to come.

After that night, Fabian turned into a constant companion, joining us regularly for threesomes. In our apartment, at swing clubs, both men took me, and Arthur even allowed Fabian to "borrow me" for a weekend alone with him. I later learned he was a wealthy businessman, owner of a huge company that produced all kind of lighting—from lamps to cables— and Arthur wanted Fabian as a regular client of his bank. His money would be good for business, and as Arthur had said, Fabian was an influential man, so it was good publicity for his bank to administrate Fabian's money.

CHAPTER SEVENTEEN

Simone – Present Day

By the time Simone put up the journal, it was completely dark outside. She had lost track of the time while reading. Madness, how old was that girl? How could she ever lead a normal sex life when all she had learned was wrong, depraved, and twisted? Simone remembered Lara's words from one of Mark's diaries: "I was forged!" That was the word—the girl had been through hell and damnation, and all her values were corrupted. She hadn't had any moral standards. Then again, her entire life had been based on what Arthur had told her was correct, so how could she?

Simone prepared her things to leave, and on her way out, she was surprised to run into Edward. She barely saw him these days; he seemed to be avoiding her.

"Hello, my friend, working late?" Simone asked him.

"Yes, I had some reports to present to the police about a case...and you?"

"Reading..."

Simone didn't want to mention she was working for Carl again; she knew Edward would be opposed to it. But then again, maybe he wouldn't care. The thought he might no longer worry about her made her sad. A knot formed in her throat, and her eyes burned with unshed tears at the thought.

"How are you feeling, Simmie? We haven't talked in a while, and I've been wondering if you're feeling better?"

His gaze showed his sincere concern, his eyes surrounded with the small wrinkles that appeared when he was worried about something, and she thought it was charming, which surprised her.

"I'm better. Working hard but already sleeping without the aid of pills." Not the entire truth, but she didn't want his concern for her as a doctor; she wanted his attention on a personal level.

"That's great news! I'm happy for you."

For a moment, she felt the old link they use to have, but then he looked at his watch.

"I have to go!" he said. "I promised to take Carla to the movies."

How nice, Simone thought...*movies...dinners...a real relationship...* She remembered it was a Friday night, and there she was, alone again. Why couldn't she find a normal man like Edward?

You did, and then you lost him by being an idiot, she told herself. *And now you have a crazy lunatic who calls your phone a million times a day and who likes to use your breasts to masturbate.*

What a life...

"Cool, have a good evening..."

"Same to you, Simmie... Have a great weekend."

And there she was, dismissed for the whole weekend again. All this rejection was starting to hurt.

*   *   *   *   *

After a lonely Friday night spent eating popcorn and watching a comedy series marathon on TV, Simone woke up to remember she had scheduled a meeting with Carl. He would drive from New York to Woodbridge, and they were going to talk at her home. Afterward, he had invited her to go out to lunch.

She braced herself to see him again after all the time that had passed. She had to admit, if only to herself, that she still had ambiguous feelings for the man, and these days, she was so needy, at any moment she might start to have feelings for the mailman... Or worse, for Armando. But no...all the neediness in the world wouldn't cause her to do that.

When it came to Carl, she had to guard her heart. For the tenth time that morning, she reminded herself he'd never love again... Not the way he had loved Lara.

And if he did, part of him would always be haunted by thoughts of Lara. Simone preferred to have a man who could give her all his attention, not one who pined silently for his lost love. It was always a hard job to compete with a ghost.

Carl arrived at 10:00 a.m., looking as handsome as she remembered, dressed in blue jeans, a t-shirt, and sneakers.

What a change. She couldn't recall ever seeing him wearing anything but a suit.

"Good morning, Carl, how have you been?"

She gave him her hand, but he pulled her in for a hug, enveloping her in his warmth and the wonderful scent of his very masculine cologne. She didn't have the perfect nose, but it was a perfume with a woodsy scent and definitively some jasmine and tobacco. Yes—there was definitely something different about him this time. He'd always treated her with distant politeness. The old Carl would have shaken her hand, perhaps given her a quick kiss on the cheek. Simone much preferred this new way of greeting her.

"I've missed you so much, Simone! Look at you. You look wonderful. The suntan suits you."

Simone was caught off guard, and she didn´t know what to do with his display of affection.

"Thanks, Carl! Let's sit and talk a little bit. Would you like something to drink?" she said after they had both gotten settled on her couch in the living room.

"No, not now. But thank you."

They made small talk about his trip, traffic, and the weather. To Simone's trained eye, he appeared as if he were merely being polite...as if he was waiting to get the pleasantries out of the way, so he could jump to the topic of Lara.

"And how is your analysis going?"

"Well, I'm not shocked because hardly anything shocks me, but it's a sad story. Have you read it?"

"Yes, I'm reading it now. Slowly, because I find I have to set aside the journal and pull myself together every so often. When Lara told me about the abuse and about Arthur, I was surprised, shocked, and revolted, but I didn't realize how horrible things were. He treated her worse than a dog! The girl in that journal...that's not the Lara I knew. The girl in the diary was a terrified kid, trying to do her best to survive. Oh, sure...I've seen traces of my Lara in that girl—especially when she describes how she'd misbehave or stand up for herself a little—but even then, I found myself comparing those actions to a dog that sought revenge by peeing on the carpet. Annoying, but you can let it go, you know what I mean?"

Carl's voice was stressed, indicating how disturbed he was by the things he'd discovered about Lara's life. If it was hard for Simone—a complete stranger and a professional—to digest the information found in those journals, she could only imagine how Carl felt. After all, he'd loved Lara with all his heart.

"She couldn't do much else. She was powerless, a helpless girl trapped by perverse adults."

"Do you believe Arthur is a pedophile, or was he really in love with Lara?"

"Hard to say...maybe both...but certainly he was a pedophile, and I don't believe an adult can be in love with a child...there's always some sort of deviance involved."

"And is there a cure for that, or do you believe he is out there molesting children?"

"A good psychologist could cure him, but first, he'd have to admit he has a sickness and seek out a cure...and, of course, there's no guarantee he wouldn't relapse. It's like any addiction, but I did some research on him. He's married, and his wife is his age. And get this... They live in New York."

"Yes, I've been doing research on him, too, but every time I think about him, I feel so much hate I think my head might explode."

Carl put both hands to his head, in a clear sign he was disturbed about the whole story.

"His behavior was hateful... I know it's not going to make you feel any better, but I can tell you that usually pedophiles are the product of a very traumatized childhood. There is a great chance he suffered sexual abuse when he was a child. But he is not only a pedophile, he is also a sadomasochist...the combination implies a very disturbed mind."

"God, my longing to kill the guy grows stronger every day." Carl made a gesture of stabbing someone with his hand.

"Don't think like that...it's not good for your health." Easy to say, she knew, but difficult to do for a man in his position.

"When I read about him hiring that hooker to make Lara fall in love with the man, my rage rose to an incontrollable level. I had to smash the glass I had in my hand... I hurt myself, and I was so upset, I didn't even feel the physical pain!" He showed Simone his left hand, which was wrapped in a bandage.

"That subterfuge, the abuse she suffered, all of it contributed to forming Lara's personality. When I read Mark's—well, your report... I still have a hard time facing the fact that you two are the same person— anyway, your report shows a woman who wanted to feel love, but she couldn't trust men enough...the roots of that behavior came from Arthur's betrayal of her trust. She thought he was a friend, and he wasn't. Then there was Adrien, the man Arthur hired to act as if he wanted her for himself. She fell in love with him, her first love, the most important one in the life of any person, and he betrayed her. Imagine how hard it was for her to trust again, after experiencing all that in her early years."

"You know, I think in the end she loved me... I have to believe she did...or I would go crazy! Of course, I don't know for certain, and I have a feeling the more I read— the farther along I get in her journals—the closer I'll come to knowing the truth, and I don't know if I'll be able to cope if I discover she didn't love me."

"I'm still reading about her younger days, but I have a suggestion. Allow me to read the entire journal first, before you finish reading it. That way, I will be prepared to really help you."

"That's a good idea. How about this... When you finish a chapter, send me a message, and let me know where I need to stop, and then I'll read up to that point. Will that work for you?"

"Yes, that's perfect. I think things will work better that way. If I'm to help you, I need to be prepared."

They talked for at least an hour and a half about Lara's diaries before Carl changed the subject.

"I have something to tell you... Peter has been calling me..."

Simone's heart began to race, her palms grew sweaty, and she felt as if something evil had entered the room. She couldn't describe it, exactly, but it felt metaphysic, as if she were suddenly surrounded by some kind of bad energy.

"And?"

"He says he loves me, and then he hangs up. And then he calls again and says he is innocent, and he is going to prove it. He calls at least twice a week. Yesterday, he called me and said he wants to come back to the country. He doesn't let me talk; he just says a few words and hangs up... I've already been to the police, and they're taping my phone calls, but so far, they haven't been able to trace them because he cuts off too quickly. He's smart. I just wanted to let you know, so you can make sure you're safe—maybe hire security and make certain your alarm is on here, because I really don't know where he is. No one does."

"God, I don't need all this again right now! I'm going to talk to my partner and see what I can do to protect myself."

"I feel so sorry for bringing all this into your life, Simone."

"You are not the one to blame...anything could trigger Peter's psycho side...and I believe it would be worse with someone not prepared to deal with psychos. I imagine those poor women he killed."

"I would never have believed Peter could be a killer. The thought of that is so unreal. He was always the funny guy, always the good friend... I can't believe I didn't know what evil lurked beneath his normal exterior."

"Don't blame yourself for not knowing. Many psychopaths create normal lives; they even have children. They can show affection, and their madness happens far away from home."

"I know...in theory...but when it happens in your own life, it's so surreal."

"It is...and I'm used to dealing with madness, but it was hard to find myself in the middle of the hurricane. I jump every time I hear Peter's name."

"Take care, Simone. I don't know what that man is

capable of."

"Anything, I'm sure. When his psycho side appears, he can do anything." A psychopath was not someone whose movements you could predict.

Disturbed by the conversation, Simone bit her lip. Her palms were moist, and she really was afraid of him.

"I'm hungry...let's have dinner?" Carl said, abruptly changing the subject.

Perhaps he'd sensed her discomfort, and she was thankful for that. She really hated talking about Peter Hay.

"My car is outside," he added. "Do you need some time to get ready?"

"No, I'm ready, I'll just get my purse."

"First woman I've ever met who doesn't need half an hour to prepare to leave!"

Simone smiled at his remark. She got her purse, and they headed out the front door. As Carl took her arm to escort her down the front steps, a taxi pulled up at the curb. The rear door flew open, and Armando leaped out. He sprinted up the sidewalk toward them.

"You bitch!" he shouted. "Is this the reason you're not answering my phone calls? You're fucking around on me!"

Carl grabbed Armando, pinning his arms to his side and immobilizing him with some kind of martial arts-type move. Simone hadn't known he had that kind of training.

"Calm down! If you calm yourself, I'll release you! I'm one of Simone's clients. Nothing is going on here."

Armando stilled, and after a moment, Carl let him go.

"I'm sorry, Simone...sir... I saw you come out of the house together, laughing, and I lost control." Armando turned to address Carl. "I'm Armando, Simone's boyfriend."

Oh, for God's sake... "Armando, you are not my boyfriend, and you know you're not. Stop this nonsense!" Simone put her hands on her head. Why did she always attract the crazy ones? What she wouldn't do for a little normalcy in her life.

"But I will be, and I'm making things clear here with your 'client'."

"Stop!" Simone shouted, finally losing her temper. Even though Carl was there, and she'd always behaved professionally in front of him, at the moment, she just didn't give a damn. "I've told you already. I couldn't have been clearer, but I'm going to say it again; I don't want you. I won't have a relationship with you. You are not welcome here! Understood?" She grabbed Carl's hand. "Let's go."

Carl had an astonished look on his face, but he didn't say a word and merely headed to his car with her.

"I'll tell you when things are over between us, Simone!" Armando shouted. "Carl, did she tell you she fucked me inside a nightclub on our first date?"

Armando's whining tone had turned to one of anger. *What an unstable man!*

Carl looked from Simone to Armando. "Sir, what Simone does or doesn't do is none of my concern, but a real gentleman never speaks of such things!"

"Oh, I get it. You must be one of Simone's gay friends. *A gentleman never speaks of such things!*"

Armando mocked Carl's words, but Carl was far too mature for such silliness. He ignored Armando and opened the car door for Simone and then walked around and climbed in behind the wheel. He started the engine and pulled out of the driveway. As they headed down the street, Armando remained standing on the sidewalk in front of her house, screaming God knew what. Again, she wondered how she always managed to attract so many lunatics.

She slumped in the passenger seat, her cheeks burning after what Armando had told Carl. She stuffed her shaking hands between her knees.

"I'm sure he'll be gone before we get back from lunch,"

Carl told her. "We'll order dessert, just to be on the safe side."

"Welcome to my life, Carl. I deal with that kind of lunacy all day long, every single day."

"I really don't know how you can."

Carl changed the subject quickly—he was good like that—and they made light conversation and joked with each other throughout the ride to the restaurant. His effort to tease her into a better mood had the desired effect. She smiled at his kindness. They chose a local restaurant and had a very long lunch, Carl reminding her he definitely wanted to be certain she didn't need to face Armando again.

Throughout their meal, she kept thinking how much she enjoyed his company, and that she would have loved to meet him under different circumstances.

Don't even think about falling in love with him, Simone. That's a certain road to unhappiness. She must remember to keep her heart from getting involved with this man.

After lunch, Carl took her home, parked in front of her house again, and to her relief, there was no sign of Armando.

"It seems the cuckoo is not around."

"Do you want me to come in with you and check the

house?"

"Not necessary, Carl, but thank you. My alarm is set, and he couldn't have gotten into the house without tripping it."

Besides, she had decided to keep a healthy distance from the charming lawyer. The less she saw of him, the better.

"Okay then. I'm heading back to the city. Thanks for everything, Simone, you make my life much easier."

He caressed her arm, a touch that meant "thank you", but she felt chills just the same.

"You're welcome, Carl! And please, try not to suffer so much over what happened with Lara...it's in the past, and nothing can be done to fix that..."

"If only I could. Fix things, that is. But I will take your advice seriously. Better if I do, or I might really go insane."

She said good-bye, and he waited for her to get inside her house before he pulled off. Simone closed and immediately locked the door and reset the alarm. She felt so secure inside her house, as if she was in a fortress.

Deciding she needed to de-stress, she dragged a thin mattress out of the closet in the spare bedroom, unrolled it, and laid it out on the floor in her home office. She sat down and had just begun to meditate when her cellphone started to ring. She looked at the phone and frowned. How odd... While at lunch with Carl, she had set the device to its "do not disturb" mode, but apparently, someone had tried to call her more than once—a signal there must be some kind of trouble. She decided to answer.

"Hello, Dr. Bennet, this is Patricia."

"Hello, Patricia, how are you? Is something wrong?"

"Not well, to tell you the truth... I have bad news. I forwarded the phone at the office so that any incoming calls would ring on my cellphone. I didn't want to miss any calls over the weekend, and someone just called for you. Remember Theodora, your new patient? She only came to see you once—"

"Yes, I know who she is. Does she want to talk to me?"

"No, she's dead! One of her family members called to say she'll be buried this afternoon."

"She's dead! But how? I saw her just last week, and she appeared perfectly healthy to me! In fact, I recall thinking she might live forever when I reviewed her medical records."

"Her heart stopped, or something like. I can't recall exactly what the man said."

"Poor woman, so full of life! Did they say where they're

holding her funeral?"

"They are going to bury her at Beaverdale Memorial Park today after a graveside service. It's at 90 Pine Rock Avenue. Do you have a pen? They gave me directions for you to get to the grave."

"Sure, Patricia, hang on one sec." Simone went into the kitchen and grabbed a pen off the kitchen island. "Okay. Go ahead."

"It's in the L section, Lot 120 A. Grave five. The funeral is at 5:00 p.m. Dr. Bennet, I took the liberty of sending some flowers in your name."

"Thank you very much for your efficiency, Patricia!" The woman was full of surprises.

"Thank you, Doctor! Do you need company?"

"No, Patricia, I'll be fine. Thanks again. Have a nice weekend."

The woman had proven to be a real asset. She was very efficient, worked weekends, and was very attentive to details.

Simone felt tears in her eyes when she remembered Theodora, a person so full of life and plans for her future. She'd seemed so healthy, but she had reached an age when complications could arise without warning. Maybe her heart hadn't been able to keep up with her. Life was like that sometimes. People who wanted to live and love ended up dying, while people who wished for death went on living... Simone decided to go to the funeral; she would do a last tribute to that woman.

She dressed in a simple, black pencil dress, took her purse, her car keys, and left the house. The cemetery was only about five miles away, but she hated to be late, and it was already ten after four. When she opened the garage and backed out her car, she glanced over her shoulder. She hit the brakes hard. A man sat on the bench in her front flower garden. She started to put the car in drive to pull back into the garage.

"Simone!"

Armando? She glanced over her shoulder again. *Oh, my God.* What the hell was that lunatic doing there? She rolled down her car door window and backed up until she was close enough to speak with him.

"My God, Armando, you scared me half to death! What are you doing here?"

"I was waiting to apologize. I regret what I said this morning. I saw the guy drop you off and leave. I really am sorry. The thought of another man in your life made me lose my temper for a moment."

"Okay. Apology accepted; you are forgiven. Now I'm sorry, but I have to go to a funeral!"

"Can I go with you? Just for support, I mean." He looked

at her like a puppy, begging for a bone, the rage he'd exhibited a few hours ago having disappeared.

Thinking if she said no, he would stalk her forever, she nodded. "Get in."

After the funeral, she would drop him at the bus station or wherever he would like to go, and hopefully, she'd be rid of him. But for now, it might be good to have some company at a time like this.

On the short drive, Armando talked like a parrot, driving her crazy. He wanted to know everything—who had died, how had she died, when had she died, and so on.

At least a hundred people surrounded the grave. People of all ages, crying and talking about what a wonderful person Theodora had been. A few people spoke about her, and Simone listened politely, feeling a little out of place. After all, the woman had been a new patient, not someone Simone had known for years. A handsome man of about fifty, his eyes red and filled with tears, started to talk, and Simone instantly realized who he must be.

"I met Theodora some months ago, and she was the best person I've ever known. It took me all of five minutes to fall in love with her."

Several people in the crowd nodded in agreement.

"I've never met a nicer, more authentic person," the

man went on. "We were in love and dreamed it would last forever. We were going to marry. I wanted to spend the rest of my life in her company, in her arms, but she decided to depart too soon... I'm thankful I had the opportunity to know and to love her; that was a privilege and an honor.

"Theodora was special. It's hard to explain, but she helped me know myself better, and she taught me how to stand up for what I wanted. In a short time, she showed me how I'd been living a lie and how different—how real—life could be with her by my side." He stopped, drying a tear with his hand, and then proceeded in a broken voice. "Her time with me was short, but her lessons will last forever. In her honor, I would like to read a poem from Alisson Matos that conveys the way I feel.

"Ah, the emptiness that leaves everything without nothing

"No happy day, no butterflies in the stomach

"Without my flesh muse!

"Without the good smell of skin!

"Without a kiss on the mouth

"No image

"No touch

"Nothing

"Just me

"Alone. ''

By the time he finished, he was sobbing, as were many other people surrounding the grave. Simone's eyes were moist, and beside her, Armando was crying like a baby. What the hell? The man was really nuts. He hadn't ever even met Theodora. Why was he acting so upset? She looked at him, brow raised.

"I'm very moved by his words. I would read that poem if it were your funeral."

Oh, great. Thanks for thinking about my funeral. Simone turned away without responding.

Simone greeted Theodora's family, thanked them for informing her about the funeral. Strangely enough, no one she talked to even knew Theodora had been to Simone's office. She made a mental note to ask Patricia who had called.

Simone and Armando left. On the way home, she dropped a very protesting Armando at the taxi station.

"You can't do that to me!"

"Yes, I can, and I will," she said, parking her car in front of a taxi stand. "Please leave, Armando."

As there were people around, he didn't make a scene, and a moment later he climbed out of her car.

"I love you," he said, before closing the door, "and I won't give up on you!"

Great news! Now I'm going to open a bottle of champagne and celebrate, Simone thought. Way too much excitement for a single Saturday!

Back at her house, Simone decided to take a long bath and then go out to the mall; she was in need of pampering herself a little bit.

＊ ＊ ＊ ＊ ＊

Simone woke up late on Sunday morning. She stayed in bed for a while, thinking about things that had happened the day before, and she decided to call her daughter. She was missing the girl a lot.

"Hey, babe, if your old mom never called you, would you ever pick up the phone to check on her?""Sorry, Mom, but it was a hard week...lots of things to do in school."

"Yeah, and you didn't have five minutes to call me..."

"I said I was sorry. Listen, I was thinking...what do you think about me going to college here?"

And here comes the bomb to start a good Sunday...her daughter wanted to stay in another country. Why?

"Well…what made you think of doing that?"

And suddenly, Simone realized her daughter must have a strong reason to want to be abroad for another couple of years.

"Are you in love, babe? With the guy you were going to have dinner with a while back?"

"Yes, Mom, I am, and the idea of leaving Marcel makes me sick!"

And the idea of losing you makes me sick, thought Simone, *but I´m not going to tell her that, or that it´s too early, since everyone knows teenagers tend to do the opposite of what you tell them to do.*

"Well, what's he like?"

"Oh, Mom, he's wonderful, he's intelligent, brilliant, he makes me laugh. I really do think I'm in love."

"Take care, honey. You hardly know this guy…"

"Of course, I know him! We've been hanging out together for almost a month!"

Yeah…and a month is a lifetime! God, how kids think they know everything. But she wouldn't say no to her daughter right now because it would provoke an argument. If you want to separate a couple, never tell them they don't belong together or they're moving too quickly. Simone bit her tongue.

"Okay, babe, I know I'm acting like your mommy, but please be safe, and keep me posted... Let's wait a little bit to talk about plans for university, okay?"

Tamara changed the subject, and they talked for another ten minutes or so. Simone could tell by her daughter's short answers she was anxious to hang up and not be questioned about her love life again.

Simone thought about taking an early morning run, but it was so good to just lie in bed. She decided to stay home and read some of Lara's journal before getting back to reality and another lonely Sunday.

Lara's Journal

One Thursday afternoon a few weeks after the party, I was in my room, being lazy. Wrapped in my rose-colored bathrobe, I was resting on my bed, watching TV. Arthur came into my room, and I immediately tensed. I sat up and pulled my robe more tightly around me. Funny how I could be so calm, but the moment Arthur approached me I would get anxious. His moods were mercurial, and I could never guess what he might have on his mind at any given moment. He might want to shout at me about something, fuck me, or simple say hello.

"Lara, you are going with Fabian to the beach

tomorrow."

"We are? Which beach?" I asked.

"No, not *we*. *You* are going." He pointed at me. "He's taking you to Cap Ferrat. He asked to spend the weekend with you, and I said yes."

"You can't be serious!"

The idea of spending two or three days alone with Fabian frightened me. He took enormous pleasure in causing me pain, and I believed Arthur's presence during our sexual encounters had been the only thing keeping Fabian from really hurting me at times. Although both men were sadists, and Arthur had become a master at following Fabian's examples and had discovered a delight for provoking pain, Fabian was definitely the more dangerous of the two.

"Yes, I'm serious, and he is coming to get you tomorrow morning, so pack a bag."

He left without further explanation, and I sat staring after him, my mouth hanging open in disbelief.

* * * * *

Fabian arrived early the next day, riding in the back seat of his grey Audi. His driver took my bag, opened the door for me, and Fabian was there waiting.

"Glad you accepted my invitation, darling. I'm dying to spend some time alone with you."

I'm not, I remember thinking. I felt no anticipation for the coming weekend, only fear.

I kept silent on our way to Orly Airport, where we boarded a private jet. I was so worried about what would happen once we arrived in Nice, I couldn't enjoy the hour-and-a-half flight. The jet was decadently luxurious, with large, comfortable, cream-colored leather couches, thick, cream-colored carpeting, tables and TV sets. Two pretty, rosy-cheeked stewardesses served snacks, drinks, and smiles, but I thought them too much crew for just two people.

When I think back now and remember Fabian, an Abba song comes to my mind. *Money, money, money. Always sunny in the rich man's world.*

We arrived at the airport in Nice, and another car was waiting for us, a silver Rolls Royce this time.

Saint Jean Cap Ferrat is part of the Alpes Maritimes in France. It's a beautiful place surrounded by nature, crystalline waters, and populated by people with a lot of money. It is one of the expensive places the wealthy people go to relax for vacations or weekend-long escapes.

I have seen few places so beautiful in my whole life, and back then it was certainly the most marvelous area I had ever visited.

We arrived at the Promenade Maurice Rouvier, a wide,

beautiful street near the ocean. We pulled up to an address hidden behind high white walls and a white iron gate. The driver punched in a code, and the gate opened. We drove through an opening in a hedge of cypress and came to a stop before an enormous white mansion.

"Welcome to my refuge, Lara."

"It's beautiful," I replied, finally finding my voice. I felt much calmer, thanks to the beauty all around me.

We entered the house via the wide-open double front doors and paused in the entrance hall. The marble floor reminded me of a chessboard with its large black-and-white squares. Palm trees planted in vases surrounded the foyer, and a huge, crystal chandelier hung from the ceiling. Two curving staircases—one in white marble to the left and one in black marble to the right—led to the second floor.

Two uniformed maids stood waiting for us.

"Bonjour, monsieur, bonjour, mademoiselle," they chorused.

"Annette, take Mademoiselle Lara to her room." Fabian didn't reply to their greeting.

I sighed inwardly. People who had money but lacked class had always disturbed me.

"Good morning, Annette and—" I looked at the second

maid and raised a brow.

"Caroline, miss," the young girl answered.

"Caroline." I smiled at them both. "It's a pleasure to meet you."

"Lara," Fabian interrupted. "Change your clothes. Put on a bikini, and meet me at the pool."

I looked away so he couldn't see me roll my eyes, thrilled to have yet another man to give me orders... One day, I would be free of all men in the world, and I would do things my way, I promised myself.

I followed Annette upstairs and down a long hallway to a room at the back of the house.

"Here we are, miss." Annette stepped aside to allow me to enter.

For a moment, I stood silent, stunned by the room's magnificent décor and the view of the ocean through the floor-to-ceiling windows along the rear wall. Done in yellow and white, the room glowed, bathed by the sun that was high in the sky, as it was almost noon. A gold metal canopy bed—the mattress covered by a thick white quilt dotted with tiny yellow flowers—occupied most of the available floor space. Two white lacquer chairs and a round table, upon which sat a jar of fresh yellow roses, sat near a set of French doors. A thick white rug covered much of the white marble floor, and I could imagine sinking my bare toes into that plush carpeting when I climbed out of bed in the morning.

I approached the open French doors to gaze out at the most fantastic view of the sea. I took a deep breath, drawing in peace and tranquility from all that natural beauty. By the time I turned back to re-enter the room, I had recovered a deep sense of inner peace.

I took a quick shower in the bathroom, which had the same white marble floor as that in the bedroom and light-yellow cabinets. An antique porcelain bathtub contrasted with the other modern facilities. After washing away the grime from traveling, I chose a pink bikini from my suitcase, slipped it on, and then covered up with a bathrobe I found on a hook on the back of the bathroom door. As I slipped it on, I noticed it still had its ridiculous price tag attached, and I quickly yanked it off and tossed it into the little white ceramic trashcan.

I hurried from the room, thinking Fabian might become angry with me for taking so long, and nearly ran right into Annette. Had she been standing there waiting for me the whole time I had been getting showered and changed?

The maid bobbed her head and smiled. "If you'll follow me, miss, I'll show you down to the swimming pool area." She scurried off without waiting for an answer. If she thought I was Fabian's lover or just a hooker, she didn't let her feelings show but treated me courteously and politely.

I shook my head and hurried after her, worried I might become lost in this great, big house if I were left to find my own way.

Fabian was sitting beneath a cabana near the pool. Dressed in shorts but no shirt, he leaped to his feet as I approached. I let my gaze drift down over his lightly tanned skin. He had a nice body, slim without being too muscular, and I could tell he had a wiry kind of strength, as if he played some kind of sport that required a lot of running around and upper body movement. I later discovered he was a tennis fanatic.

"There you are, my dear." Fabian took my hand and lifted it to kiss the back of my knuckles. "You look wonderful in that shade of pink."

I murmured my thanks and then slipped into the nearest chair without waiting for him to ask me to join him.

Fabian leaned over the table and picked up a bottle of Crystal champagne. After removing the cork, he filled two crystal glasses and gave one to me.

"To the most beautiful girl I have ever met. Thanks for accepting my invitation." He lifted his glass in a toast then took a quick sip.

"Thank you, Fabian," I said, accepting the glass.

"I'll have to thank Arthur for his generosity. When I invited you both, and he told me he couldn't come, I would never have expected him to allow you to come alone."

"We have a very open relationship." What more could I say? Arthur had told me Fabian had invited me and only me. But then again, maybe Fabian was the one lying.

"I can see that! Very modern, indeed… If Arthur wasn't an old shark, I would believe he trusted me with his beloved fiancée…"

At that moment, I decided to put Arthur in the fire.

"He told me the invitation was only for me…and he basically told me I had to come here…"

"I believe you. I just don't understand how he could do that…you deserve more consideration from your fiancé. And yet, you accepted…"

"It's hard to explain our relationship…" I stopped there because I could not find an excuse for a man who loaned out his girlfriend—or whatever title I had—to his friend.

I took a sip of the bubbly champagne while he continued staring down at me silently, until I began to grow uncomfortable. My hands started to shake a little, so I set the glass on the table. The moment I did, Fabian grabbed my hand and yanked me back to my feet. I yelped in surprise, but he pulled me into a tight embrace and devoured my lips. I shivered, having missed his violent kisses. I always felt as if he could suck out my soul with his voracious lips, and my body responded instantly.

"I've missed you, darling, but I didn't want to share you with your fiancé... I had to invite you both, but, to my luck, he is an ambitious bastard..."

So he knew exactly what game Arthur was playing.

"I thought you were friends."

"We have common interests...like you, for example..."

"I'm not a thing."

"Of course, you are not. You are a precious girl. I would steal you from him if you would allow me."

"You just did."

"No...he sent you to me for now...but I know it's not forever...for just one weekend...and I intend to enjoy every minute of it. You intrigue me, Lara. You seem so innocent and young. I still can't figure out if you play along with Arthur or if he is using you, as he does with everybody else..."

What could I say? Tell the truth of my life to another old shark? I just stood there, sipping my champagne.

He positioned himself at my back and started to massage my shoulders, and then he gave me kisses on my neck.

"You have the ability to turn me on like no other woman; all that mystery around you is an aphrodisiac. It seems to me you hide a world of secrets in those green eyes. Come with me."

He led me to the other side of the cabana and opened a door in the back wall. I followed him inside what looked like some kind of a pool house, complete with a bed, a couple couches and tables, and a large TV mounted on one wall.

Without hesitating, Fabian removed my bikini top and bottom and tossed them onto the floor. He then stepped out of his shorts, before pulling me back into his embrace, crushing my breasts against his chest. His hands felt as if they were everywhere, all at once, caressing my body. His expert touch left behind fiery trails, and he used his nails, scraping them up my back and giving me chills. My skin was very sensitive to his touch, and his lips didn't leave my mouth as he continued caressing me, patiently working me into a heightened state of arousal. That was the one thing I admired about him—he was the kind of lover who always took pleasure in giving his partner pleasure. I could tell he took great pride in his achievement every time he made me come.

He pushed me gently back onto the bed, opened my legs, and dove between them, attacking my pussy with his lips and tongue, licking and sucking, caressing me with his fingers, applying just the right pressure to my clit, using just the right stroking rhythm with his tongue until I had a mind-blowing orgasm. I felt as if all the blood in my body was concentrated in my throbbing clit, and my bones felt as if they melting, so great was the physical release of coming.

I decided to repay his kindness, so I climbed from the bed, grabbed his hand, and made him stand. I fell to my knees on the floor in front of him and put his entire cock into my mouth. I tipped back my head, and the first inch or so slipped down my throat. I held his gaze as I took him deep. I sucked him hard, making my tongue dance over his cock as I allowed him to fuck my face. I could see he was reaching his peak as he pushed a little deeper inside me.

"You're a natural at this," he said, "And you make me crazy, but I want to fuck you. There will be plenty of time for me to experience the pleasure of coming in your mouth."

He eased his cock from my mouth and helped me to my feet, then he guided me down onto the mattress, positioning me on all fours. He took the time to cover his shaft in to a condom and entered me from behind, quick and deep, and began ramming in and out as he spanked my buttocks with his hands. The pain and the pleasure melded, and I was about to come when he suddenly withdrew his cock. I fell facedown onto the bed.

Taking advantage of my position, he thrust his finger into my pussy and gathered my juices, and then he used them to lubricate my anus. When he got me good and wet, he positioned himself behind me and drove his dick inside me.

I screamed at the top of my lungs; the pain was unbearable. I shouted and kept shouting, until I slowly began to become accustomed to his invasion. But just as my body had adjusted and agony had turned into a dull ache, he leaned forward and wrapped his hands around my neck and started strangling me. I fought for air and struggled to accept the pain in my ass, but he was strangling me and fucking me violently. Just when I thought I was going to pass out and my mind grew fuzzy, he alleviated the pressure on my neck, put his hands on my clit and rubbed it in a quick, circular motion. At the same time, he increased his pace, ramming his cock in and out of my ass, and to my surprise, I had the most strange and violent orgasm. I felt as if my whole body was connected to his dick, and I felt something like a spark, filling me with the most exquisite energetic sensation.

I cried out again, a sound of pleasure and pain, and he came hard inside me, dropping to slump over my back. The sensations were darkly erotic, so difficult to explain.

The kind that energizes you when you come, but when it's over, you are destroyed, overtired.

"That was amazing. You are so fucking hot, you drive me insane."

"You hurt me," I accused him. My ass felt as if it was on fire, burning from his assault.

Fabian chuckled and shifted to lie beside me. "But you loved it. You know you did. When I squeezed your neck, you couldn't think… The lack of oxygen forced you to focus on what your body was feeling at the time, and that's when you experience the best orgasms. When we simply feel, when we lose control, and we are lost." He shoved his hand between my legs, scooped up some of my juices with his fingers, and then lifted them so I could see. "The evidence is right here," he said. "You can't deny it."

The whole weekend was like that, sessions of savage sex, spanking, strangling me to the brink of unconsciousness, and making me come.

He alternated that behavior with being the kindest man in the world. Outside the bed—or the table or the floor—he was courteous, he tried to learn more about me, asking questions I couldn't answer…not because I was mysterious but because I couldn't answer without revealing my whole situation.

By the time we had packed our luggage for our return

trip I had become completely addicted to mixing pain with my sex. Without Arthur's company, Fabian took time to introduce me in the arts of masochism. I especially loved the sensation of having a man's hands wrapped around my throat.

I didn't know it then, but I'd become a masochist, and that one weekend forever changed my life.

When we arrived back in Paris, Fabian "returned" me to my and Arthur's apartment.

"I want to see you again. I must have you again, Lara," he said, twisting around in his seat to face me."

"I would like to see you again..." I said in a strangled voice...I had to admit I had lost my fear of him, and I was lusting for him, but I had also developed some kind of bond with him. He treated me very well, and he was a completely contradictory man—savage in bed, sweet everywhere else.

"We will..."

I dragged my feet as I walked into our apartment building. Once away from Fabian, I sank back into a state of melancholy—seemed as if I was always sad as a kid. After all, I had no friends, not a single soul I could confide in. Dogged by feelings of guilt, abused, and treated like dirt, I constantly feared what might be lurking around the next corner. What new, terrifying, demeaning surprise would Arthur have for me next? As

I entered our flat, I particularly worried about how he might react. After "lending" me to another man, how would Arthur behave? Would he punish me for complying with his wishes, for following his orders?

Thankfully, I didn't have to face him right away. The apartment was empty, and I released a relieved sigh and headed to my room. But I couldn't shake the nervous fear as I anticipated the next storm, so I made a quick detour into the living room to fix myself a whisky.

I discovered drinking alcohol was a great way to alleviate fear, and I had started drinking every day... All sense of guilt disappeared after a few glasses of whisky or champagne...and I always had at least a glass at bedtime in order to fall asleep. But sometimes, I drank just for the taste of the drink...from liquor to whisky...with ice, cowboy...

Arthur didn't come home until late. I had already fallen asleep, but I woke when I heard him come in. I held my breath as I heard him approach, only releasing it and relaxing after his footsteps passed my room. After several minutes, I felt confident he would leave me alone...at least until morning...and I drifted back into an uneasy sleep.

Nothing lasts forever, they say, and our time in Paris came to an end with a phone call the next day. Arthur's mother was very sick, and he needed to return to Washington immediately. He took the first available flight, and arrangements were made for Sabine to come to take me back home.

Again, my life had turned upside down—one chapter ended, another about to begin. I decided the time had come to put my plans into practice and get rid of Arthur and Sabine...hopefully, for good.

CHAPTER EIGHTEEN

Simone — Present Day

Simone felt bad after reading Lara's account of how she'd become a masochist, but as a professional, Simone understood it had taken much more than a few sessions of deranged sex to change that girl. Her mother's betrayal, the ordeal she had to withstand in order to please her mother, Arthur and all the lunatics around them—Lara had found an escape in pain, turning all the pain she had been through into pleasure...into a way to escape her reality. Under different circumstances, Lara would have been a normal person; masochism had become her way to cope with her reality. If she had to endure pain, her brain changed the experience into one of pleasure. But that was not pleasure; that was sickness.

After another lonely Sunday, on Monday, Simone went into the office, hoping she could speak with Edward. He'd been very distant lately and busy with his FBI-agent girlfriend. Simone missed the close, special relationship she and Ed used to have, missed hanging out with him, and just then, she needed to see him, to hear his voice.

She arrived earlier than usual because she wanted to organize her notes a little bit, and to her surprise, Patricia had arrived even earlier and had organized her desk to perfection.

"Patricia, good morning! Here I was, thinking I'd have at least an hour's worth of paperwork to sort through, but you've already organized everything."

"Good morning, Doctor. Yes, I'm a morning person. I've already left your schedule for the week on your desk. I believe you're going to have your hands full. You have no more than an hour for lunch in the middle of the day, so if you like, I'll be happy to order something for you. Just give me a list of foods you like to eat."

"Well, Monday is a low-carb day for me, so anything will do if it doesn't have carbs."

"Understood!"

Simone went back into her office and took a seat behind her desk. The silver-framed photograph she kept there caught her eye, and she picked it up. A smiling, four-year-old Tammy stared back at her. In the picture, she had her arms wrapped around Simone, hugging her close, but Tammy's face was toward the camera, her little cheek pressed against Simone's. Simone felt a pang of nostalgia. Tammy was much more than just a daughter. Simone had raised the girl to trust her, to be a friend, and she missed her very much. She worried about the idea of Tammy going to college abroad and thought about how good it would be to have her company again...at least for a while...because soon, she was going to college—either in the U.S. or France. And although Simone would be sad, she had to face reality. Kids grew up and moved away from home, and hers wouldn't be any different.

She felt alone, and Tammy's idea of staying abroad had increased that sensation. A sad way to start her week...she never felt so alone before because she'd always known she had Edward nearby, but unfortunately, she was just realizing that now. She didn't think their friendship would ever be the same, and she missed his kindness more than she thought would be possible.

Maybe it was time to really think about finding a boyfriend...but where? All the men she knew who were close to her age were married. Single men over forty tended to turn into lunatics. Divorced men always came with lots of baggage, such as complicated relationships with their ex-wives, and young men didn't interest her.

Armando appeared to be a great guy on the surface, but the more she knew about him, the more she wanted to put a lot of distance between them. That man definitely had issues—this, coming from a psychiatrist who dealt with people's strange habits all day long. She hadn't pinpointed his exact problem yet, but she knew he was not normal. She sighed and set the photograph back on the corner of the desk. She didn't see any clear answer to her situation. Maybe she should consider a cat. But then again, as the joke goes: if no man wants you, why force a poor cat to live with you? Okay, no cat for now.

And there she was, trying to cope with the restless sensation in her chest that life was passing her by, and she was just watching the show and not taking part. But how to change that?

She glanced at her schedule, which lay neatly in the middle of her desk. Patricia had been right...this week looked very busy, every hour filled except for one opening on Wednesday, the slot that used to be Theodora's. Another wave of sad washed over Simone. She didn't want to wait until she was eighty years old to find someone to love. She wanted someone special in her life now.... Yes, she definitively was prepared to love someone... *C'mon, Prince Charming, introduce yourself,* she thought.

She concluded she would start to get out more...try to find someone nice...maybe some wine-tasting lessons...there were always a lot of men at those things. But no... She shook her head. She just wasn't the type to go out looking for men as if she were desperate.

"Enough of these ridiculous thoughts. Time to get to work. Staying busy is always the best remedy for sorrows and pains," she told herself.

She decided to read Lara's journal until her first patient arrived. But as Simone found her place in the journal, she wondered when she was going to face her own life in a way to improve it. With no immediate answer, she got to work.

Lara's Journal

Back to Washington

To return home was not easy as I thought it would be. Although I had been Arthur's property in France, I'd also had a certain amount of freedom and could come and go pretty much as I pleased. I had my schedule, and I even had command of our house. Back home, things were completely different. For one thing, I had to deal with Sabine on a daily basis. She was the boss, and you don't put two lionesses in the same cage... I was happy to once again be near Dad and the kids, but I couldn't touch them. As a girl in my late teens, I didn't know how to hug people or how to receive affection; I was always worried how people would read my gestures, and I had a hard time touching people. I could have sex, but I couldn't do intimacy or tenderness.

Emms was still forbidden to come to the house, but I could meet her outside if I wanted to. However, I couldn't face her...I felt so ashamed about everything I had done, and I was positive she'd be able to read it on my face, or she would guess...and I couldn't trust her or anybody with my secret. Besides, Emm's was a very affectionate person, and I couldn't deal with that.

Arthur had an apartment, and we met there, which was good, in a way, because I didn't have to be around him all the time. However, it was also strange—and this is a little hard to explain or to understand—because I missed being near him sometimes.

The worst part was going back to school. Kids my age were...kids...and I was emotionally an adult, having lived the life I'd lived in France and having experienced the things I'd experienced. I really didn't know what to say to other people my age. I didn't dress like they did, and I felt like an alien as I listened to them gossip about boys and parties. So not a part of my world... I suffered a wave of sad amusement when I considered what I might say to them. *So, do you like to be strangled while you have anal sex, too?*

I felt lost...so lost I would search the sky to see if the mother ship had returned for me. I was displaced, and worse, I really couldn't concentrate. But I started implementing my plan and posted an ad on the school bulletin board, offering to tutor other kids in French. Four days later, my first student contacted me when I was leaving the class.

He was a boy from my school, a tall kid, taller than I was but around my age, and he wore glasses. He was handsome but in a different way. He had a shy but handsome smile, his hair was black, his eyes dark brown, and his skin was as fair as a baby's, as if he never had been out in the sun.

He was outside the class, waiting for me.

"Hello, my name is Oscar." He extended his long hand in greeting.

"Hi, Oscar, my name is Lara." I took his hand but released it quickly, unable to bare much contact with people back then.

"Nice to meet you, Lara. I'm interested in the French tutoring sessions you advertised. Do you really speak French? Where did you learn it?"

"Let's sit on that bench"—I pointed to a bench under a nearby tree—"and I'll explain."

"Sure."

We sat on the bench, and he turned to me, seemingly very interested in what I had to say.

"I was in France until last week, and I studied there," I told him.

"So you really know the language."

"Yes, I do!"

We continued talking, and he became my first student and my first real friend in life. Not in the common sense of the word "friendship" because that would have included a level of trust and affection I wasn't capable of expressing in those days, but I discovered I needed him much more than he needed tutoring in French. He was smart, and he would often explain to me in very easy and funny ways about things I had trouble learning during class because I was always daydreaming about other people, places, and things.

We hung out together at school all the time...and I remember my heart feeling heavy whenever I had to leave him to go meet Arthur or to go home. Oliver was always making me laugh, and I recall thinking it had been a really long time since I'd had a good laugh. I felt like a teenager again when I was with him, and although there was nothing sexual between the two of us, we developed a real friendship. He tended to act a little immature, as boys his age often did, but even that made me laugh. He was so full of dreams, and I didn't have any left.

We were sitting on the grass near the school lake, a spot we both loved to visit, both with our legs crossed.

"What do you want to be when you grow up, Oscar?" I asked him one day.

"Grow up? Who said anything about growing up? I never want to get old!"

" Be serious!"

"I am serious, Giraffe," he said, using the nickname he'd given me due to my height.

"We are the two giraffes! And you definitely look like one."

He was skinny, and he had a long neck.

"Want a mirror?" He contorted his neck in a very funny way, imitating a giraffe.

I shook my head and laughed. We spent a lot of time together, being silly kids, mocking each other.

I had the good sense not to tell anybody about him. He was my secret, and God knows I'd become good at keeping secrets.

I used to go to school, and then afterward, I'd meet Arthur at his apartment for a session of sex. Not every day, because he was working at his family's bank, and he had a busy schedule...and also because I could feel a decrease of interest from him. And besides, in the U.S., we couldn't risk being seen together; people might start asking questions.

I missed him when we were apart, and I hated him whenever we were together. Talk about a confusing situation!

One afternoon, some twenty days after my return, afternoon classes were canceled. I don't remember why, but I recall I had decided to go to Arthur's apartment a little earlier than normal that day. He wouldn't be there until after 5:00 p.m., and I was in the mood to be alone somewhere quiet. At home, I never had any privacy. The kids were always messing around.

I had my own key to Arthur's place, and when I arrived and opened the door, I heard voices. I paused to listen, recognizing the speakers as Sabine and Arthur. They were talking in the guestroom, and I crept down the hallway, wondering what they were doing back there. When I reached the door, I peeked inside to see them lying on the bed, both of them naked.

I spun around and left quickly without them realizing I'd ever been there, making my way back outside in a state of shock. Sabine was betraying my father, but not with Arthur. The voice I'd thought was his actually belonged to his father, my uncle Ruggierio. How could he, I wondered? His wife was very sick with cancer, and he was off fucking Sabine!

Shaken, I called Arthur to tell him I was going to go directly home. I was feeling sick. I really was. I knew Sabine was a scumbag, but I hadn't known how deep that bag was.

I didn't say a word about what I'd seen to anyone. I didn't know whom to trust. I tried to put what I'd witnessed out of my mind, but the next day, I couldn't think about anything else. At lunchtime, Oscar came to my empty table to sit and eat with me as he usually did.

"Hello, Miss Distracted... I bet you didn't hear a word the teachers said in class today. Where were you? Back in Paris?"

I frowned and shook my head, fighting back angry tears.

"Hey," he said. "Are you okay?"

"No...I'm not okay..."

Oscar tried to take my hand, but I pulled away.

"Tell me what's going on," he insisted. "I can see something is really bugging you."

I knew I could trust him, and I had to trust somebody, or I would explode, so I took a deep breath and told him.

"My mother is having an affair..."

"How do you know that?"

How could I explain without telling him about Arthur,

his "love nest", and all the rest?

"I saw her yesterday kissing one of my father's friends," I told him. "I don't know what to do!"

"You have to tell your father!"

I shook my head. Bad idea... "He won't believe me; he trusts her..."

"So then you need proof. I have a camera...it's a Polaroid. It's not very good, but you can try to catch her with that...I can help you."

In that moment, an Idea formed in my mind. If I had proof of Sabine's betrayal, I would have her in the palm of my hand. The following week, I borrowed Oscar's camera and went whenever I could to Arthur's apartment, but they never showed up.

"They are not meeting at the same place," I told Oscar.

"I'll bet they meet on a specific day of the week... Next week, go there on the same day you saw them this past week."

And once more, the smart kid was right. I went back to Arthur's on the same day—a Wednesday—that next week, and the two lovebirds were there. As I entered the apartment, I could hear them back in the bedroom giggling. Once again, I crept down the hallway, but they'd closed the door this time. I stood and thought a moment, then decided I had no other choice. I eased it open, holding my breath and praying it wouldn't squeak. I had no idea what I'd do if they saw me. My heart beat fast, and my hands were shaking as I looked inside. They were having sex, so wrapped up in each other they didn't notice me. I quickly took a picture and then got the hell out of there as fast as I could.

The picture showed Sabine's face to perfection, but her lover's was hidden, pressed into the crook of her neck. But that wouldn't be a problem; his almost white hair was recognizable. I hid the picture in the same hole I used to hide my diary in my room, but at the moment, I didn't know how I would proceed. Still, I had my first weapon to defeat Sabine.

Another month would pass before I figured out what to do.

I never really considered all the consequences—I simply knew I had to escape Sabine's and Arthur's control. I couldn't die their slave. I didn't know how I would feel afterward, how my life would be, but I sensed I'd lose everything, and that was the reason I put off bringing things to a head. In the meantime, I continued gathering my courage, money, and jewels—even though Arthur was not that generous now that we were back home. I kept making excuses for not using the picture, but finally, one day, things changed.

CHAPTER NINETEEN

Simone – Present Day

Simone´s phone alarm pulled her from the world of Lara. In few minutes, her first patient would arrive. She had a few minutes to send a message to Carl, telling him where she was on the story and giving him her thoughts on what she had read the last few days. She recorded a voice message and sent it to Carl through *What's App*.

Lara´s life was a nightmare with no daylight between one bad dream and another, she thought. The girl had been through hell since she was a kid. Simone spent most of her time reading hoping things would change for the girl. At least she was back with her family and

Arthur had less control over her.

Simone sighed and focused her attention on her next patient's file.

* * * * *

Philip, her first patient that morning, arrived on time, a smile on his face and a little box in his hand. She had to admit, if only to herself, that she grew excited at the sight of those little pastry boxes of his. Each week, he baked her some new, sugary delight, and although she never ate them, they gave her the sense of being home.

"Doctor, I baked these cookies bright and early this morning. I even made the praline—entirely homemade." He set the box on the edge of her desk and took a seat in the chair across from her.

"Thank you very much, Philip! I can see you're pretty happy today."

"Oh, I am. I'm worried about the hearing, sure, but I'm happy, too. I broke up with Leonora, and I'm back with my wife!" He lifted his left hand and wiggled his ring finger, proudly displaying his wedding band back in place.

"In the blink of an eye... What changed?"

"Well, I was honest about my feelings with Leonora, and she was very understanding...well, to tell the truth, she threw the whole house at my head, but I survived...

Then I went to my wife's apartment and told her to pack her bags because this nonsense of hers was over, and she needed to come home."

"And what did she say?"

He grinned. "She asked me what took me so long to come after her!"

"That's good if you're happy, but did she leave her...boyfriend?"

He nodded. "We reached an agreement. I will allow them to fuck if I can watch, but only at home and under my supervision... And the two of them cannot develop an emotional attachment. It's a good arrangement, and we already had our first encounter. He came home with us Saturday, and we had some beers together. He's a funny guy."

Back to normal? Yes...that was Philip's idea of a normal life...

"And?" she asked.

"And after a few hours of just socializing, I started to kiss my wife, and I invited him to join us. It was sensational!" He acted as if he was describing a basketball game or something. "All the other times, I watched her, or she was alone with other guys, and I listened, but to be actually take part—that was amazing."

In his excitement, he was literally spitting his words, and Simone casually relocated to a chair a little farther away from him, claiming she needed a firmer place to sit. *It's either this,* she thought, *or I grab my umbrella.*

"We kissed her together, our tongues tangling inside her mouth, and then we both sucked one of her breasts... I let him fuck her first, and since they'd had an affair already, we agreed he wouldn't use a condom... And oh-my-god, that was so incredible for me because he came inside her, and I could see his cum in her pussy, which turned me on, and I felt like a mad man."

You are mad... No thoughts about AIDS, STDs, nothing?

"I fucked her so hard, and he was sucking her breasts, and she was coming and coming, and suddenly, when I came, the three of us were entangled, and we just stayed that way, cuddling, and we slept together that night! The next day, he thanked me for sharing her. I believe it's a great deal we have!"

"*I* believe you're trying to learn how to share Mommy, but your wife isn't your mommy. She is the love of your life, as you've always claimed, so why share?"

"I've been thinking, Doctor...maybe this is just what I need to become really excited...it's not a disease or a result of some trauma..."

"It stems from a trauma, definitely, but if you're happy, truly happy, we can consider it a way of life..."

"I'm thankful to have my wife back. I confess I felt a pang of jealousy when I watched her with her boyfriend, but then when I saw him leave, and she was still with me, well, I felt gratitude..."

"For being left with the crumbs? Can't you think about having the whole cake?"

"What do you mean?"

"Maybe you don't have to share your wife, Philip...maybe you could talk, and try a normal marriage, just between the two of you. You already lost her once, and in my opinion, she left you because she doesn't like to be shared or borrowed. She wants to be important to you."

"She is my world!"

"But you are not telling her that when you say it's okay to share her with another guy..."

"Sex is so good when I do that!"

"I can believe it...you achieve the satisfaction of the pain sadomasochism brings to you... I'm just not sure your wife is really okay with all that, regardless of what she might be telling you now..."

"What do you suggest, Doctor?"

"How about bringing her the next time? I would like to talk to both of you together…"

He nodded. "Okay. I'll ask her. Maybe that's a good idea…"

"Talk to her, Philip. I want to hear both sides on this subject."

They talked about the hearing, which was schedule for the following week, and Simone promised she would be there to support him. He also showed her the results of his follow-up drug test, and he was absolutely clean—no trace of any controlled substances.

He left, and Simone barely had time to make notes in his file before the next patient came in. And that was her week—dealing with patients and troubled minds, dealing with self-pity over being alone and over her daughter wanting to be away for much longer than planned.

* * * * *

Wednesday afternoon, Simone talked to the general again, via Skype. He seemed more relaxed, and to her amazement, he was wearing a t-shirt! He was always a formal kind of man, and suddenly, he seemed younger and more at ease… Even his hair was different.

"Good afternoon, Cezar, how've you been?"

"Great, Dr. Bennet. How about you?"

"Fine, thanks. You seem happier…"

"I am! Very much so. But I'm also very worried…"

"What happened to make you happy and worried at the same time?"

"Tereza! I followed your advice. By the way, I'm in Paraguay right now. I came back home, and I called Teresa, and I told her I had to have a serious talk with her. Doctor, she is prettier than ever!"

"And how was the chat?"

"I told her everything… I thought about it a lot, and I came to a decision. I'm an old man, and this may be my last chance for happiness. I had fifty percent chance of hearing a no…but I also had fifty percent of chance of hearing her say yes. So I told her everything, that I couldn't get her out of my mind, and I wanted to know why she had left me…"

"Did she explain?"

"Yes! She told me she wouldn't settle for leftovers— that she doesn't want another woman's man. She was in love with me, but she loved herself more, and she wouldn't live her life in the shadows. She wants it all, me—all to herself—or nothing!"

To Simone, Tereza seemed to want what a normal and

reasonable person wanted from a relationship. *At least someone is a little normal,* she thought.

"And how about you?"

His shoulders slumped. "That's what's disturbing me...what should I do? Divorce? Embrace a life with a woman years younger than me? Leave my family? I have grandkids! But I promised her I'd do exactly that, and now...I don't know what to do!"

Why would you promise if you didn't know you could keep your word? Simone closed her eyes and counted to five.

"Doctor?"

She opened her eyes again. "Yes, Cezar. Let me ask you a question. If you knew you were going to die tomorrow, or better yet, at the end of the week, would you divorce your wife for Teresa?"

"Of course I would, but that's not the case! I don't love my wife anymore. I haven't loved her in a very long time. But we have a family...and I respect her... It's not that simple..."

"I'm going to give you some news, here, Cezar... You don't know when you are going to die, okay? So enjoy your life the best you can. Live as if every day is the last day. Let me tell you something that happened this weekend...one of my patients...she was eighty, and she had just met the love of her life...and then she died. Not from any disease or illness...this happened unexpectedly. Can you imagine if she had decided she was too old to love? She would have spent the few months she had left alone and sad. At least she died happy, loving and living."

"Very philosophical, Doctor, but not very practical... I have properties. I will have to share..."

"If you leave with fifty percent of what you have, wouldn't that be enough for you to have a good life?"

"Half of what I have would be enough for at least four lifetimes..."

"So, think about what is more important to you. It's a matter of values...what do you value more? Your children are always going to be your children, and besides, they are not children anymore. Do you want Teresa and do you want to live a love story? It's all about measuring what is more important for you."

"Ah, Tereza...and it worked, Doctor! You were right..."

"What worked?"

"My dick! When she arrived at our meeting, he greeted her...he stood up for her like the gentleman he is, and he remained hard all the time I was near her."

Simone coughed to cover a chuckle, imagining a cock wearing a military kepi, standing at attention.

"I love that woman. I love her scent, I love her body, I love her mind! And she is a devil; she is not going to give in to me until I'm divorced!"

"So...you have to make a decision. Think well, Cezar, life is short, and coffins don't have pockets..."

Simone suddenly realized what she had said. What was happening to her? *I'm going crazy,* she thought, *telling something like that to a patient.* Maybe Theodora's death had shaken her more than she thought.

"You are right! I'm going to think about that..."

They talked for another half an hour, with the general listing all of Tereza's finest qualities, and then he suddenly changed the subject, his expression turning serious.

"Doctor...I have to tell you something here...I've been informed my son has been wooing you..."

More like stalking, she thought. "Well... I'm not sure what to say to that, Cezar..."

Her face grew hot. She had to do something to put an end to that—this mixing of her personal life with her professional life was growing beyond her limits.

"Well, I hope you're not considering him... I have to tell you, Armando is a good boy, but he is weird when it comes to women. He is always the Don Juan or the dog..."

"The dog?"

"Yes, wagging his tale and humiliating himself if the women don't want him..."

"And if they do?"

"He runs like hell. He says when they are too eager, you mustn't trust them because it's either rotten or it's burned—no one offers a good meal for free like that."

Like a piece of meat, good way to think about women, Simone reflected, but she also silently thanked the general for his information...he had just given her an idea of how she could get rid of Armando...

"I really don't intend to pursue a relationship with your son, Cezar. It was a summer fling, but it's over."

"I have to warn you...that's not what he's telling people. He is telling everybody he has found the love of his life...so I'm worried he is going to stalk you..."

Too late... He was already making her life hell, but she kept her thoughts to herself, unwilling to share her problems with a client. "I can handle him," she said, as much to herself as to the general.

Simone said goodbye to Cezar and then decided to finish the day reading another chapter of Lara´s incredible journey.

Lara´s Journal

One afternoon, Arthur told me to go to the apartment. When I arrived, to my surprise, he was there with another man. Since we'd left Paris, we'd only had sex together—just the two of us...no third party. The moment I entered the room and saw the guy, a man much older than Arthur was, I could sense the sexual energy in the air. The guy had a round belly hanging over his waistline and almost no hair. Big lips dominated his round face, and I shuddered. Not in a million years would I fuck that aberration.

"Come here, honey, I want to introduce you to James, a friend of mine."

"Hello, James." I spoke from a distance, refusing to approach the sofa where they were sitting and sipping on some kind of alcoholic drinks.

The man ignored my hello and talked to Arthur.

"My friend, she is a beauty."

"Help yourself...her skin is as soft as velvet, you will see."

Arthur just offered me up like a piece of meat—a habit he'd developed during our time in France. But he had never chosen a man like that one, and it made me nauseated just to think about James putting his hands on me.

"No, Arthur, I won't let him touch me."

Arthur looked at me with a very surprised expression. "Sure you will. Let's put this collar on you."

He had a dog collar he used with me when we were in France, and he rose up and came in my direction.

"No way! I told you! He is disgusting."

"Shut up, you little bitch! You belong to me; you do as I tell you to do! Come here."

"Arthur, if she doesn't want to, don't insist. I would not have a woman against her will..."

"She is just playing hard to get, James, don't worry."

"I'm not! I don't want you!" I screamed at the man.

Arthur came to me, grabbed me by my arm, and threw me toward the sofa. "Touch her!"

"No, Arthur, sorry, my friend, but I won't take part in this."

He got up to leave, and I could see Arthur was furious.

"She is just a bitch. We can have her whenever we want. She is well paid for her services."

I couldn't bare his name-calling any longer; I was no

bitch!

"I'm not. I'm not a bitch. I'm a student!"

"Arthur, I'm leaving now," said the man. He looked at me. "Are you going to be okay, girl? Wanna come with me?"

"She stays!" Arthur shouted before I could answer.

As soon as the man left, Arthur grabbed me by the hair and dragged me into the bedroom and to his bed. I fought him with everything I had. I wouldn't allow him to touch me, not today. Today, my courage was with me; today, he made me feel more degraded than I could imagine it was possible to feel, and so I fought. He was stronger than I was, and he tore my blouse and raised my pleated skirt and ripped off my panties.

He was crazy; I could see that. I think he was under the influence of some sort of narcotic, because I had never seen him like that before. I fought hard, and he punched me in the face for the first time since our sick relationship started. He hit me with a closed fist, and I passed out with the pain. When I woke up, I was alone in the apartment, and it was dark. I had semen between my legs. He had raped me while I was passed out! My survival instincts told me it was time to finish this. Before he killed me or I murdered him; he was becoming violent, and something bad would happen.

I saw my face in the foyer mirror on my way out the

door, and I gasped. My eye was swollen, my face all red, my hair in total disarray. I combed my hair with my fingers, arranged my clothes as best I could, and left the apartment.

When I arrived downstairs at the front door, the doorman didn't ask me what happened; he simply turned his face away, but I wasn't surprised. Life, I had already learned, was like this sometimes. Some people turned away from things that disturbed them. As I stepped out onto the sidewalk, more concerned with how I would get home, the door of a nearby parked car opened, and James called out to me from inside.

"Come here, girl, I will take you where you want to go. What did he do to you? Sorry, it's my fault. He told me he had a great hooker...but you are so young... Here, let me take you home."

I was in no condition to deny him or to reply. I climbed into his car, gave him the address, and he left me off in front of my house. I had forgotten the keys and had to ring the bell. Just my luck, my father opened the door to me, and I could no longer hold back my emotions. As if a dam had broken, my tears started to roll down my face. I couldn't talk, I was sobbing so hard. He took my hand and led me to my room, gave me a glass of water, and patiently listened to me.

I told my father everything. I couldn't pretend anymore. I told him everything that had happened from day one—about Arthur's invitations for ice creams, about our trip to Paris—only leaving out the part about Adrien and the other men Arthur and I had sex with. I don't know why I kept those things secret, but I did.

I was crying so much, sobbing, and he was just listening, and when I finished the story, he sighed.

"Why didn't you talk to me or to your mother? To Emms? You always loved her. Your mother took you to France. She could have prevented you from going, babe."

The moment I feared most in life had arrived, but I had to tell him the truth. I didn't have the strength to lie anymore.

"I told Sabine…she was the first person I told, that first day Arthur touched me…and she slap me and told me I was a liar. Again, when he rapped me, I told her, and she called me the guilty one and said I had to have sex with him whenever he wanted me to because his family helped us. I told her I was going to tell you and Emms, and you were going to stop him from touching me, but she told me…"

I couldn't finish my sentence. I started to sob again, hard. That was the moment I feared most in my life, the moment of the truth. My father hugged me and waited for me to calm down again.

"What did she tell you, Lara?" he asked after a bit.

413

"That I'm not your daughter…she was pregnant with someone else's baby, and the man wouldn't marry her…so she chose you… I'm not your daughter, and she said she would tell you everything, and I would lose you, Emms, and the kids. She said she was going to send me to live with Sheila!"

"My God, Lara, what we did to you! Forgive me, baby, for being an absent father. How could I have not seen all those things going on right under my nose? Lara, love, you are my daughter; you look exactly like your grandmother. Your mother lied to you. You are my oldest and dearest daughter, and I love you so much, please forgive me!"

My father was crying, and I realized he'd always trusted in me and would have never doubted my word. He believed in me, and he told me I was his daughter!

We hugged each other and cried together for a while, and I felt safe in his arms.

But then Sabine arrived…

"What happened here? Are you both okay?" she asked, striding into the room.

"What do you think, Sabine? Are we supposed to be okay?"

"Well, I don't see why not. Everything was okay this morning." And then she saw my bruise. "What happened to your face, Lara? Did you get into a fistfight?"

She looked back and forth between my dad and me, and I could tell she was starting to get worried as she tried to guess what had happened. Then suddenly, my father leaped to his feet and grabbed her by her neck.

"I'm going to kill you, Sabine; I'm going to kill you with my bare hands!"

My mother screamed and began to struggle. A maid rushed in and tried to help Sabine, and I jumped in between her and my father, trying to separate them. The last thing we needed was my father going to jail for killing that reptile. She wasn't worth it.

My father regained his senses and backed away.

"You disgusting excuse for a human being," he shouted at her. "How could you do such a thing? To your own daughter! You sold our daughter!"

"I don't know what she has been telling you, but she's lying!" Sabine said, trying to defend herself without knowing exactly what I'd revealed. "Everything she told you is a great, big lie!"

For a moment, I worried my father would believe her, but then I remembered how I'd felt when he'd wrapped his arms around me, and I straightened my spine.

"And your affair with Uncle Ruggierio?" I asked her. "Is

415

that also a lie?"

Both my parents fell silent for a moment, and then Sabine turned on me and tried to hit me. I ran over to my dresser and got down on my knees to open the hole in the back of it. I withdrew the Polaroid picture and took it to my father.

He stood there, staring at the photograph for several long moments, and then he took Sabine by the arm and hurried her out of my bedroom and down the hall to theirs. Their bedroom door slammed, and for the next twenty minutes or so, I listened to them shout and cry. After that, the house fell silent.

I stayed in my room, not knowing what else to do. A maid brought me dinner, but I couldn't eat. Thankfully, she also brought me ice for my face, which helped ease the pain a great deal. Afterward, I slept. I'd learned to sleep deeply in order to escape from reality. When I was in big trouble or very upset about something, I could disappear into my dreams.

I awoke the next morning to Emms entering my room. She was carrying a breakfast tray, and she smiled at me as she set it down on the bed beside me. *I must be dreaming,* I thought, but she sat with me on my bed and caressed my hair, and then leaned in and hugged me. I let her hold me, and I started to cry again, suddenly all the repressed emotions of those years were back and I couldn't stop the tears.

"Cry all you want, Lara. I will be here forever. You don't need to talk. I just want to tell you I love you, and I'm your grandmother, and nothing in this world can change that. I promise I will do my best to keep you safe! I'm so sorry you felt as if you couldn't trust me, so sorry I couldn't protect you as I should have, but I won't fail you again!"

"I love you too, Emms, I'm so sorry I had to lie to you and Dad. I was so afraid I'd lose you!"

"Don't talk, little one. I know everything I have to know. You don't need to tell me anything you don't want to. I'm here for you now."

"Where is...she?"

"Sabine left the house, baby, and she won't be coming back."

CHAPTER TWENTY

Simone – Present Day

Simone felt a sense of relief as she read about the end of Lara's parents' marriage. *Poetic justice,* she thought. She sent a message to keep Carl, updating him on her progress, and then decided to go home to rest. She deserved a break after such a long day. As she left her office, she was surprised to feel a wave of happiness, brought on by the turn in Lara's circumstances. She always had gotten a rush when good triumphed over evil!

* * * * *

On Wednesday, after another busy day at the office,

Simone was preparing to leave in order to attend Philip's hearing when Patricia buzzed on the intercom.

"Doctor, there's a woman on the phone. She says her name is Nora, and she's Philip's wife. She wants to talk to you. I wasn't going to bother you, but she sounds very distraught."

"Okay. Yes. Go ahead and put her through. Thank you, Patricia."

Simone hung up the phone, and a moment later, a call came through on line one. Simone punched the button and picked up the handset. "Hello? This is Dr. Bennet. Can I help you?"

"Oh, thank God I reached you. You don't know me, but I know how good you are for Philip. I'm in the hospital with him, and the doctor just told me he's dead! I don't understand what's happening here. No one will tell me anything else, and they won't let me in to see him. How is this possible? He simply can't be dead! Could you come here? I have no one else to call. You're a doctor. They'll have to explain what happened to you!"

Simone felt as if someone had punched her in the stomach. Philip was dead? Impossible! The sound of his wife sobbing over the phone line broke through Simone's shocked silence, and she gathered her wits enough to try to calm the poor woman.

"I'm glad you called me. Which hospital did you say you

were at?"

"Yale New Haven," Nora said, "Please, Doctor, can you come?"

"Yes...yes, of course, I'll be right there." Simone checked her watch. Traffic shouldn't be too bad this time of day. "Give me twenty minutes, okay?"

Nora mumbled something that sounded like "hurry", and then the line went dead.

Simone grabbed her purse and keys and left the office in a hurry. She drove as fast as she could, her mind racing with thoughts of what could have possibly happened to Philip. How on Earth could he be dead? Maybe his wife was mistaken. Maybe he was merely unconscious...or even in a coma... But no, that made no sense, either. The doctors wouldn't have told his wife he'd died if he hadn't... God...how could this be? She hadn't thought to ask Nora where she'd be waiting. Yale New Haven Hospital was a pretty large facility. Had Philip been taken to the ER? Simone couldn't remember Nora mentioning anything about calling 9-1-1.

After parking her car in the emergency department lot, she rushed through the sliding double doors and approached the front desk, digging in her purse for her wallet. She introduced herself to the receptionist and showed her credentials.

"I'm here to see about a patient who was brought in

earlier today," Simone said and gave the woman Philip's full name. "Can you tell me which section of the hospital he's in?"

The attendant, a middle-aged woman with a kind, round face, typed a few words on her keyboard and then nodded. "Yes. Here he is. Second floor, Vascular Neurology. Looks like Doctor McMillan is in charge up there at the moment."

"Thank you." Simone turned and headed for the bank of elevators at the far end of the emergency room waiting area. Vascular Neurology? What in God's name had happened to poor Philip?

The elevator doors opened and Simone stepped inside. She pressed the button for the second floor and leaned against the wall, her knees suddenly going rubbery. She closed her eyes and took a couple slow, deep breaths in an effort to pull herself together. The doors swished open, and she stepped out. The atmosphere up there was completely different from the emergency department. The lights were a little dimmer, and the seating area was empty except for a petite woman with short dark-brown hair and large brown eyes. She looked lost and very fragile, occupying a chair among many empty chairs, and she was sobbing softly into a wadded-up tissue. Simone approached her carefully.

"Nora?" she said.

The woman lifted her head, but her expression

remained blank. She blinked wide, tear-filled eyes.

"Hello, I'm Doctor Bennet. We spoke on the phone just a little bit ago?"

Nora leaped to her feet and threw herself into Simone's arms with a cry of despair. Simone awkwardly patted the woman's back and tried to comfort her the best she could, but she was shaken by the news, and wanted more details. When Nora calmed a little bit, Simone disentangled herself from the woman's embrace and took a tiny step back.

"Why don't we sit down?" she said, and helped Nora back into her chair. "Can you tell me what happened? How did Philip end up in the hospital?"

"I don't know. Everything was fine—we were at home, and he was working in some papers in his office, and then suddenly, he said he wasn't feeling well. We waited a little while, but he started getting worse, so I insisted we come here...and then the next thing I know, some doctor is telling me they think my Philip had an aneurysm...but then they said they aren't sure..." Nora began sobbing again, her small body shaking in her chair.

"An aneurysm?" Simone whispered. They could happen to anyone at any age, but Philip? Simone couldn't believe it. Life truly wasn't fair. She was angry at the universe. "I'm going to find the doctor. I'll be right back."

Simone left Nora sitting in the waiting area and went in search of Dr. McMillan, whom she knew, as they were colleagues, and he was also a professor at Yale. She found him signing some papers in his office.

The door was open, but she knocked anyway.

"Hello, Charles."

He looked up.

"Simone Bennet! How are you?" Charles straightened and held out a hand. "Haven't seen you around in a while. Enter, please "

"Yes...I've been...I took a leave of absence," Simone told him, shaking his hand. Charles was an exceptionally handsome man, and he had one of those calm, deep voices that immediately put his patients at ease.

"My patient, Philip Raymond was brought in earlier. His wife called me to say he'd just died. She's extremely distraught, and to be honest with you, I'm pretty shaken up, too. Can you tell me what happened? Nora—his wife—said she was told he'd suffered an aneurism!"

"Ah, yes. I'm afraid it's all a bit of a mystery. He arrived here several hours ago, and emergency thought he'd had an aneurysm, so they sent him to us, but less than half an hour later, he was dead. We did our best to help him, but I'm afraid he didn't die of an aneurism... I believe he may have overdosed."

"An overdose? Of what?" Simone thought about Philip's LSD episode, but she decided to remain silent. At least, for now.

"We still don't know for sure. We're going to send him to autopsy..."

"Autopsy?"

"Yes, any time a physician suspects a patient died of an overdose, we have to check. You know...he has insurance, and so..."

"Sure, but is it possible the ER doctors were right, and he had an aneurism? He wasn't an addict."

"The chances are slim, I'm afraid. But as I said, once they've completed the autopsy, we'll know for certain."

Simone really hated doctors. She was one of them, but when she was on the receiving end, a physician's calmness was disturbing. "I suppose I should go tell his wife. I don't know how she's going to feel about all this." *And I don't know how I'm going to keep calm enough to give her the news when I'm torn up inside, too.*

"I understand. Death is difficult even when it's expected. Something sudden like this...well, I imagine his wife is a mess." Charles shook his head.

Her and I both, Simone thought. "Thank you for filling me in, Charles. I'll talk to you later."

Simone headed back into the neurology waiting area. Although she dreaded telling Philip's wife what she'd learned, Simone felt as if she owed Philip at least that much. She was heartbroken...her chest ached, and she had trouble drawing a full breath. None of this seemed real to her... She had really loved Philip and would miss him and his stories and his pastries like hell. She wiped the tears from her eyes so Philip's wife wouldn't see them.

Nora was in the same spot she'd been in when Simone had gone to talk to Charles, still. Simone approached, sat by her side, and touched her shoulder.

"Nora...I know how difficult this must be for you," she said. "You and Philip had only just gotten back together..."

Nora raised her head and looked at Simone. "We were both so happy, Doctor... I can't understand how fate can be so miserable...so evil to take someone like Philip. He was the best of the best!"

Simone took Nora's small hands in hers, looked at her, and said, "He really was a good man, and he loved you very much. I can tell you he loved you more than anything."

"Thank you for saying that, Doctor." She started to sob all over again.

Nora was inconsolable; nothing Simone said seemed to

make things better, and in fact, when Simone informed her about the autopsy, the situation grew worse.

"Why are they are going to cut him into pieces? He's not a junkie! I know my Philip. The man didn't do drugs!"

"I know...but it's a formality; they have to rule out an overdose...for insurance purposes..."

"I don't care about insurance! I care about not having my man cut into pieces!"

"It's not like that! Calm down, Nora," Simone patted the woman's hand. "It's actually a good thing to know what caused his death."

Nora stopped arguing, but she continued to cry as if she'd never stop.

"You should go home," Simone told her. "Get some rest. There's nothing more you can do here. Not now."

Nora shook her head. "No. I don't want to leave him all alone here..."

"Oh, honey...he's not here anymore. That's just his body down there...the vessel that held Philip's spirit." Simone paused then asked, "Nora, do you believe in God? In Heaven?"

"Of course." Nora sniffed. "Doesn't everyone?"

No...actually, Simone thought, *some of us don't.* But she needed to calm Nora down, and so Simone kept her thoughts about the existence of God to herself. "Well, then you know Philip isn't down there on that autopsy table, right? He's in Heaven, and he's not in any pain, and he wouldn't want you sitting here crying your eyes out, would he?"

Nora sniffled some more. "I... I suppose you're right. I hadn't thought of that..."

Simone sighed. "Good. Then let me walk you out to your car, okay? You did drive here, didn't you? Or did you ride in the ambulance?"

"I drove." Nora sighed. "Gosh, that seems like days ago now."

Simone knew the feeling. "Come on. Let's go home. The doctors will call you when they have the autopsy results."

After walking Nora to her car, Simone circled around the hospital, her head spinning as she tried to find a reasonable explanation for Philip's death. She approached her car, wincing at the terrible job she'd done parking when she'd arrived earlier. Her vehicle took up two spaces in the emergency department's parking area. Thank god they hadn't had the damn thing towed. She unlocked the door and climbed inside, fastened her seatbelt, and put the key in the ignition, but then her hands started shaking. Her whole body started shaking, and she hugged herself and sat hunched over, forehead resting on the steering wheel.

The floodgates opened, and she began to cry, awash in waves of sadness and anger over the loss of one of her dearest patients, over how stupid life could be sometimes. Her anguished sobs came from her soul, and she didn't try to stop the tears. No one needed her to be strong now, and she was tired of being the tough one all the time.

Some time later, she lifted her head and looked around. The sun was on its way down, and she heaved a sigh, considering she should take her own advice and go home and get some rest. A little calmer—calm enough to drive, at any rate—she started her car and pulled out of the lot, but she cried the whole way home.

* * * * *

On Thursday morning, feeling the heavy weight of reality, Simone resumed her normal daily activities. Her heart still ached...as if something were crushing her chest. Her eyes were red and swollen from crying so damn much. She had literally cried herself to sleep the night before, and makeup and concealer wasn't enough to cover the dark circles and blotches on her cheeks.

When she arrived at her office, she met Edward in the hall. He took one look at her and shook his head.

"Oh, Simmie...I am so sorry. I heard about your patient." He opened his arms. "Come here. You look terrible."

Sobbing, she threw herself into Edward's embrace and buried her face against his shoulder. He hugged her close, caressing her hair and telling her everything was going to be all right.

God, it was so good to be back in Edward's arms. She had missed him so much. He could calm her like no other person in the world. But when her tears subsided a little, he disentangled himself from her embrace, albeit gently, and took a half-step back, putting some space between them again.

"Okay now?" he asked her, his hands resting on her shoulders as he looked her in the eyes.

Although she'd love nothing more than to spend the day in his arms, buoyed by his kindness and supportiveness, she straightened and stepped back a little.

"Um. Yes. I'm okay." But her voice quivered. *Damn it.* She had to find a way to shut off those damn waterworks.

"Yeah. Right. Patricia?" Edward called to their secretary, who sat at her desk in the adjacent waiting area. "Dr. Bennet is not feeling well. Will you please cancel all but her most urgent patients for today?"

"Oh, no—that's not—" Simone began to refute his request.

"Yes," Edward said, his tone telling her he wouldn't listen to any argument.

"There's nothing urgent on her schedule, Dr. Reynolds," Patricia said, coming to stand in the entry to the hallway. "Just her regular patients, and I can call them to reschedule. No problem." She glanced at Simone. "I'm very sorry about Philip, Dr. Bennet. He was a very nice man."

"Yes," Simone said softly. "He was."

Patricia nodded and returned to her desk.

"Okay, it's settled." Edward put a hand on Simone's shoulder. "You're taking the day off."

"I don't know, Ed... I really don't want to go home alone..."

"Stay here, then. I'll keep an eye on you."

In the end, Simone hadn't the strength to argue, and she spent the next several hours just hanging out with Edward and Patricia. The two of them were very understanding, and their kindness helped her a lot with her pain. But at noon, she decided it was time to go home.

"Okay, hon... If you feel well enough, go on home," Edward said when she told him she was heading out. "But if you get sad, you call me, you hear?"

As she headed out to her car, she realized Edward had done more than lift her spirits. She felt almost...hopeful again. As if life wasn't completely horrible, after all... Edward was acting like his old self, and in that moment, she didn't feel quite so alone and utterly depressed.

When Simone arrived home, she went to the kitchen and grabbed an apple from the refrigerator. Although she wasn't hungry, she needed some sustenance. She took the apple, a bottle of water, and her purse with her and went into her in-home office.

She had two options, she thought, as she slumped into a large, overstuffed chair in the corner. Either she could sit around and feel miserable, or she could try to distract her mind by doing something useful. She decided to spend some time reading. She took Lara's journal from her purse and found the spot where she'd last left off.

Lara's Journal

The day after what I began to refer to as "Lara's Independence Day", things got worse. Sabine had left the house, but my father was acting really crazy. I don't know what pissed him off more—my story or Sabine's betrayal. Maybe both, and my revelations were obviously too much for the poor man to bear. He seemed to be on the verge of a nervous breakdown.

Emms installed herself in our house to be closer to everything and to help us, and that morning, I left my bedroom to find her. As I approached the kitchen, I heard voices, and as I got closer I realized Emms and my father were having a conversation. I paused outside the doorway, held my breath, and listened.

"I'm going to kill that bastard. I'm going to smash him *and* his scumbag father, and then I'm going to kill Sabine!"

"Son, what are you planning?" Emms sounded worried.

"I'm going to confront the little shit, and then I'm going to see to the rest of them! You were right all the time about Sabine, Mother... I'm sorry I wouldn't listen."

I couldn't see my father's face, but his voice sounded tired. No doubt he hadn't gotten any sleep the night before.

"Larry, don't do anything stupid. You have three kids who are depending on you."

"Yes, I know, but he's still going to pay for what he did."

And in a clear example of how messed up my head was back then, the very first thing I thought about, upon hearing my father's words, was Arthur's safety. Instead of silently cheering the idea that my torturer—my molester—would finally get what he had coming to him, I cringed with fear at the idea of my father hurting him.

How crazy and mixed up my feelings were back then.

I rushed into the kitchen, interrupting their conversation. Four stools stood before a countertop bar created by a little center island, and Emms was occupying one of them, while my father stood next to her. I approached him and touched his arm.

"Dad, please don't hurt Arthur!"

My father and Emms looked at me as if I'd just sprouted horns and a tail. Emms put her hand to her open mouth, and my father sat down stiffly onto one of the barstools.

"He is not that bad." I tried to explain what I couldn't explain to myself. "He took care of me... It was— I mean... He just lost control yesterday, that's all. I don't know why, but—"

"Baby..." Emms interrupted me, her expression grave. She raised one eyebrow like she always did when she was upset or angry. "What he did to you... That was not taking care of you! I know you might think it was, but the truth is, he stole your childhood. He is *not* a good person."

"Lara, I don't want to hear you say another word in that scumbag's defense!" My father was shouting. "I can't believe you! How could you possibly defend a man who raped you, used you, and made you lie to your family?"

"Larry, calm down! We all have to calm down here, and I'm going to look for a counselor... I don't know if we can deal with this situation without help."

"I'm leaving. I have to think!" My father grabbed his briefcase from the counter and stormed out of the kitchen.

"Lara, do you want to talk about this?" Emms asked gently.

"I don't know," I said truthfully. "It's hard to talk about it... My feelings are all mixed up. Over the last few years, all I wanted to do was get rid of Arthur and Sabine, but now... I feel as if I don't belong. Not here...not anywhere. I don't feel as if anyone wants me... Arthur wanted me, Emms... I feel completely lost, and I miss him!"

"Come here, honey." She opened her arms wide.

Emms hugged me close, and I let her, but I had run out of tears to cry. I was just scared—in that moment, life seemed so big and so complicated.

"Lara, I understand. That was your life for the last...what? Three years?"

"Four," I murmured, eyes downcast.

"Bad or evil, you were used to it, and it'll take time to adjust to a new reality. But everything will be okay. I promise. All I ask is that you trust me. I won't disappoint you. You can share your feelings with me—no matter what they are—and I will try to help you."

"Is it bad to miss him?" I managed to ask her, even though I feared the answer.

"What do you miss exactly, babe?"

"I don't know...his attention...knowing he would be there waiting for me...wanting me..."

"Did you like to have sex with him?"

"Yes, I did... Not at first, obviously, but after a while, yes..." I was ashamed to admit it, but I had promised to myself no more lies for Emms.

"I suppose sex can be good, even when it's bad..." Emms reflected.

"Do you think one day life can go back to normal, Emms?"

"Babe...I don't know. First, we have to try to establish some normality so we can recognize it when we see it. And then we'll have to try to live according to those standards. Don't push yourself right now, Lara...wait...give things time. Time is like magic; it can heal everything. I don't know if we can forget, and maybe we shouldn't. But we can learn lessons from the situation and go on."

I released a sad, deep sigh. "I'll try. My father is upset

with me."

"No, he's not...he's blaming himself for what happened to you, and he's upset because he was so blind to Sabine's lack of character."

"I blame myself for what happened to me. I liked to have Arthur around when I was younger; I loved being the center of his attention. He's the one who first told me I was to blame—he said I bewitched him."

"Lara, never think that way. No child has the power to bewitch an older man. This is not your fault—this happened because Arthur has a complete lack of morals!" Emms glanced at her watch. "I have to take the kids to school. Do you want to go with me?"

"No, I don't want anyone to see me with my face like this."

Until my black eye went back to normal, I didn't want to return to school or be seen out and about. My dear friend Oscar called me, and I told him I was sick. He wanted to visit me at home, but I said my illness was contagious... So many lies...

Chaos reigned in our lives from the day I told everything to my father. I lost control—if I ever actually had any—over my life. Things were happening, and I felt like the only survivor of a fire that had destroyed the whole house and everything in it. I had to gather the pieces of my life, try to fix the family album with the remaining photos of another era, and I had no clue how to do it.

CHAPTER TWENTY-ONE

Simone – Present Day

The ringing of her cellphone interrupted Simone's reading a short time later. Although she didn't recognize the number, she decided to take the call, anyway.

"Simone? Good afternoon."

She recognized his voice immediately. "Charles. Hello. Good afternoon."

"I'm happy I caught you," he said. "I wanted to talk to you before talking to Mr. Raymond's widow."

"Yes. Of course. I'm guessing that means you have bad news...?"

"Very bad, indeed. Do you know if Mr. Raymond had any enemies?"

"Enemies? Philip? I don't know...but I can tell you he was a very passive man...no trouble with any kind of aggression..."

"Did he have thoughts of suicide?"

God, why wouldn't he get to the point? He was making her crazy!

"No," she told him. "Well, once he mentioned something about death being a release, but it wasn't anything serious, and he never tried to harm himself or anything like that... And during our last meeting, three days ago, I recall thinking he seem very happy. He'd never kill himself. Now, can you please tell me why you're asking me these things?"

"I suspect he was poisoned, Simone. When the doctor opened him up, he didn't find any traces of internal bleeding...no evidence of drug abuse or an aneurism, but he was very intrigued, and suddenly he smelled bitter almonds..."

"Potassium cyanide?" Simone frowned.

"Yes, they sent samples to the laboratory, and the results were conclusive."

"It can't be! Who would kill a man like Philip?"

"I have no idea. But obviously, we have to report this to the police. It's possible—I would say likely—that we have a crime on our hands. They'll want to launch an investigation."

"God, poor Philip!" Simone slumped in her chair. "Okay. Well. Thank you for calling and telling me. If you learn anything else, please let me know."

"No need to thank me." Charles sighed. " Now I have to explain all this to the widow. She's back—in my office as we speak—and she's waiting for an answer."

"Oh. Poor Nora. Good luck, Charles!"

"Thanks. I have a feeling I'll need all the luck I can get. This is the worst part of our profession..." He sighed again. "I'll talk to you later."

In a daze, Simone hung up the phone. What to make of all this? Could someone have killed Philip, or had he had some kind of bizarre accident? Maybe Leonora, the dominatrix... Would she...? Simone's mind twisted and turned, trying to find answers.

The doorbell rang, startling her. She walked into the front entry, still mulling over the possibilities.

"Yes?" She opened the door. "Oh! Edward!" Just the sight of him standing there lifted her spirits, and her cheeks grew hot as she realized she must sound ecstatic to see him. Still, she couldn't help her reaction. In a more moderate tone, she added, "So great to see you. Please, come in."

Edward stepped inside and followed her into the living room. "Are you okay, Simmie? I just came to check on you."

"Take a seat, Ed!" She waved toward the sofa.

"No, thanks." He shook his head. "I can't stay. I just wanted to make sure you were all right."

"I'm feeling completely lost, actually." Simone shook her head. "I just received news that Philip was poisoned!"

"Poisoned? But I thought the guy died from an aneurism...?"

"No. The autopsy results came back today. Somehow, Philip ingested enough potassium cyanide to kill him."

"That's awful!"

"Yes...I can't imagine who could have done such a thing. He was one of the kindest people I know. He never mentioned enemies, never said a mean word about anyone. And apart from his sexual troubles, he seemed to lead a normal life."

"Suicide, maybe? Did he have access to that kind of substance?"

"He was an accountant, Ed." Simone scoffed softly. "And I'm positive he didn't take his own life."

"Did he have any insurance? Maybe his wife...?"

"No. No way. I was with her shortly after she received the news he'd died. Her pain was genuine."

Edward shrugged. "Well, I'm all out of ideas. I really am sorry, Simmie... I know you liked him a lot."

"Thank you." She drew a deep breath. "Anyway. Would you like to stay for dinner?"

Simone would love to have Edward's company. Indeed, she needed him to comfort her, but she couldn't tell him that.

"Oh. Um, no..." He shook his head. "I can't stay. I'm taking Noah and meeting Carla for dinner." He checked his watch. "In fact, if I don't get going, we're going to be late."

She showed him to the door, gave him a hug, and thanked him again for coming to check on her. As she watched him walk to his car, her heart sank. Taking his son to meet Carla for dinner? Must be turning into a serious relationship if he was taking his child with him. And he'd left her to face another lonely night.

Simone was disappointed, and it really hurt to know her friend would leave her alone, knowing how sad she was, so he could go have dinner with his girlfriend. Suddenly,

Edward seemed a different person to her, more selfish than the man she was used to.

Simone, go back to work and shake this man from your thoughts, she commanded herself, *forget your old friendship; that doesn't exist anymore.* She went to her home office and took Lara's journal with her.

Lara's Journal

Two days later, my father was in jail. As I think I've mentioned before, I have a bad habit of eavesdropping on adult conversations. From what I'd managed to overhear between my father and Emms, Dad was in trouble. What I couldn't figure out was why. I entered the living room where Emms had just hung up the phone from talking to him, thinking I could find out what was going on.

"What happened, Emms?"

"Your father beat the shit out of Arthur! Larry went to Arthur's apartment and smashed his face, broke his nose, some ribs, and sent the guy to the hospital. Ruggiero pressed charges, and your father called me to bail him out. That was him on the phone just now."

"What are you going to do?" I longed to ask how Arthur was, but I didn't dare. I was worried about my father.

"Try to bail him out."

She got her bag and the car keys from off the back of the sofa, but as she headed toward the door, I had an idea.

"Don't go to the jail," I told her. "Talk to uncle—to Arthur's father, and tell him that if he doesn't drop the charges, you're going to take the photograph of him with my mother and turn it over to the press."

Emms stared at me, obviously surprised at my suggestion. I suppose she would have been, though. I wasn't the little kid she'd known four years ago—a lot had changed during my time with Arthur. I could tell she wasn't exactly pleased with me for suggesting that she use blackmail, because she tightened her lips and frowned. But she didn't scold or admonish me.

"Give me that picture," she said. "Let me see it."

I raced to my room, retrieved the picture, then hurried back down and handed it to her. The photograph was a little wrinkled, but the image was still clearly visible.

Emms called her lawyer and told him about the fight, the picture... I was worried she was going to tell him about what had happened to me—what had led to my father storming over to Arthur's—but the only thing she said was that my mother had been having an affair... Of course, that didn't explain why my father had smashed Arthur's face and not his father's, but the lawyer didn't ask questions. He merely listened then told her he was going to fix everything. She also told him my father wanted custody of the kids. After providing the attorney with all the information he should need for that moment, Emms hung up and turned to me.

"Let's have some tea," she said. "Everything is going to be fine..."

"I'd rather have a glass of whisky," I said without thinking. During my time in Paris, I'd drunk whenever I wanted to, without ever asking for permission. Since returning to the States, I had continued to drink but was smart enough to know my father and Emms would not be pleased, so I kept my new habit a secret. Until that moment, anyway...

"Excuse me? Don't tell me he allowed you to drink!" Clearly, Emms was upset.

I should tell her the truth, as I promised myself I would do, but the truth was I'd practically drank my way through my time with Arthur, boosting my courage with alcohol, hiding behind a bottle rather than facing my fears. I thought a moment, considering how I might answer. Emms and my father were blaming Arthur for everything right now... And honestly, I decided, it only seemed fair to let him pay. In that moment, I felt one overwhelming feeling toward Arthur—a longing for revenge. The idea took me by complete surprise, and once more I decided to lie, overcoming completely my promise but forgiving myself with the idea it was not a lie, it was revenge. But I also didn't want Emms to think I was a total lost cause.

"Well...yes..." I said, dropping my gaze. Despite having rationalized that everything wrong about my life could be traced back to Arthur, I still couldn't look Emms in the eyes.

"And how often do you drink?"

"Once a day...at least."

That was apparently too much for Emms to hear. She dropped to sit on the couch, her face a mask of emotions, and I could tell she was being strong for me, or she would have cried at that very moment. She looked destroyed, and she had tears in her eyes.

"Baby...we need to have a serious talk here. You can't go on like this. You're scaring me. You have a series problem if you're drinking every day. That's alcoholism!"

I could see Emms was worried as hell. She seemed to have aged over the last few days, so many wrinkles forming around her forehead and eyes. She was staring at me, and I felt as if she was trying to see inside me, trying to figure out the extent of my damages. I couldn't worry her like that.

"Emms, I can stop if I want. I'm no alcoholic." But I

wasn't so sure about that, as I remembered I was also Shirley's granddaughter, and she was an alcoholic, so maybe I had inherited that bad seed.

"We are going to figure out something together, my sunshine. No granddaughter of mine will be an alcoholic."

And I felt sure I wasn't going to be one, no matter what, Emms wouldn't let that happen.

CHAPTER TWENTY-TWO

Simone — Present Day

Simone could sense Lara's grandmother's sadness over all the traumas and ugly revelations in such a short period of time. The older woman had been a lioness, determined to help her family and to try to help Lara without pushing the kid. Obviously, she'd been a good and wise woman, and also a strong one, Simone concluded.

Simone sent Carl a message about her progress and he responded quickly with just a smiley-face icon. Did that mean he was happy about her progress, but just too lazy to answer? She hated when people answered a message with an icon!

Simone needed to clear her head a little bit, and to her, there was no better way to do that than to organize something. She decided to work on her closet. She went to her room, opened the door to her closet, and started with the dresses. For the first time, she realized what Peter had meant when, after he'd snuck into her home and had gone through her things, he'd said her clothing was boring.

All dark colored, slim-lined dresses, designed for work, plus the two more colorful ones she'd bought during her trip to Miami, thanks to Arami, who had told Simone she must show a little a bit of her shoulders. Simone grabbed all the dresses and threw them onto her bed. She began to go through them, choosing a few to donate to Goodwill, but for the most part, she decided to hold on to the dresses she wore to work. However, she promised herself she'd go as soon as possible to buy new ones more suitable for hours outside the office. Even if her life wasn't about fun, at least she could dress in a way that made her feel a little more feminine, a little prettier.

Two hours after entering her closet, she had at least five bags of clothes to donate and a lot of space in her wardrobe. You need space in your life if you want new cloth... The same goes for a new relationship. She could buy new clothes now, and since she didn't have anybody in her life, maybe she would find someone to fill that empty space, too.

* * * * *

Simone woke up early on Saturday, and she decided to go out for a run. The wind in her face and the effort made she feel alive, and she was feeling better as she made her way back home.

When she neared her house, she noticed a car parked out front and a man knocking on her door.

Oh, no, not Armando. Not today.

She'd been avoiding him like the plague, but he was an insistent man. He called her cell at least ten times a day the previous week until she blocked his number, but then he apparently discovered her office phone number, where a very clever Patricia avoided him. But then he started to call Simone's phone at the house. A real pain in the ass.

Simone got very upset and thought about telling him to go to hell, but then she remembered her last meeting with the general and decided to try a change in her tactics to get rid of him.

"Hello, Armando, so good to see you here!"

He seemed surprised, as he raised his eyebrow at her cheerful greeting. "Good to see you, darling girl. You look absolutely marvelous in those gym clothes!"

She offered her sweat-coated face to him for a kiss, and

to her displeasure, he pressed his thin lips against her cheek. She got her keys from inside her short's pocket, but at the very same moment, Lola, her maid, opened the door to her.

"Doctor Bennet, good morning, I heard the bell and didn't know it was you."

"Good morning, Lola, this is Armando, a friend. Please take care of him while I take a quick shower."

Simone spent at least forty-five minutes bathing, hoping the delay might annoy the guy, but apparently he had the patience of a saint. When she finally joined him in her living room, there he was, all smiles, with a very attentive Lola serving him coffee and speaking Spanish to him.

"How are you, Simone? I've been trying to reach you all week!"

"Oh, I know...but I had a very difficult week. I just lost another patient. He was poisoned, and I was not feeling well..."

She silently apologized to Philip for using his death as an excuse.

"Sorry, I didn't know that! You should have told me. I would have been here immediately!"

"I didn't want to bother you with my problems. You might think I only call on you when something goes horribly wrong. Would you like a stronger drink, or are you okay with just coffee?"

"A glass of scotch would be great."

Simone went to the teacart she used as a bar, took a bottle of golden label Johnny Walker, and poured a shot into a short, crystal glass.

"Ice?"

"No, cowboy would be great..."

"Here is your scotch." She handed him the glass.

"Thank you. I've really missed you, Simone. So badly, that I decided to come here, even though I hadn't been able to reach you."

"I've missed you, too, and I want to have a serious talk with you..."

"About?"

"About the two of us. I've been thinking, and you're right. We need to be together... I can't be afraid."

His smile turned into a big grin, and she continued.

"And I think we should marry soon. I'm too old for a long engagement. Plus, we'll want to get settled in Miami before my daughter arrives... I don't remember if I told you, but I have a daughter...a complicated girl...drug problems, you know?" Simone barely kept a straight face, but she was desperate to get rid of the guy and willing to try almost anything. "I've sent her abroad to rehab, and she's going to be back soon, so she'll have to live with us."

"Are you kidding me?"

"No...but don't worry, she's clean now. At least, I hope she is..."

Simone made a face, pretending she didn't believe what she was saying.

Armando appeared very uncomfortable with the situation... He stared at her, a strange look on his face. Simone recalled the general's words. *Run to him, and he will run from you...*

"Don't you like my proposition, Armando?"

"Sure, I do... I'm so surprised and happy. I came here thinking I was going to be rejected, and now this... I'm so happy, Simone! I've just discovered you are the love of my life, and now you propose to me! You are such a wonderful woman, so modern."

Simone was stunned... What the hell? Why wasn't he running? Shouldn't he be halfway out the door by now? How to get out of this? She'd acted like an idiot for nothing!

"Armando...I was joking... Really, I don't have the same feelings for you. I...sorry...but no...we can't be together…we are not going to be together. I was trying to sound ridiculous so you could see that we don't fit together."

"How dare you make fun of me? What do you think I am? One of your crazy patients?"

He dropped his glass to the floor as he jumped up from the couch, and Simone didn't have time to react before he was on her, his hands wrapped around her throat.

"Listen to me, bitch! And listen carefully! You are not going to make fun of me; you are going to start respecting me!"

Simone was getting dizzy from the pressure of his fingers against her throat, and she couldn't fight anymore.

"Dr. Bennet! What on—!" Lola rushed into the room. She flew at Armando, little fists swinging, shouting what sounded like a thousand words of Spanish, none of them good.

Armando had to release Simone's neck to defend himself from Lola's attack, and they shouted at each other in Spanish for several seconds.

Lola grabbed Armando by the sleeve and started to drag him toward the front entry. As they reached the foyer, someone knocked on the door, and Armando stopped resisting. Simone pushed past him and opened the door quickly, startled to find two policemen standing on her front porch. Had Lola called the police? When?

Beside her, Armando assumed a calm expression.

"Dr. Bennet?" One of the policemen spoke up. "I'm Officer Alfred, and this is Officer Montgomery. Sorry to bother you on a Saturday, ma'am, but we would like to talk to you about your patient, Philip Reynolds? Do you have a moment?"

Absolutely. Stay as long as you like, she thought. "Good morning, Officers, you can come in. My...friend here is just leaving."

She kept the door opened after the two officers entered her house, and Armando passed her as he left, leaning in to whisper.

"If you think you are going to get rid of me so easily, you are greatly mistaken..."

"Please, Lola, accompany Armando outside while I talk to the officers."

Simone turned to the policemen and invited them to follow her into the other room and take a seat. How bad was it when she felt grateful to have two officers appear at her front door? Talk about an unsettling Saturday morning!

"Dr. Bennet, we are starting to investigate the murder of Philip Reynolds. Can you tell us what you know?"

"Of course. He was my patient for some time, and I was very fond of him."

"Did he talk to you about any enemies he might have had? Or indicate he was afraid someone might kill him?"

"Never! He seemed to be a kind person and never talked about getting into fights or anything like that."

They asked her several standard questions, and they wanted her to remember anything that could help them.

"He was involved in trouble some time ago, and he had taken some drugs," Official Montgomery said.

"Officer, I'm positive someone drugged him that night. He was afraid of drugs. I also think someone gave the poison to him. He wasn't the kind of man who would have committed suicide, and he wasn't some big party animal."

"Are you sure?"

"Yes, I'm pretty sure."

"How about his wife?"

"He was in love with her, and he seemed happy. They had been apart for some time, but they'd gotten back together recently."

"Did he have any lovers?"

"While he was separated from his wife, he had a girlfriend; she was a dominatrix… And I believe you should investigate her a little bit further because the day he had problems in the nightclub, she was there, and he was poisoned right after they broke up."

"Do you think someone killed him out of some sort of revenge or something like that?"

"I don´t know, and I don´t want to point fingers here, but his relationship with the dominatrix always sounded weird to me. Maybe I´m being biased because of her profession, but you can´t call a relationship normal when one of the partners keeps the other tied up in ropes."

Simone gave them all the information she could about Leonora and Philip's association, and the officers seemed satisfied.

"Thank you, Dr. Bennet, we appreciate your help. If you remember something else that can help us, please give us a call."

Officer Montgomery gave her a business card. She felt like she was in a movie.

"Please let me know how things go. I real would like to know what happened to Philip."

As the officers walked toward the front entry, the

telephone rang, and Simone excused herself to answer the call. She said hello, but no one responded. All she could hear was some kind of music playing in the background, but no words. *Armando.* He knew all about her kidnapping...he must have decided to pretend like he was Peter and try to terrify her.

When the officers left, the telephone rang again and again. Each time she answered, it was the same. *Yes,* she thought. *This has to be Armando.* The timing was just too coincidental.

"Armando, let me tell you something. Go to hell! Stop stalking me, or I'm going to talk to your family, so they can have you locked up. I'm also going to talk to the police next time you come near me. I didn't do that today out of respect for your family, but my patience has reached its end."

She slammed down the phone.

For the rest of that day, she received several more calls, all of them the same. Frustrated beyond belief, she phoned Arami and explained the situation. Arami told Simone not to worry because she was going to deal with her cousin.

But the phone calls continued throughout the week, and Simone started to think about getting a lawyer— one she already knew—to advise her about getting a restraining order. On Wednesday evening, she called Carl.

"Hello, Carl, how are you? If you're not too busy, I would like to discuss a situation I'm having with you. It's a business matter, so if you want, I can call you tomorrow."

"No, Simone, of course not... You are a friend as much as a business associate. No need to wait if there's something I can help you with."

He considered her a friend? She was happy to hear that, even if she couldn't see being friends with a man like him—he was too damn charming to be classified as just a friend.

Simone then explained the whole Armando problem to Carl and told him about the phone calls. She ended by asking for his advice.

"Simone...I'm afraid the phone calls you are receiving are not coming from this Armando. I'm afraid they are coming from Peter. I've received the same kind of calls; remember me telling you about them the last time we saw each other? I'm going to go to the police station this week. I meant to go sooner, but I didn't have the time..."

Simone had completely forgotten about that information. How was that possible? *Maybe my subconscious doesn't want to deal with Peter Hay again.* That had to be it. Otherwise, she would have realized sooner that it had to be him, and would have at least remembered Carl talking about the subject.

"Do you think he's back in the country?" The idea of Peter Hay being anywhere near her again gave Simone chills.

"I don't know. I don't know how he'd get in—he's on every wanted list, and everybody knows his face, thanks to the media's coverage of your kidnapping. But he called me, as I told you, to tell me he wanted to come back. I told him if he did, I'd hand him over to the police. He hung up on me, and since then, I've been getting those strange phone calls."

"My God, I hope it's just a coincidence. I don't know if I can stand much more of this."

"I don't believe it's a coincidence. I'm going to take precautionary measures tomorrow, Simone, and I advise you to do the same."

She started to shake, overwhelmed by all the traumatic events the past weeks. Two dead patients, Armando stalking her, and now the specter of Peter again, hanging over her head. She thanked Carl and hung up the phone, then sat on her couch for a long time, wondering what she should do next.

She decided to call Edward.

"Hello. This is Carla."

Simone looked at her phone, momentarily confused. Had she somehow managed to dial the wrong number?

But no...she'd called Edward's cell. Apparently, he and Carla were serious enough that she felt comfortable answering his calls. A pang of jealousy rattled Simone's confidence. She cleared her throat.

"Hello, may I speak to Edward, please?"

"Sure, who's calling?"

"His partner, Simone..." She thought it best to keep it formal.

Silence filled the line, and for a moment, Simone wondered if the other woman had hung up. Bitch hadn't even said goodbye.

"Hello, Simmie, what's going on?" Edward asked.

Relieved to hear his voice, Simone began telling him what was going on, so nervous she couldn't stop the flow of words.

"I'm afraid," she said, once she'd finished filling him in. "And I don't know what to do."

"I'll be there shortly," he told her. "Hang tight."

To calm her nerves, Simone decided to read until Edward got there. Once again, she escaped into Lara's troubles to keep her mind off her own.

Lara´s Journal

My father was out of jail by the end of that same day. By the end of that month, he had divorced my mother and had started to prepare us for a move from Washington, D.C. to New York City. He already had business there and was going to transfer everything.

Meanwhile, Emms was worried about my drinking problem. She caught me drinking once or twice and ended up taking me to a local AA meeting. God, talk about weird! In fact, after the third session, rather than have to go back there, I immediately stopped drinking. But not before I'd met one really handsome guy.

The sessions were held every Saturday in the back of a church. The meeting room was ugly and bare, with only a circle of uncomfortable, wooden chairs arranged in the middle of the floor. There were all kinds of people there—old, young, ugly, pretty, and strange—but there was also a very good-looking guy...the person responsible for managing the meetings. He was around thirty years old, I believe. He told us his story and asked us to tell everybody ours, but of course, I couldn't do that. No way...

"My name is Frieda," one woman said.

"Hello, Frieda," everybody greeted her with enthusiasm.

She started her miserable story about how her miserable life had led her to alcohol, and how alcohol had further destroyed her life.

By my third meeting, I already pitied everybody...even the handsome guy—Jordan—who had kicked the habit some years ago and now helped others.

"Hello, Lara, why don't you tell us your story?" he asked.

I hadn't shared a thing since I'd joined their group, but I shook my head. "No. I don't have anything to say... I'm really here just to listen..."

Everyone was staring at me, and my cheeks grew hot, and my palms started sweating. Thankfully, he didn't push me, but when the meeting was over, Jordan asked me to stay and talk with him.

"Sorry if I upset you earlier. It's just that you'll heal more quickly if you talk about your drinking problem."

"I don't have a drinking problem. My grandma caught me sipping a drink and insisted I come here. My issue is nothing like the problems I've heard here."

"And why did you start drinking?"

"Because I was sad..."

"Lara, you can't do that—not without asking for big trouble. You can drink to celebrate but never to mask problems. Everyone here started drinking for the same reason—we were sad and alone and lost—but I can promise you're not going to find happiness, solace, or your true self inside a bottle."

"Thanks for the advice. I'll keep it in mind."

They had the habit there of hugging each other; I guess it was their way of showing their support. Jordan stepped close and gave me a hug, but I guess I wasn't used to being in a man's embrace unless he wanted something more. Before he could release me, I lifted my face and kissed him.

He jerked back. "Hey! I'm afraid I must have given you the wrong impression or something," he said, taking another step back and putting more space between us. "I'm probably twice your age, and I'm definitely not a pervert." He shook his head and ran a hand through his hair. Now he was the one who looked embarrassed. "You really need to be careful. You keep doing stuff like that, and you're going to find yourself in big trouble someday."

I felt so ashamed and knew my face had to be bright scarlet. Apparently, I'd been missing the physical contact more than I'd realized, and I hadn't thought...had just reacted to his hug.

To make a long story short, I hightailed it out the back door of the church, and I never went back. I don't know if Jordan talked to Emms or not, but she and I came to an agreement. She'd lock up the liquor cabinet for a while, and I would do my best to control myself. If all went well, I'd never have to go to another AA meeting. That, alone, was enough motivation, another motivation was to think about my grandmother Sheila— I never wanted to be like her—and I had faith I could abstain. Mostly. Of all my problems, alcohol was one of the least, and I sought to find a balance. I never quit drinking completely. I continued having a glass of wine or a scotch now and then, and I cut loose a little bit while I was in college, but I never developed an addiction, thanks to Emms and her quick intervention.

CHAPTER TWENTY-THREE

Simone – Present Day

Simone admired Emma's wisdom—the woman was really very smart, and in a short time she'd found a way to cure what could have been a huge problem. Mostly because alcoholism can be hereditary, and Lara's grandmother was an alcoholic. A knock on Simone's door took her from her thoughts, and she realized, to her pleasure, the reading had done it's job. She was calmer and composed when she set aside the journal and headed into the front foyer.

She answered the door to find Edward there, a very pretty woman by his side. She was one of those curvaceous females, with a heart-shaped face, high cheekbones, deep-blue eyes surrounded by very long eyelashes, and chestnut hair. To make matters worse, she seemed to be much younger than Simone. *At least he could have chosen someone a little older... I didn't realize he likes them younger.*

"Hello, Simmie, this is Carla, my...girlfriend..."

He seemed to hesitate on giving her the title of girlfriend, which Simone took as a good sign, but then she chided herself for even thinking such a thing. Why did it matter what he did? He and Simone were only friends...

"Nice to meet you, Simone."

"Nice to meet you, Carla."

They shook hands, and Simone noted the woman had a very vigorous handshake. Carla's curious gaze moved from Simone's face to her toes and then back again, as if the woman were taking Simone's measure.

"I brought Carla with me because she's an FBI agent. She's been working on Peter Hay's case, and she can give us some ideas."

The phone on Simone's kitchen counter rang, and everybody turned to look at the device.

"May I?" Carla asked.

"Sure!" Simone nodded. "I'm sick of listening to silence or background music. Feel free."

Carla answered the phone. She held the handset to her ear for a few minutes, and then replaced it in its charger.

"More of the same?" Simone asked, although she already knew the answer.

Carla nodded. "I'm going to inform my people. If that's our friendly psycho, Peter Hay, then my agency will want to know. We'll probably have to start taping all your calls... I'm sorry, but we'll have to follow standard procedure here."

"Don't worry about it," Simone said. "You can record them." It wasn't as if they'd get anything other than those lunatic phone calls on tape, since her life sucked big time these days.

They talked for some time, and then Edward and Carla left, leaving Simone alone to cope with her fears by herself. And if Carla and Carl were right, Peter was back, which could only mean Simone was in danger. And did Edward give a shit about that? Nope... He was too busy with his pretty new girlfriend. His pretty, *young*, new girlfriend. Edward had changed...a lot. Simone was really sad about that.

She went back to reading the journal, putting aside her self-pity and her sudden anger at Edward.

Lara´s Journal

We sold our house in D.C. and moved to New York. I was sad to leave behind my only friend Oscar.

He had tears in his eyes when he came by my house to say goodbye. "Hey, Giraffe, I'm going to miss you...a lot..."

"I'm going to miss you, too, Oscar."

He gave me a clumsy hug before spinning around and racing back down the sidewalk. And that was the end of my first real friendship and of my tutoring career; Oscar had been my one and only student. I cried as I watched him go. It seemed nothing was permanent in my life.

We—Dad, Emms, and I—established a kind of democratic way of living at home. We would discuss everything and make decisions together. We decided together that we would move to New York. We discussed our new home, furniture, and even schools for kids. I felt like an adult, and I could see Emms and my father—the latter only with a great deal of effort—treated me as if I were grown. Only a few months ago, I had lived the life of an adult. To pretend I could go back to acting like merely a teen wouldn't have made sense.

Dad and I decided to buy a nice apartment on 70

Charlton Street, Soho. Emms bought a small place for herself five blocks away on Hudson Street.

I didn´t need to sell my jewels, and Emms decided to keep them inside her safe for a while. We talked and together we decided I wouldn´t need to wear them any time soon—I rarely went anywhere those days—and they didn´t bring me much happiness. Years later, they left that safe, when I could forgive myself for the way I had gotten them, but I sold them, piece by piece, and gave the money to a home that cared for abused children.

What can I say about that period in my life? I was often depressed because I was dealing with so many changes, but on the other hand, I felt safe. I had ups and downs—mood swings, Emms called them—all the time, and finally, she said we should all go to see a family counselor. Of course, that didn't work out so well, and after only two sessions, the therapist recommended I see a psychiatrist on my own, since I couldn't open up in front of my whole family.

I started to see Dr. Jordan Dominick, a fifty-year-old psychiatrist whose chestnut-colored hair was just starting to go grey at his temples. I remember he always wore the nicest clothes—always a dark suit with a brightly colored tie. We had sessions twice a week, every week, but I wasn't anywhere near ready to tell him about Arthur and everything we had done together.

So instead, we focused on other things. Dr. Dominick diagnosed me with ADHD—Attention Deficit Hyperactivity Disorder—and explained that was one of the reasons I had a hard time learning certain things. He told me people with my condition are geniuses when it comes to a topic they love but that they can be totally distracted when they didn't like something.

I've described having ADHD as something like this: Sometimes my head is full of ideas, and my thought are like dancers performing the can-can. They are so bright, so colorful and alive; I can't find any peace. My brain jumps from one thought to another, from one interest to another, and I grow tired with all the noise inside my mind. During those times, I would do almost anything to have peace, a moment of quiet calm, but I could do nothing to control my racing thoughts.

When I explained this to my psychiatrist, he ran some tests, and I finally had a diagnosis. God, it was good to finally know what was wrong with me, why I couldn't concentrate. I'd always felt stupid for not being able to learn certain things, and the news about ADHD lifted a huge weight off my shoulders. If I was suffering from a physical condition, I wasn't an idiot!

Dr. Dominick prescribed some medication for me— Ritalin—and asked me to pay close attention, to watch for any improvement. That first day, I took my first small, oval-shaped white pill and washed it down with water while my father watched over me. As the doc had requested, I waited, hoping for some sign of improvement in my ability to concentrate.

"Well?" Dad asked after ten minutes had passed.

"Well...nothing." I shrugged. Maybe it was too soon.

Another ten minutes passed, and my father gave me a look. I shook my head sadly. Still nothing... Finally, after twenty-five minutes, I sat up straight.

"What is it?" my dad asked.

"I feel..." I tried to find words to describe the light igniting my mind. "At peace."

I grinned at my father, and he looked relieved.

"Well, that's good." He nodded.

Good. Yes. Great, even. The dancing thoughts in my head seemed to leave the stage, one by one, until finally the stage stood empty, ready for a presentation, but this time, I could choose the play.

Doctor Dominick also gave me an antidepressant, saying he thought I would need one to help me face and adapt to all the changes I'd have to deal with.

The medicine helped me through my student years, but when I finally graduated, I decided I wasn't going to take it anymore, and I was going to stop going to my psychiatrist for a while. I wanted to be normal, and I thought normal people didn´t need medication or doctors.

CHAPTER TWENTY-FOUR

Simone — Present Day

The description Lara gave about her dancing thoughts was a poetic version of what Simone´s patients with ADHD used to tell her...hard for a person with that kind of condition to lead a normal life. First of all, they weren´t like other people, and second, their thoughts were always flying. That explained Lara's ability to cope with all she had been through; she could imagine being with another man, or she used her imagination to escape, emotionally. In a way, Lara´s deficiency had helped her to survive her years of abuse.

* * * * *

Simone was in her office on Tuesday, sipping some tea in the middle of her break, when her secretary told her two agents were there to talk to her. Simone thought it was the agents who had been to her house on Saturday, but when she went to the lobby, she found Edward's girlfriend, Carla, in the company of another man. A tall and very serious man wearing a dark suit.

"Hello, Agent... Good afternoon. Hello, Carla." Simone greeted them.

"Hello, Simone. There's been a development, and we need to talk to you. I decided I should come, since you already know me."

Neither Carla nor the male agent returned Simone's greeting, and neither of them smiled.

"Nice to meet you, Dr. Bennet. I'm FBI Agent Oswald Neville," the man told her, showing his credentials.

"Nice to meet you, Agent Neville. You've come at a good time. I was just taking a break." Simone nodded toward the hallway behind her. "Why don't we step into my office?"

She turned, and the two agents followed her.

With the office door closed firmly behind them, she pointed toward the couch and said, "Please take a seat."

They sat, and Carla started the talking.

"The police searched Philip's home, and they took what they considered to be several pieces of evidence, one of which was a bottle of medication." She paused and looked directly at Simone. "They tested that medication and found potassium cyanide."

Simone slumped back in her chair. "Oh, my God."

"Yes. But there's more," Carla said. "The label on the bottle indicates that you were the prescribing doctor."

"But... That's impossible. Incredible. How did potassium cyanide get into Philip's medication?" Simone asked.

"That's the reason the FBI is involved. Potassium cyanide is the same poison we found in the unsolved cases involving Tylenol years ago. That one was a case of product tampering that lead to the deaths of many people in the Chicago area. The FBI coded it as TYMURS—the Tylenol-poisoning murders."

"Yes, I heard about that on the news, but that was years ago. Do you believe there's a connection between those cases and Philip's death?" Simone wasn't following their line of reasoning here.

"That's what we're trying to find out. There were several copycats crimes after the original case, all of them using the same poison inside pills, trying to pass themselves off as being connected to the Tylenol crimes, but all those later cases were solved, and they were not linked to the Tylenol murders. Most of them had something to do with someone trying to receive insurance money or get rid of someone."

"And now do you think this one might be linked to the original Tylenol case?"

"We don't know...but Philip didn't have any insurance to justify someone trying to poison him. We talked to his former girlfriend before coming here, and she didn't know about his death. She seemed genuinely shocked and saddened when we gave her the news. And besides, she was out of town last week. We checked her alibi—airport surveillance videos and so on—and although we're still investigating, right now, she seems clean."

Simone sat forward, propping her elbows on her desktop. "How can I help you at this time?"

"We just need to ask you some questions, Doctor," said Agent Neville.

"Did you recommend a specific drugstore for Philip to get his prescription filled?"

"Absolutely not." Simone shook her head. "That's illegal! Doctors can't recommend pharmacies to their patients. I write the prescriptions, and they buy their medication wherever they choose; Philip was not an exception." Simone couldn't keep her irritation and indignation from showing in her tone of voice. She prided herself on being ethical, and those types of questions really pissed her off.

"When was the last time you gave him a prescription?" Agent Neville asked. If he sensed Simone's annoyance, he didn't show it. He sat hunched over his iPhone, apparently using it to take notes.

"During his last session, actually," she told him. "His prescription was about to run out, but I suppose he must have taken one or two out of this new prescription, even though he still had some left from the other one," Simone said, thinking out loud.

"One laced pill would be enough, but there were several poisoned in the bottle. Someone wanted him dead. This was not an accident."

"But who? And why? I really can't imagine... I'm a sex therapist, but my patients tell me about their whole lives... I'm making an effort here to remember if he ever mentioned having any enemies." She touched her forehead with her index finger. "Maybe one of his brothers. I seem to remember him saying he had some issues with one of them. Nothing serious, more like sibling rivalry, but that's all I can remember him complaining about. Well, that and his mother... I remember he told me he employs his brother, but I can't remember the man's name."

"That's good to know. Usually, the killer is connected to the victim in some way. We are going to talk to his family. Thank you very much, Simone," Carla said.

The two agents rose to leave.

"Feel free to come back. I'm going to check his files to see if I can remember anything else."

"Files? You have files? Can we have copies of them?"

"Of course, I have files. I take notes on every patient. I see different people all day long. I can't remember everything. And yes, if you think it's important, you can take them with you. But I would like to have copies for my records and research."

"Certainly. Can you get them for us now?"

Simone checked her watch. "Do you mind if I ask my secretary to get them? I have patients waiting..."

"Of course! Sorry to disturb you in the middle of your workday, but it was very important for us to speak with you. I'm sure you understand."

"Yes, no problem. It's also important to me to find out what happened to Philip. I was very fond of him."

They said goodbye, and Simone asked Patricia to search the file room. Simone and Edward shared one room in the house, where they stored their medical records. They kept the room locked, and only she and Edward had access. Just recently, they had given Patricia one key, trusting the woman to deal with the files with utmost discretion. She had been going in there now and then to organize the files and to help them with their schedules, always having everything together and waiting on Simone's and Edward's desks before their first patients arrived.

* * * * *

Simone worked hard for the remainder of the day, but her heart felt heavy. As she had established a routine, at the end of the day, she decided to resume reading Lara's journal, which she had abandoned for several days, because her head was full of her own problems, but she had promised to help Carl, and she had to analyze the rest of it, whether she wanted to or not.

Lara´s Journal

One day, six months into my weekly therapy sessions, I arrived at Dr. Dominick's office in a terrible mood. Suffering from a serious bout of depression, I sat there waiting for him to call me in, gazing around the waiting room, looking for something to distract me from my thoughts.

"This place is so...beige," I said to myself and laughed quietly. But it was true—the entire room...walls, carpeting, even the couch and chairs—were done in various shades of beige. The whole thing cried out for some color.

He had a small waiting room, where a lovely secretary

organized his schedule. Her name was Nina, and she always greeted me with kindness, a welcoming smile brightening her cherubic face. That day, she was either busy or had grown tired of trying to make conversation with me without getting much of a response, so I continued to sit in silence, lost in my own thoughts.

The door to Dr. Dominick's office opened, a patient left without looking at me—I'd discovered that no one wants to be recognized in a psychiatric's office—and the doctor called me in. Nina followed on my heels as she always did, carrying my chart.

I installed myself on yet another beige couch near the mullion window with—of course—beige courtains, hugged a beige pillow, and looked at him. He positioned himself across from me on a dark-brown couch, crossed his legs, rested his notebook on his lap, and tapped it with his pencil while he observed me with his penetrating eyes.

"I'm sad! I miss him!" I told him.

"Okay... Well, it's certainly okay to be sad, but who is 'him'?"

Finally, after months of weekly sessions, I started to tell him about Arthur and me. I laid it all out there, from our first encounter until the day I confessed everything to my father. I didn't hold back a thing—I told the doctor about the threesomes in Paris, about Adrien and the other men... I pretty much spewed the whole dramatic tale over the course of the next forty-five minutes or so.

When I finished, Dr. Dominick got to his feet, pressed the button on his intercom, and told Nina to cancel his next apointment. He then returned to sit on his couch, took off his glasses, and ran his hands over his face. Then he replaced the glasses and started to talk.

"Lara, you've been through a lot! And it's very normal for you to feel confused and sad. It's even normal for you to miss Arthur—it's not healthy, but it *is* normal."

"How can it possibly be normal for me to miss someone who abused me so badly?" I asked in disbelief.

"Well, first of all, victims of sexual abuse—and you, my dear, are a victim of sexual abuse—often take personal responsibility for the abuse. I can tell you feel this way simply by listening to you describe what happened to you. Everything you said about Arthur and how he approached you and so on...you made it very clear that you liked his attentions, and because of that—because you enjoyed being the object of his desire—you have decided you are to blame for his actions."

"He used to say that all the time...that I was to blame, and I believed him."

"But it wasn't your fault. You were a child; in certain ways, you still are. Children must have sexual experiences at the appropriate time, with other children their age. An adult should never force himself upon a child. Never, under any circumstances."

"I thought he was my friend..."

"From what you tell me, he was very smart...he knew exactly how to lure you, how to gain your confidence. You trusted him, you believed his words, and he bonded with you."

"Yes...in the beginning, I really liked him."

"He is a predator, and predators do that. They create a bond with their victims. They groom them...lure them in a little at a time. He convinced you to lie to your family, and he made it seem as if doing so was something special—a little secret between the two of you, not a bad thing, because adults don't understand...but *he* was an adult."

"He used to say he was a child inside an adult's body..."

The doctor made some noise with his tongue before continuing. "Another way of bonding with you, made worse because of your ADHD. You have a strong imagination. I bet you could see the kid inside him."

I nodded. Yes, that was exactly the way I had felt back then.

"You must get rid of your guilt, Lara. We have to work on that. How do you feel right now about everything that happened with you and Arthur?"

"Confused, lost... I have flashbacks sometimes. I try to fit in with my family, and I can do that sometimes. But most of all, I really don't know who I am, and I feel deeply guilty about my parents."

"Don't! I can assure you, you are not responsible for anything that happened between your mother and your father!"

"But I destroyed my father's life, his family! My siblings are suffering; they lost their mother."

"Lara, think back. Think about what your mother did. She destroyed the family with her selfish, abhorrent behavior. She didn't protect her family; she betrayed you all. You are not the guilty party in this situation. Your mother is to blame for everything."

"I hate her, and I feel guilty about that, too."

"Hate her as much as you want to, but don't hate yourself."

"I really would like to smash her face or see her run over by a huge truck."

He laughed. "Rage is a good thing. All those years, you repressed your true emotions. To express rage is very healthy." He paused then said, "I have an idea. Why don't you shout about hating your mother?"

"Shout? When? Where?"

"Here. Now, if you feel like it. Those walls are soundproof…"

"I hate Sabine! I hate her with all my heart!" I shouted and was amazed at how yelling helped relieve some of the anxiety I'd been feeling lately.

"How do you feel now?"

"I still hate her, but I feel better. But sometimes, I feel guilty because she is my mother, and I should love her."

He shook his head. "There is no law that states you must love your mother because she is your mother. Love is not a genetic thing. Love must be earned. If she doesn't deserve to be loved, if she deserves to be hated for all she did to you, then hate her. You owe her nothing."

"But she is my mother…I owe her my life…"

"No, you don't. While she did give birth to you, she was never truly a mother to you. Not by any true definition of the word."

"Sometimes, I miss Arthur. Today, for instance, I was sitting in my room all alone, and I started missing him."

I laid out all the details of my life for Dr. Dominick to review, in the hopes of resolving everything, right then and there…as if I could perform surgery and cut out all the bad stuff.

"Lara, as I said before, he bonded with you before molesting you; he created deep ties of friendship. You told me he wasn´t bad at all. If you did what he expected you to do, he was good to you."

"Exactly."

"You are suffering from something called Stockholm Syndrome, which is a type of post-traumatic stress syndrome that links you to your abuser. Generally, a victim suffers from this when the abuse lasts for long periods, and you were abused for four years. Stockholm Syndrome is a survival mechanism."

He cleared his throat and then continued.

"You were in a sort of captivity. He was the powerful person in your world. He provided for you, gave you gifts, had sex with you, did anything he wanted to do to you, and you had practically no rights. You couldn't say no. He started to be like a god in your eyes. When this kind of situation occurs, the brain has a mechanism to dissociate good from evil in order to help the person to survive. Since you couldn´t leave or get out of the situation, you had to tell to yourself it was not that bad, or you would have gone crazy."

"Yes, but now I´m out of it, and I still miss him."

"No, you don´t. You are still afraid of him and what he can do to you...or you're worried the same situation can happen again...it´s your subconscious preparing to fight, so it's better to tell yourself he is not that bad, because if it happens again, you are going to be prepared."

"I miss sex."

"I believe you...you had an intense sex life for several years, and then...nothing. But remember you never had sex with Arthur—you always imagined you were somewhere else or with someone else when you were with him. Can you name one time when you focused on the fact that it was Arthur having sex with you?"

"Never..."

"So you don't miss *him*...you miss *sex*. It's not wrong to miss sex; it's natural."

After listening to his explanation, I felt as if the hands that had been smashing my heart had suddenly disappeared. I released a long breath and smiled.

* * * * *

I spent many years on Dr. Dominick's couch. He helped me find my emotional independence from Arthur. My guilt slowly subsided, and I started to see Arthur and Sabine for the evil pieces of shit they really were. I hated them for what they had done to me, and I allowed myself to hate them because doing so was liberating.

But my scars ran deep, and the traumas I'd suffered through were complex, and it was hard for me to bond with anyone. Apart from my little family, I couldn't trust anybody, and I had an especially difficult time relating to boys.

As I grew older, I resumed my sex life, always trying to choose boys my age, but I was never satisfied with the kind of sex they had to offer.

CHAPTER TWENTY-FIVE

Simone — Present Day

At least Lara had a good professional, one who was able to lead her through her healing journey. If she hadn't stopped seeing him at some point after college, as she'd made clear in her journal, she would have had a different life, Simone thought. Maybe she would even be alive.

She sent a message to Carl, informing him of where she was in her reading and telling him he could proceed to that point. When Carl had originally approached her, prior to her kidnapping, he'd done so under false pretenses. When he'd finally admitted to her that he was the "Mark" who had accidentally killed Lara, Simone had promised to help him, to take him on as a patient... But then the situation with Peter had happened, and since then, Carl hadn't asked for much help. She was just helping him by reading the beginning of Lara's journals, the parts about her abuse and her years in Paris, which had seemed to be more difficult for him to handle. The last few chapters hadn't bothered him as much. That was a good sign, in Simone's opinion; he was dealing well with the story, but she was prepared to help him as soon as he asked her to. She had promised, and she always kept her promises.

* * * * *

Two days later, Patricia buzzed Simone's intercom. "Dr. Bennet, those two agents are here again. I told them you had patients scheduled all day, but they are outside waiting. How should I proceed?" The woman sounded out of breath as if she was very disturbed about the agents' presence.

"Are you okay, Patricia?"

"Yes, Doctor...just came running from the kitchen..."

"Okay. Send them in, and hold my next patient, and call the next one to tell them I'm going to be late today...at least half an hour."

"Certainly, Doctor."

Simone was behind her desk when Carla and Agent

Neville came in, and she pointed at the two chairs in front of her. She was not in the mood to be nice. They were interrupting her routine again, and she hated that.

"Agents, I assume you have news on Philip's death?" Simone put down her glasses and looked at Carla and her partner.

"No, Doctor, we want to talk to you about another one of your patients. A Helen Northstrond?"

"Helen? She didn't come to her session this week, but that's not entirely unusual. What about her?"

"She didn't come this week because she's dead," Carla said.

Simone's heartbeat accelerated, and her hands immediately started to shake at the news. She could sense the other woman watching closely, as if gauging Simone's reaction to the news, but she was truly shocked. Helen was only about thirty years old. What could have happened to her? Maybe an overdose? Simone recalled the woman's problems with drugs.

Simone took three deep breaths, trying to calm herself. "How did she die? An overdose? She used to have a drug problem, but I thought she'd gotten clean."

"She went to the hospital Saturday night. At first, they suspected an overdose, and then an aneurism, and she died less than an hour after arriving in the ER. The same doctor who attended Mr. Reynolds was on duty that evening, and he suspected there might be some connection, because she showed the same symptoms, so he sent her for an autopsy. The results came back yesterday...she was another victim of cyanide. We've searched her house. Can you guess what the lab discovered in the prescription bottle we collected from her home? A prescription bottle with your name listed as the prescribing doctor?" Agent Neville asked.

"It's not possible!" Simone said, putting the facts together in her mind. "Potassium cyanide?" Her throat grew tight. She could see her world crumbling around her again. There must be some connection to her...to Peter's phone calls. There had to be. "Three deaths in three weeks! I've lost three patients in the last three weeks. This is insane." She shook her head and put a hand to her chest, feeling as if the ground had fallen from beneath her feet.

"Three, Simone?" Carla asked.

"Yes...but the first one had a heart attack. She was eighty years old."

But Simone could see by the look in Carla's eyes she didn't believe in coincidences.

"So she already had bad health?"

"No. On the contrary, she was in great shape. I saw her medical reports before prescribing some sleeping pills to her. You don't think—?"

"I don't think it's a coincidence," Agent Neville said. "Can you give us the woman's name and contact information for her family?"

"Sure."

"What process do you usually follow when prescribing medication, Simone?"

"First, I ask for the patient's medical reports, and then I prescribe according to the patient's symptoms and according to any previous health conditions."

"Do you know where your patients buy their medication?"

"No, I have no idea. That's not a question I would ever ask."

"Okay, I'm going to tell you. They all went to the same pharmacy—"Health Care Drugstore."

"I didn't know that..."

"You don't know anybody who works there?"

"I don't know; I can't remember anyone. But Health Care Drugstore is right around the block, isn't it? Maybe that's why they went there?"

"Have you prescribed medication to any of your other patients?"

"Of course, I have. This is a psychiatrist's office! I deal with all kinds of psychological problems here every day! What now, Carla, do I need a lawyer?"

Simone was shaken by all the news and grew impatient with their questioning. She had been treating people for years, and she took pride in knowing her job.

"Calm down, Simone... I´m asking because I think you will need to contact those patients and have them bring their medication for analysis. Without creating a panic, of course. Just tell them there may be a problem with expired medication or something. All we know for sure is that we have two identical crimes involving two— maybe three of your patients. The cyanide was found in medication you prescribed. We're afraid the psychopath who kidnapped you might be back. And maybe he's up to a lot more than making a few nuisance phone calls..."

Rather than growing calmer, Simone grew more upset at Carla's words, which sounded like something she'd learned during a pillow-talk session. Simone could imagine Edward, holding Carla in his arms as he talked to her about Simone's personal issues. The embarrassing thought filled Simone with uncommon rage.

"I feel like I'm never going to have peace in my life again!" Her hands were shaking, her stomach burned, and she was positive her gastritis was back. Not a surprise with all she had been through the last few months.

"For now, I'll need you to stay in touch with me," Carla said. "If you notice anything suspicious, please let us know immediately. We're already taping your calls. I'm worried about your safety. We can't know for sure it's the same guy, but what are the chances of two different psychopaths disrupting your life in such a short period of time?"

"I don't know, but none of this has his signature, does it? I mean, in the past, he only killed women, and he didn't poison them. This person—whoever he or she is—has killed at least one man, and he's using potassium cyanide. He used to leave his sperm at the crime scene..."

"Yes, but every victim—before and now—had some kind of connection to you, or the crime happened near you. We think he is trying to get you involved in someway, and we really suspect the same guy."

Agent Neville spoke up. "Doctor, it's rare but not impossible that he simply decided to change his methods. Some psychopaths will try to find other ways to commit their crimes if they believe the police are closing in on them. They are clever, intelligent, and they tend to plan everything, right down to the last detail."

"I can't believe that's the case with Peter...he really seemed disturbed to me...delusional. I got the impression he was a little guy trying to kill the same woman all the time. I could be wrong. After a while, I think I was delusional, but he showed me a side of his personality that came across as a very frightened child."

"Doctor, they're as clever as the devil, and he could have played you. We'll only know if we can put our hands on him, and that's not going to be easy. We still don't have confirmation Peter is our guy. We weren't able to apprehend him, so we weren't able to gather samples of his DNA to compare to the DNA found at the crime scenes. We need to find him, but at the moment, he seems to have vanished. Or he's back but doing a great job hiding from us, and although that would be difficult, with all the surveillance we have in this country, it's not entirely impossible.

"Simone, I promise you, we are doing our best, but we think you're at risk again. We're going to assign a couple agents to protect you," Carla said.

"Here we go again... Please find this guy! I'm sick to death of all this!"

Carla and Agent Neville left Simone's office, and she decided to go back to work. She would go crazy if she started thinking about all she'd just learned. After she saw her last patient, she gathered her things to head home. She no longer felt safe, staying alone in the office. As she was leaving, she met Edward in the hallway.

"Simmie, Carla called me. I'm very worried about you. I'm going to hire that security guard we hired last time, just to keep an eye on things around here. What do you think? The FBI is going to assign a couple agents, but I feel like we need extra protection at the office. And I can ask if he has someone he can put at your house, or the guard we used last time can go from here to there when you leave each day. I'm not thinking very clearly here, but I believe that psychopath is out there somewhere, just waiting for a chance to get to you."

"Please, Ed, yes. Give the security company a call. I don't think I'll be lucky enough to survive if he gets his hands on me again." She didn't have the emotional energy to play the strong woman right now. She felt threated and frail, and she needed someone to take practical measures for her.

"I'm going to take you home."

"Thanks, Ed, I really appreciate that."

She desperately needed some company and to feel reassured. Edward took her home, and when they arrived, he walked through her house to make sure everything was okay.

"Please turn on the alarms as soon as you close the door, okay?" he asked as he prepared to leave.

"Sure," she told him. "I will. Promise." Simone couldn't summon an ounce of enthusiasm. In the past, Edward would have offered to stay with her or would have invited her to sleep at his place. But now...he planned to leave her to deal with her problems... *Don't be unfair. He checked the house, and he drove you home,* she told to herself, but she still felt abandoned.

When she locked the door, she looked in the mirror on the wall in the foyer. Her sunken cheeks and wide, frightened eyes made her look older and tired. The suntan she'd gotten in Miami had faded, leaving her gaunt and pale. No wonder Edward preferred to be with the younger, adorable, vibrant-looking Carla! And Simone had to admit she was jealous as hell of their relationship.

For Christ's sake, Simone, you're in the middle of a tsunami, and you're worried about your looks? She reproached herself.

She sat on her couch and tried to rest a little bit, but after a while, she discovered she still couldn't calm her rattled nerves. She tried meditation, a long bath, controlling her breathing...but she still felt anxious, and worse, she couldn't eat.

She thought about going for a run, but she didn't feel safe enough to do that, at least not at night.

Simone's phone beeped, and she saw she had a message from Carl.

Have you made any more progress? I just finished to the

point you told me to read.

She felt guilty because for two days she hadn't touched Lara's journal, so she decided to work on it now.

I'm in the process of reading, she wrote, *and I will let you know soon.*

And to ease her conscience for telling a little white lie, she quickly grabbed the stack of papers and started to read.

Lara's Journal

For two years of my life, I lived without sex, other than masturbation, which I admit I had to resort to on a daily basis. I was afraid of becoming intimately involved with men, and boys were a source of boredom to me. I didn't find them attractive. They were too young, too immature, too naïve...too...well, I simply had nothing at all in common with them.

"Lara, my girl, I think it's time for you start looking around for a boyfriend. Find a nice guy to date. It would be good for you," Emms said.

We were sitting in Starbucks on 2379 Broadway, sipping coffee, after a show she'd taken me to. Emms had put herself in charge of my cultural education. She loved taking me to shows, museums, and movies, and she gave me books that we'd discuss after we'd both read them. At least once a week, we would go to a show, an exposition—good ones and bad ones—and these were our special moments, spent together with no interruptions.

Emms made it a point to spend one-on-one time with all her grandchildren. She had one day for Sean, when they engaged in activities he enjoyed—he was a teenager now—and she'd spend another day with our little girl, Debbie, who was nine and loved dolls, princesses, and fairy tales. She was adorable and naïve...a normal "little girl" who took piano lessons and still enjoyed the occasional bedtime story.

I didn't have much time for my brother and sister these days because I was studying hard. I had finished Barnard College with praise and was accepted into Columbia's Graduate School of Architecture, Planning and Preservation—*gasp!* And to think there'd been a time when I couldn't even follow along enough in class to make passing grades! I'd actually been accepted in all the universities I applied to, but I didn't want to be far away from home. The children didn't have a mother; Emms had her hands full... I don't know if I mentioned this before, but Emms worked as an architect, and when my family relocated to New York City, she'd agreed to assist my father with his business. Prior to us moving, she'd had her own business, a small one, designing residential homes. My father's company dealt with large commercial and governmental projects, but with Sabine gone and us changing locations, my father and Emms had decided it was better for her to work with him. She had to work less because she wanted to keep an eye on the kids...but one thing was for certain; both her eyes were constantly on me.

Did that bother me...constantly being scrutinized? No, not really. Emms loved me unconditionally—I understood that now—and I appreciated knowing she cared.

"Emms," I said, setting aside my coffee and resting my elbows on the table, "I don't know... I haven't met anyone I found interesting or attractive in a long time. Boys my age are stupid, and I'm avoiding older men... Dr. Dominick would kill me if he found out I'd gone out with a guy twice my age. He's adamant that I find a way to act my age."

"And I agree with him. But you're in college. Surely there are at least a couple nice-looking young men there. Try the football team..." She paused to giggle. "They usually have such hot bodies!"

I laughed. Emms could always make me laugh, and I often felt as if I were out with a girl my age. I probably haven't mentioned that we've been riding around New York City on her motorcycle. She has a group of friends who ride Harleys. They're a lot of fun. Unlike me, Emms has a ton of friends... I'm still working on that... It's still very hard for me to trust people.

But Emms did have a point. I really should try to meet guys in college. I decided to gather my courage and resume my sex life—I was eighteen by then, and God knows I needed some physical attention! But the initial result of my re-entry into the dating pool was disappointing, to say the least. Boys make love—I don't make love; I never did, except in those rare moments with Adrien, but even then, things tended to get a little rough. I tried to go along with the guys I dated, doing things their way. The result? I turned into a serial dater... I went from guy to guy, hoping to find one who could satisfy me. I was afraid to teach them things...to tell them what I really liked...probably because I was afraid to tell those things to myself.

I decided I should discuss the matter with Dr. Dominick, his advice might not exactly be what I would like to hear, but he was a wise man, and following his guidance gave me peace in life. On my scheduled day with him, I decided to bring up the subject in our conversation.

"Dr. Dominick, I can't go on like this anymore."

"Like what?"

He was sitting on his beige couch wearing a beige suit. Nowadays, I believe he had some kind of compulsive obsession for that color. He and the sofa matched so well they could have been covered in the same upholstery material. Of course, he would be the matching pillow...

"Trying to have sex with young men who don't know where to put their hands. I'm frustrated, I'm nervous about it. I'd like to grab them by the collar and say, 'C'mon, let me teach you how to fuck'!"

"Okay..." he said. "So go ahead and do that. They're inexperienced, so you have to teach them. No, don't grab them by the collar, but you can still instruct them in the art of pleasure. You'll need to be kind and patient, or they'll run. Older men hate hearing a woman say they aren't satisfied, but younger men are only concerned with their pleasure, so give it a try. Explain it to them nicely, and see how it goes."

I took his advice and achieved a bit of success. Some of the guys were hopeless causes, but others caught on quickly and improved their technique. Still, the problem was within me... I longed for some violence, for a bit of struggling, a man's brute force... I had to face facts; I was a sadomasochist, and there was no cure, but I couldn't even talk to Dr. Dominick about that part. He worried something bad would happen to me if I pursued that lifestyle.

"People die doing those things, Lara," he told me, the one time I brought up the subject.

I never talked about those things with him again.

I was studying hard, and I only had weekends to relax with my family. Emma had bought a house in Westhampton for us to stay at when we needed to relax, and I really loved to go there.

Years passed quickly while I stayed busy with college, helping with two younger siblings, and being an intern for my father. I had a few disastrous sexual encounters that were so boring they don't deserve to be mentioned. For six years after the end of my relationship with Arthur, that was my life.

I was in my last year of school, I would graduate in six months, and I was twenty-two years old. Once again, I was in search of something better, from a sexual standpoint, and I had decided to follow Emma's advice and take a look at the football players. I was sitting on the sidelines, watching one of their practices, when I saw the most gorgeous African-American quarterback, ever. As tall as I was, all muscles and testosterone, he made me wet just looking at him. I decided I would approach him after the game.

I positioned myself so he had to pass in front of me to go to the locker rooms.

"Well played!" I told him.

He looked at me with a beautiful smile. His hair was very short, and to my surprise, his eyes were so light brown they looked green in the sun. He was gorgeous, and I wanted him.

"Thank you!" He leaned close to one of his fellow players and whispered something, then jogged over to me.

He gave me his hand. His touch was warm and powerful. "John Mayer," he said.

"Lara Parker."

"Nice to meet you, Lara. Never seen you before; don't you like football?"

"I do...but it's my last year, and I've had to really focus on my classes..."

"I know... It's a lot to juggle, right? I'm almost finishing here, but I still have years ahead of me—my internship at a hospital, and of course, the rest of my life studying. I had to pick a profession that requires constant research if I'm to be a success."

"What are you studying?"

"I'm in med school. I'm going to be a doctor."

Nice. Beautiful, brains, and a working knowledge of human anatomy—talk about perfect!

"Hey, John, we're going to go have a beer. Are you coming, or what?" One of his teammates called out to him.

"Sure, hold on a second." He turned back to me. "I have to go, Lara, but how about a movie one of these days?"

"Okay!" How about my bed? I'd enjoy that much more

than an over-priced movie. But of course, I kept those thoughts to myself.

"How do I find you?"

"Architecture...but here's my phone number..."

I gave him my number, which I had written on a piece of paper before I ever approached him. He put it in his pocket, and with another wonderful smile, he left.

"See you," I said.

He called me the next day. I just loved a man who could make up his mind quickly. He invited me to see a movie and made arrangements to pick me up at home.

He picked me up in his silver Ford Escort and took me to the movies. Afterward, he asked if I would like to go to Hoboken to see the view of Manhattan. Since I was nowhere near ready to end our date, I said sure.

It was a cold night, windy...the end of the winter. We parked the car and tried to get out for a little while, but we didn't last long. The wind was glacial. So there we were, sitting inside his car, neither of us speaking, just watching the lights of Manhattan, and suddenly, John leaned over and started kissing me. A savage kiss that had me curling my toes. Oh, God, how I'd missed that! He drew my tongue between his lips and started sucking it, and I felt as if he wanted to eat me with his kiss. He pulled up my blouse and touched me, and then he bent lower and drew my nipple into his mouth and bit it hard.

I moaned in pleasure, encouraging him with whimpers of delight, and he continued his exploration, running his fingers inside my panties and touching my clit. He groaned as his fingertips discovered my wetness. I reached for his dick, opening his zipper and reaching in to wrap my hand around the shaft... Holy shit! That old stereotype about the size of a black man's dick was certainly true in this case. He had a huge package, the size of a Coke bottle! I tried to take him into my mouth, but it was impossible. I could lick it, even suck the head, but it would never fit inside my mouth. I did the best I could, and he must have enjoyed my attempts to pleasure him with my lips and tongue, because his deep moans sounded loud in the enclosed space of the car.

I don't know how, but a few minutes later, we were both half naked in the back seat, me in just my blouse and him with his pants lowered to pool around his ankles. We kept hitting our long legs on doors and seats, trying to find a semi-comfortable position. He climbed between my legs to touch my clit, using his fingers to open my pussy and caress it until I was good and wet.

He rose up to his knees, leaned over the seat, and fished around in the glove compartment. After sheathing his cock with the condom he'd retrieved, he positioned himself between my legs and drove his huge dick inside me. I came immediately, and as he started to move, he grabbed my hair and pulled it hard, and all the pleasure that provoked within me was incredible. He kept moving until I came again, and then he followed me.

"God, you are *so* good. I could live inside you."

We shifted, trying to get into a more comfortable position for a new round when a knock came at the car window.

John hit the button, and the window rolled down. A policeman leaned down to peer into the car.

"Get dressed and get out of here, you two kids! You're lucky I'm too tired to deal with a couple of punks fucking in a car, but if I see you again around here, I'm going to haul you both to jail. Now you have two minutes to get your clothes on and disappear."

We didn't need one. John pulled up his pants and jumped into the driver's seat. He had the car started and was pulling out before I could climb over to the front seat. When we'd put some distance between the angry cop and us, we looked at each other and started to laugh.

"God, I don't know how we got away with that. I was scared shitless I'd end up in jail and have to call my grandma."

"Yes, my heart's still racing." John got my hand and put it on his chest. "See?"

"I do..."

He held my hand there. "I don't want this night to end yet, Lara. I really need to have you again...and again...that was so amazing..."

He turned his face to me to see my reaction and then quickly looked back to the road.

"I'm having fun, too. And I want you again—I haven't had enough of you yet. Not by a long-shot!"

"You are amazing, a girl who doesn't play hard to get. Let's go to my apartment?"

"Sure!"

I couldn't deny his description of me. If a man excited, I wouldn't deny myself the pleasure of taking him to bed. Especially since so few men turned me on back then.

He drove like a crazy man to his place. He shared an apartment on West 171st Avenue with two other college students. It was a beige brick building, not far from the university. The apartment was nice, surprisingly organized for a man cave. Simple furniture filled the combined kitchen, dining area, and living room—a round, white Formica table with stools, a refrigerator, a stove, a microwave oven, and a sink. The couch looked like leather, but I couldn't tell for sure without touching it. We went directly to his room.

The minute we stepped inside, he took my purse and threw it on the armchair beside the twin bed. He then sat on the bed and pulled me to stand between his legs. He lifted my skirt and lowered my panties, then he lowered his head and started licking my pussy, nipping at my pussy lips and nibbling on my clit. He drove two fingers inside me then pulled them out and brought them to his mouth.

"Mmm, delicious," he said, licking them dry. "Girl, you are so gorgeous; I need to bury myself inside you again."

He pulled me down onto the bed, took off my panties, put on a new condom from a collection he had inside the nightstand drawer, and drove his large dick into my pussy. He moved inside me hard, in long, deep, merciless thrusts, and when I came, he rolled me onto my hands and knees, and I felt him licking my ass!

"I want to fuck you like this," he said. "Would you like that?"

I hesitated. A lot of years had passed since I'd last done that, and John wasn't exactly what I'd call "small". In fact, I'd never—ever—had a dick that large *anywhere*, let alone...there.

"I'll be gentle; I promise. I have a wonderful thing here that will help..."

He stood up, searched around for something in his drawer, and then showed me a small, plastic tube.

"What's that?"

"Dentist anesthetic pomade. I got it from a colleague..."

"No." I shook my head. "I want to feel... I enjoy a little pain," I found the courage to tell him. I didn't care if he decided to run afterward; I was only concerned with my pleasure.

He tossed aside the tube and went back to licking my ass and caressing my pussy. Just when I thought I couldn't take another moment of such intense pleasure, he leaned back on his knees and slowly started to penetrate me, using one finger, at first, then adding a second one, taking his time to stretch me.

"Guide me here, Lara...tell me how deep I can go..."

"As deep as you want... It's so good, John. Go on. Just don't stop..."

With gentle control, he put his huge dick to my anus and pressed inside. He slid deeper, until his cock bottomed out, buried inside me. Amazingly, the pain was minimal, and I was so excited, my pleasure was overcoming my initial anxiety. God knew it had been a long time since I'd been fucked so well.

"Move now, and move fast!" I told him. I decided I was going to be myself with this guy, and fuck what he thought of me afterward.

He lost control and started moving deep in my ass while he spanked me with his hand. I came three times before he pulled out, changed the condom, and made me ride him while he held my breasts, squeezing them until it hurt. I don't know how many times I came that night, but when I climbed from his bed at five in the morning, he had fallen asleep.

I grabbed my clothes and got dressed, trying my best not to wake him. I used my cell and called for a cab as I left his apartment, heading home satisfied for once, after a long time of starvation.

I arrived home and went directly to my room. I took a long shower, thinking about how great that night had been. I went to bed and I was happy, but I didn't relish the idea of seeing John again. Girls like me were not meant to be girlfriends...

CHAPTER TWENTY-SIX

Simone — Present Day

After staying up late to read the journal, Simone slept in. She awoke more tired than usual, and before leaving for the office, she sent a message to Carl, updating him on her progress.

She arrived at work to find a message lying on her desk. The FBI had gotten a judicial order to exhume Theodora's body, and they planned on digging up the casket that day.

Simone spent another busy day seeing patients, and as she was finishing up her notes and wrapping things up, she received a text message from Carl. He wanted to talk to her on the phone that night. She messaged him back, saying she'd be available after seven, and then left for home.

Back at her house, Simone changed into sweatpants and tennis shoes and went for a run. Before she talked to Carl, she needed some fresh air to clear her mind and to relax.

* * * * *

At 8:00 p.m., Carl called. "Simone, how've you been?"

"I'm okay, how about you, Carl?"

"Trying to catch my breath after reading more of the journal. I have an idea, and I want your opinion. I'm thinking about giving John Mayer a copy of Lara's journals. What do you think?"

"At this point, I don't think it's a good idea. We don't know what's going to happen with them. Let's finish reading it, ourselves, and then we can decide."

"Well, John loved her, you know?"

"I remember reading about him in your diary. He said she crushed his heart. But if you give the journal now, we might end up hurting him even more. Like I said...let's finish reading them...find out how things ended between Lara and John, then we can decide."

"You're right, as always. Thank you very much for all

you're doing. I know your life isn't easy right now, and here you are, helping me with my troubles."

"Don't worry about it, Carl. It's good for me to keep busy…"

They talked for a few more minutes, and then said goodnight. Simone decided she needed to go to sleep early for a change. She ate some chicken and asparagus Lola had left for her and then went to her room. After a long shower, she went to bed. She turned off the lamp and fell asleep within minutes of her head hitting the pillow.

She heard steps, and she knew somebody was inside her house. She wanted to run, but she couldn't move her legs. As hard as she tried, her legs wouldn't respond. She needed to at least reach her phone. She should call Edward; he would help her. She stretched her arm to get her phone, but Carla suddenly appeared. The woman snatched up Simone's phone and ran to the door, laughing.

"Give me the phone; I need help!" Simone shouted.

She awoke to the sounds of her own screams.

"God, not the nightmares again… I can't go back to sleeping pills. But after trying hard for at least half an hour to go back to sleep, Simone got up, went to the bathroom, filled a glass of water, and took one of the little pills. She turned on the TV and waited for sleep to take over.

* * * * *

Two days after the exhumation of Theodora's body, the results of her autopsy were concluded. The report came back the same as Philip's and Helen's. Cause of death, potassium cyanide poisoning. Once again, agents discovered the poison in pills Simone had prescribed, and as Helen and Philip had done, Theodora had filled her prescription at Health Care Drugstore. No doubt in Simone's mind—she was definitely at the center of all these crimes.

That being the case, she began calling her clients one by one, telling them they should bring in medication as she'd been told there'd been a mistake involving the expiration dates. But news of Theodora's exhumation had gotten out and had been widely reported, and suddenly all Simone's clients were calling or coming into her office. They voiced their fears about taking their medication, but thankfully, not even one of her patients believed she had anything to do with the deaths. They were all worried about her and her safety. Out of precaution, she gave new prescription to all her patients and, per the FBI's instructions, advised them to smell the pills before taking them. If they noted the odor of bitter almonds, they were to contact the local police immediately. They were also recommended to avoid Health Care Drugstore.

Of course, two clients—the kind of people who read

about the possible side effects associated with a particular medication, then suddenly start to feel all the symptoms—went to the police station, taking their medicine bottles because they believed they had smelled bitter almonds. The pills were sent to the lab and tested for potassium cyanide, but the results were all negative.

One patient—an elderly man who lived alone—had been unreachable by telephone, and when the police went to speak with him, they discovered him dead. Potassium cyanide, and again, the poison was discovered inside a pill Simone had prescribed to him for depression, which he'd gotten filled at the same drugstore as the other victims had patronized.

FBI agents had been sent to interrogate the employees at Health Care Drugstore, but so far, they hadn't found a suspect.

Agents were watching Simone's house and office, and her private security guard, Gregory, accompanied her everywhere she went over the following days. The strange phone calls continued, and the records indicated they originated from an unknown number from Asia. Unfortunately, none of the calls lasted long enough to exactly pinpoint the caller's location, and the FBI couldn't discard the possibility Peter had entered the country, bringing an foreign cell phone number with him.

Every TV network was covering the latest murders, and many of the headlines described "Psychopath Peter Hay" who'd come back to terrorize Connecticut. His photograph appeared on every national broadcast.

Simone was at home when her phone rang. She answered it, and for the first time since that horrible day, she heard Peter's voice, and immediately her heart started racing.

"Stop with that shit, bitch! I'm not to blame for your problems, so stop telling everyone I am, or I'm going to kill you! Just stooooooopppppp."

"Peter, where are you?"

"Me? I'm in the fucking hell you sent me to!"

The line went dead, and again, he hadn't stayed on the phone long enough to get his position. The FBI had told Simone to try to keep him from hanging up right away, but he was obviously too smart to fall into their trap.

FBI agents searched for security cameras in the houses of all victims, but they hadn't found any suspects going in or out. It seemed a dead end... Simone's head was in turmoil; she didn't know what to think. Had Philip really returned to begin killing off her patients, or had he been telling the truth about not being involved?

That same evening, she took Lara's journal and sat on her couch. She would continue reading about Lara and

John Mayer. Afterward, she'd be better able to advise Carl regarding whether he should give a copy of the journal to John. And besides, Simone was really curious to find out how Lara had ended up breaking John's heart.

Lara's Journal

Although I hadn't planned to see him again, John apparently had other ideas, and he called me in the middle of the next morning. I didn't answer the phone.

On Monday, he was waiting for me near my class, leaning against the brick wall with one leg bent, foot propped against the bricks. A navy-blue t-shirt revealed all his muscles, and he scared me because I wasn't expecting him to be there.

"Hey, girl, you know how to make a man feel like trash."

"Hello, you scared me. Why do you feel like trash?"

"You fuck me that way, and then you just leave? You don't say a word; you don't answer the phone... Did I do something wrong?"

"No... I just thought..." Actually, I figured that after what I'd let him do—what I'd *encouraged* him to do in bed the other night—he'd be scared as hell and on a one-way flight to China.

"What? I can imagine what you thought...just a party for the night?" Obviously angry, he practically spit the words.

"No...it's hard to explain... I had to go. I have two small siblings to take care of, and I couldn't stay. We—my brother, sister, and I—have no mother. I—"

"You don't want to see me anymore, fine. I just wanted to be sure."

"No. I want to, but I figured my behavior the other might have scared you, and I thought you didn´t want to see me anymore." I told him the truth, thinking I had nothing to lose.

"Why? For the first time in my twenty-four years, I find a beautiful and intelligent girl, *and* she likes to fuck the way I like to fuck, and you think that scared me?"

My bones practically slumped with relief. His language was rude, but he was upset, so I could forgive him. Besides, he didn't think I was a lunatic—he had enjoyed what we'd done as much as I had! I gave him a spontaneous hug, then took a step back and gave him my famous smile, the one I'd practiced using since I was a kid to disarm people. He seemed relieved, too; his shoulders relaxed, and he returned my smile.

"That's good to hear because I really liked being with you," I told him, running my fingernail down the side of his neck. God, he turned me on. I really loved the smell of his skin.

"Let's have a beer tonight? Oh, no, shit, tonight I can't. I have night-duty at the hospital. Tomorrow?"

"Tomorrow is okay for me. I don't have anything planned."

He gave me a light kiss on my lips and left, humming some song I wasn't familiar with. I watched him go. I don't think I could ever get tired of watching that man's ass...

* * * * *

I started seeing John on a pretty regular basis. I have to confess, the sex he and I had was the best I'd had in years. He was rough, and I could tell him about the things I liked... Still, I worried I might be pushing my luck, because every time we were together, I would introduce a new "game", and then I'd wait for him to throw me out. He never did, though, so I'd proceed to next step.

He taught me to appreciate beer. After years of drinking champagne and whisky, I could finally name two or three beers I enjoyed now and then, and although an icy cold draft wasn't my absolute favorite choice of beverages, at least drinking one made me feel my age for a change.

We were having a beer in his room, both of us naked and lying on his bed. Actually, he was lying on the bed; I was sort of lying on top of him, draped across his luscious body while he caressed my breasts. Since we were both so relaxed—and I was a little tipsy—I decided it was the perfect moment to introduce the subject of using a whip. I had brought one with me to his place— one small enough to fit in my oversized purse—and I had to see what he'd say if I asked him to use it on me. I turned my head to look at him and dropped the bomb.

"Hey, John... I was wondering... How would you like to try something different tonight? Are you up for another new experience?"

"If it's not a gay thing," he said, using a phrase I'd heard several times before. "I'm in." He smiled.

I'd never understood what he meant by "a gay thing", but I decided now wasn't the time to ask him to explain. Instead, I pushed forward with my agenda. I reached down and grabbed my purse, pulled out the whip, and tossed it to him. He looked down at it and then looked at me. If he was surprised, he didn't show it.

"What you want me to do with this?" he asked, lifting one dark brow.

"How about trying it on me?"

The little whip had black leather with fringes. He took it, analyzed it, caressed it, and immediately gave my buttocks a light blow. He left the bed and pushed me against the mattress, already starting to play. He began caressing me with the whip, passing the fringes over my body. I shivered at the cold touch. He teased my breasts with it and passed it over my pussy. I shivered again, this time with excitement. He turned me on the bed, and I lay facedown, and he did the same caress on my back, and then, very gently, he whipped my buttocks. God, I'd missed that. Missed it like a so-called "normal person" misses breathing, but his touch was too light for my taste.

"No...harder..."

He hit me again, putting more force behind it, but the blow was still far from what I wanted.

"Harder, beat me. I promise it's okay."

A second passed, and then I felt him tense beside me. I tried to relax, to prepare for his next strike and just go with it. The crack of the whip against my ass sent a fiery pain rushing over my skin. My pussy reacted as if someone had turned on a spigot. I moaned in satisfaction as he hit me two more times, then he threw the whip aside and drove his dick as deep inside my pussy as he could, taking me from behind. He covered me with his big body and fucked me without looking me in the eyes, grabbing my hair, hitting my ass with his bare hands. I was moaning, crying, and moving my hips, and suddenly, I felt the melting sensation in my pussy growing and my clit throbbing as if it contained a heart inside it. The sensation climbed, spreading over my stomach while my heart raced, and I started to come nonstop in a beautiful, ongoing series of orgasms.

When it was over, I couldn't speak. My entire body hurt, my face buried in the pillow, John still over my back, kissing my nape. He was so tender and yet at the same time so brutal in bed.

"Are you okay? Did I hurt you?"

He pulled my hair aside to see my face, sounding worried.

"Hurt me?" I laughed weakly. "You made me come like crazy; you didn't hurt me. I loved what we just did."

"You drive me crazy, girl! I don't know my limits with you. Just the smell of you turns me into a psycho!"

"I like that!"

He rolled off me to sit on the bed, and I got up to gather my clothes, ready to go.

"Hey, where are you going? Can't you spend the night?"

I couldn't. It was to intimate for me to sleep with someone. Too much for my head.

"I can't, John, I have—"

"I know...siblings... But just for one night? They have your father! I would like to hold you in my arms for a while. You're always running. I need more intimacy."

"More than we just shared?" I pointed to the bed.

"That's not intimacy, Lara. That's sex. I want to know you better. You are so mysterious. I never know what goes on in your head. You're so hard to understand sometimes."

"What's so hard to understand?"

"You never talk about your life. I don't know much about you. We fuck, we go to the movies, but you don't accept an invitation to go out with my friends. It seems as if you don't want to be seen with me. The first thing regular girls want to know after having sex is when you're going to introduce them to the team as your girlfriend, but you don't seem to care about that."

"I am not a regular girl...I never will be." I wasn't hurt because he'd tried to compare me to other girls, but I felt like shit when I thought about my life. About the things I'd been through. The shit he would never know, because I would never tell him about my shameful past. I simply couldn't.

"Why do you look so sad?" he asked. "Let me in, Lara. Don't close the door on me like that."

I shook my head. "This is just the way I am. I don't know how to be different. I'm not sad; I'm just thinking..."

"Okay, girl... You obviously have your limits. I'll respect that. Just don't disappear on me, okay?"

"No, I won't. I promise!"

I left his house, leaving behind a man who had a worried expression, little wrinkles he hadn't had before forming on his forehead. Despite what he'd said about respecting my limits, obviously, he was still worried about something.

* * * * *

Emms and I were at home, lying around being lazy on the sofa. She had her feet on me, and I was massaging them. She always loved when I rubbed her feet.

"Mm, good!"

"Emms," I said, "I'm seeing this guy from school."

She immediately sat up to look at me, a small smile forming in her lips. Obviously, my news made her happy.

"And…?" she asked.

"I don't know what to do with him." I sighed.

"Tell me everything…" She had an amused expression, and her eyes had the sparkle of a teenager waiting for her girlfriend to tell her the latest gossip.

"Well, I met him at a football game. He plays on the team. He's gorgeous, his body is soooo great…and he's black."

"And...? Is that the problem? That he's black? Who cares what color he is?" She dismissed the idea with a wave of her hand.

I shook my head. Emms wouldn't have any bias. She was all about love and peace for the world.

"No, Emms, that's not a problem. The problem is that while the sex is really great with him—he's the first guy who's satisfied me in a really long time...since Paris— but he wants me to meet his teammates, his friends, go out with him. And I don't know what to do..."

"How do you feel about him, Lara?" Emms took my hands and looked me in the eyes.

"It's hard to say. I really would like to say I'm in love with him. I wish I could feel what I felt for Adrien, that romantic kind of feeling I've read about in books. The kind of love where you want someone so much, you forget about yourself, but I can't. I can't feel those things, and that hurts me. It's like a hole inside me...an empty hole. And I can't fill it, and I don't know why!"

"Love implies trust. You've been through a lot, my dear, and it's hard for you to trust."

"I can deal with sex, I can deal with passion...but feelings, Emms? I can't, I just can't! I know how to give a man pleasure, and I can feel pleasure. I can leave my body and go to another galaxy during an orgasm, but I can't love. I can't."

Some people might think it's weird to talk like that to their grandmother, but I didn't. Emms had always played a dual role in my life. She was the perfect girlfriend when she wanted to be and the perfect grandmother when I needed one. And in that moment, she was being my best friend.

"Explain to me what you feel. Tell me more about this hole you think you have. Maybe I can help."

"It's like an eternal hunger, Emms, a desire I can't satisfy. It's like needing sex but not getting any, but it's inside the heart." I put my hand over my chest and continued. "I really would like to fall in love with John. He's special. He understands my physical needs. I think he could be the one for me, but I don't know how to fulfill the silent demand I see in his eyes. I don't know how to give love, Emms! I only know how to fuck!"

"Babe, that's not true! You are a loving and caring person. I see you with your siblings, and you are always trying to compensate for your mother's absence. You love them, you worry about them...you have a tender heart inside your chest, Lara."

She touched my face, and tears filled my eyes.

"Maybe I just don't know how to love men."

"Give yourself a chance, sunshine! Just give yourself a chance, and don't push yourself to love someone. If you enjoy being with this guy, try to go a little bit further…go out with his friends, invite him to come here…be his girlfriend for a while. You don't need to promise him eternal love or marriage, but if you like him, give it a try."

"I like him, and I love you. You are so special, Emms!"

"See! You know how to love! And please don't forget condoms. That's how I got pregnant with your father…"

She opened her arms, and I hugged her, and laughter replaced my tears.

* * * * *

I took Emm's advice and started going out with John. To my surprise, I found his teammates enjoyable, and he opened a whole new world for me.
Friends…beers…bars…a life I'd never known. I discovered how to laugh with people my age, and I was trying hard to let things run their course.

CHAPTER TWENTY-SEVEN

Simone – Present Day

Simone sent a message to Carl to tell him where she'd stopped in her reading, but he didn't answer. Maybe he was busy, she thought.

And what about Edward, she thought. What had he been up to lately? They rarely talked, and she had to admit she really missed him...and worse, she was jealous. Her chest ached every time she thought about him laughing with the beautiful and young Carla. The woman tried to be nice to Simone, but she couldn't deny she hated her—after all, Carla had stolen Simone's friend!

She definitively had to analyze her feelings, but not now. No more of that kind of thinking so late at night, she decided. She made a detour into the kitchen to grab a quick snack before bed. Some day, when she had a clear and rested mind, she'd analyze her feelings for Ed. Now, she would open a bottle of wine, serve herself a glass, and make a toast to loneliness and hard work, the two constant companions of her life.

* * * * *

On the way home from work the next day, Simone went to the supermarket to buy a few groceries. She had to get some food in the house, or soon she would starve.

Simone entered her house through the garage to avoid to been seen. The press had been harassing her, and it was hard to go from home to work and back. Besides the FBI agents were always watching her. They were in front of her house and her office 24/7—for her protection—and she felt like a fish living in a bowl.

Simone put away the groceries and then went into the living room to lie on the couch and relax for a while. She would read in a little bit, but for now, she would do nothing...just rest from her tumultuous day.

She was putting on her glasses to start reading when she heard noises. She looked up, got to her feet and went to see what was going on outside. She crossed to the window and pulled back the curtains a little bit, and her heart sank. Standing there in her front yard was a very angry Armando, an FBI agent searching him from head to toe.

"Hey, stop that; I'm Dr. Bennet's fiancé!" he shouted.

Oh, God. The last time she'd seen him, he had tried to pass himself off to Carl as her boyfriend. Now he'd upgraded his status to fiancé? She was going to strangle that idiot.

Simone went out the front door and stormed down the sidewalk.

"You can leave him alone, Agent," she said. "He's an idiot but a harmless one."

"Are you sure, Doctor?"

"Yes. I'm certain."

"Told you!" Armando told the agent, sounding like a child who'd been rescued by his mommy, which had probably happened a lot during his life. Just one of the reasons he was such a spoiled bastard, reflected Simone.

Simone half expected him to stick out his tongue or stomp his foot at the poor FBI agent.

"Armando, let's go inside."

Simone's life was already so exposed; she didn't want to talk to Armando on her front lawn. She turned and went back into the house, having no doubt Armando would follow. Once they were in the foyer with the door firmly closed behind them, she turned to face the man whose behavior had grown dangerously close to that of a stalker.

"Are you not going to invite me to come in and sit down, Simone?" He pouted.

"No, I'm not. What are you doing here again? Don't you have a life in Miami, Paraguay, or whatever?"

"I do...but I needed to see you! I saw the news, and I was worried. I thought you would want to go somewhere safe. We could go together to my family's farm in Paraguay...even the general suggested that would be your best course of action."

"I know. I've already spoken to him. Thanks for the offer, Armando, but I'm not going anywhere. I have patients who need me."

"I need you! You can't die!"

He tried to hug her, but she pushed him hard. Before he could recover, she spun around and stalked away, into her living room, needing to put some space between them. Unfortunately, he followed.

"Hey, you could be more kind. After all, I came all this way just to protect you!"

Simone spun around. "Armando, you are here because

you want to be here, not because I asked you to come; let's be clear about that. And I hope you don't make a scene this time. Did you see the agent outside? I'll be happy to call him back to get you!"

Armando was searching for something inside his backpack, which he had thrown onto her living room floor. Simone frowned and shook her head. Had the pig-headed man heard a single word she'd said? Finally, he straightened, a triumphant smile on his face and a small, square black box in his hand. He lifted the lid on the box and showed it to Simone.

"Simone, marry me! I can protect you from the world!"

I am literally surrounded by crazy people. If he was going to protect her from the world, what was he...an alien? Simone blinked at the gold ring with its ridiculously huge, heart-shaped stone inside the box. She was furious, she felt invaded by Armando's presence, she was upset by his ridiculous marriage proposal, her stomach was hurting, and she really wanted to be strong enough to literally kick Armando's ass She'd never felt the urge to beat someone before, but now she did, and she finally could understand why people lost their temper and hit each other.

"And who would protect me from you? Armando, how many times do I have to repeat myself? I don't want you! I don't love you, I don't want to marry you, and I don't want you near my home or in my life. Is that clear now?" Her voice was loud and her tone angry.

"Not to me…you're playing hard to get…"

"No, I'm not! I'm telling the truth. I'm being as honest as I can be! Get your stuff, your rock, your backpack, and your stupid face, and get out of my life, please!"

"You are a real bitch, you know that? You just broke my heart! You deserve all you're getting! You don't deserve a good man like me; you deserve to have a psychopath destroy your life! You are going to pay for this, Simone! You did everything to get me to fall in love with you, and then you discard me like an old rag!"

He was threatening her but in a very low tone of voice, no doubt remembering the FBI agent just outside her front door. But his face a mask of anger, his mouth turned down at the corners, and he was clenching his teeth. Simone was afraid of him, but she couldn't show her fear.

She nodded toward the front entry and opened the door quickly, shouting to attract the attention of the agent in front of her house. "Please leave now, Armando…we're finished with this conversation. Hopefully for good!"

He left quickly without looking back. Simone hurried to the window and watched him as he approached the agent who had searched him. As he passed the man, Armando switched his backpack from one shoulder to the other, swinging it wide so he hit the agent in the arm. Simone shook her head. *God, what a spoiled child.*

Simone went to the kitchen and filled a glass with water. She drank it slowly, calming her nerves, then she opened went into the medicine cabinent in the powder room and grabbed some antacids. Her stomach would kill her if her life continued as it had been. She really needed to find peace again.

It took half an hour for her to calm down for her breathing to return to normal and her hands to stop shaking. She returned to her spot on the couch, put on her reading glasses, and picked up Lara's journal to read a little bit more.

Lara's Journal

I arrived home earlier than I usually did, and the scene I found in our family room stunned me. Sean was there, kissing another guy! Christ, what a shock. I'd known he was different—for instance, he'd always loved playing with dolls while he'd mostly ignored his toy cars—but I'd always assumed he was just sensitive or something. What should I do? Talk to him?

I went to the kitchen before they could see me, and I made a lot of noise so they'd realize I was there.

I was eating a sandwich when Sean entered the kitchen, his "friend" on his heels.

"Hey, sis, you're home early today!"

He seemed surprised and really uncomfortable. He stood near the table, kicking the leg, clearly uncertain about what he should say or do next.

Sean was taller than me and very skinny. He wore glasses, his hair was brown, and his eyes were the exact same color as mine. He was going to be a handsome man, but for now, his hands were too big and his bones too visible for my taste.

"Yes, I'm tired, and I'm sick of the library. Aren't you going to introduce your friend?"

"Peter." The stranger gave me his hand. He had brown hair, green eyes, and was very handsome with his wide smile.

"Lara, Sean's older sister."

"Nice to meet you, Lara. I thought you were God."

"Nice to meet you, too, Peter. God? Why?"

"Sean is always talking about you, but I never met you before, so I had to believe he had a gorgeous sister. Like God, everybody believes, but nobody sees."

The guy was trying to be funny.

"How old are you, Peter?"

"Twenty-one."

"Are you studying?"

"Just finished business school, and I'm starting my own business."

"Oh...what kind of business?"

"I'm buying clothes from China and selling them to retailers in the U.S...."

"Interesting...and it's a good business?"

"One day it will be, but so far, I couldn't buy you a beer. Sorry!"

"Nice. Thank God, I'm not that fond of beers. Good luck. I have to go to my room to study, so you two take care."

Sean had remained silent during my conversation with Peter—a very guilty mute, in my opinion. Peter talked too much with his hands. I didn't think he looked Italian, so I figured he was nervous.

I didn't know what to do, and when Emm arrived home that night, I was waiting for her.

"Emms, I believe Sean is gay..." I greeted her with this news.

"Oh, well, hello to you, too, miss. And yes, he is. The

sooner we all accept that, the better. I'm surprised it took you so long to notice."

"No! You knew already?"

"Since the day I did his birth chart. I think it's pretty obvious, though, don't you? He's not the least bit masculine. Never has been. But how did you find out?"

Emms was an amateur astrologer, and she was always doing charts for her friends and family. She was very good and very serious about it. Back then, I didn't believe much, but after some years, my curiosity increased, and she even taught me how to do charts and analyze people's personalities.

"I arrived earlier than usual and saw him kissing another guy...an older guy..."

"Aye, that's news! Until now, I didn't think he was a practicing homosexual. I guess it's time for me to have a talk with him. How much older was this guy?"

"Five years older than Sean."

"Shit! That's a lot! Who is he? Were you able to find out more?"

"Peter something. I don't remember if he told me his last name. I was in a state of shock!"

"Oh. Yes. Peter. He's a nice kid. Don't worry. He comes from a good family—all lawyers, I believe."

"But he's older…"

"Yes, that's a concern, but at least he's not crazy. Well, I have to do his chart to know for sure. Did they know you saw them?"

"No. They didn't see me. What are we going to do about this?"

"First, I'm going to talk to your brother, and then I'll need to speak with your father. That will be difficult…"

"Why? What do you plan to say to him?"

"He needs to embrace Sean's sexuality. Your father is not the kind of man who will accept having a gay son very easily. He is too strict."

"But are you not going to try to convince Sean to…I don't know…like girls?"

"No chance. If a person is gay, they're gay. There is no way to force someone to be something they're not. If he's not accepted by his family, he'll have a life filled with hiding who he is, disguising his desires, and suffering as he tries to fit in. I won't allow that to happen to your brother. He's adorable, and he has been through a lot with your mother's departing. He needs support. It won't be easy, but it's going to be worse if we don't support him."

"Do you think that's normal, Emms? To be gay?"

"What I know is that it's not a choice, and a person is gay or they aren't. Sean is, so the sooner we face that, the better. It's a hard decision he will have to make, to decide if he is going to embrace his homosexuality or if he is going to try to hide it. If he decides to come out of the closet, he will need courage. Society isn't very accepting of homosexuality, but if we are by his side, it'll be easier."

"I don't know what to think."

"Think with your heart, not your brains. He is your brother. You love him, you accept him how he is. Why would that change? His penis is not his heart, and being gay is his problem, not yours. Just love him, kid."

This was the first time I had to face the subject of homosexuality. I didn't know what to think, but I loved my brother. I was going to support him, no matter what.

CHAPTER TWENTY-EIGHT

Simone — Present Day

Enough for today, thought Simone. From a psychiatrist's perspective, Lara had a very interesting family. A family filled with problems that revolved around sexuality, betrayals, homosexuality, and pedophilia... Simone was glad she had focused her career helping people who had deviate sexual issues, as she was positive they were the at the root of all other emotional problems.

Simone decided to take a shower. The water running over her body would do wonders for her, she thought, and then she would end her day with a nice meal and a sleeping pill. She was afraid of another nightmare, and as the pill took at least half an hour to produce the necessary effect, she decided to take it before going to the kitchen.

* * * * *

Saturday morning, Simone overslept, thanks to the pill but also thanks to not having any nightmares. She got up, and after taking a quick shower just to wake up a little more, she dressed in sweatpants and a t-shirt. She would go for a run after breakfast. She was positive the agent following her would not be happy about that, but he would follow her anyway. When she entered the kitchen, her breakfast was ready. Her maid, Lola, had arrived earlier and had prepared a lovely table.

"Good morning, Lola, thank you very much! You are so kind. How are you today?"

"Good morning, Doctor. Not feeling well, I'm afraid. As usual, my stomach is bothering me."

"Oh, Lola. If you're not feeling well, you should go home. No need to be here today if you're—" Simone gasped. "Lola! Are you okay?"

The maid swayed, her eyes rolling back in her head, and then she fell to the floor at Simone's feet.

"Lola?" Simone kneeled at the woman's side. "Lola, can you hear me?"

The older woman had turned deathly pale, and foam

oozed from between her lips and drizzled down her chin.

Simone leaped to her feet, dug her cellphone out of the pocket of her sweatpants, and quickly dialed 9-1-1. As she gave her address to the dispatcher, she hurried to the front door and yanked it open.

"Help, Agent Wilson, please!" she called for the FBI agent. "I believe my maid has been poisoned!"

Agent Wilson rushed inside the house. He kneeled beside Lola, and, after clearing her airway, he began CPR. Simone stood nearby, watching and ringing her hands. She felt impotent. Even though she was a doctor, she couldn't think clearly or find the necessary calm to help. Who would have hurt her maid? How could someone do such a thing? The presence of foam coming from Lola's mouth made Simone certain the poor woman had been poisoned.

The wail of a siren disrupted her thoughts, and she ran to the front door to flag down the ambulance.

Five minutes later, the paramedics rolled Lola out Simone's front door on a gurney. Simone grabbed her purse and keys off the table in the foyer and followed them. She waited impatiently while they loaded the stretcher into the back of the ambulance.

"I'm going with you," Simone said, stepping forward before they could close the emergency vehicle's back door. She didn't wait for assistance but climbed in to sit beside Lola. As she sat on the bench in the back, she saw Agent Wilson on the sidewalk, putting a pair of handcuffs on a very upset-looking Armando.

"What happened agent?" she shouted from inside the ambulance.

"Don't worry, Doctor. I just found this guy parked in front of the house and acting very suspicious. Go with your maid; I'll take care of this."

Simone sat back on the bench, and the doors slammed closed. The ambulance lurched forward, sirens blaring. Once again, Simone watched quietly as a paramedic checked Lola's vital signs and added some kind of medication to her IV. Thankfully, the poor dear was still alive. Simone said a hasty prayer for the maid's full recovery. Her thoughts turned to Armando. Could he be responsible for Lola's sudden illness? He'd gotten into a confrontation with the maid on one of his previous visits and had promised he'd seek revenge against Simone for dismissing him as she had. Her head spun at such horrible thoughts, but what about the other deaths? Why would he have hurt anyone else?

* * * * *

Lola died before noon, and according to the doctors, she'd somehow ingested potassium cyanide. Still in a state of shock, Simone sat in one of the hospital's tiny waiting areas. She hadn't moved in hours... Not since the attending physician had come in to tell her Lola hadn't made it. Simone didn't know what to do or where to go.

"Simone, are you okay?"

She looked up. *Edward.* How had he known where to find her?

"I heard the news... Carla called to tell me the agent had reported in about you coming here," he said, as if he'd read her thoughts. "How is Lola?"

"Dead...going to autopsy...she was poisoned!" Simone's voice cracked, but her eyes were dry. She still couldn't process the pain. Lola has been with her for more than ten years. She was family!

"Poisoned!" Edward shook his head. "Well, that's it then. You're going home with me! No way you are going home alone."

"But I never prescribed any kind of medication for Lola!"

"Calm down, Simmie. We still don't know what's going on." He held out a hand to assist her to her feet. "Let's go home."

"Did Carla tell you anything about the guy they arrested in front of my house?"

"Yes, they are questioning him. As soon as I have any

news, I'll let you know."

* * * * *

Edward dropped Simone off at his apartment before heading over to her house to collect some things for her. She couldn't think clearly; she felt sorry for Lola, and she felt guilty.

Lola is dead because of me! The thought kept whirling through her mind. Why? Who would do this? If Philip was really abroad, who had poisoned her maid? Armando? Am I so blind? Did I unwittingly drive a true psychopath to violence? If that's the case, I should rip up my diploma. If she'd slept with Armando without realizing he was capable of killing people, then her judgment was truly compromised, which meant she could be a danger to her patients. Maybe the kidnapping had messed up her head, maybe she couldn't trust her judgment. She remembered the advice she'd given her patients recently and felt badly about that.

Her head was like a labyrinth; she couldn't find the solution to the puzzle.

When Edward arrived, Simone was sitting in the same chair she'd been in when he had left her forty minutes earlier.

"Simmie, I'm going to run a bath for you. It'll help you relax."

Once again, he took her by the hand and led her to his guestroom. She waited, standing in the middle of the room while he went into the connecting bathroom. A moment later, she heard the sound of water running. When the bathtub was full, Edward came back into the guestroom.

"Will you be okay alone?" he asked.

Simone nodded. "Yes," she whispered. "Thank you."

He nodded. "I'll wait for you in the kitchen."

Simone took a long bath, got dressed in a pair of pink panties, blue jeans, and a t-shirt she had found in the suitcase Edward brought for her. She then headed back to the kitchen barefoot, her wet hair hanging down her back.

Edward had prepared lunch. It had to be after three in the afternoon, but although she'd barely touched her breakfast, she had no appetite.

"Eat a little bit, honey. You've been through a lot lately."

That did it. His kind words created cracks in the fog shrouding Simone's mind, and she started to cry, hot tears running down her face. She felt so impotent, so guilty, and so lost.

Edward pulled her close and wrapped his arms around her. As he ran his fingers through her hair, for the second time in one week, she cried on his shoulder.

"Shh, you're safe now, Simmie. I'm not going to let anything happen to you. I promise."

He moved his head as if to kiss her cheek. Simone turned her face at the same time, and their lips touched. Driven by an instinctive need to feel alive...for human contact, she kissed him. Thankfully, he responded in kind, pulling her closer instead of pushing her away.

Their tongues tangled in a deep kiss. Simone put one hand at the back of his neck and reached for the buttons of his shirt with the other. Once she'd created a large enough opening, she slipped her hand inside to caress him, running her fingers through his thin chest hair and drinking in his warmth. After a few moments, they paused, and Edward lifted his head. Simone met his hot gaze as she drew in a few shaking breaths. The look in his eyes asked her if she was certain this was what she wanted. After a beat, Simone slowly nodded.

Apparently, that was all the invitation Edward needed, because he scooped her up in his arms and carried her to his bed. Neither of them uttered a word. Instead, they used their hands and fingers and lips and tongues to communicate their mutual desire as they stripped off their clothes in a desperate race to feel skin against skin.

The smell of his sandalwood cologne invaded her

senses, a familiar aroma and one that had never turned her on before. But today, for some odd reason, the scent fired her blood and made her want him even more.

"Lie back," he told her, "I need to touch you."

Simone smiled. "You are touching me, silly," she said, but she complied with his request and moved to lie on her back, her head propped on one of his thick, down pillows.

Edward lay on his side and began to caress her body, and although her flesh responded to his touch, her focus was on his expression. Never had she seen a look of such smoldering admiration. He traced her curves, his touch gentle, until he'd touched nearly every inch of her, and then he did the same thing with his lips, licking and kissing her from neck to ankle, stopping only to lavish his attention on her breasts. He moved slowly, obviously in no rush and clearly enjoying the foreplay.

Edward swirled his tongue down her belly, leaving behind a trail of fire, until he finally reached her clit. He drew in a deep breath, touched her with the tip of his tongue. Simone was already contorting under his touch, and when she moaned, he started to move quickly, sucking her clit and caressing her pussy with his fingers until she was wet and ready.

She reached to touch him, but he grabbed her hand and gently moved it away.

"Not today...I want to feel you...I've wanted this for so long..."

He rose up until their pelvises were aligned and then slowly entered her.

"You are much more incredible than I thought you would be, and that's saying something," Edward told her. "It feels so good to be inside you."

Desperate to come, Simone urged him to move faster. She lifted her hips quickly, and Edward increased his pace to match hers. The friction of his cock inside her, invading her, started a hot sensation that spread all through her pussy. Her clit pulsed, her body craving the final release. She moaned, shifting her body until she felt Edward's cock moving against her G-spot, and she let go, coming hard and exploding in a sensation of fulfillment. Edward's orgasm followed shortly after hers, filling her with his hot cum and causing her to shiver and quake beneath him.

They lay there quietly, side by side, friends for more than twenty years and lovers for only a few minutes, and amazingly enough Simone didn't know what to say. She feared that no matter what came out of her mouth, she'd break the idyllic atmosphere surrounding them like a warm shroud. She thought about telling him how good it was and how great she suddenly felt, but she was too shy. Edward was the first to break the silence.

"What do we do now?"

"About?" she asked.

"Us?"

"I don't know...I didn't plan this...and you have Carla."

"Yes, I do, but I love you. That never changed, Simmie. I've loved you since...forever, and you know that."

"I don't know what to say, Ed." She sighed and rolled over so she could see his face, propping her head with her arm. "I don't know what to call how I feel, but I know one thing for sure. Being away from you is torture to me, and I just can't do that anymore...and I can't pretend I don't mind you seeing Carla or pretend I don't mind you being distant."

"That sounds like love to me, Simmie, and I'm happy with that! We'll figure out what to do. Just stay here for a while; let me enjoy having you today."

Edward pulled her into his arms, hugging her close to his side and supporting her head on his shoulder.

"You...didn't use a condom."

"I know. I'm sorry—I wasn't thinking about safety. I really didn't think about it."

"Don't worry about that...it's okay...no worries... I don't think you're the kind of man who sleeps with every girl in town, and I have an IUD, so we're okay. I hope..."

"Oh, well, if you're worried about pregnancy, don't... After Noah was born, I had a vasectomy, remember?"

She shook her head. "I forgot...sorry."

Simone closed her eyes and relaxed, enjoying the sensation of safety and comfort she felt from being in Edward's arms. For the first time in a long time, she felt as if all was well in her world.

* * * * *

Later, when Simone and Edward were eating the dinner he had prepared, his phone rang. He answered the call, listened for a few moments, and then he thanked the caller and hung up.

"Your friend has an alibi. He claims he wouldn't have had the time to do anything to Lola. He was on a flight, and then he drove directly to your place. He had airline ticket stubs, a contract for renting the car, and he said your neighbor greeted him when he arrived. The FBI has to confirm everything, but if it all checks out, it sounds as if he's in the clear."

Simone was relieved. Maybe her judgment wasn't so bad at all. She always thought Armando was a spoiled jerk, not a psychopath, but one never knew for sure.

"I have cameras at my house, Ed. The agents can have copies of the recordings. I believe they go back seven days."

"By now, I believe they already have those records. I hate to tell you this, but they've been searching your house for evidence."

"I wouldn't have expected anything different."

* * * * *

Simone and Edward were having breakfast the follow morning when he received another call from Carla. Simone paid attention to their conversation, although she kept her eyes down, gazing at her plate. To her relief, their conversation sounded professional rather than personal, and Ed kept the call brief.

"Your friend is clean," he said after disconnecting the call. "His alibi was confirmed, and the records in your house show he appeared after the ambulance was parked. He is not a suspect anymore."

"Thank God!"

I knew he wasn't crazy, Simone thought. *He's just a pure pain in the ass.*

* * * * *

Over the course of that weekend, Simone and Edward spent most of their time in bed, making love, but they didn't talk much. No promises were made. She didn't know what Edward had told Carla, but he hadn't left his apartment to talk to her.

He and Simone were enjoying themselves, and she

didn't want to think about their future—assuming they even had one. If she survived all the craziness happening around her, she would think about tomorrow. For now, her recent decision that life was too short would guide her thoughts and actions.

Sunday evening, she decided to spend a little time reading Lara's journal, as Edward needed to look over some paperwork he was doing for a lawyer on a criminal profile of a rapist.

She got Lara's journal from her purse, and as she climbed into bed, she looked at Edward. He lay propped against the headboard, his laptop on his legs, squinting at the screen, despite the fact he wore his reading glasses, and she felt enormous pleasure to be by his side, even if they were finishing their weekend working.

Lara's Journal

The next day, Emms told me she had talked to Sean, and he'd said he was very reticent about coming out of the closet. As with all teenagers, he wanted to be accepted, and he didn't want to be different. Emms had told him how important it was for him to accept himself if he wanted to be happy, but for a while after that, none of us talked about the subject. We would see him hanging out with Peter, either at home or at Emm's house in Westhampton every weekend, until one day at dinner, my father started a conversation I knew wouldn't end well.

"Hey, Sean and Peter, can't you find girlfriends? You're always alone. Time to find a couple nice girls and have some fun, don't you think? You're men now."

I held my breath, waiting for Sean's reaction. He faced my father and raised his chin.

"I'm not going to find a girlfriend, Dad; I'm gay, and Peter is my boyfriend!"

I glanced at Peter, and his red face and mortified expression spoke volumes. Poor guy looked as if he wanted to hide under the table.

"You pervert, I'm going to kill you. What did you do to my boy?"

My father sprang from his chair, sending it toppling backward onto the floor. He pointed at Peter, but before Dad could reach out and grab him, Sean took hold of his father's arm.

"Stop, Dad. He didn't do anything to me. I'm his first boyfriend. We discovered we are gay together. There's no one to blame here."

"Sir, it's not my fault. We fell in love!"

Peter tried to defend himself with words, but he stood half hidden behind Sean, using my brother as a shield. I could tell immediately he was not a very strong person.

"Larry," Emms said, thankfully deciding to intervene. "Calm down, and let's talk. We are a family, we are together, we love each other, and we are going to support Sean right now. It's hard enough for him to have found the courage to tell you. I would have done so for him if he would have allowed me, but he told me when he was ready, he would do it. He did, and he deserves our respect! He has more courage than a thousand people I know!"

"Yes, Mom, I have no doubt you approved this nonsense! You're nothing but a crazy lunatic!" He stormed away from the table, and a moment later, the front door closed with a bang.

Sean appeared devastated; his eyes filled with tears. Peter was trying to calm him, and I decided it was time for me to use the lessons I had learned in my life for a new purpose: never judge, accept differences, and try to understand. I rose from my chair and went to Sean. I hugged him and let him cry on my shoulder.

"I love you, bro. I'm by your side, forever and ever. I don't care if you're gay. I just want you to be happy. You will always be my little brother."

Peter hugged us, too, and Emms joined in. As always, our little family was going through tumultuous times, but together, we would solve our problems.

It took some time for my father to accept how things were, but Emms did a nice job convincing him he needed to do just that. In the end, he decided he couldn't do anything to change the situation, and he was not going to lose his only son because of Sean's sexual preferences. We had been through so many storms, what with my problems and my parents' divorce, so Sean being gay was not going to tear us apart. We were one family, and we always would be.

CHAPTER TWENTY-NINE

Simone — Present Day

"Hey, girl, let's get some rest."

Edward's voice and his kiss on her shoulder broke Simone's concentration, and she looked up from the journal.

"That's a good idea," she told him, suddenly realizing how tired she was.

She set aside the journal and cuddled up in Edward's arms, thinking what a nice way that was to finish a Sunday night.

* * * * *

On Monday, before starting her day, Simone went to see Dr. Edgar. She really needed therapy to help her make it through the turbulent times.

Dr. Edgar Rhivas was one of the best psychiatrists Simone knew. Not only was he known for being a researcher and having years of experience in his field, but he also used unorthodox methods when dealing with patients. He tended to be very direct and clear with his advice, which was highly unusual in their field. Most psychiatrists, including Simone, tended lead their patients to think and analyze by themselves regarding what would be their best course of action, but not Dr. Rhivas. He was the kind of doctor who would kick a patient in the ass, if necessary, in order to make the patient understand his professional point of view.

Dr. Rhivas was a short man, around five feet tall. He had a mustache and was always wearing a suit. His greenish-gold eyes looked like those of a cat, and when he stared into his patients' eyes, no one could lie to him. Simone had been his patient for at least fifteen years.

She entered his office, a symbol of success, all marble and wood furniture, very modern but also very cozy. He always had a fire in his fireplace when it was cold or the windows open for a fine breeze when the weather was good. That Monday, he had the windows open, and the transparent curtains were dancing in the wind.

Simone always sat in the same spot, but on that specific day, she was so unsettled she chose another chair.

She was already sitting there when Dr. Edgar came out of the attached bathroom. He fixed his eyes on Simone immediately and made a light remark about her changing her seating preference.

"I'm guessing someone is going through changes in her life... Hello, Simone. I'm not going to ask how you've been because the news runs faster than our meetings."

"Well, you may not ask, but I'm going to tell you, anyway. I feel like a real piece of shit...about my patients...my maid... I feel as if I've lost members of my family over something I can't explain but that is somehow linked to me. I can't imagine who could do such horrendous, evil things. I have no enemies—at least, none that I'm aware of. The police can't find a suspect, but they think it's Peter again. I can't say I agree, because this killer's M.O. is so different from Peter's. I'm in the middle of the most chaotic, craziest time of my life, and what do I do? I spend the whole weekend making love with Edward."

"Well, before we go any further, let's start with this; take a deep breath, Simone. Your brain requires oxygen to think straight. I thought you knew that by now..."

Dr. Edgar was always making fun, in his dry-humored way...

Simone inhaled deeply, filling her lungs, and then let the air out slowly. "Sorry," she told him, "I guess the pressure's been building with all this, and my words came out in an explosion." She sighed. "I really don't know what to do."

"Well, let's start with your most recent news. About Edward...can you explain what happened and what you're feeling?"

"I don't know! That's the reason I'm here... I can't explain!"

"Why did you sleep with him? During our last session, you said he had a girlfriend."

"He does..."

"So you played the seductress?"

And to Simone's dismay he blinked.

"No, Dr. Edgar, of course not! I was shaken. I am shaken...and he was trying to comfort me."

"And it sounds as if he was successful!"

Simone could tell he was teasing her. Even if he hadn't moved a muscle of his face, his voice sounded amused.

"Nice. Very funny. Yes, he was successful...for the weekend, anyway, but now... Well, this is just one more thing I have to cope with."

"And you still haven't managed to define your feelings for him?"

"The sex was amazing! Really good. He is the kind of lover I most appreciate!"

"Marry the guy! You're not going to get anything better. It's very hard to find an adequate sex partner, so when someone tells me she's found the kind of lover she most appreciates, I recommend she ties the guy to her bed!"

"Edgar, have any of your patients ever told you that your methods are unorthodox?"

"If they didn't say so, I'm certain they at least thought as much, but why beat around the bush?"

"I don't know if I love him."

"Oh… Love? Love is bullshit Hollywood created to fill our heads with nonsense. Do you know what real love is? It's a relationship between two friends who respect each other and love each other's company. And if the sex is amazing, bingo, you won the lottery!"

"I don't know. What about butterflies?"

"Butterflies?"

"Yes, you know…that feeling you get…like you have butterflies in your stomach…"

"Take some medication because that's a sort of sickness. Butterflies in the stomach are for teenagers, not for people like you who know the human soul and mind. Do you really believe you could fall blindly for someone? Without analyzing the person's psychological profile? No, you couldn't. When we analyze a person, love is gone. We all have huge flaws, and falling in love requires one to become blind, foolish, and deaf! If you could fall in love without thinking, you would have done that with the lawyer you are working for...but you can't because you tell yourself he is not for you."

Simone thought about Carl. Could she fall in love with him? Only if she decided to go blindfolded into his arms, ignoring his obsession for Lara, his tormented past, and all the guilt he had to cope with over taking someone's life...but he gave her the butterflies...

"I'm not sure, but I really enjoyed myself this weekend."

"Give it a chance... C'mon, Simone. We both know your relationship changed the moment he told you he loved you, and there's no going back. And now that you've explored each other's...feelings... Well, as I said, there's no going back. So give him a chance, or forget about him, and let him live his life. You can go on pretending he's your friend, but he's not. Well he is, but he also wants the benefits."

"Yes, you're right..."

"As always, my dear, as always. But now, about your

losses..."

He proceeded to give her the most unusual advice a doctor can give to his patients, all pertinent, all good ideas. When Simone left his office, she was feeling better, lighter, and strong again, ready to face life, the FBI, the police, and...Edward.

* * * * *

Simone breathed deeply before opening the door to her office. A very hard week lay ahead of her, and she had to be strong—for her patients and for her own good.

She found Edward and Patricia at Patricia's desk, looking over some paperwork. Neither appeared to have noticed Simone's presence, so she took a moment to just look at Ed. It was as if she was seeing him for the first time. He was a handsome man, with dark-brown hair, fair skin, and deep-blue eyes. He had a sprinkling of gray in his dark hair, he was taller than Simone by several inches, and although he appeared a little skinny beneath his dark suit, Simone knew he wasn't skinny at all. While he might not have a six-pack abdomen, he had a perfectly proportioned body.

He looked up, and their gazes met. He stared at her for a moment before flashing her his brightest smile. A warm sensation travelled throughout her body, and she didn't know how to behave, what to say.

"Hello, Simone, how are you this morning?" His lips twitched as if he were fighting back his amusement over trying to behave in front of their secretary after all they had shared that weekend and after the crazy love they had made to start the day.

"Great, Edward. Good morning, Patricia. I'm going to my office…"

"Good morning, Dr. Bennet, Agent Neville called. He would like to speak with you today. He asked me when you had a free moment, and I scheduled him for one o'clock. Is that okay? It's your only free time today. And even then, I had to shave thirty minutes off your lunch hour. Your first patient, Mr. Shermman called to say he is sick, and he is going to see a "normal" doctor"— Patricia made quotes in the air—"I didn't call you because he just called fifteen minutes ago, and I knew you were already on your way."

"That's okay, Patricia, thank you."

"Well, you girls have a good day," Edward said. "I need to get to work, and I'm sure you do, too."

Whistling, Edward went down the hall and into his office.

"Dr. Reynolds seems very happy today…"

"Yes, indeed he does, Patricia."

Simone went quickly to her own office before Patricia noticed how embarrassed she was.

As Simone had her first hour free, thanks to her patient's cancelation, she would read a little bit more of Lara's journal.

She went to her desk, took the journal pages from her purse, drew a deep breath, and picked up where she'd left off.

Lara's Journal

John was a wonderful guy, and I was having a great time with him—in bed and out. He was fun, friendly, and kind, and he was also a rough and amazing lover.

We were in his room, having some fun, and I had brought a dildo because we were going to try a little double penetration.

"Hey, girl, couldn't you have at least brought a black cock?" he asked me, looking at the fake phallus I'd handed him.

"I tried, but they didn't have any, and I was too shy to ask them to check the stock."

"Sometimes, I can't believe you. You can be the most liberated girl in bed, but try to get you to talk about sex, and you become the shyest person on the planet."

"I don't like to talk about sex; I like to do it."

Talking about sex didn't make me shy, but the problem was, whenever I had to talk about sex, I also had to police myself not to reveal things I didn't want him to know, so it was better to let him think I was just extraordinarily reserved when it came to discussing the topic.

I took the dildo from his hands and put it in my mouth, pretending like I was sucking his cock.

"Crazy, delicious girl, come here."

He took me by the waist and put me on his bed. We both kneeled on the mattress, and he took the dildo from me and put it aside. He licked my lips, and I started to kiss him violently, biting him, sucking his tongue, devouring him until I tasted his blood in my mouth.

While kissing me, he pinched my nipples until they hurt, and I grew wet. Reaching down between my legs, he began caressing my clit, gathering my moisture on his fingers.

He got the dildo and slowly inserted it into my pussy. It was cold and too hard, but the sensation brought about by playing like that was so good.

He put the dildo all the way inside me, moving in slow increments.

"Hold this thing inside you for me."

He moved behind me. I was fucking myself with the

dildo when he scratched my back with both hands. Pain mixed with pleasure as he leaned my body forward, spit on his hand, and spread the makeshift lube on my anus. Once he had me good and wet, he started to press his huge cock at my back door while I supported myself against the wall with one hand and played with the dildo with the other.

We both moaned as he pressed forward, slowly entering my ass. The sensation of his huge dick inside me burned and yet filled me completely. I was preparing myself for a double orgasm with the dildo and John both inside me. Chill bumps covered my entire body, and my skin burned and throbbed. Embracing the approaching release, I squeezed my inner muscles around the two cocks. I moved back and forth to receive John's strokes as he fucked me hard, grabbing my hair. He inclined his head and bit me—really hard—while he continued to drive the entire length of his giant cock inside my ass. I came in the most violent of orgasms, screaming, moving my hips as fast as I could and feeling as if I was going to die. I grew so lightheaded, I felt like I had left my body on a wave of powerful sensations.

"Oh, God. I heard screams. Excuse me… I am so sorry."

I looked over my shoulder at the black lady standing just inside John's room, and all the air left my lungs in a whoosh. Who was she? How had she gotten in without us hearing her?

In the next instant, the lady spun around and hurried back out the door. John withdrew from my ass so quickly he hurt me.

"Shit! My mother!" He sprang up from the bed.

He left the room wrapped in a bath towel, then returned about ten minutes later.

"It's okay," he said. "I managed to calm her down..."

"She is still here?" I asked.

"No, she left. She never just shows up without giving advance notice, so I don't know what happened."

John was running his hands through his hair, and I was mortified. Not for getting caught fucking—that was old news to me—but getting caught by a guy's mother? This was a first.

"She invited us for dinner...for a...um...proper introduction..."

"Never in my whole life! I can't. Not after what she saw. She will think I'm a whore!"

"She will not. She's going to be happy. She thought I was...um...gay."

John simply didn't know how to lie, and the truth was obvious in his silly expression.

"You're lying. She did not."

"Yes, I'm lying, but c'mon. Let's have dinner at home, and after you get to know my mother, you're going to like her."

I had no intention of having dinner with John's mother—I had to get out of this situation. The only way I could think of getting his mind off the subject was to pull off John's towel and take his flaccid member into my mouth. Soft as it was, I was able to fit it entirely into my mouth, but a second later he was ready to do battle again.

"You are not going to get out of this by trying to distract me with sex, woman."

I glanced up at him and smiled then did a kind of corkscrew movement on the head of his dick, sucking it while running my tongue 'round and 'round. A moment later, he forgot about everything else, including his mother.

* * * * *

Unfortunately, John regained his senses before too long. Two days after our disastrous encounter with his mother, we were returning from a game in John's silver Escort when he brought up the subject again.

"Lara...my mother wants to know when we are going to come over for dinner."

"I...I don't feel comfortable doing that."

I stared out the window, trying to think of another way to avoid his question, a way to get out of the situation, but John pulled over and parked on the shoulder of the street.

He caressed my hair, and then he made me turn toward him. "Hey, girl…one day, you are going to have to meet my mother. You can't keep putting it off."

"Yes, I can. I really don't have to meet her."

I couldn't imagine how someone could make me do something I didn't want to do.

"Yes, you do because I'm deeply in love with you, and I want to spend the rest of my life with you, so eventually, you're gonna *have* to meet my mother."

I stared at him with my mouth hanging open. My chest grew tight, and I had a hard time drawing a full breath, as if someone had sucked all the air out of the car. Talk about shocked. I was not prepared for his response, and all my fears came galloping back to me. I remembered when I had told Adrien I loved him and what he had done in return. I was afraid I was going to lose myself to someone else again, and I would feel the unbearable pain of being fooled, used up, and tossed aside. I felt as if I was suffocating, and John was looking at me, and I didn't know what to say and do.

"I love you, girl, more than I can explain with words. I would do anything for you."

Take me home. But I had no voice to say even that, and in order to get him to stop speaking—which was only making matters worse—I leaned in and kissed him. I must have kissed him for at least ten minutes before my mind grew calm enough, and I found a way to answer him.

"Okay," I told him. "I'll meet her. But give me some time. This is all too new for me."

"Sure, babe, whatever you need. We'll do this on your schedule. I want you to be comfortable."

Thank God he didn't ask me to explain why the idea of meeting his mother had me so freaked out, and he had the good sense not to ask me if I loved him back. What would I have said if he had? Love scared me shitless.

CHAPTER THIRTY

Simone – Present Day

Simone could understand Lara's fears. Her first love had betrayed her badly. How could she find the courage to trust another? But if Simone's intuition was right, Lara was well on her way to falling in love with John. Clearly, she couldn't leave him alone, and they were obviously like fire and gunpowder in bed... But Simone supposed she'd have to wait and see where the story went.

"Doctor?" Patricia's voice came over the intercom. "Your next patient is here."

Simone sighed. Time to get to work...

* * * * *

After the morning patients, Patricia entered Simone's office carrying a cold chicken salad and an orange juice. She put everything on Simone's desk.

"Thank you, Patricia," Simone told her. "You truly are a wonderful asset. I am very happy Edward and I hired you."

"You're welcome, Doctor. Enjoy your lunch. I also really appreciate my job here. It's...entertaining..." Patricia left the room, closing the door softly behind her. Despite her kind words, she hadn't shown even a hint of a smile. Didn't she have any feelings? What a weird woman...

* * * * *

After lunch, Simone waited for Agent Neville, who arrived ten minutes late and alone. After greeting Simone in his somber way and his ogre-like husky voice that reminded her of Captain Caveman, he took a seat in front of her desk.

"Dr. Bennet, we have to talk. I need some explanations. The killer must have entered your house at some point, since that's where your maid died."

"I don't believe that's necessarily true, Agent Neville. He must have gotten access to her some other way. After I was kidnapped, I had alarms installed all over the house, and I have video surveillance monitoring. I was informed the police already confiscated all those recordings. I can't imagine how he could have gotten to her, and besides, she was not my patient, I've never prescribed anything to her—"

"Tums!"

"What?"

"We found her purse in your house. Cyanide was inside a bottle of Tums."

"That morning, she told me she was not feeling well. She was sick to her stomach. But how did the cyanide get into her Tums bottle? Those aren't prescribed—she could have bought them at any pharmacy in town."

"That's the million-dollar question. She must have gotten the bottle from someone."

And Simone, who spent her life interpreting other people's expressions, easily read the suspicion in the agent's eyes. She should hire a lawyer soon. Could Carl work as an attorney in her town?

"You should talk to her daughter; try to figure where she bought the bottle."

"We are going to do that today. Yesterday, we were at your house searching for evidence..."

"In my house?"

"Your house is considered a crime scene now, Dr.

Bennet. We met Dr. Reynolds there, and he let us use his key. Once you left with the ambulance, we did a thorough search."

"You could have given me a call at least."

"Doctor Reynolds asked us to not disturb you because you were under a lot stress over your maid." This time, his face didn't give much away, but the tone of his voice sounded as if he didn't believe she'd been upset at all.

After all, she thought, *I'm not rolling around on the floor, pulling out my hair.*

"And did your men discover any other evidence in my house, Agent?"

"Nothing, so far...we dusted for fingerprints to see if there were any other than yours or hers inside the house. After the first crime scene examination, we can't do any more searches on the premises without a warrant, don't worry."

"I'm not worried, and you don't need a search warrant. Just let me know when you want to go in; that's all I require. I'm staying with Dr. Reynolds for a few days, but I would like to have access to my house. Is that possible?"

"Yes, absolutely. Whenever you want."

Agent Neville asked a few more questions, all concerning Lola's death, and they were very neutral in tone and content. After some time, he seemed satisfied, and he got to his feet.

"Am I a suspect agent?"

"At this point, Doctor, I'm sorry to inform you everybody is a suspect. The last victim was murdered inside your house, after all, and the others were your patients. I can't discard the fact that you're linked to the crimes, but you're not a direct suspect."

"Good to know..."

"If you're thinking about leaving town, please inform me first."

Not a direct suspect, my ass, Simone thought.

* * * * *

The rest of Simone's day was spent focusing on her patients, and at five o'clock, she decided to read more of Lara's journal, so she could get caught up a little bit. The lighting in her office was good for reading, and she felt safe there with all the surveillance the FBI was doing. She reclined back in her chair a little bit until she was more comfortable, searched for the journal inside her purse, and started to read.

Lara's Journal

I was really worried about John's declaration love, and I didn't know what to do about it, but I knew someone who could give me good advice.

Emms was getting ready to go out, and she was acting rather mysteriously. *She has a secret life,* I thought—a boyfriend or something that she was trying to keep hidden. Well, she wouldn't be the first member of my family to have a skeleton in her closet; that was for sure.

Emms was dressed in a pair of tight jeans and a nice shirt. It was amazing how beautiful she was, even at almost seventy years old. She had a cute little body, and she seemed much younger. But as far as I knew, she'd never had any kind of plastic surgery or liposuction or anything... She was naturally beautiful—inside and out.

"Someone has a date..."

I teased her as she passed by me, probably searching for her car keys...again. She seemed to lose them every other day. If attention deficit disorder was really genetic, then I knew where it came from in this family...

"Yep, but I can't find my keys..."

"They're on the kitchen table. You put them there when you got home earlier."

"Thanks, babe. One of these days, I'm going to think seriously about taking one of those pills you take; I really need them." She gave me a kiss on the cheek.

"Can we talk, or are you in a hurry?"

"I have time now. Besides, I love to make men wait." She winked. "What's happening to form that little line in your forehead, young lady?"

"John. He said he loves me, and I don't know what to do."

"And why do you have to do something?"

"Because... Oh, I don't know. When someone says they love you, aren't you supposed to say 'I love you' back?"

"No. He was expressing his feelings for you, not telling you how you have to feel about him. You never want to tell a man you love him if you don't... That's very unfair and can cause you all kinds of heartache, sooner or later."

"I don't know what I feel for him..."

"I'm sure. We almost never know, but some of us decide to try to reciprocate, anyway, no matter the cost. Be true to yourself, Lara. Never tell somebody you feel something you don't feel."

"I won't, but I can sense he's disappointed."

"That's another thing. You can't be responsible for his feelings for you. Don't hurt the guy on purpose—that's not what I'm telling you here... At some point, he will require some commitment from you if he loves you. That's how this 'love' thing works..."

"What kind of commitment?"

"He'll want you to declare your feelings, maybe even agree to marry him."

"Marriage, Emms? No. No way. I can't become another man's possession. Not again. Marriage isn't for me. Just the idea gives me chills..."

"A good marriage is not about belonging to a man, but so far, I've never witnessed a good marriage. So when and if the topic comes up, you have to be prepared for an answer, and the answer must be true to your feelings."

"Okay, Emms, thanks. Now go find your lover boy."

She laughed but she didn't deny my words. After giving me a quick kiss on the cheek, she left.

* * * * *

For several days following my conversation with Emms, John didn't mention the "L-word" again. I said a prayer of thanks for the reprieve, but, yes, he brought up the topic of having dinner with his mom—several times— and eventually, I caved and said yes, just to put an end to the torture.

He picked me up at home for the ride to his parents'

house in Connecticut. The drive didn't take long—only about an hour from New York to his family's front door—but those felt like the longest sixty minutes of my life. I gripped the box of Godiva chocolate Emms had recommended I pick up for his mom, and stared out the window in silence.

"You are going to like my people, Lara. They're really nice."

"I'm sure I will, but that's not the question. The question is: are they going to like me?"

I didn't pay attention to his answer but continued looking out the window, immersed in my own thoughts.

We arrived at a beautiful, stone, Georgian house, the outside of which was covered in some kind of green vines. A white, iron balcony jutted out from the center of the second floor. The place surprised me—John seemed such a simple man. He lived in a small apartment with other guys, his car wasn't anything special, and he didn't flash around a bunch of money all the time.

The front entry was even more amazing, the floor covered in cream-and-beige marble, and a curving, black iron staircase wound its way up to the second floor. An enormous, wagon-wheel-shaped black chandelier hung suspended two stories above our heads.

We stepped into the living room, which had two fireplaces, one at each side of the room, and antique-bronze French doors covered with heavy, velvet curtains led to the outside. Several beige-and-blue Persian rugs covered the marble floor. Classy.

John's mother entered the room to receive us. She was a charming woman, but I felt very shy, unable to forget she had caught her son and me in bed together.

"Hello, Lara, we are very happy to have you in our home. Thank you for accepting the invitation."

She was all smiles, but something about the way she looked at me set me on edge.

"Thank you for having me, madam."

"Please call me Diane, Lara." She then ignored my hand and kissed me.

Suddenly, an older man appeared, an older copy of John. His grandfather, perhaps?

"Lara, this is my dad, William."

Oh. Thank God I'd kept my mouth shut for once. I cleared my throat and smiled. "Hello, sir, it's a pleasure to meet you."

"No 'sir' here, Lara. I know I'm an old man, but we hate formalities."

"Okay... William," I said, almost gasping. I'd never met any boyfriend's family. Then again, technically speaking, John was my first official boyfriend, and I was nervous.

"Kids, you're late. Dinner is ready, so no aperitifs for you today. Let's go to the table, shall we? William, darling, is that okay with you?"

"If you say so, my love..."

We were directed to her twenty-person table, all dressed in linen with a beautiful arrangement of fresh lilies in its center. Thank God the woman hadn't decided to be formal about the seating; she would have needed a megaphone to talk to us from the other side of the table.

Dinner was great. Will and Diane turned out to be very funny and super polite, and it was easy to see the love that family felt for one another. John's parents behaved in a way that showed great intimacy between them, and they genuinely seemed to enjoy being in each other's company.

How could I ever fit in with a family such as this? They were normal—no past tragedies, no big issues. Would they be as polite and nice if they knew about my past? Would they approve of their only son hanging out with a girl like me? How could I ever have a real relationship with John—or any man—when I had so many hidden things in my past?

The nicer the Meyers were to me, the more worried I became.

After the meal, we spent a little more time visiting in the living room, where Will served after-dinner liquors. Finally, his mother led us up to our room, and she surprised me once again by putting us both in the same bedroom. I wasn't terribly pleased. After all, I'd never spent an entire night with John...

"Hey," I said, once we were alone. "You didn't prepare me for all that luxury...and the daddy and mommy stuff... They are perfect; they could be on the cover of some family-oriented magazine."

"What exactly would you have wanted to know that I didn't tell you?"

He was sitting in a chair, and he grabbed me by the waist and sat me down on his lap. "My parents are fifteen years apart, but they love each other deeply. I'm an only child, my father's money comes from oil, and my mom is a typical housewife, only she has four maids to do her job."

I laughed. "And how about your apartment, your car...you don't live the life of a rich son of a millionaire..."

"No...my father raised me to follow in his footsteps. As you can see, he has no one else to do that. But I always wanted to be a doctor, to take care of people. When I decided to go to medical school, he told me I'd have to fend for myself because he was not going to support that sort of nonsense. Well, then I was accepted into college, and I found a few odd jobs here and there, which was really hard because I didn't know how to do much. Now I can tell you I'm a great waiter and a wonderful dish washer.

I had to laugh, thinking in John washing dishes, and he continued.

I was living in a rat hole for long time, but I was happy. But then my mother found out what I was doing, and she got really upset. She decided to buy an apartment in NYC, but I told her if it was a luxurious place, I wasn't going to live there. So she bought the place I'm in now, and I told my friends I found us a better deal on rent, so we moved... But, of course, we did all the decorating, not her!"

"Yes, I could tell..." I mocked his taste in plastic furniture.

"Bitch."

"I'm not...I'm a future architect, remember? I have...taste..."

"Yes, I know, so do I, but my friends and I didn't have the money for expensive furniture..."

"So your friends don't know about this life?" I waved at

the luxurious room around us.

"Nope...they would feel betrayed, and I really love my friends. Now...no more talk of my family. I really want to have you in my arms, and finally, I'm going to have you for a whole night!"

"Yes, thanks to your mom. They are very nice, John. I really liked them."

"And I can tell you, young lady, they loved you, as I do."

I wasn't so sure about that. At least, not when it came to his mother, Her cold, coal-colored eyes were always undressing me and analyzing me, as if I were a some kind of bug under a microscope, but John was so happy, I wouldn't spoil his feelings voicing my suspicions.

John hugged me, and I started to kiss and undress him. His chocolate color always made me horny. I ran my fingers over his body, inserted them into the waistband of his pants, and touched his cock. It was ready for me, and the tip was moist.

He lifted me into his arms and threw me onto his canopy bed, all signs of tenderness gone now that we'd started to have sex. He knew I didn't like sweetness...he knew exactly how to turn me on. He landed by my side in the bed and bit my nipples, making me moan, and then he delivered a couple sharp slaps to my buttocks.

"I'm going to fuck you hard, girl. You were the most

delightful lady at the table, but I know you better.
You're a little slut, *my* little slut..."

He whispered in my ear, his hot breath giving me chills.

"Stop talking and fuck me; I want your dick inside me."

I turned and slapped his face lightly. I wasn't the only
one who liked it rough.

No foreplay this time. I wanted him quickly. I
unbuttoned his shirt and opened it, and then I opened
his trousers and drew out his cock. I licked the tip, and
then I started sucking him hard while looking into his
eyes, knowing how turned on he got when I did that.
Apparently, he couldn't handle it tonight, because he
closed his eyes and moaned.

"Little bitch... You drive me crazy..."

"Get me a condom," I told him when I could see his
excitement was high.

"No. Let me taste you."

"No! No foreplay. I'm already wet, and I want to feel
you hard inside me."

He got a condom from his wallet and gave it to me. I
opened the wrapper and held the tip of it with my lips
and started to unfold it down over his cock with my
mouth.

"Crazy, delicious bitch."

Then I turned my back to him—one of his most favorite positions, since it allowed him to stare at my ass—and I mounted his cock, taking him completely inside my pussy. I began to move, riding him hard, supporting myself with my hands on his knees and giving him a full view of my pink ass.

He gave me a slap on my buttocks and then another one, causing pain and a wonderful wave of pleasure, and I had my first orgasm. My juices coated his dick. He switched positions and thrust back inside my pussy. He pinched my nipples, increasing my pleasure, and my whole body was at his mercy. When he bit my neck and scraped down my torso with his fingernails, my skin tingled at his touch. I felt as if I had turned in to some sort of liquid, so well did my body join with his.

We were moving our hips, and he fucked me faster.

"I'm going to come," I told him. "Squeeze my neck."

One thing I always loved about John; he was game for anything. Without hesitating, he put his hands around my neck and started to squeeze, fucking me harder at the same time. My inner muscles kissed his cock, tangling to its rhythm, and the more he squeezed, the more pleasure I felt until I came, screaming my release, my body succumbing to the orgasm he'd just given. A few moments later, when I was calmer, I pushed him off me and onto his back. I got on my knees, removed the condom, and sucked his dick until he filled my mouth with his salty cum.

"God, woman, you are going to be responsible for my death, no doubt in my mind."

He hugged me and supported my head on his shoulder, and we both fell asleep, wrapped around each other, exhausted from the great sex and wine.

CHAPTER THIRTY-ONE

Simone – Present Day

Simone decided to stop reading, as the sun had begun to set. She left work and went directly to Edward´s apartment and waited for him. He'd told her he was going to be late arriving because he had some errands to run. Simone had let herself in, using the key he'd given her years ago—just as she had given him one for her place. She settled in on the couch in his living room and clicked on the television to provide some background noise. A short time later, she heard the front door open and shut.

"Hello, Simmie, I've brought something for our dinner!"

Edward greeted her from the door, balancing several grocery bags and his briefcase.

Simone ran to help him. "That's great news. I'm hungry, and I was considering trying to fry an egg."

"Please, no fires in my home." He smiled. "Just kidding..."

Edward gave Simone a small kiss on her lips, and the action seemed very normal to her. *We almost could say we are a couple,* reflected Simone.

They went to Edward's kitchen—or his "kingdom", as he called it, because he loved to cook. He'd had the space remodeled recently, and it was fresh and bright. White furniture and vintage red appliances gave the place a happy atmosphere. There was a huge island in the middle of the room, where Edward always cooked. Six tall red leather stools surrounded the island, and Simone took a seat on one so she could watch Edward prepare their food. From the looks of the ingredients he had laid out, he was cooking some kind of Chinese dish with vegetables and chicken.

He got two wineglasses from the cupboard, opened a bottle of 2012 Corison Kronos Cabernet, and poured. He handled one glass to Simone. She took a sip and sighed.

"Damn, that's good," she said.

"Hmm...yes. Very good," Edward agreed. He set his

glass aside. "I broke up with Carla today."

"Really?" Simone shifted on her stool. "We don't have to talk about this if you don't want to. You don't owe me explanations."

"Yes, I do... I told her I couldn't continue going out with her because my feelings for her where not enough to proceed.

"Oh, Edward, you didn't! That's cruel!"

"No, it's not. It's the truth." Edward smiled. "And do you know what she said? She told me she already knew, and she wished me luck...and then she added that she hopes you can make me happy..."

"Did she know?"

"I believe she could tell. You women are like that. You have an intuition about certain things."

"You're right; we do, but her attitude was still very civilized, in my opinion." Simone was surprised because she had seen the girl, and she thought she was very attached to Edward.

"Yes, indeed! I thought it would be more difficult."

"Ed, I'm happy here with you... In the middle of all the chaos in my life, being here with you is one of the few good things I have to look forward to. I have to confess, I was jealous of your relationship with Carla."

"I could see that, and I had hopes when I saw you were very bothered by her." Edward flashed a small, mischievous smile, showing his pleasure with her jealousy.

"I'm sure I wasn't that obvious." She sipped her wine and avoided his gaze.

"Maybe not to anyone else, but when it comes to you, I can tell exactly what you're thinking. And I played you a little bit, I have to confess here."

"You did not!"

That was a side of Edward she hadn't known existed. So he had a manipulative side... Interesting... She'd thought she could predict all his movements, but she had been wrong

"I did. My relationship with Carla was not as serious as I tried to make you think it was. We were two lonely people going out together, waiting for the right one..."

"Thanks for telling me that, Ed. I don't know if we have a future, but I'm very happy we are together now."

"Let's not push things. You're in a very fragile emotional state right now. I don't want to rush you. When all this other garbage is in the past, we can talk about us. Right now, I'm just happy you're here with me. And it's even better than in my dreams."

He turned off the stovetop and came around the island

to Simone. He wrapped his arms around her and hugged her, his nose buried her hair, and she realized how much she loved to be in his arms.

"You are a great guy, Ed." She hugged him back, thankful he wasn't pushing her into making some kind of commitment now, when her life was upside down again.

"I have good news!" He released her and stepped back, changing the subject and breaking the romantic mood.

"So tell me! I'm in need of good news…"

"You know the FBI interrogated all the workers at Health Care, right? Nobody knows who you are. They told the agents they just know your name, so that's good news. The bad news is they all seem to be innocent. They gave direct answers; no one showed an unexplained increase in his or her bank account, none of them have criminal records. So far, there's nothing to implicate any of them in the crimes. We still don't have a suspect."

"So the bad news is that we still don't know what is happening around us…"

"For now…but the police and the FBI are working together, so it won't be long, Simone. And you're safe here…"

"The person who is doing this isn't just trying to kill me;

he's killing my patience. I don't understand why someone wants to mess with me like this."

"It sounds to me like revenge. Peter Hay couldn't kill you, and you told the world about him, and he had to leave the country. He can't come back, or, if he is back, he has to hide like a rat. I'm positive he blames you for all his miseries. I bet my last dollar it's him."

"I don't know. These crimes aren't the same as the last ones. But he is calling my house... I really don't know. My head spins when I try to figure it out."

"So does mine, and I'm worried as hell about all this. Many times, I saw your pain, and I wanted to be near you, but you wouldn't miss me if I did that, and I needed you to miss me."

"You are a bastard, Ed. I was so miserable missing you!"

Edward's cellphone rang, interrupting their conversation, and he answered. Simone sat at the island, munching on pieces of raw celery, mulling over Edward's words while he walked into the adjoining room. Lost in her thoughts, she looked up, startled, when he came back into the room some ten minutes or so later.

"That was Carla," he said. "The police received an anonymous tip. Apparently, Health Care didn't declare all their employees because they were using illegal immigrants for their janitorial needs. The FBI is tracking down those people now. Maybe we'll get lucky. Carla thinks they are on the right track because earlier today, they talked with Lola's daughter, and she told the agents the only different thing in her mother's life was a recent friendship with a Cuban woman. Maybe the two things are linked."

"I hope so, my friend! I would love to have all the answers."

They had dinner and talked about everything, from their kids to their office, and then they went to bed for another night of passionate love.

Two days after the anonymous caller phoned in their tip, Simone was at her office, making notes on one of her last patients, when Edward entered to bring her up-to-date on the latest in the police investigation. There were three illegal immigrants working for Helth Care; one was a Cuban woman, but after the FBI showed up and started interrogating the staff, she had vanished. The address the pharmacy had for her was false, and she'd given them a fake name, but they had a picture of her, taken at an office party without her knowledge. The FBI had sent the picture to the press and had issued an arrest warrant after Lola's daughter confirmed the woman in the photograph was the same person who had been hanging around with Lola just before she died.

"A woman? Why would a cleaning lady get involved in

something like this? Surely, she's not the primary killer?" Simone was astonished.

"Hard to say. Poison is one of the weapons women choose when they want to kill someone…"

"But that makes no sense at all. I don't know her, and the crimes seem to be directly linked to me!"

"Well, you're probably right. She must be working for someone. Peter Hay can't come back to the country, but he could hire someone to do his dirty work. We have to catch her to know. I hope they can find her soon," said Edward.

"No more than I do, my friend."

"Hey, lady, watch it with that 'my friend' stuff. I don't want to be just your friend anymore. I want to be your boyfriend."

"That's okay with me."

And as simple as that, Edward's status in my life has progressed, thought Simone. *I have to be careful, or I'll wake up on my honeymoon!*

"I'm very happy, Simmie, and I hate to leave you, but I have to work now…" Like a teenager, he approached her desk and stole a kiss, and then he left quickly.

They were very careful not to mix business with pleasure in the office and to keep the appearances of work colleagues.

Simone had some time left before her last patient, so she decided to call her daughter; after dropping the bomb about wanting to stay abroad for college, the ungrateful kid had been avoiding Simone's phone calls.

"Hey, Tammy, are you alive?" Simone said in response to her daughter's breathless hello.

"Oh, don't be so dramatic, Mom. Yes, I'm alive, but I'm busy with a lot of things, and besides, there's the time difference…"

"Hmm… I can imagine how busy you are if you can't even talk to me for five minutes. I just need to know you're okay, baby."

"I'm okay, Mom, really. I miss you, but I'm happy. Did you and Dad talk about me staying in Europe so I can attend college?"

"Me and your dad? No, why?"

"Because I've talk to him, and he says he agrees if you agree."

"I'll have to call him, I guess. I didn't know you had talked to him about that…"

Simone felt betrayed. How could her daughter have discussed the issue with her father before discussing it with Simone? And sure, she could imagine he would agree. He had married again and had two small children, so of course, he didn't want to be bothered with a teenager. Simone grew angry at the thought.

"Mom, don't make me feel guilty. You already knew what I planned to do. All I did was call Dad and get his input, too."

"Sure, Tammy. Glad to know you're okay. I have my next patient in a couple minutes, so I have to go."

"Okay, Mom. I can tell you're upset, but I love you, and I'm happy here, okay?"

"Bye-bye, Tammy."

Simone hung up the phone and leaned back in her chair. Tears burned her eyes, and her hands were shaking a little. She felt as if her link with her daughter was getting thinner. Thank goodness she had this new element in her relationship with Edward, or she would feel even worse. Life...you raised a child and then you lost her as soon as she grew up. *Why do people have kids?* she asked herself. In Simone's case, Tammy had been an accident, but Simone loved that accident above all things. Only she was not a priority in her daughter's life anymore, and the thought made her feel blue.

Her intercom buzzed, and she hit the button. "Yes, Patricia?"

"Your next appointment is here, Doctor."

Simone sighed. *Life must go on. Time to get out of this bad mood.*

"I'm ready," she said, forcing a cheery note into her voice. "Please send him right in."

* * * * *

After her last patient left, Simone took Lara's journal from her purse and began to read again.

Lara's Journal

I woke up before John did, disoriented at first, wondering where the hell I was. How strange to awaken in a man's arms. And surprisingly, how wonderful it had felt to sleep snuggled up next to him. I ran my hand over his torso and breathed in his scent— a mixture of citrus cologne and sex. He was deeply asleep, so I slowly left the bed, went into the bathroom, and took a long, hot shower. For the first time in a long time, I was feeling happy.

After I dressed, I left the room without waking John. It seemed the whole house was still asleep. It was a Sunday morning, but when I entered the living room, the French doors were open, and I stepped out onto the terrace. Diane was there, taking care of some flowers.

"Good morning, Lara!"

"Good morning, Diane."

"Hope you slept well...?"

"Yes, thank you." I suddenly felt shy for having slept with her son.

"How serious is your relationship with John?"

She didn't beat around the bush, obviously. But that was not her concern.

"We've been dating for a while..."

"And having a very busy sex life, or so it seemed the other day..."

My cheeks burned with my mortification. How rude. But she didn't stop there.

"I don't know if you realize it, but my son is black, Lara..."

No! And all this time, I thought he just had a really good tan. What kind of question was that?

"That's a big deal when it comes to marriage. People who marry outside their race often experience real problems."

"The color of his skin never crossed my mind," I told her. "I couldn't care less what color he is."

"That may be true, but not everyone feels that way.

There are a lot of people out there who will give you a hard time. And any children you might have—they'd be mixed blood. It's going to be hard on everyone."

"We've never even talked about marriage, Diane."

"Soon, you will. And before that happens, I wanted you to know what I think."

"I don't believe that's what you think. I believe the problem is that you saw me fucking your son, and now you don't think I'm good enough for him." I really wanted to shock her with my words as much as she had shocked me with hers.

"Oh, yes, there is that, too. I'm old-fashioned, Lara. I don't think girls who have sex with men the way you two were doing it are to be taken seriously. And I really didn't like witnessing *that* kind of intimacy."

"I'm sorry, but if you had called first, you wouldn't have seen anything. We do know how to behave."

"My son knows how to behave...but you? C'mon, Lara. Let's be clear here. I hired a private detective. You lived in France with some rich man twice your age for almost a year. I know your type. You are a sorceress, and you are going to damage my son's life. So think well before doing anything we all are going to regret, or I will have to tell my son about you. Let him in on your little secret. And please, don't bother trying to deny it. I know everything I need to know... And if you tell my son about this conversation, I'm going to deny it ever happened. Just remember; I will keep your little secret as long as I don't ever see a ring on your finger."

"You know nothing about my life, nothing!" Hurt and humiliated, I longed to disappear, to vanish from the Earth. I fled, running directly to the bedroom, where I woke up John. I lied, telling him I had to return to New York immediately because my father was ill. What was one more lie in my huge collection of secrets and deceptions?

* * * * *

We departed before breakfast, and I couldn't handle seeing John for three days. I gave him all kinds of excuses while I was thinking what I should do. I missed him like hell, but his mother was going to be another Sabine in my life, cold and manipulative. I could practically hear Sabine's voice when Diane had been talking to me that morning. I was feeling sick, and my heart was once more in pieces. I had been rejected like trash. Her private detective had told her things that had led her to believe I'd had a "sugar daddy". How would that viper react if I told her my sex life started with a rape when I was twelve years old?

I couldn't talk about any of this with Emms; she would kill Diane, and then what would I have left of any value in my life? I couldn't deal with the idea of the world knowing about my life with Arthur. It hurt too much to have lived through that horror. To have people knowing it would be unbearable.

During the three days away from John, I did a lot of thinking, and I knew I had some decisions to make about my life.

* * * * *

Eventually, I began taking John's calls again. He and I continued dating through the rest of my college months. Whenever he mentioned going back to his parents' house, I invented some excuse. I was nearing graduation, which is a time when students have to study hard, and I was also working with my father, doing some projects already, so John believed me when I told him I had too much going on.

We were happy together, other than the issue with his mother hanging over my head. We got along well, and we laughed together, and we always had a great time. His mom never told him about me, but she'd warned me...no ring, or she would...

CHAPTER THIRTY-TWO

Simone – Present Day

Lara would not have peace if she wouldn't forgive herself for her past, Simone thought. Her fear of being discovered was palpable, and John's mother arriving close to the truth was the worst that could have happen to Lara at that time.

Abused children carried around so much shame over what had happened to them in the past. As a means of coping, some children even developed amnesia and forgot about everything—sometimes for a lifetime, other times remembering when some new traumatic event triggered their memories. Unfortunately, Lara hadn't been that lucky; she knew everything that had happened to her, and the knowledge caused her a great deal of shame. To have her past exposed—even if John´s mother were miles from the truth—would have destroyed the girl.

Simone texted Carl with an update and then went to Edward´s house.

* * * * *

Simone and Edward were holding hands and sitting on Edward's couch in his home theater room. They were watching the news, which Simone didn't like to do, because they always seemed to dwell on the horrors in the world. As far as Simone was concerned, life was difficult enough without dissecting every ugly thing that happened. When she wanted information, she usually went online and read different articles from a variety of sites in an effort to get a balanced view. Better that than being spoon-fed other people's opinion.

They had turned on the TV because Carla, who seemed to have accepted very well the breakup of her affair with Edward, had phoned to tell him that Maria Helena Gomez, the Cuban woman who was now the main suspect in the murders of Simone's patients, had been arrested in Las Vegas. The FBI had tracked her down five days after her photo was released to the media, and she was being transferred to New Haven for interrogation.

"Tomorrow, when they begin the interrogation, I'm

going to be there. I want to hear what she has to say," Edward said.

In the past, Ed had worked with the police on an ongoing basis. He'd helped them by developing psychological profiles of criminals, and as the police and FBI were cooperating to solve this case, he had been summoned by the chief of police to participate in the interrogation.

"That would be great, Ed. I just can't imagine why that woman had to kill my patients and my maid. To me, it doesn't seem similar to the Tylenol crimes. There's nothing random about this. She had to have carefully chosen her victims."

"I agree with you, Simmie. If only your patients were killed, the motive for the crimes could have been similar to that of the Tylenol killer. All of them bought the medication in the same pharmacy. But when you factor in Lola, that theory stops making sense, and these events certainly seem to be connected to you. The FBI, the police, and I all think this is related to Peter Hay."

"I almost hope you're right. If you're wrong, that means there's someone else out there who hates me as much as Hay does." Simone sighed her frustration. "Ed, do you think it's safe for me to return home? I love being here with you, but I would like to go home."

Edward's expression told her he didn't want to let her go. "If an agent stays at your door, you can go back if you need to," he said, despite his obvious wish that she would stay.

Simone appreciated him keeping his promise not to push her. "Well, I think tomorrow will be soon enough," she told him and moved in close to wrap her arms around his neck. "Tonight, I want to stay with you, Dr. Reynolds."

Simone leaned in and kissed the base of his neck, breathing in his scent. Things were so different now, she thought. She noticed things she hadn't noticed before their relationship turned intimate. His cologne was intoxicating, and smelling him turned her on. They started to kiss, slowly, at first; Edward always seemed to be savoring her as he slipped his tongue past her lips to dive into her mouth.

They caressed each other, and Simone opened Edward's shirt, running her hands over his body. She then left the couch to kneel in front of him and opened his trousers. She took his dick and put it to her mouth and started to suck him, making circular movements with her tongue and stroking it with her hand. Edward's reaction was immediate; he grabbed Simone by her hair and moaned.

"God, you're crazy, woman..."

Simone continued to suck him until she felt his cock pulsing, and his groans grew in volume. She then got to her feet, helped him take off his pants, and took off the dress she was wearing. She didn't bother taking off her panties. She just moved them aside and climbed onto his lap.

"No…I want to touch you, Simmie. Let me."

"No, not now…I want you like this…"

She mounted his cock, in a hurry to feel him inside her. She sat down slowly, allowing him to sink fully inside and their bodies to meet, flesh to flesh.

Edward helped Simone to move, his hands on her hips. They moved at the same pace, the pleasure growing, and Simone felt her orgasm approaching her. Chills covered her skin, her heart raced, and sweat covered her body from the effort of riding him savagely. Each thrust inside her wet pussy brought her that much closer to the finish, until she couldn't hold back anymore, and she abandoned all her thoughts for the full sensation rushing through her veins.

As she started to come, Edward began to kiss her again, his tongue inside her mouth and his cock inside her pussy doubling the pleasure. Her orgasm hit her with enormous strength, stealing her breath and making her head spin.

When she came back to Earth and opened her eyes, still sitting astride Edward, she found him observing her, a very satisfied and proud expression on his face, a small smile forming in the corners of his mouth. He seemed pleased with the reactions he had provoked in her.

Simone felt a little bit shy in that moment. She had forgotten the world, only to be reminded now that Edward was her friend and business partner. She lowered her eyes and started moving again so she could escape his gaze.

"Don't be shy...you are amazing, and it makes me so happy to see you come like that. I love your abandon. You make me feel as if I'm the best lover in the world." He grinned.

"Stop reading me, Doctor. You make me feel naked."

They laughed at the irony in her statement, and Edward changed positions, laying Simone on the couch. He covered her body and penetrated her again, and this time he was able to touch her breasts, lick them one at a time. He wasn't in a hurry; he wasn't a kid anymore, and his pleasure came from giving pleasure to Simone. That much was clear to her.

He thrust inside her and started to move, slowly again, as if he had all time in the world to enjoy her. He coaxed her steadily toward release, and when she grew close, he picked up his pace, but before she could come he slowed and then started the whole thing all over again. She was crazy to come. He was denying her orgasm, and it was unbearable, the need for satisfaction growing to a point she was in pain. Finally, he must have driven himself beyond his ability to control his release, and this time, when he started moving faster, he didn't stop. Their hips smacked together, moving in an erotic dance that sent them to the stars, both of them coming at the same time.

They lay on the couch, legs and arms entangled, not speaking. After a bit, they slept, lulled by the pleasure of being in each other's arms.

* * * * *

Simone awoke the next morning in his bed. She must have been exhausted the night before because she had no memory of him carrying her, naked, into his bedroom.

The door opened, and an equally nude Edward came in, carrying a tray with her breakfast. I'm going to marry this man, she thought. And let all the butterflies in the world be killed if he makes me come like he did yesterday every day.

Two hours later, Simone went to her office, where she kept busy with her patients the whole day. At the close of business, instead of going to her place, she decided to go back to Edward's house. One day more wouldn't kill her...

Edward had gone to observe the Cuban woman's interrogation, and he hadn't made it back yet. While she waited for him to get home, Simone decided to read more of Lara's journal.

Lara´s Journal

Graduation was only a few days away, and I was very happy to be getting my degree. I was talking to Susie, the fiancée of one of John's friends. She was a great girl, and I really liked her. She was studying to be a dentist. She always seemed to be in a good mood, always looking at the bright side of life.

"Hey. Do you prefer oval, square, or round?" she asked me out of the blue.

"Is this a new game?"

Suzie loved those ridiculous, childish games like rock, paper, scissors, so I figured this was something similar.

"No, silly, your engagement ring..."

"Never thought about it." I remembered the ring Arthur had given me. I still had it, and it was a hateful symbol of ownership in my opinion.

"John is going to propose...he wanted my opinion. I told him you seemed like a square type of girl..."

The ground seemed to shake under my feet. My legs were quivering, and my heart was racing like a group of savage horses. "Propose?"

"Yes. I'm so happy for you both! You are going to have a rock on your finger, girl!"

"Susie, I have to go. I need to get a book from the library for my final exams. Sorry. We'll talk about this later."

"You are the first girl I've ever met who wanted to postpone talking about marriage. Go on, girl. Go get your book, but it will be square if you don't tell me what you like."

I didn't respond, and I literally left running. As the days passed, and John didn't mention marriage, I thought maybe Susie had been mistaken, and I relaxed. I took all my exams, and I passed with excellent grades.

Graduation day arrived, and I was excited about it. As I walked out onto the stage, dressed in black with my black hat, following other students in alphabetical order to the sound of the Pomp and Circumstance march, I felt a mix of emotions—happiness at having accomplished this step in my life, and sadness because my college years would soon be in the past, and certainly I would lose contact with friends and great professors. This had been one of the happiest times of my life.

I saw all my family occupying their seats. I could see the proud faces of my father and Emms and the happy faces of my siblings. Debbie was so beautiful in her white dress. She reminded me of myself at her age, but thank

God, she was all innocence, and her life was all about fairy tales, makeup, and dresses. At fifteen, she was already a beauty, but she had a lovely family taking care of her.

Sean and Peter were there, laughing about something. John waived to me from his seat, and then I had the displeasing vision of his mother by his side. *God, no!* What was that bitch doing there? I wouldn't allow her to spoil my day.

The illustrious and notorious architect, Lucciano Strabello, an Italian from New York City, had been chosen to give the graduation speech. His words, delivered in a strong, beautiful accent, moved and inspired me.

"My young professionals...yes...you leave here today as professionals, and a whole world awaits your talent. I have some advice for you. You can follow it, or you can do things your own way...and eventually follow it one day. Architects don't build houses or buildings. They build homes and places for work. Never think of anything you design as a way to make money; think of them as a way to make people's lives better, and the money will follow...

"Most of all, I hope, during your career, that you never build egos. Construction is not about what you like and don't like; it's about understanding the client's dreams and necessities, and using your knowledge to help them achieve those goals..."

The speech was long, and my attention deficit disorder wouldn't allow me to follow it along to its end, but during my whole life, those first words were always present in my mind. I always tried to fulfill my client's dreams and to build homes or places where people could work and feel comfortable. The one thing I always took seriously and performed responsibly was my work.

CHAPTER THIRTY-THREE

Simone – Present Day

Edward called Simone around 9:30 p.m. that evening, and the phone ringing interrupted her reading.

"Hey, girl. I'm leaving the police department now. Have a ton of news to tell to you, but I'm really tired. I'm going to go home, eat something, and crash. How's it feel to be back home?"

"I'm not at home...well, not my home, at least. I'm at your house...didn't have the heart to go to my place and spend the night alone. Do you mind?"

"Do I mind? Are you kidding me? That's the best news

I've had all day!"

"So come home. I've ordered Chinese, and it'll be here soon."

"God, I love you, woman!" He disconnected the call before she could answer.

When Edward arrived, she was setting the table. He gave her a kiss.

"Simmie, it's so good to find you here, waiting for me and...heating food..."

She laughed; he was mocking her for her inability to cook.

"Tell me everything," she said.

"Maria Dolores is a tough one! For three hours, the only thing we could get her to say was, 'No English'. We all knew, but she kept her mouth shut. She only started talking after four hours of constant questioning, and then she told us she had killed your patients because she wanted to... She had decided they were meant to be dead."

"Do you believe her?"

"Nobody did... She was crying, sobbing, really. She didn't act like a cold-hearted psychopath, bragging about her crimes. She is a very simple woman, her English is terrible, but she seems to be a hard-working woman. I can tell you one thing; she is not a killer..."

"But then...who?"

"While she was being interrogated, the FBI discovered she had followed her son to the U.S. He just got arrested and is being transferred here, and she was in a real panic when they gave her the news this evening. She started crying and praying and telling everyone to let her son go, that he has kids, he has a family, that she killed everybody. She said she had confessed, so why arrest her son?"

"So...he is the main suspect now?"

"Yes, he is, and they'll have him at the police station soon. He's a pretty rough character, despite his mother's claims to the contrary. He's been arrested and convicted for minor offenses in the past—stuff like burglary, auto theft, drug use—I'm surprised he hasn't done more time than he has. Apparently, he had a pretty good attorney."

Edward's phone rang, interrupting their conversation. He picked it up and looked at the display.

"Sorry, Simmie...it's the police chief. I have to take this."

This time, Simone paid attention to this side of the conversation, and based on what she could hear, the chief was inviting Edward to go back to the police station.

"I need to go," he said after ending the call with a tired sigh.

Simone glanced at her wristwatch. "I heard," she told him, "but it's 10:00 p.m., Ed! You're going to be so tired in the morning. You don't have to do this just for me. We can always get an update in the morning."

"I'll be fine," he told her, scooping up his car keys off the counter. He leaned down to give her a kiss on the cheek. "Nothing could stop me from being there to hear what that guy has to say. Then we're going to bring his mother back in and ask her some of the same questions...see if we can trip her up. As far as I'm concerned, the more tired she is, the better."

"I'm not going to lecture you about human rights because I don't think she deserves any consideration. Not after what she's admitted to doing."

Edward left, and Simone knew he wouldn't come back soon, so she decided to read. There wasn't anything she could do to help now, and reading might make the time seem to pass more quickly.

Lara's Journal

After all the graduation procedures, my father invited my friends for a party at a local restaurant. Emms had organized the entire affair, and she'd done a beautiful job.

John approached me with his mother.

"Congratulations, Lara! I really hope your career is wonderful, and I pray for your success!" the viper said.

I was positive inside her mind she added, "Provided you stay far away from my boy."

"Thank you, Diane! And welcome to my party." I decided I would ignore her and have fun with my friends.

It was almost eleven o'clock, and everybody was half drunk, dancing, laughing loudly, and John and I went to a quiet corner to take a short break. He hugged and kissed me and was all about happiness for me.

"Girl, I'm so proud of you. I also have some good news. I was accepted at Presbyterian University Hospital to work with the neurosurgery team!"

"That's great news, John!" I hugged him. "But I thought you wanted to go to John Hopkins...?"

"Yes, but that would have taken me away from you, and that's not going to happen. The hospital is going to pay me a salary, even though I'm technically still considered a student. And there's something I need to ask you."

He took a black box from his pocket and opened it,

revealing a stunning, square diamond. This ring was nothing like the ridiculous, giant stone Arthur had given me. The stone in this one was maybe half that size, but it was beautiful. And the meaning behind this ring was one of love and happiness. Of course, that only made me feel worse.

Diane stood a few feet away, watching us, and I could read her shocked expression.

"Marry me, Lara. I love you more than anything in this world, and I promise I will make you happy every single day of your life."

"No one can promise to make someone happy, John..."

"I can, and I will. I love you, Lara! I will do everything I can to make you happy if you marry me."

"I can't..."

To say those words hurt me more than anything, but I could read the message in Diane's eyes. *A rock on your finger and the truth on the table.* I couldn't let that happen. I could imagine the hatred in John's eyes if he discovered the truth, and if Diane told him her version of the truth, I would have to tell him the whole story. I couldn't do that. I had a hard enough time just remembering those details, and I remembered the pain in my father's and Emms' eyes... To this day, those memories still hurt me. But I would never get over knowing John hated me for what I'd gone through, for the things I'd had to do.

"Are you kidding me?"

"No, I'm going to France...for an extension in architecture..."

"But that won't last forever. We can marry when you get back...and be engaged while you are abroad. I can visit you..."

"No, we can't. Because... I don't love you, John, and I never will." I had to cut him out of my life, or things would come to a point of no return. "I'm sorry if I gave you the wrong idea about my feelings. I enjoyed going out with you, sex between the two of us is amazing, but it's just that—not enough to marry. And besides, we're too young for a step like that!"

Hurt and tears filled his eyes. "You've broken my heart, girl. I thought you loved me. I gave you my whole heart, unconditionally, and you just threw it in the trash."

His voice was husky, and I could tell he was trying not to cry.

"I'm sorry, John. I'm really sorry..."

He turned and left, so he didn't see my tears rolling down my face. My heart was broken, too...again...again, my past was responsible for my present misery, and I knew at that moment how much I loved him, how much I would have loved to have accepted his proposal and to marry him. But I couldn't do that because you can't start a relationship without being totally honest, and that was the only thing I couldn't do. Maybe he would accept the truth, but I couldn't bear to tell it.

I ran from the party. I passed Diane on my way out the door, and I saw her victorious smile, the bitch. I got a cab and sobbed the entire ride home, crying over a lifetime of failure, a lifetime written by mother when she'd decided to sell me to a horrible man, written by Arthur, who, in his sickness, had used and abused me. That story was not over; it would never be. Wherever I went, I knew it would haunt me; it would destroy any chance I might have to be happy. I hated Sabine and Arthur with all the strength I had at that moment, and I couldn't stop crying. Losing John was much worse than anything that had happened to me, and telling him I didn't love him and breaking his heart was the worst thing I'd done in my life, and I wouldn't forgive myself for that.

I fell asleep still crying. I felt destroyed, my heart ached, I couldn't stop thinking about all the good times John and I had, and the only thing that prevented me from calling him and telling him I loved him and that I didn't give a fuck about anything else, was the certainty I had in my mind he wouldn't love me after I told him the truth, and the truth was too shameless for me to try my luck.

About going to France... I'd been reading some

brochures about extensions, but I hadn't made up my mind because I had the same feelings John put into words—I couldn't be away from him, but now it was a necessity, and I would discuss with my father the possibility of going abroad once more.

CHAPTER THIRTY-FOUR

Simone – Present Day

So Lara had loved John, and her fear of the truth had made her give him up. What a sad story. They could have been happy if only Lara had given him a chance and had trusted him. What had she had to lose? If she'd told him the truth, there may have been a chance for them, and if he hadn't loved her enough to get over her past, then she'd have been no worse off than she had been by walking away. But Simone knew that a girl of twenty-two—who had a recent past still haunting her—wouldn´t have had the necessary courage to open the book of her life to the man she loved. Emotionally, Lara probably couldn't have handled it if he'd responded negatively to her truth.

Simone texted Carl, telling him where she had ended her reading and asking him to get in touch with her after he'd read up to the same point, because she needed to talk to him.

She then turned on the TV to watch a movie, but she was so tired she fell asleep on the couch. She awoke early the next morning to Edward returning from the police department. He seemed tired, so she made breakfast for him, and after showering, he ate quickly, gave her a kiss and went directly to bed, and she went to work.

In the middle of the morning, Carl sent her a message.

I need to talk to you. Just finished the chapter on John.

Call me at 1:00, Simone texted back.

Done.

At noon, Simone was sitting at her desk, finishing the salad she'd ordered for lunch, when Edward popped his head inside her office door.

"Hey, beautiful. You busy?" he asked.

She shook her head. "Nope. Come on in."

"I have some more news," he said, dropping into the chair in front of her desk.

She set aside her fork. "Tell me..."

"Now we have two people admitting they're murderers."

"What?"

"Ovídeo, Maria's son. When we confronted him with the fact that his mother had admitted to the crimes, he said she was lying, that he was the killer. But he doesn't even know where Health Care is—he doesn't even know what street it's on. Hell, we had to tell him it was a pharmacy. So obviously, he's lying to protect his mother."

"And his mother is lying to protect...who?" Simone frowned. She'd thought for sure Maria had been covering for her son. None of this made much sense.

"That's what I'm going to find out this afternoon." Edward leaned forward, snatched a tomato wedge from her bowl, and popped it into his mouth.

Simone shook her head. "I would give my kingdom to be a fly and listen in on those interrogations. I'm so sick and tired of all this..."

Edward got to his feet and came around her desk. He reached down and hugged her from behind, then gave her a kiss on top of her head.

"Just wait. I'll keep you posted. By the way...can you see two of my patients? They really need prescriptions, and

I can't be here."

"Sure." She squeezed his hand that lay on her shoulder. "Ask Patricia to make arrangements for them to see me. She'll find a way to fit them in."

"Great. Thanks. About Patricia...Keep an eye on her. I could be wrong, but it seems to me some files are missing. I was searching for a couple folders I needed, and I couldn't find them, as she is the one who handles archiving all our files..."

"Did you ask her about it?"

"Didn't have the time..."

"I'll check for you. Which case or cases?"

Edward told her the names of the patients, and she made a mental note to check later. He dropped another kiss on her head.

"Thank you again, beautiful. I have to fly. I'll see you later, okay?"

Simone nodded. "Be careful. And thank you, Ed. I really appreciate you giving up so much of your time to help me with this."

"No problem. Anything for you."

She stared at the door for a long moment after he left then sighed. She'd be really happy when this whole investigation was over and done with, and they had the killer behind bars.

Her phone rang, interrupting her thoughts. She checked the caller ID. Carl. Was it really one o'clock already? Simone sighed and accepted the call.

"Hello, Carl, how are you?"

"Fine, and you?"

"Great, things are improving here. The FBI has two suspects behind bars."

"That's excellent news!"

"Yes. So, what did you think of Lara's explanation about what happened with John?"

"Well...I never expected that. I knew John's side of the story, but I would never suspect Lara had loved him."

"And I suspect she loved you even more than she loved John. She just wasn't able to disclose her true feelings. But even if she never said the words—and remember; she never said them to John, either—she must have had deep feelings for you. She told her story to you, and she couldn't do that with John."

"Simone, I really want to believe that; I really *need* to believe that."

"I can imagine."

"I've decided to give a copy of her journal to John. He deserves the truth. We're friends now, and he is not a happy guy. He's already gone through two failure marriages. I believe he still loves her. Maybe if he knows how she felt about him—"

"Does he know the whole story?"

"I don't know. I've never told him, and Lara didn't. I suppose he doesn't."

"Go slowly, then. Ask him to meet for a drink, tell him you have the journal, and then ask him if he is prepared to know the truth. Some people can't face reality very well."

"I'll do that. Simone, I don't know how to thank you for all you're doing for me."

"You don't have to thank me. It's my job."

"No, this is more than just doing your job, and you know it. You're a wonderful human being, Simone. You've done so much to help me."

"Thanks, Carl, it's good to know I can really help you. Make sure you let me know how things go with John. Meanwhile, I will keep you posted on my progress with the journal."

"Will do. Thanks again."

They said good-bye, and then Simone disconnected the

call. She could tell the guy was happy—he sounded so much better, and she felt an immense pleasure at his words. After all, that was her mission in this life—to help people to be happier—and she was proud of herself.

* * * * *

Since Edward would be out until late, Simone decided to go home. She left him a message, letting him know when he didn't answer her call.

An agent accompanied her to her house. She opened the door, but this time, she didn't feel the same pleasure at being back there. So much had happened—in less than a year, her house had become the site of two deaths. Her daughter wasn't going to come home any time soon. Why keep a place that size? For the first time, she thought of selling the house, and the idea didn't bother her.

Edward called, and she told him to come to her place. She told him she was going to order some dinner for them, and he could tell her the latest news.

* * * * *

When Ed arrived, he rang the bell. She opened the door to him, and they hugged as he entered.

"Ed, use your key next time."

He grinned. "I've missed you, girl."

"I missed you, too."

"I have a gift for you…" He took his cellphone from his pocket, pressed a few buttons, then said, "Listen to this."

"What's this?"

"Maria's statement. Or rather, the parts of her statement that interests us. I recorded it for you. Now you don't have to be a fly to hear what was said."

"Ed, are you crazy? You can go to jail for that!"

"We're not going to use the recording outside this room. You deserve to hear this firsthand. It must be awful to be in the center of this garbage and not know what's happening. Please start listening while I shower."

"Okay…use the master bathroom."

Edward grinned. "What a guy has to do to get into a girl's room. Just risk his neck. But I've made progress…from the guestroom to her bedroom…"

Edward went to her bathroom, whistling, and she touched the play button on the phone.

"Mrs. Gomez, how are you?" A man's voice filled the room.

"Tired…" a woman answered.

"Well, I brought you a sandwich. You must be hungry,

too."

Simone recognized the speaker as Carla.

"Thank you, but I'm not hungry."

"Maria, I have good news for you. You're free to go. Your son confessed he was the guilty one here and the true killer," Carla said.

"No! My son is not guilty. My son is good; he is no killer! I did this thing. I kill those people."

"No, Mrs. Gomez, you didn't. Your son told us he did," a male agent said.

"What's going to happen to my son?" Maria answered, and the terror she felt was present in her voice.

"He'll go to trial, and since he committed so many crimes, he will likely be sentenced to life in prison without parole," Carla said.

"I don't understand what that means." Maria was sobbing.

"That means, Mrs. Gomez, that your son is going to spend the rest of his days in prison. He is not going to get out alive, and he is lucky this state has abolished the death penalty, or he would be dead. Do you understand now?"

The male agent's rude tone contrasted with Carla's soft,

kind voice, and Simone realized they were playing "good cop, bad cop".

Maria started to cry louder. "No, no, no," she repeated between sobs. After a few minutes, she drew a shuddering breath.

"I don't believe my son confessed to something he didn't do," she whispered.

"He signed a confession, Maria, it's right here."

Carla must have shown Maria her son's confession because the sound of rustling paper came over the phone's speaker.

Simone looked up as Edward came back into the room, his hair still wet from his shower. He didn't say anything, just flashed her a grin as he took a seat beside her on the couch.

"No, he is lying," Maria suddenly shouted. "She is the one to blame. I didn't know people could be killed. She told me she was going to give something for them to sleep better."

"Who, Maria? Who told you that?"

"I'm not going to tell you if you won't guarantee my son is not going to spend the rest of his life in prison!"

"Do you want to make a deal?"

"Yes, I do!"

"Do you have a lawyer?"

"Do I look like I have one, Agent? I'm a poor person. I work hard to survive!"

"Okay. Let me see what I can do."

Edward reached over her shoulder and pressed the stop button on the phone.

"They got her a public defender, and she's talking to him. They're going to offer her a plea deal if she tells the truth. As soon as she makes a decision and they bring her back in to talk, they're going to let me know so I can sit in on their questioning."

"You'll have to go back to the police station?" she asked him.

He nodded.

Simone sighed. "Okay, then I guess we better eat before you get called away again."

"I'm starving! What did you make?"

"Nothing...but I ordered a wonderful lasagna."

"Excellent! Let's go check it out."

They had a quiet dinner, and luckily, they'd finished before Edward was called back to the police department.

"Don't wait up for me, beautiful. Well, that's assuming you were going to invite me to sleep over?"

"Please, Ed, come home when you finish."

"I liked that: come home."

She smiled, surprised by her own words, and kissed him goodbye.

Simone went to bed right after Edward left. She was exhausted and anxious to be in her own bed.

Nothing like sleeping on my own pillow, she thought, before falling into a deep sleep. No need for pills that night. She was feeling so much better now that things were progressing with the investigations. She was almost feeling safe again.

* * * * *

It was lunchtime when Edward arrived at work that day. He entered Simone's office and closed the door behind him.

"Do you have time to hear the truth?"

"Absolutely! Always!"

"Maria's lawyer worked a deal to have her charges reduced to conspiracy, and she'll get two years, at the most. I recorded everything. Do you want to listen?"

Edward showed her his phone, and she reached out for it, anxious to hear what had happened.

"Okay, have fun. I'll leave you alone. I have to check with Patricia about those missing files."

Simone nodded absently, pressing the play button on the phone. "Okay."

"Maria, we have an agreement, but it depends on what you have to offer us," Carla said. "We need the truth. Who is responsible for those murders? Who asked you to change the medication?"

The sound of Maria's deep breathing came over the phone.

"The prosecutor, the one taking care of the rape case of Brigit," she said.

"Who's Brigit? Did this crime happen here? In New Haven?" a male agent asked.

"Brigit Gillmond. No…in Hartford."

"What's the prosecutor's name?"

"I just know her last name. I always called her Mrs. Morelli"

"Can you check on this, Jordan? See if you can find a rape case involving someone by the name of Brigit Gillmond, and see if there's a prosecutor with that name in Hartford," Carla said, finally providing Simone with the male agent's name.

"I'm going to check that right now."

The sound of a door opening came over the speaker, followed by several seconds of silence.

"While we wait, Maria, why don't you tell me truth? You already have your deal."

"My son...people said he participated in a rape, but he is innocent. He was sleeping at home; I swear. But somehow they say he was involved. And Mrs. Morelli was in charge...she told me if I did some errands for her, she would let him go free."

"And you accepted?"

"She told me it would be easy. She just wanted to put some people to sleep. I just had to replace the pills, and nothing bad would happen."

"But didn't you see that someone died? On TV?"

"I didn't until they dug up that woman. But then it was too late."

"But after that, you gave the Tums to Lola, didn't you?"

"She made me do it. She told me she was going to come to public and tell everyone what I had done, so I would end up in jail to make company to my son."

The woman started to sob and cry all over again.

Some minutes later, the sound of a door opening could be heard again.

"Deena Hay Morelli is the prosecutor on that case. Does that name ring any bells for you?" Agent Jordan asked.

"Of course. Peter Hay was the serial killer behind the previous deaths. Obviously, they must be connected!"

Simone couldn't listen anymore. She pushed the pause button and looked at Edward, who had just entered her office again.

"Ed... Deena is Peter's sister. I remember from Mark's journal. She was a prosecutor, but she was being considered for a *federal judgeship*... She should be a judge by now."

"Having a brother as a serial killer? It astonishes me she is still a prosecutor."

"I believe she told Carl she would turn down the nomination or something like that...but...why would a person like her would do such a thing? It doesn't make any sense."

"I don't know. When does murder ever make sense? Maybe she was seeking revenge for her brother, or maybe psychopathy runs in their blood. That's actually not unusual."

"Or maybe she's always been helping him? Maybe she had something to do with the other crimes, too?"

"I never thought about that. It seemed he acted alone."

"The FBI is going to have a hell of a job trying to figure this out."

"I'm going to check in with them...see if they have any updates. Can I have my phone, please?"

Simone handed the cellphone to Edward and waited while he placed a call. She half-listened for several moments, thinking about everything she'd just learned from Maria's interrogation.

"Simmie, you can relax now," Edward said. "Deena was arrested at the airport. She was trying to leave the country."

"Let me guess...for China?"

"Exactly!"

"That means Peter never came back here."

"No, he didn't. His sister must have acted alone. At least this time. Remember, I told you poison is a typical weapon for some women. You were right... Peter didn't do it."

"We'll see... But at least now I can breathe. Have a little peace again."

"Yes. Finally. And you need a little peace. This has been one heck of a year…"

"As the queen of England said once, *'Annus horribilis'*— a horrible year."

"It's over now. Come here, girl."

They hugged and stood there for a while, wrapped in each other's arms, enjoying the good news and each other's presence.

* * * * *

The following day, the local police questioned Deena Hay. She denied everything, but a search revealed she had been postponing the trial of Ovidio Gomez. Even then, she continued to deny she'd done anything wrong, telling the media she'd been "framed". Investigation would proceed.

Over the following week, life slowly resumed a normal rhythm. Simone was finally calm and relaxed, her patients were all feeling safe and well, and she was having happy days in the company of Edward. They still hadn't found time to talk about their relationship— Edward had been at the police station every day since Deena's arrest, listening in on her interrogation. She was still denying her involvement in the crimes, and until now, no physical evidence linked her to the crimes, only the testimony of Maria. But Simone and Edward were happy with each other, and at the moment, that was all that really mattered.

Simone decided to surprise him with a home-cooked meal. She found what sounded like a delicious recipe on YouTube and set everything up—the ingredients, utensils, and her laptop—on the island in her kitchen. An hour later, she had just added the last bit of herbs to her Fettuccine Alfredo sauce and had the water heating for the pasta when Edward arrived, a bottle of wine in his hand.

"You look so beautiful cooking, Simmie!"

She frowned. She'd just lifted the lid on the boiling pot, and her face was coated in water vapor. She felt a slimy mess. "I hope you think the same after you try my meal."

"I'm sure I will. I will find you beautiful when you are eighty, I'm have no doubt."

Edward kissed her on the lips and then dug around in the utensil drawer until he found the corkscrew. He opened the bottle and poured two glasses of wine.

"What are we going to toast?" she asked, lifting her glass.

"Wait," he said. "First, let me put on some music for us."

Edward got his phone and connected it to the speaker she had in the kitchen, and a beautiful piano solo started to play.

"That's beautiful! I've never heard it before!"

"That's for you. *The Look of Love,* by David Gurwin."

"I love it, Ed, thank you." She stood on tiptoe and kissed him.

"Now, our toast...to..."

The phone rang before she could finish her sentence. She considered not answering, but that could ever happen. She was a doctor, and she never knew when one of her patients might need her.

"Just a second, Ed, hold that glass, and don't think about drinking before we toast." She answered the call. "Hello?"

"You find a way to tell everybody the crimes were your fault, bitch; take my sister out of this...take me out of this mess..."

Simone cringed at the sound of Peter's voice. She just had the time to push the speaker to allow Edward to listen.

"You are both a couple of psychopaths!" she shouted.

"Yes, indeed, but this psycho has your daughter, and you are never going to see her again if you don't do as I say..."

The phone went dead. Obviously, Peter was smart

enough not to stay on the line long enough to allow the police to pinpoint the origination of the call.

Simone turned to Edward. Her legs were like jelly, but before they could exchange any words, the phone in her hand started ringing again, and she jumped. Heart racing, she answered the call.

"Mom, I'm here with Peter. Mom, you need to do something. I'm so afraid..." Tammy was crying, but it was definitively her voice.

"As I said, I have your daughter. I always wanted a pet. Now I have one. And in a little while, I'll have a corpse, unless you do what I told you to do."

He hung up again, and Simone felt the floor disappear below her feet. She couldn't react, talk, or cry. Her nightmare was back, only this time, it was worse than she could have ever imagined possible.

ABOUT THE AUTHOR

A. Gavazzoni is the Brazilian author of the newly released novel *Behind The Door*, a sensual romance now available through Amazon.com. She is a lawyer by day and former professor of law; she writes (novels and legal books), but she is also a voracious reader and a writer by night and currently has a law book about international contracts published in Brazil.

She speaks four languages: English, French, Portuguese, and Spanish. She also studies Chinese and hopes someday she will master it (but it's been a challenge!). Her favorite countries, no surprise, are Italy, France, and the USA. When she is not practicing law, she enjoys many interests and is a very active person. She loves to dance (Tango) and workout. She also enjoys travelling, loves good wine, and has been studying astrology for fifteen years. She paints and loves to cook.

She has two poodles—Gaia and Juno—and loves all animals. She is an aunt to four nieces who enjoy painting and cooking alongside their aunt. She lives in Brazil and has just finished writing Lara's Journal, the sequel to Behind the Door. She invites readers to visit her website for updates on upcoming books and events, and join her on her blog, where she loves to interact with readers and other authors. Readers can also follow her on Twitter @a_gavazzoni.

Made in the USA
San Bernardino, CA
27 February 2017